The Perfect Manhattan

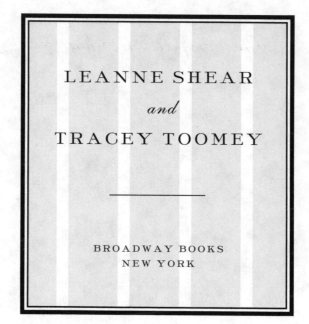

LEANNE SHEAR
and
TRACEY TOOMEY

BROADWAY BOOKS
NEW YORK

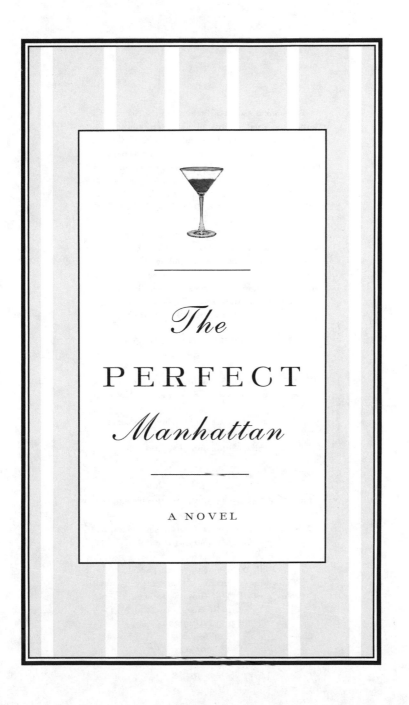

The
PERFECT
Manhattan

A NOVEL

THE PERFECT MANHATTAN.
Copyright © 2005 by
Leanne Shear and Tracey Toomey.
All rights reserved. No part of this book may be
reproduced or transmitted in any form or by any means,
electronic or mechanical, including photocoping,
recording, or by any information storage and retrieval
system, without written permission from the publisher.
For information, address Broadway Books,
a division of Random House, Inc.

PRINTED IN THE UNITED STATES
OF AMERICA

BROADWAY BOOKS and its logo, a letter B bisected
on the diagonal, are trademarks of Random House, Inc.

Visit our website at www.broadwaybooks.com

First edition published 2005

Book design by Jennifer Ann Daddio

Library of Congress Cataloging-in-Publication Data
Shear, Leanne.
The perfect Manhattan : a novel / Leanne Shear and
Tracey Toomey.—1st ed.
p. cm.
ISBN 0-7679-1849-5 (alk. paper)
1. Young women—Fiction. 2. Bartenders—Fiction.
3. New York (N.Y.)—Fiction. I. Toomey, Tracey.
II. Title.
PS3619.H4P47 2005
813'.6—dc22
2005042123

1   3   5   7   9   10   8   6   4   2

Why they came east I don't know. They had spent a year in France, for no particular reason, and then drifted here and there unrestfully wherever people played polo and were rich together.

–THE GREAT GATSBY

The bartender is the aristocrat of the working class.

–COCKTAIL

PROLOGUE

I was drowning in a sea of sopping bev naps, searching frantically for the bottle of Grey Goose, while hordes of people thirty deep with contorted red faces and bulging veins were screaming drink orders at me. They clawed their way toward the bar, yelling "Seven Ketel tonics! Twelve sour apple martinis! Fifteen Captain Cokes! Thirty shots of So Co lime!" There I stood behind the bar, paralyzed. There were no glasses, no ice, no lemons or limes, no plastic stirrers. All the bottles I grabbed were empty, and the crowd was growing more and more hostile. A crazed woman in a beaded Zac Posen top and Yves Saint Laurent miniskirt in dire need of a raspberry mojito mounted the bar, threatening to gouge my eyes out with her impossibly long, air-brushed fingernails.

"Cassie, wake up," Annie urged, shaking my shoulder. "We're going to be late for work."

Totally disoriented, I opened my eyes and looked around at the stained, mildewed walls of the share house. The roar of my housemates playing beer pong on the front porch echoed up the stairs. Still bleary-eyed, I checked my watch—to my horror, it was seven-thirty in the evening. I'd been sleeping the entire day away since I'd arrived home at nine that morning, exhausted and still drunk. I struggled out of bed, pulled on my grubby uniform, and slathered on some lip gloss, all the while dreading the hysteria awaiting me at Spark. As I tucked my bottle opener into the waistband of my skirt, I asked myself, How the hell did I get here?

One

SHIRLEY TEMPLE

An unruly pile of spiral-bound notebooks, final exam schedules, and dried-up highlighters were scattered across my sky-blue comforter as I stared intently at the ad in the *Village Voice*. A large, cartoonish picture of a mustached bartender enthusiastically shaking a martini smiled broadly back at me.

I was sitting in my cramped Columbia University dorm room in Hartley-Wallach Hall chasing that ethereal dream of finding an apartment south of 14th Street that was both spacious and cheap. But instead of finding the last rent-controlled one-bedroom on the tree-lined West Village sanctuary of Bank Street, I found Martini Mike.

For weeks prior, I'd been strolling around Columbia's Morningside Campus in a daze, transfixed by the frenzy of activity raging inside the Lerner Student Center. Every time I walked by the Career Services office, I saw professionally dressed seniors milling around, waiting to be interviewed by whatever top banking, law, or consulting firms happened to be recruiting that day. The firms themselves were easy to identify on account of the brightly colored banners strung outside the building: COLUMBIA WELCOMES DELOITTE AND TOUCHE! COLUMBIA WELCOMES ACCENTURE! COLUMBIA WELCOMES WHITE & CASE! Whenever possible, instead of taking College Walk to travel to and from class, I'd take Broadway or Amsterdam and cut across 114th Street just to avoid the spectacle of eager job-seekers.

"Hey, Cass," Jocelyn Van Der Wal had called out to me only the day before as I hurried to my fiction thesis tutorial. One of the many willowy blond heiresses in my class, Jocelyn had been primed for a career in investment banking since birth. She had beauty, brains, ambition, and it didn't hurt that her father was the CEO of Lehman Brothers. "How are you?"

"I'm okay," I said, adjusting my heavy backpack. And then inevitably, "How are you?"

"Fabulous!" she bubbled. "Just finished my third-round interview with Lehman. I think it went well, but I don't know. I'm really nervous."

It was hard to sympathize with a girl waiting on pins and needles when her dad was the reigning monarch of the financial world.

My roommate Alexis, another investment banking prodigy, was at the moment in a final round of interviews at Morgan Stanley. I, on the other hand, was still in my pajamas at two o'clock in the afternoon on a beautiful spring day, eating Healthy Choice microwave popcorn and flipping dejectedly through the paper. I couldn't leave the security of my dorm room, afraid of the questions that lurked outside: "Where do you see yourself in ten years?" or "Have you found a job yet, Cassie?" I was graduating with a BA in creative writing with a concentration in comparative literature. That and a $2 MetroCard could get me on the subway.

Still, my friends and professors innocently laid their expectations on thick. They came at me from all sides.

"So have you decided yet?" Alexis had asked the previous Monday. She was staring at her reflection in the mirror, expertly applying Nars eyeshadow.

"When I figure it out, you'll be the first to know," I said testily.

"Well, I think you should take the job at *Us Weekly*. Then we could get into all those parties and meet celebrities!" she suggested brightly.

I sat wearily on my lofted twin bed and yanked on the black, pointy-toed Coach boots that had cost me two weeks' salary at my work study job at the law library. I'd been agonizing for months over what to do after graduation. The only job I'd been offered, an editorial assistant position at *Us Weekly*, paid a whopping $22,000 a year. Alexis had trouble getting her head around the fact that my parents, unlike hers, weren't able to supplement my income

After summer internships at *New York* magazine and *Glamour*, there was one thing I did know for certain: I wasn't cut out for an "office" job in corporate America. The fluorescent lights and sterile air seemed to suck all the creativity right out of me. Plus, I knew that in any entry-level magazine position, 90 percent of the work I'd do would involve mindless tasks such as copy-editing two-hundred-word sidebars entitled "QUIZ: Are you stalking him? Ten questions to help you figure out if you're a Bunny Boiler." Though I desperately wanted a career as a writer, serving as a cog in Wenner Media's machine seemed like a *Groundhog Day*–type nightmare where every day was eerily similar: wake up, brush teeth, grab green tea, ride subway to work, sit behind desk for eight to twelve hours, ride subway home, order take-out, collapse into bed. Repeat.

Expectations were running high in my family as well. My parents couldn't help but notice the stacks of dog-eared journals, diaries, and salt-and-pepper notebooks that lined my shelves, busting at the seams with my evolving insights and outlines for novels and plays, and they tried their best to support my fervor for writing. They attended all the plays I wrote and directed in high school, but never failed to remind me of the paltry wages and high probability of unemployment that came with the turf.

For their part, my parents weren't in any sort of financial position to help me out. Unlike many of my college friends who'd grown up "in the city" and attended tony private schools like Spence or Horace Mann, my family had no connection to the names Tisch, Rockefeller, Steinberg, Hearst, Trump, or Vanderbilt. I would be leaving school with approximately $40,000 in student loans, even though my parents had taken out a second mortgage to finance my education. The irony of it all was that my friends who needed money the least were the ones who were entering the highest-paying careers. Take Alexis—she had an untapped trust fund in the high seven figures, her parents still paid for her every bill and whim, and she was entering a field where year-end bonuses were enough to put a down payment on a five-bedroom home in Westchester County.

During junior year, I'd started writing screenplays, and had submitted one of my shorts to a contest at NYU, where—to my utter joy and amazement—it had been selected for production. It was a thirty-minute screenplay I'd scratched out spur-of-the-moment on the train home to Albany for Christmas break, about a demoralized hooker in Lower Manhattan. A few nights prior I'd been leaving a Christmas party thrown by Alexis's father's law firm at Capitale, a swanky nightclub housed in a 1930s bank building designed by Stanford White. Balancing on my borrowed D&G spiky heels and trying to hail a cab in the dark underworld of Grand Street and the Bowery, I noticed a young girl about my age saunter up *Pretty Woman*—style in six-inch platforms with clear plastic heels to a black Lincoln Town Car that had pulled up to bid on her services for the evening. Fleetingly catching the unmistakable look of vulnerability in her eyes, I'd said a silent prayer that the presumably wealthy stockbroker in the backseat was a Richard Gere of sorts who would rescue her from the "oldest profession on earth." In my screenplay, the man in the Lincoln didn't turn out to be your stereotypical Wall Street prototype, but a best-selling novelist. Compelled by my heroine's plight, he takes her in and uses her as the inspiration for a Pulitzer Prize—winning epic based on her life story. My next mission was to develop the existing script feature-length version entitled *Glass Slipper*. That, and to have Focus Films produce it (but I'd settle for Miramax—just so long as Harvey Weinstein didn't plug polished Gwyneth into the roll of my working-girl heroine).

So here I was, months later, on the eve of commencement, with only a few days left before my release into the real world, desperately in need of a savior of my own. I had no job that would support me, no money, and no trust fund that would activate upon graduation.

The raunchy ads for strippers, phone sex operators, and call girls splashed all over the back of the *Voice* practically devoured Martini Mike's ad, and if it wasn't for the strategically placed dollar signs scattered throughout the type, I might have missed it. I read it a second time, then a third, thinking I'd heard somewhere that Bruce Willis had been working as a bartender in New York when he'd been discovered by a high-powered agent. . . .

G raduation was on a Thursday, and on Wednesday night my mom and dad arrived in the city to take me out for a precommencement dinner. My mother had a habit of reading Zagat like most people read the newspaper, and after weeks of careful study, she'd decided we should dine at the Gotham Bar and Grill, an elegant restaurant in the Village.

"Are you sure?" I'd asked her when she told me she'd made the reservation. "It's pretty expensive."

"Of course I'm sure," she responded. "It's not every day your daughter graduates summa cum laude from one of the best universities in the country. We're so proud of you, Cassie." What was left unsaid was that my dad would likely have to work overtime at the Albany Fire Department and pick up extra shifts at Joe's Plumbing, where he moonlighted on his days off, just to pay for the appetizers.

"Do you have a reservation, miss?" asked the model-cum-hostess when I arrived.

"Yes, actually, but I'm early," I said, unconsciously straightening my shoulders in hopes of mimicking her ramrod-straight posture. "I'll just wait at the bar."

I carefully picked my way through the well-heeled crowd. "Rum and coke, please," I said to the gray-haired bartender, who was wearing a neatly pressed black tuxedo and mixing cocktails with the precision of a chemist.

For the first time in all my years as a bar patron, I took an interest in how everything was set up and watched him carefully. At the moment, he was mixing a frothy, fruity, multi-ingredient drink I couldn't identify, but overall, his job looked pretty easy. And as the Bacardi settled warmly in my stomach, my fears about the future dissolved—nothing like two ounces of hard liquor to make the specter of telling your parents that you were abandoning a corporate career path with benefits and a 401K in favor of slinging drinks a lot less daunting.

My stomach growled as waiters bustled past with steaming plates of grilled lobster tail and Kobe beef. I glanced at my watch—still ten minutes until my family was due to arrive. When the bartender turned his back to me, I reached across the bar and snuck a couple of cherries out of the fruit tray conveniently placed right in front of me.

"Times that tough?" asked a man who'd materialized on the bar stool next to me even though every other stool was vacant. As he reached into his pocket to retrieve his BlackBerry, the course tweed of his Paul Stuart blazer grazed my bare arm.

I smiled, mildly embarrassed.

"I bet Sam'll overlook it this time," he said with a wink, nodding toward the bartender.

"Yeah, but only because she's so pretty." Sam grinned at me. Then he shrugged. "It's not like they're a big commodity anyway. We only use them for manhattans and the occasional Shirley Temple." I took mental note of this bartending wisdom, and turned back to my rum and Coke.

"I'm Dan Finton," the man on the stool continued.

"Cassie Ellis," I said, accepting his outstretched hand.

As I took in the crisp white button-down shirt and argyle pullover vest, he reminded me of Indiana Jones's alter ego—the straightlaced college professor, with the smoldering good looks underneath. Take off that tweed blazer, and he could be perfectly capable of trekking through the desert and rescuing both the Holy Grail and the damsel in distress.

"Hey, Dan, wanna see a menu?" Sam asked.

Dan nodded imperiously, and Sam returned a moment later with a wineglass the size of a fishbowl and placed it in front of him along with an elaborate, leather-bound menu. He then presented him with a bottle of red wine (which, from the looks of the ornately scripted label, was really expensive) and opened it expertly. He poured a small amount of wine into the glass, and I watched out of the corner of my eye as Dan, in one motion, grabbed the glass, swirled its contents, then leaned forward to breathe in the aroma deeply. He took a small sip and seemed to chew it in his mouth for a few seconds.

"It's less tannic than the '97 Qupe Bien Nacido Reserve, and I like the warm chocolate overtones," he mused sybaritically. "Still, it's a touch too angular." Sam finished filling the glass as Dan studied the menu. I concentrated on my own drink and listened curiously to what he would select.

"I'll start with the fois gras, and then I'll have the rack of lamb—very rare," he said.

I'd never had fois gras before, but I vaguely remembered hearing it had something to do with geese and liver, and that was enough to deter me from ever trying it. And while I couldn't get enough of the burgers at Corner Bistro—a famous West Village dive with a line that frequently stretched out the door—I never could wrap my mind around eating lamb because, well, all I could picture was a furry little lamb frolicking happily in a field.

As I stirred the narrow red straw around in my rum and Coke, I caught Dan stealing glances at me and became strangely self-conscious. I sucked in my imagined beer gut, ran a hand through my long, dark hair, and again forcefully straightened my posture—shoulders back, chin up.

"So, Cassie, what do you do?" Dan asked, squaring his shoulders so he faced me directly.

"Actually, I'm a bartender," I said, trying on my new profession for size, and leaving out the fact that I still had to go to Martini Mike's and earn my certificate of mixology. Not to mention that, at this point, my drink-mixing skills were limited to a college repertoire of vodka tonics, Jack and Cokes, and the occasional screwdriver made with OJ procured from the corner deli. Throw in Jell-O shots, Milwaukee's Best (Beast), and that was just about the extent of my drinking knowledge. But Dan's ears perked up.

"I'm actually in the bar business as well," he said. "I own a bar downtown called Finton's—it's kind of an upscale Irish pub."

I shifted uncomfortably on my stool, certain that given his line of work he could sense I was lying. I buried my face in my glass and felt the blood rush upward and imbue my ears with a dark purple hue.

"You should come down and check the place out sometime," he volunteered.

"Um, okay," I said, as he proffered his business card.

"I'm actually looking to fill a couple of bartending positions," he went on thoughtfully, raising an eyebrow. "If you ever need a job, give me a call."

"Okay," I said, dropping his card into my bag.

"I think you'd be great," he said. "A girl like you . . ." A smiled played around the corners of his mouth, and he held my gaze just a little longer than was necessary. I looked away.

New York was full of men like Dan Finton—older, polished gentlemen who wouldn't hesitate to flirt with a girl twenty or thirty years their junior. My friends and I had been bumping into them at restaurants and clubs all over the city for years, and as a struggling college student I'd occasionally been guilty of taking them up on their tempting offers for things like Dom Perignon and strawberries at 3:00 A.M. at various bars and lounges, at the exact moment I ran out of money and was starving to boot. I'd learned that while it was always fun to drink a $1,000 bottle of champagne, nothing came free. More often than not, these Cialis-fueled men grew more aggressive as the champagne dwindled.

Fortunately, Sam returned to our end of the bar and began filling his fruit trays with limes, lemons, and twists, and as he replenished the cherry supply he winked at me.

"How are the kids?" he asked, turning back toward Dan.

"They're doing great," Dan said without missing a beat. "Taylor just got the lead in the school play, and Alex has taken up tennis. They're keeping us busy."

"How's the wife?" he asked.

"Linda's fine," said Dan.

"Cassie!" I heard my mother's voice behind me. She was standing at the entrance of the restaurant with my dad. Even though she was smiling, I could tell she was nervous, and feeling about as out of place as Sean Hannity at a Hillary Clinton fund-raiser. I watched as the maître d' explained to my father that the restaurant required coat and tie and that he'd have to give him a jacket before they could be seated. He disappeared and came back with a blazer that looked like it came straight from the Ralph Lauren purple label collection at Barney's.

"Perhaps you'll be more comfortable in this, sir," he said, slipping it over my father's shoulders.

I turned back to the bar. "Can I get the check, please?"

"I'll take care of it," Dan said.

For a moment I hesitated, but my mind was on rescuing my parents from the stuffy maître d', and I was, frankly, too broke to protest. Plus, what were the odds I'd ever see him again? "Thank you," I said, smiling at him uneasily. I slid off the stool and headed over to meet my parents at the door.

Twenty-six bucks for a salad!" my dad lamented after we'd been seated at a table in the dining room.

My mom gently kicked him under the table. "We're here for Cassie," she said. "Let's just enjoy ourselves."

After the waiter had taken our order, I decided it was time to break the news. "So I was thinking," I began. "You guys know how confused I've been about what I'm going to do after graduation. And you know how expensive it is to live in Manhattan. So I've been looking into some different options, and I think that for right now, I'm going to bartend."

"Cassie, what are you talking about?" my mother gasped, utterly bewildered. "What happened to that position you got at *Us Weekly*? I thought you wanted to be a writer."

"I do want to be a writer, Mom, but I don't know if that's the right magazine for me. I'd be an editorial assistant, and my salary wouldn't even cover rent in *Albany*."

"Well, you have to start at the bottom, sweetheart," my dad cut in. "You work your way up—that's how it goes in the

real world." If there was one thing my dad had tried to in-
still in me, it was the importance of hard work and paying
your dues.

"I understand that," I said, leaning in, "but what you
guys don't understand is that it's really expensive to live in
New York City. This will only be a temporary situation so I
can support myself while I focus on my writing. I really want
to work on my screenplay, and I'm going to try to pitch some
freelance articles to other magazines as well. I don't want to
be stuck writing hundred-word captions about J. Lo and her
latest wedding. And I know you guys can't help me out, especially after helping me pay for college." I regretted those
last words immediately when I saw my dad's face fall. "I'm
sorry. I didn't mean it like that. You guys have been amazing, but I need to take care of myself from now on. And I'm
going to need money quickly if I'm going to sign a lease on
an apartment." They remained silent, so I continued. "I
found this bartending school where they promise they can
get you a job where you make a lot of money—up to a thousand dollars a night! I'll only need to work one or two nights
a week. And I can spend the rest of my time writing."

"But what about the late hours?" my mom asked. "You
always get run down if you burn the candle at both ends.
What about getting your master's? If you're so worried about
money, why don't you try to get a job at Morgan Stanley like
Alexis? You said she's going to be making a terrific salary."

"Mom, Alexis got a job in *investment banking*. I haven't taken
a math class since freshman year of high school. And she's
going to have to work over a hundred hours a week. I'd never
get to work on my screenplay." I could tell just by looking at
their crestfallen faces that convincing them was going to be a
hell of a lot harder than I'd anticipated.

"What are you going to do about health insurance if you

don't have a real job?" My mother was working herself into a panic. "Our insurance won't cover you now that you're out of college. What if you get sick?"

I twisted the napkin on my lap and stared at my knees. I hadn't even begun to think about things like health insurance. "I haven't had a chance to look into that yet—but I will."

"Health insurance is really expensive if you don't get it through an employer. Are you going to be able to spend five hundred dollars a month just on insurance?"

"Yeah, I am. Mom, I'm going to be making thousands of dollars a month easily."

My mom took a deep breath and clutched my father's hand on the table. "Cassie, your father and I have worked hard our whole lives so that you'd have opportunities. You're brilliant, you're beautiful, and we think you're capable of anything and everything. We want the world for you. We want you to have stability, a steady income, benefits, and not to have to worry about money like we've had to do our whole lives. You're graduating from *Columbia University* tomorrow. You can do *anything* you want to do. Why bartending?" she wailed.

"Mom, what I'm trying to make you understand is that bartending isn't what I want to do with my life. It's just a means to an end. I want to be a writer. You have to trust me. I know what I'm doing."

The waiter arrived with our salads, and delivered the delicately arranged plates of mesclun and frisee into the midst of our stony silence. "How much does this 'school' cost, and how are you planning on paying for it?" my dad finally asked.

The truth was that even though I'd saved up my last two work study checks, they amounted to a grand total of $313, and I was definitely going to need a loan if I wanted to survive for the next few weeks, not to mention pay for the bartending course.

"Five hundred dollars," I mumbled. "But it's an investment! I'll be able to make the money back in my first night of work."

A long pause followed. My mother finally broke it. "Cassie, you're an adult now, you're graduating college tomorrow, and you're right—we don't support you anymore. So I guess you need to do what you need to do. We'll be proud of you no matter what."

They both attempted to be lighthearted throughout the rest of the meal, but even as they raved over the mustard seed—encrusted salmon, I could tell they were distressed. After dinner I went with my dad to return his borrowed blazer to the maître d'. When we were alone, he pulled me aside and handed me a check.

"Your mother and I were going crazy trying to think of the perfect graduation present for you." He sighed. "Looks like you'll be needing this."

My eyes filled with tears as I looked at the amount: $500. At that moment, I committed myself to learning to mix the finest cosmopolitan Manhattan had ever seen. I would live up to everything Martini Mike's ad had promised, while simultaneously getting my screenplay produced. I would make my parents proud.

Welcome, future bartenders!" chirped the female instructor on the first day of the weeklong intensive class. She was perky, petite, and didn't look old enough to drink legally. "My name is Britney, and in just one short week, I'm going to teach you everything you need to know so you can become part of New York's fabulous nightlife!"

Over the past few days, I'd been deliciously anticipating all the knowledge Martini Mike's was going to impart, knowledge that would not only enable me to easily make back the cost of the course in one night, but would also leave me with ample money for all the things I'd always coveted in the city: decadent brunches at Felix, lunches at Michael's, and dinner at Cipriani's. I was so excited planning all of the other things I was going to spend my newfound money on (an iMac to write my new screenplay, a brand-new apartment rental in the West Village) that my student loans had nearly evaporated in my mind. I couldn't wait to breeze through to my second diploma in one week. Once I had that certificate of mixology in hand, everything else was going to fall into place.

"Okay, so here's the breakdown," Britney continued as she distributed copies of *The Martini Mike Bartending Manual*. "Today you're going to learn the ingredients of basic cocktails as well as basic bar etiquette, pour levels, and customer service skills. There'll be a quiz at the end of the class. Tomorrow we'll go over different types of wines—red, white, rosé, and also beers—lagers, ales, pilsners, you get the idea. The next two days will focus on scotches, liqueurs, cordials, ports, cognacs, and specialty drinks. Your final exam will be on Friday. Any questions?" and without waiting for an answer, she moved on.

"First things first. There are your three basic levels of liquor: well, which is the least expensive and housed in 'the well,' which is the rack—technically called 'the speed rack'—in front of the bartender, below the soda gun. You use well liquors when someone just orders a generic vodka and tonic or gin and tonic. Then you have your call liquor—brands like Absolut, Stoli, Jack Daniel's—which you use when people 'call' what type of alcohol they want. Finally you have top shelf, which refers to the most expensive liquors, like Ketel One, Grey Goose, Bombay Sapphire—they're always located on the top shelves, got it?"

My hand rocketed across the page and my head spun as I tried to notate every detail she spewed forth over the next two hours. The class ended with a practical exam, where we were each called up to the front of the room to make a drink. Looking at the equipment behind the makeshift bar—shining stainless steel shakers, bottle openers, zesters, and wine openers—I felt like a prisoner eyeing instruments in a torture chamber. Much to my embarrassment, I failed—because I couldn't make the "simplest of drinks," a vodka tonic. It was the first time in my life I failed a test of any sort. To make matters worse, my poor performance was followed by that of Jack, my round-faced classmate who not only made a cosmo with a deft hand and style to boot, but was hilarious, opening with a classic bar joke: "A brunette walks into a bar . . ."

On the last day of the course, Britney pulled me aside. "Cassie," she began, "you're a nice girl, but I think you need a little more training before you can become a certified bartender, because you don't seem to perform well in front of an audience. Bartending is all about showmanship—you're an entertainer, the life of the party, the hostess who makes sure everyone is having a great time! If you're interested, we offer a second round of training at a reduced price."

My stomach sank. I'd failed bartending? I'd just graduated from an Ivy League university, and I'd failed a course on mixing drinks? Too stunned to argue, I ignored her offer and turned and walked out into the chilly late-spring night. The air in the city was heavy with humidity and the smell of ozone, and even though it was early evening, the night felt as thick and black as a pint of Guinness.

Panic set in. I'd wasted my parents' graduation money on

Martini Mike's. And just two days ago, after spending fruitless hours searching through the *Village Voice*, Craig's List, and nofeerentals.com for a cheap studio apartment, I'd realized that there was no way I could afford to live in Manhattan on my own and had impulsively signed a lease on an apartment with Alexis. Rent loomed. My work study checks wouldn't even cover the first month, and on top of it all, I now owed Alexis's dad $3,980 for my half of the broker's fee and security deposit. It was a full-fledged disaster.

My mind raced. Temping was my only real option for fast cash, but even if I made $12 an hour and worked a full forty-hour week, I'd still bring home less than $300 a week after taxes, and that would never cover my living expenses. I'd hit a brick wall. How was I going to afford to eat? I'd feel like such a loser moving home to Albany. And I couldn't even afford to do that. Moving costs money, especially when you don't even have a car. I quickly calculated that I could survive a maximum of two and a half days in Manhattan without working.

By the time I reached the subway station, I'd all but given up. Feeling decimated, I resigned myself to breaking the news to Alexis that I couldn't take the apartment and calling my parents and begging them to come back to New York and rescue me. Fighting back tears, I fumbled through my purse, looking for my MetroCard. Among the handful of old receipts and gum wrappers, my fingers curled around what turned out to be not my monthly subway pass, but a dog-eared business card.

Suddenly the heavens seemed to clear, and the night changed from Guinness to Amstel Light. With shaking hands, I reached for my cell phone.

Dan Finton answered on the first ring.

Two

SICILIAN KISS

Finton's was tucked in the quiet corner of Grand Street and Centre Market on the border of Soho and Nolita, with Chinatown and Little Italy mere steps away. If I hadn't gotten explicit directions from Dan himself, I would've walked right past it, even though it was situated at the nexus of at least five eclectic New York neighborhoods.

As I surveyed the red brick facade of the building, which was softened by expansive bay windows, I imagined backroom deals being brokered inside under thick curls of cigar smoke. I would later learn that the bar's clandestine location had provided a safe haven for drinkers during Prohibition. Rumors still lingered that a brothel had existed upstairs, along with an underground tunnel that ran between the bar and the old police headquarters across the street. According to neighborhood lore, the policemen would travel surreptitiously through the tunnel to visit the speakeasy or brothel. Commissioned by Teddy Roosevelt in 1908, the headquarters—a stately stone building with a Greco-Roman portico—now housed some of Manhattan's most luxurious apartments and famous (or infamous) tenants, notably Madonna and Monica Lewinsky.

I raked a hand through my hair to tame the frizz (full-blown New York humidity had set in, even though we were barely into May) and yanked down on my skirt to maximize its coverage. Earlier that evening I'd had a hard time deciding what to wear. When I'd asked Dan if there was a uniform or dress code, he'd replied, "All black. Whatever you decide, I'm sure you'll look great." After a brief pause, he added, "But I do *prefer* the women to wear skirts."

I'd holed myself up in my new nine-by-eight room and stared at every single black piece of clothing I owned, which I'd spread out on my twin bed. Fortunately, I had a lot to choose from. Any rational woman will agree that after spending an extended period of time in New York, at least 75 percent of your wardrobe will be black. I shuffled and rearranged, trying to assemble an outfit, and after ten minutes, items were covering the floor and even dangling from my lamp. I finally settled on my favorite knee-length black skirt from H&M and a slim-fitting long-sleeved button-down shirt from J. Crew. For good measure, I unbuttoned one extra button. The small silver cross necklace that my grandmother had given me for my confirmation peeked through on my exposed neck.

I was checking myself out in Alexis's floor-length mirror when she sauntered into the room. She took one look at me and rolled her eyes.

"What?" I demanded, annoyed.

"Is that what you're wearing to work?"

"Yes," I said, shooting her a withering look over my shoulder. "I know I look like I'm going to a funeral, but Dan Finton said we have to wear all black."

"But you don't have to dress like you're *Amish!*" she said.

"It's my first night, Lex! You dress conservatively for work too!"

"Yeah, but I'm a banker. You're a *bartender*. You're going to work at a *bar*. They want you to look sexy, and *you'd* better want to look sexy too if you're going to make any money." She noticed my crestfallen face and then suggested, "Why don't you wear that Marc Jacobs skirt I bought you for your birthday? It looks adorable on you."

That Marc Jacobs skirt was about three inches long. I'd never worn it. "I don't know, Lex, it's really short."

"Cass, you're *supposed* to look hot. It's in the job description." As I scowled, she continued. "Think about when we go out—all the bartenders and cocktail waitresses are always practically *naked*, but they probably make more money in one night than I make in an entire week! Come on, just try it on."

I'd reluctantly left my apartment in the hip-hugging miniskirt and a snug tank top that Alexis had pulled out of her underwear drawer—but just to be safe, I'd stuffed my long-sleeved blouse in my backpack, within easy reach should the need arise.

A brunette walks into a bar . . ." Jack's joke popped into my head as I pulled open the heavy mahogany door and stepped over the threshold. The lighting fell softly on the overstuffed, red-upholstered couches. The bottles behind the bar, lit from below, cast colored shadows on the wood floor, and drink specials were ornately written in white on the mirror-covered wall, French bistro style. White, gauzy curtains billowed in the warm breeze, drawing my eye to the black-and-white photographs of historic New York adorning the walls. Candles reflected off the shiny brass of the beer taps built into the middle of the bar.

The ceiling was especially striking. Intricately carved out of what appeared to be mahogany, I would soon learn that it had lain hidden under a thick layer of plaster for more than a hundred years until Dan Finton had accidentally exposed it during a renovation. He discovered that it had been shipped from Vienna in the late seventeenth century and, according to appraisers, was priceless. Dan had it cleaned and restored, and now modestly likened it to the Sistine Chapel.

As my eyes adjusted to the dim light, a dowdy blond wearing elastic-waisted cotton pants, flat shoes, and an oversized oxford shirt that concealed her less-than-fit figure approached me and offered her hand, but not before outwardly scrutinizing my outfit. I wondered if Alexis's smallest, tightest camisole from La Perla had really been the right choice.

"You must be Cassie," she said.

I nodded, giving her my best firm handshake.

"I'm Laurel," she supplied tersely, adding, "the general manager here at Finton's." She had a cropped hairdo reminiscent of the bowl cuts my grandma had issued me when I was in third grade and a shrewd, judging gaze.

Laurel handed me a memo on Finton's bar policy that

looked about as reader-friendly as the *Communist Manifesto*. As I paged through the introduction, I was immediately overwhelmed by the volume of information that a Finton's bartender had to commit to memory and the severe penalties that followed if the rules weren't strictly adhered to. For instance, if a "sanitizing tablet" wasn't dissolved thoroughly in the rinsing sink, the bartender would immediately be "dismissed" because the Board of Health could come in and close the place down. The opening and closing procedures went on for twenty pages, accompanied by more threats that would be executed should any of the said tasks be overlooked. My anxiety mounting, I looked up from my reading and found Laurel studying me critically.

"If everything works out tonight and I decide to put you on the schedule, then I'm going to need to know your availability," she said. "I know Dan promised you Thursday, Friday, and Saturday nights, which I'm sure you know are the best shifts, but he didn't consult with me about this, and I need to revisit the schedule. Hopefully we'll be able to figure something out that works for all of us. Are you available for day shifts, or do you have another job during the day?"

"Well," I said taking a deep breath, "I don't have an actual nine-to-five job or anything, but ideally I would like to keep my days free, because—"

"Are you trying to be an *actress*?" she asked with obvious condescension.

"No, I'm not an actress," I said with all the confidence I could muster. "I'm a writer."

"Interesting," Laurel said insincerely. "You're going to have to work at least one day shift. That's the rule, if you don't have a *real* day job."

In the back of my mind, I could already hear my mother

now: "I thought you were bartending so that you could keep your days free, so what are you doing bartending on a Wednesday morning?"

But the cold, hard truth was that I didn't have much choice. I didn't exactly have the funds to retake Martini Mike's course, even at the reduced rate. In fact, I'd be lucky if this woman agreed to hire me at all, given that I'd never set foot behind a real bar.

I continued to pore though the mandatory reading material, the churning in my stomach mounting again. I hadn't even considered things like serving minors or the difference between Burgundy or Bordeaux wineglasses. I read terms like "end-of-the-night drop," "register ring," and "comp checks" and I tried desperately to organize in my head everything I knew, didn't know, and needed to learn—and fast. After enduring a short quiz on her excessive policies, Laurel granted me access behind the bar, where a handsome man of about thirty-five was mixing drinks with a style that I surmised could only come with years of experience.

"This is Billy," Laurel said brusquely. "He's been working here for seven years. You'll be training with him. You better get to work." And with that, she made a purposeful exit down the long flight of stairs to the left of the kitchen.

Billy was tall and fittingly Irish in appearance, complete with reddish cheeks and sandy brown hair with wild curls that framed his boyishly alluring expression. His blue eyes sparkled when he smiled, complementing his distinct dimples. I felt a tingle of attraction as well as a sense of relief—I was pretty sure that it would be easier to win over a man than a woman. If the difference between Dan Finton and Laurel was any indication, pure chemistry could count for a lot in this business.

"Hey!" I said. "My name's Cassie. It's great to meet you."

"Jesus. Are we really training another girl?" Billy said to no one in particular. "That makes, what, five in the last two weeks?"

I felt a further prick of fear. How many girls had they trained there? Did any of them pass the training test and graduate to bartender status? Flashbacks of the monstrous failure I'd suffered at bartending school blazed in my mind. I wasn't good at enduring criticism, and Billy was already giving off a whiff of outright hostility. What if I couldn't pull this off?

"Well, hopefully, after tonight you won't have to train anyone else," I said, trying to diffuse the tension he'd created.

"In the entire history of this bar," he replied, polishing a champagne flute and avoiding my gaze, "no woman has *ever* cut it as a bartender."

I tried to squelch the bubble of feminist anger rising within me. Whether he approves of female bartenders is irrelevant, I told myself. The point is, I have to make this work. I continued to try to talk to him, but Billy wasn't biting.

"When I have customers, get out of my way—they come first," Billy instructed, before rattling off Finton's bar details at a fast clip. "The white wine's on ice, backups are in the far cooler along with backup fruit and grapefruit juice—all other juices are on the gun. Red wine is stored in the second cabinet from the left, and the backups are downstairs in the wine cellar. As for beer, the imports are in this cooler and the domestics are over there at the end. All the pint glasses are stored below the taps—be careful, the Guinness glasses are mixed in, and it really pisses me off when people pour Harp or Brooklyn Lager in a Guinness glass, because we only have about ten of them. I always work that side of the bar. This is your side of the bar—the service end. I stay on my side, you stay on yours . . . am I going too fast for you, *sweetheart*?"

I shook my head dumbly. I still wasn't sure what he meant by "service end" and hadn't known Guinness deserved its own special glass. That hadn't been covered in Martini Mike's course.

"The Burgundy and Bordeaux glasses are over your register. We carry a Cabernet from Argentina, a Shiraz from Australia, a Pinot Noir from France, and a Merlot from California by the glass. White wine glasses are in the lower shelves, we have a Sauvignon Blanc from France, a Chardonnay from California, and a Pinot Grigio from Italy. When making mixed drinks, don't pour too heavy—an ounce and a half is more than enough—your well is full, and all your call liquor is behind you—single malts are in the middle, and you've used Micros before right?"

"I don't think so," I said.

"Really?" he asked, genuinely shocked. "It's the most basic system there is. Every bar I've ever worked at uses it. What system have you used?"

"Umm, just one of those old cash registers," I said, somehow managing to pull a scrap of an image out of my head from *Cocktail* when Tom Cruise is working his first shift at T.G.I. Fridays.

"Where did you use *that*?" he asked, his eyes boring into mine.

"This place uptown," I said, shakily.

"What place?" he pressed.

It was only twelve minutes into my first shift, and I was already on the verge of a breakdown. Thankfully, at that exact moment, a yuppie in a Brooks Brothers suit approached the bar and ordered a Jack and Coke, unknowingly rescuing me from Billy's Gestapo-like interrogation.

"So you honestly have no idea how to use this?" he asked, indicating the Micros computer, when he returned from making the drink.

I shook my head.

"Great," he snorted. "Sean'll have to teach you. I don't have time for this. He's also gotta show you how to do the bartender switchover from day to night." He moved down the bar to where a flock of women were singing his name. They were all ultra-fit and wore tight Citizens of Humanity jeans and trendy skin-baring tops. Upon further inspection, however, the creases on their necks and the thick makeup they used to mask the crevices around their mouths and eyes showed they weren't nearly as young as they were trying to be.

I looked at him, unsure of what to do, until Sean, a slender, dark-haired bartender, who, according to Laurel, worked all of the day shifts, approached me with a smile.

"Hi, love," he said, his speech colored by a warm Irish brogue. I felt my shoulder muscles unknot a millimeter at the sound of a friendly voice.

"Hi," I said warily, attempting an easygoing smile.

"How's it going so far?" he asked solicitously.

"Okay, I guess. It's a lot to take in all at once."

"You'll be fine. Remember, love, it's not brain surgery."

I was grateful for a little perspective.

"So," he began, "here's how it works: when the day bartender is leaving and you're coming on, we just have to make sure your register bank is back at three hundred so you have change right at the beginning of your shift." He led me carefully through the rest of the procedure, which miraculously—perhaps on account of his laid-back and supportive delivery—didn't seem so hard. Giving a customer change for a twenty, counting out the money in your drawer before starting a shift, and filling a glass with ice before putting in the liquor was hardly nuclear physics.

After he'd taught me how to use the Micros computer (a maze of different-colored buttons and screens that referenced a practically encyclopedic compendium of different drinks), I watched longingly as Sean gathered his belongings, poured himself a pint of Carlsberg, and left me to drink his beer on the other side of the bar. I'd known the guy for five minutes, but I already wished fervently that I could attempt my virgin bartending gig under his tutelage instead of Billy's.

Once he'd gone, I took in my new vantage point behind the bar. Facing the crowd and being the focus of attention was strangely intoxicating.

Sean had left used pint glasses with rims of dried caramel-colored foam, half-empty bottles of Beck's, and bar rags soaked with a rainbow of cranberry juice, various whiskeys, and Guinness on every imaginable surface. Just as I was about to attack the dirty glasses that were piled up, Billy traversed the back of the bar and appeared beside me in all of two seconds.

"Your side is a fucking mess," he declared.

"I-it, was Sean's mess," I stammered, "I was just about to clean—"

"Don't blame it on Sean, just *do* it," he directed, and then continued in militaristic mode. "Let's go over drink prices. Pay attention. Domestic beer is five, imports are six, except for the Paulaner, which is seven. Glasses of wine are eight, well liquor is seven, call is eight, top shelf is nine, and then there are the martinis . . ."

After he finished rattling off the laundry list of drink

prices, Billy abandoned me to attend to the customers gathered at his end of the bar. As his side got busier with the happy hour crowd, most of whom wore suits and greeted him warmly, he started barking orders at me. I was his designated workhorse running up and down the stairs, to and from the basement, which was home to the bathrooms, Laurel's office, the storage area, liquor room, and the wine cellar. First, he needed more beverage napkins ("bev naps," as he called them) and little red stirrer straws. The second I tore back up the stairs and delivered those, he shoved an empty bottle of Absolut at me and shouted "Bring two!" as I bolted back down to the liquor room. When I finally arrived back behind the bar, he immediately needed two bottles of Jack Daniel's. Laurel didn't even glance up as I huffed and puffed by her office five different times. She sat hunched over a pile of paperwork in her dimly lit, cinderblock cell.

It was now approaching seven-thirty, and I settled back behind the bar as the initial happy hour rush receded. There were still no customers on my side, so I pretended to look industrious. After I finished cleaning up Sean's mess, I took a cloth and wiped down the bar, polished the beer taps along with every glass on my end, and scrubbed every metal surface with Fantastic until my side of the bar sparkled like Harry Winston diamonds. I looked around at all the bottles, trying to familiarize myself with my new environment, so that when I actually did have customers, I wouldn't be completely lost.

After about twenty minutes of excruciating boredom, I noticed two people walking toward Billy's end of the bar. I was wiping down the bar for the fiftieth time and saw that Billy was too busy chatting with an attractive redhead in a crisp oatmeal-colored Jil Sander suit to attend to the couple now seated comfortably on bar stools and looking for service. Determined to seize the opportunity and show that I was a capable bartender, I hustled over to where they were sitting.

"What are you—some kind of idiot?" Billy snapped. "This is *my* side of the bar and *that* is yours. Understand?"

I nodded dumbly, trying hard to let his anger roll off my back. *Don't cry!* I chastised myself. But I could feel the tears welling so I quickly turned my head and let my long brown hair hide my wounded expression. No matter what happened, I wasn't about to give him reason to gloat to Laurel that another girl couldn't cut it behind the bar at Finton's.

"Remember, I've been doing this since you were in diapers, kid," he added wryly, rubbing thick margarita salt in my wounds.

Another hour dragged by, and my side of the bar remained deserted. Time seemed to stand still. I kept checking the clock on the Micros computer: 8:17. I checked again after it seemed like hours had passed only to find that it was 8:23. The one thing I'd learned from my training shift so far was that nothing is more painful than a slow night as a bartender. You're literally stuck in one small space, unable to pick up a book or make a phone call without looking unprofessional. At least when I'd been bored stiff at my internships, I'd been able to occupy myself by jotting down screenplay ideas and making to-do lists that I carefully edited and revised. To kill a few minutes, I grabbed a bev nap and a felt-tip pen and jotted down the description of a man in an expensive pinstripe suit, figuring I might be able to use it for my screenplay.

I folded up the napkin and put it in my pocket, then scanned the scene around me and sighed. I felt like I'd wiped down the bar 450 times in the span of two hours. I polished the glasses again. I rearranged the straws and napkins, all the while wondering how I was going to endure the rest of the night—and if I still stood the smallest chance of actually getting hired.

"Hey, kid, make these two nice people each a vodka martini, extra dirty, straight up," Billy yelled suddenly from his end of the bar. I straightened up. I knew this was a test, because he could have easily handled the order himself.

I vaguely remembered from Martini Mike's that a "dirty" martini was one made with olive juice. So I took a stainless steel shaker, scooped some ice in it, and started pouring the amount of vodka that I guessed was about right for two people. I added olive juice. I couldn't locate the dry vermouth. Hopefully, they wouldn't notice. I pulled two frozen martini glasses out of the cooler (proud of myself for remembering their location) and placed them carefully on napkins in front of the customers, but not before I placed three olives in each glass, because, according to Martini Mike's, an even number of olives in a martini was bad luck.

I placed the smaller shaker on top of my vodka and olive juice concoction and triumphantly started to shake. I felt a splash of something cold land on my face and immediately realized, much to my horror, that the smaller shaker hadn't been secured properly over the larger one. Worse yet, I had just shaken two very dirty martinis all over the two customers who had just ordered them.

Billy dove toward me and grabbed the shaker out of my hand.

"What are you doing?!" he hissed.

Flustered, I grabbed a bar rag and began to wipe down the bar and cabinets. "I-I'm sorry," I stammered.

Billy grabbed the rag out of my hand and said through

clenched teeth, "Serve the customers first—and give them some napkins. They're soaked!" Turning to the customers, he continued. "I'm so sorry. It's her first day. She doesn't know what she's doing. Those drinks are on the house."

Thoroughly humiliated, I turned to the customers—two good-looking men wearing the standard Wall Street uniform—pinstriped Hickey Freeman suits, Thomas Pink French-cuffed shirts, and Ferragamo ties—and said, "I'm really sorry. Can I pay for your dry cleaning?"

They both smiled indulgently, and one of them said, "Don't worry about it, honey. It's not the end of the world."

"Your blue eyes more than make up for it," the other one agreed.

I flashed them both my biggest, most winning smile and caught Billy rolling his eyes.

I set up for another try, and this time managed to make their drinks successfully. Though my shoulders were still permanently brushing my ears from all the tension, I felt better when I saw that they'd actually left me a $20 tip! I hoped it was an omen of good things to come and made sure Billy saw me drop it in the tip jar.

As the clock ticked toward ten, a rowdy group of older, Italian-looking men came in—not surprising since Finton's was only a stone's throw away from the trattorias and pasticerias of Little Italy. As soon as they were assembled at Billy's end of the bar, they directed him to put on Barry White and "turn it up," and he surprised me by immediately following their commands. I wouldn't have pegged Billy for a fan of the infamous icon of love. One of the men, who was plump and balding and wearing a flashy red silk shirt, climbed up on the bar and started waving his chubby hands above his shiny head while he crooned along to "Can't Get Enough of Your Love, Babe" in a deep timbre. The rest of the men had formed a circle and were dancing around a shorter, scrawnier man. The other customers in the bar looked on, both baffled and bemused.

I warily walked over to Billy, careful not to cross onto his side, and asked in a low voice, "Who are those guys?"

"They're from *the neighborhood*. Try to keep an eye on them. They like to be taken care of, know what I mean? The skinny one in the middle is Baby Carmine. He just got out of prison. That's why they're celebrating."

"Why was he in prison?" I asked, but before Billy could answer, Baby Carmine himself swaggered over to the bar.

His hair was greased back and he had beady, penetrating eyes as black as the shining onyx stone on his pinky ring. He wore three gold chains adorned with ornate images of Christ and a diamond-studded bull's horn—the Italian symbol of masculinity. Nestled in his thick nest of black chest hair, I could see a Miraculous Medal bearing a picture of the Virgin Mary. His gray velour jogging suit was zippered halfway down, giving the overall impression that he had just wandered off the set of *The Sopranos*. Still, it was hard to imagine him killing someone or pulling off a major heist. There was an air of calm about him. I attributed it to his newfound freedom.

"Hey, honey, how's about giving me a good ol' Sicilian kiss?" he asked.

"What?" I stalled, with a nervous laugh not sure if he was serious. I'd seen *The Godfather* enough times to know that men like Baby Carmine wouldn't take no for an answer.

"It's a *shot*!" Billy smirked from his perch three feet away. I thought I detected a glimmer of amusement in his eyes. "Amaretto and So Co. Chilled."

"I know," I answered testily, and then threw a glittering smile out to Baby Carmine as I started mixing, hoping that

So Co was what I thought it was—Southern Comfort. "I'm Cassie," I said with a hint of flirtation, determined to make my way into his good graces, since he seemed to exert so much power at Finton's. Three days ago, I reflected, the notion of willfully charming a low-level New York City mobster would have been unthinkable. Times had changed.

"Cassie, it's a pleasure to meet you," he said as he grandly grabbed my free hand and kissed it. "I'm Baby Carmine." He stepped back and studied me admiringly, yet somehow not in a lecherous way.

"Nice to meet you too, Carmine," I said sweetly.

"It's *Baby* Carmine, sweetheart, and don't you fucking forget it," he said as his wide smile disappeared briefly. Clearly this was a man whose temperament could turn on a dime.

"Oh, I'm sorry," I said, silently wondering why anyone would adhere so strictly to a juvenile nickname. Flustered, I concentrated on pouring out his shot.

He slammed it back and then said loudly, so that the other guys could hear him, "Cassie, you're a great Sicilian kisser. Keep it up, honey!" They all laughed uproariously as he threw a $100 bill at me. He walked away with a wink and a "Keep the change."

The price of the shot had been six dollars. That meant a $94 tip on one drink.

"Billy!" I squealed. "He left us a *ninety-four-dollar* tip!"

"No," Billy quickly corrected. "He left *me* a ninety-four-dollar tip. You're still training, remember?"

I'd read earlier in Laurel's manifesto that trainees didn't get to keep any of the tips until they were officially on the schedule. Apparently that was a standard practice in the bar industry, but I'd foolishly hoped Billy would make an exception in lieu of my hard work—or maybe even my short skirt. "I know," I acknowledged, "but that's still pretty amazing."

"Not really," he replied coolly. "He comes in here and throws money at me all the time."

After Baby Carmine had rejoined his group of raucous cohorts and was safely out of earshot, Billy leaned in close and whispered, "Baby Carmine's a 'made man' in Gotti's family. He started off as a garbage man, but now he has enough judges on his payroll to shorten a federal prison sentence."

"Really?" I asked. Both of our eyes traveled back to Baby Carmine, who continued to laugh and drink with his entourage. I marveled that these men had actually spent their lives hustling on the street, maybe even killing people, in order to ascend the pyramid of organized crime. As I dutifully wiped down Billy's side of the bar, my mind raced with possibilities. I might be able to incorporate elements of this seamier side of New York City into my screenplay. Audiences loved a rags-to-riches story, not to mention a violent Mafia twist.

Around 10:30, two young guys wearing NYU sweatshirts strolled into the bar and ordered Budweisers. I patted myself on the back for remembering to check their IDs as Billy hovered over my shoulder.

"Look at that. You didn't even screw up," he said, but not without another small glint of amusement in his eyes. "I thought for sure you'd forget to card those guys, seeing as they're practically your age."

"That'll be twelve dollars please," I said, ignoring him.

The guys pulled crumpled singles from their pockets and combined them into one pile on the bar, topping it off with six quarters, three dimes, four nickels, and a handful of pennies. I counted the money: twelve dollars exactly.

Baby Carmine watched the exchange thoughtfully.

"Whassa matta wit' you?" he yelled in their direction.

They looked up blankly at him.

"You didn't tip your bartender," he said.

Fascinated, I waited for their reaction.

"We're sorry," they mumbled sheepishly. "We don't have any more money."

"You shouldn't be drinking in a fuckin' bar then!" Baby Carmine bellowed. "Do me a favor—next time, grab a six-pack at the deli and drink alone in your apartment."

I hid a smile, and Billy burst out laughing.

I glanced back and forth between Baby Carmine and Billy, wishing I could pull out my notebook and dissect the different ways they treated me. Baby Carmine seemed to want to protect me—probably because he thought I was a cute, defenseless "barmaid," a babe in the woods, while Billy resented working with me for the same reason. I couldn't decide the best way to move forward. If I "toughened up," Billy would probably respect me more, but I suspected Baby Carmine preferred docile women, and he seemed to have already become an unlikely ally. I shot another engaging smile at Baby Carmine, lowering my lashes, while I effortlessly lifted the case of Budweiser that Billy had put on the bar and stocked it in the cooler.

Just then the door chimed ceremoniously. I turned around and watched, captivated, as an older gentleman inhaling a cigar strolled into the bar. He hummed "Fly Me to the Moon" as he approached my end, slipping off his Burberry trench coat and draping it majestically over a bar stool. He had a Napoleonic presence, as though he'd just come back from conquering half of Europe, and a thick head of white hair. His round belly caused his black Canali suit to pucker around the midsection. He wore a patterned Hermès tie and carried a cane with an ivory handle in one hand and a beige fedora in the other.

I stood at attention, cognizant of the tangible energy shift he engendered in the room, not unlike the one Baby Carmine had caused. He smiled at me, flashing nicotine-stained teeth.

"Hello, darling," he said. His voice was gruff.

"Hi," I said, scrupulously wiping down the area of the bar in front of him.

"Don't believe I've ever seen you here before," he said. Finton's certainly had a team of loyal regulars, and it was rapidly becoming clear that I would have to memorize all of their names and respective drinks as soon as I mastered the fundamentals of bartending.

"It's my first day," I confessed.

"I'm Martin Pritchard. I'm a good friend of Dan's." He offered me his gnarled hand.

"Nice to meet you. I'm Cassie. Would you like something to drink?"

"I'd love a Maker's Mark manhattan."

I once again visualized the Martini Mike manual in my head, trying to conjure up a mental picture of the manhattan recipe. Manhattan. Manhattan . . . whiskey, sweet vermouth, dash of bitters . . . up or rocks?

"Would you like it up or on the rocks?" I asked.

"Up, please," he replied.

Grabbing the metal shakers once again, I filled the larger one with ice and poured in the Maker's Mark and sweet vermouth, dashed it with bitters, placed the smaller one on top, and began to shake vigorously, confident that I wouldn't repeat the night's tragic earlier events and spray manhattan all over his striking tie.

"What are you doing?" Billy called out from his end of the bar, startling me.

"Making a manhattan?" I ventured.

"You don't *shake* a manhattan," he said, rushing over. "You *never* shake a manhattan. You *stir* a manhattan. If you shake it, it will bruise."

"Bruise?" I asked. "What are you talking about?"

He rolled his eyes, grabbed my drink concoction, and threw the contents down the drain.

"Try again," he commanded.

I focused on Martin's cocktail for the second time. Finally I presented it to him grandly, sick with worry and frustration, while he brought the glass to his lips. He took a sip, savored the liquid for a moment, and put it down.

"A perfect manhattan," he declared.

I couldn't help myself—I beamed. At that moment, my small bartending victory felt like an accomplishment akin to getting Jude Law to star in my screenplay. I glanced over my shoulder, hoping Billy had heard. He caught my eye and gave an appreciative nod.

As the night finally drew to a close, Dan Finton breezed into the bar, and Laurel and several of the regulars flocked to greet him. I tried not to draw attention to myself as I mentally reviewed the night's mistakes. I'd covered two customers in olive juice, assumed that a famous mobster wanted to make out with me, "bruised" Martin's manhattan . . . It seemed like the chances of me actually getting put on the schedule were slim at best.

Unable to wait for the moment when Billy reported all the details of my incompetence to Dan, I decided to zip up my navy blue Puma backpack and prepare to bolt. Just as I slung the heavy sack over my right shoulder, I saw Dan making his way toward me.

"There's my girl," he said proudly as he looked me up

and down. I could feel my cheeks turning red. There was something about the way he looked at me that definitely wasn't innocent. I felt naked.

"What did I tell you?" He smiled. "I knew you'd look great behind my bar. So how'd it go tonight?"

Before I could answer, Billy appeared at my side. I felt a stab of trepidation and took a deep breath, bracing myself for his condemnation. "She was great," he said. I looked up at him, surprised. "She didn't run and cry when I told her what to do, like all those other girls you brought in."

"Of *course* she was great. I knew that from the moment I saw her," Dan enthused. Then he turned back to me. "Cassie, have you met Martin? He's one of New York's most esteemed art dealers and collectors, and a very close friend of mine."

"We just met," Martin answered for me.

"Are you in for dinner?" Dan asked him.

"I'm meeting a couple I know for some drinks."

"Anyone I know?" Dan asked.

"No. Actually, I hardly know them myself. But it seems we have similar interests." Martin shot Dan a sly smile.

"Cassie, I need to see you in the dining room," Laurel snapped from the service end, which I'd finally learned was the end of the bar where the waitresses ordered drinks for their tables.

I wearily followed her to a deserted table where she'd spread out several documents.

"I need you to fill out this W-4 form and bring me a photocopy of your driver's license and social security card," she instructed.

"Does this mean I'm officially hired?" I gasped.

"We're willing to try you out on the schedule. We had to fire someone last week and I need to fill shifts immediately.

And Billy seems to tolerate you. You can work tomorrow night, right?"

I mentally canceled my dinner plans with Alexis at La Bottega at the Maritime Hotel. I couldn't afford it anyway.

"Of course," I said. I couldn't help beaming.

"Great. The shift starts at seven, but I think you should come in a little earlier—maybe five-thirty or so—to reorient yourself. It looked like you were having a little trouble back there, and Thursdays can be busy. I want to be sure you know what you're doing."

I mentally canceled my five o'clock yoga class.

"I'll be here at five-thirty," I said.

"And another thing, all staff members have to memorize all of our menu selections. Here's a lunch menu, a dinner menu, a bar menu, and a dessert menu. You should memorize the dessert menu first, before tomorrow's shift, because it lists all of our after-dinner drinks including ports, cognac, Armagnac, and cordials."

"No problem, I always prefer to start with dessert." I smiled, but Laurel remained stone-faced. I opened the dessert menu, which listed five desserts. My stomach rumbled—I hadn't eaten since lunch. Of course my eyes immediately gravitated toward the flourless chocolate cake, served with a scoop of Tahitian vanilla gelato and raspberry coulis. "Why is it called 'Four Devils Chocolate Cake?'" I asked.

"Well," said Laurel, "I'm sure you've noticed our hand-carved ceiling."

I nodded.

"There are three panels." She gestured. "And the center panel is engraved with the faces of four devils."

I looked upward at the menacing visages. In my boredom behind the bar I'd spent a lot of time gazing at the ceiling, but hadn't noticed the devils.

Laurel got up and walked away without another word, her sturdy flats clicking on the hardwood floor. I sighed happily and glanced back at the bar one last time before slipping out the front door. I did it. I had the job.

As I headed down the sidewalk, passing the large glass window to the left of the entrance, I could see Dan engrossed in conversation with a young brunette who demurely sipped a red cocktail. Martin was lighting another cigar as Billy mixed him a second manhattan. I followed the tendrils of cigar smoke as they traveled heavenward and shrouded the faces of the devils watching over the bar.

Three

THE "PERFECT" MANHATTAN

Between bartending, setting up my new West Village apartment, and the occasional mango margarita at Dos Caminos with Alexis, work on *Glass Slipper* fell behind on my priority list. Of course I continued to scribble and jot ideas in my notebook—that was the easy part. I was sure that once my bills were paid—I planned to have all my debts settled in the next two months—my screenplay would come into focus. The problem was, by the time I woke up, exercised, came home, showered, blew out my hair, and got dressed, it was time to go right back to work.

With two weeks of bartending under my

belt, I'd learned that Martini Mike's ad in the *Voice* had grossly exaggerated the nightly income of a New York City bartender. I was working four shifts a week, and according to Martini Mike, that should've amounted to roughly $4,000 a week. But the truth was, I was euphoric if I pulled in $500 in any given week. Sure, there were high-rollers like Baby Carmine or the occasional Wall Street magnate who liked to throw money around, but most people left a dollar tip per drink, and I certainly wasn't serving a thousand drinks per night. Wednesday nights were pretty steady. We always had a regular crowd, but it never got slammed, and Billy and I usually made anywhere from $80 to $100 apiece. We never made more than $250 on weekend nights. Even worse was the day shift I worked on Tuesday, where I was lucky if I could scrape together $10 in tips. No one ever came in for lunch, and the shift lasted nine painful hours.

I became obsessed with the financial spreadsheet in my head. My rent was $1,000 a month. Student loan payments would be kicking in shortly, and my lenders estimated I'd be paying $200 a month. My utilities totaled $250 a month. All this before I even factored in dinners and nights out, my YMCA gym membership, health insurance, new contacts and glasses every year, and the occasional new Fresh lip gloss from Sephora. Then there was the slippery slope of credit cards. My brain short-circuited whenever I tried to calculate the exact amount of debt I was in. I called Laurel and told her I was available day or night if she needed me to cover any shifts.

Time is money both for you and Dan Finton."

Billy repeated this mantra for the umpteenth time, as he showed me how to pour liquor out of a bottle and soda out of the gun at the same time. I'd also learned how to massage the foil seal off a bottle of wine with one quick hand motion, instead of taking the time to cut it off with the little knife attached to the corkscrew on what bartenders called a wine key. I'd mastered pouring two beers from the taps at once. I could even make a perfect bishop's collar on a pint of Guinness (the phenomenon that occurred when the beer's white head extends beyond the glass).

I quickly realized that Sean was right—bartending wasn't brain surgery. With each shift another mystery would unravel. On my third night, I'd learned that Syrah and Shiraz came from the same grape and were actually the same wine with different names (Syrah in France and Shiraz in Australia). If someone ordered a scotch or whiskey "neat," that meant it should come without ice, not chilled, just poured straight from the bottle. (I also learned that "scotch" is exactly the same liquor as whiskey, except that it's made in Scotland.) I already knew from Martini Mike that a "dry" martini meant light on the vermouth, but I quickly learned that even when people didn't specify "dry," it was still best to add no vermouth at all (unless someone requested the very rare "wet" martini). "Common tastes have changed with the times, and dry vermouth is becoming a thing of the past," Billy had explained.

Laurel left early much of the time (after dipping into too much red wine, which she liked to gulp as she pored over her paperwork), so Billy and I held the unofficial keys to the kingdom.

On Friday and Saturday nights Billy and I worked with a bar back (a bartender's assistant) named José. José got a $35 shift pay and 10 percent of the bartenders' tips. In return, he set up the bar, brought us ice all night, washed glasses, cut extra fruit, took out the huge trash bins two to four times a night, replenished the liquor supply, stocked beer, picked up dirty glasses and plates from the tables, and managed all the cleanup at the end of the night. When Billy went down to the basement to drop the money in the safe, I would always sneak José an extra $20.

Most nights I met Annie, one of the waitresses, for a postwork drink at Spring Lounge. Annie was a five-foot-nine blond Brazilian bombshell, who immediately after work swapped her boring black Finton's outfit for brightly colored, ruffly short skirts, tight camisoles, and dangly beaded earrings. It was necessary to have a friend with whom I could rehash the night's misadventures—from married men asking us to meet them at their hotel, to jealous girls shirking on tips if their boyfriends paid too much attention to us. After being on my feet all night, running around behind the bar, I was so wound up at 3:00 A.M. that sleep wasn't in the cards. All bartenders, I learned, needed a wind-down drink—anything to prolong the party.

After José, the waitresses were the second lowest on the totem pole. (The bartenders were the second highest, directly behind the manager or owner.) Waitresses had to ask the bartenders for every single drink and made about half the money that we did on a nightly basis. They did, however, have more access to the food. Annie and I worked out a mutually beneficial system—I gave her drinks, and she snuck me food from the kitchen when my stomach was growling at 2:00 A.M.

Shifts seemed to fly by when I worked with Annie. When the bar was quiet we huddled around the service end and chattered. Laurel would furiously disperse what she called our coffee klatch, but since she spent most of her time downstairs in her office, we spent the majority of our time deep in conversation, occasionally to the annoyance of customers waiting for drinks or to place food orders.

I'd met Annie on my second night of work. "It's Cassie, right?" she'd asked as she dexterously balanced six Bikini martinis on her tiny cocktail tray. The turquoise cocktails were Finton's Friday night special, and Sean had just taught me how to make them: 1 ounce of Stoli Vanilla, 1/2 ounce of Liquor 43, a splash of lime juice, and just a drop of Blue Caracao to give them their electric color.

"Yeah," I said, extending my hand foolishly, before realizing that she couldn't accept it without losing a martini.

"I'm Annie," she said brightly.

"Nice to meet you."

"You too! I'll be right back, I just gotta deliver these drinks."

I watched as Annie smiled playfully at the six Suits—straight out of an ad for Today's Man—who'd ordered the drinks, tossing her curls and tilting her head to the side.

"These aren't very manly drinks, gentleman," she said with a flirtatious smirk, while gracefully bending over and placing a martini in front of each one. They erupted in laughter, clamoring and competing for attention from their pretty cocktail waitress.

"Don't worry, beautiful," one of them said, "I usually drink scotch, but Roger over here insisted we try these." Roger started to protest, but Annie was already strutting back toward the bar.

"What a bunch of losers, huh?" she said to me with an exaggerated roll of her big green eyes. "They were in here last week, and one of them ordered a Grey Goose and cranberry—

so transparent. They only order Grey Goose because it's expensive, and they think they'll sound cooler—I mean, why spend ten bucks on vodka and then ruin it by adding that syrupy crap from the gun? Anyway, the guy with the eight-dollar haircut was bragging to his friends that he could only drink Grey Goose because he gags if he has cheap vodka. So just as an experiment, I had Sean give him the well shit for his second round, and the idiot didn't even know the difference."

I grinned. "Have you been working here a long time?"

She looked up reflectively and seemed to search her brain for the answer. "Almost a year. God save me! I'm becoming a professional waitress!"

"Come on, one year isn't that long," I reasoned.

"I know, but when I graduated from Tisch last May, I promised myself I'd only do this for six months while I found a way to become famous."

"You went to Tisch?" I asked, "What'd you study?"

"I majored in modern dance. How about you?"

"I studied creative writing at Columbia. But I took some screenwriting classes down at Tisch last summer. I loved it."

"Perfect! You write a screenplay, and I'll star in it, and then we'll *both* be famous, and we'll look back on our days at Finton's and laugh!"

"Sounds like a plan," I said.

Annie was definitely gorgeous enough to be a movie star, and with her slight Brazilian accent, she was evocative of Brigitte Bardot. Her olive skin contrasted sharply with her golden hair, and her full lips could morph from an alluring smile to a sexy pout without missing a beat.

"I've been just *dying* to break into acting," she went on.

"You never *stop* acting," Billy said wryly. He had a habit of suddenly materializing over my shoulder.

She gave him her best pouty smile and then laughed. "I guess you're right, but it'd be nice to start getting paid for it. Why won't someone just discover me? I wouldn't forget all my friends slinging drinks back at Finton's—" Her words drew to an abrupt halt as her eyes trained to a tattooed man with a shaved head walking in the door.

"Oh my God!" Annie moaned, throwing half of her body on the bar and shielding her face with her hand.

"What?" I asked.

Billy looked over at the guy and smiled impishly as his face lit up with recognition.

"That's L.A., isn't it?" he whispered.

"Yeah," Annie croaked.

"Who's L.A.?" I asked.

"Oh, I'm sure Annie can tell you all about him," Billy teased.

"Shut up!" Annie hissed.

"What's going on?" I asked in a low voice.

Annie quickly jerked her head to the right, indicating I should follow her into the dining room. The expression on her face let me know that it was urgent.

"Are you okay?" I asked after we were both seated at table twelve, a two-top nestled in the back of the dining room.

"No!" She put her head in her hands. "Did you see that guy that just walked in?"

"Yeah, I saw him."

"Well, he's the guitar technician for *Metallica!*" she said, her eyes widening. "Isn't that insane?! He came in a couple of weeks ago and stayed all night, and we had sex in the kitchen right on the countertop."

I made a mental note not to eat any of the vegetables that were chopped and prepped on that counter.

"Anyway," she continued, "I kind of like him, but I don't know what to do, because Allen is coming in any minute."

"Who's Allen?" I asked.

"One of the guys I've been seeing. I really like him too. And Marc is supposed to come in later if he gets out of work before I'm done. Marc's the guy I met at Marquee last week. This is a fucking mess. You need to help me."

"Okay," I said. "What do you want me to do?" I twisted around to look over my shoulder. I was waiting for Laurel to realize I'd left my post behind the bar and march up and hand me a pink slip. She usually insisted that we remain caged back there for the duration of the night.

"I'm going to take L.A. downstairs, give him a blow job, and send him on his way."

I burst into incredulous laughter. "Are you serious?"

"Yeah! Did you see how hot he is? And his dick is enormous."

I'd never known any other Brazilians, but if Annie was any indication, they seemed to have a tendency toward too much information. "But if Allen comes in while I'm gone— Marc definitely won't be in until much later—I need you to tell him I'm downstairs doing inventory, and keep him occupied until I come back up."

"But I've never even met Allen. I don't know what he looks like."

"Billy does. He'll show you," Annie said confidently. She had an answer for everything.

"Okay," I said, regretting the word as soon as it came out. I'd only just met her five minutes ago and was already heavily entrenched in her histrionics.

"Thank you *so* much!" she exclaimed as she threw her long arms around my neck. "I owe you one."

Annie disappeared downstairs with L.A., and I returned to my station at the service end of the bar, where a pyramid of dirty glasses had piled up. Ten minutes later L.A. emerged from downstairs looking like the cat who just ate the canary and slipped stealthily out the front door. A minute afterward Annie appeared, straightening her short, pleated skirt and rearranging her bouncing curls.

"Looks like you need a shot, you Brazilian nut," Billy called as he arranged three shot glasses on the service bar and filled them with Jameson Irish Whiskey, the only acceptable shot at Finton's.

"Staff shots," I had quickly realized, had a funny way of keeping us from our duties. Billy was usually the ringleader, and on a half-hourly basis he would line up three shots of Jameson for me, Annie, and himself. It was a bonding ritual that started our nights with a bang and fueled us intermittently through the hours of trying customers, boredom, cheesy songs, bad pickup lines, and, in some cases, depression.

"God, that was like my ninth shot tonight," I wailed, after I'd knocked it back and felt the smooth burning on my tongue and down the back of my throat where it spread warmly in my stomach. "I'm becoming an alcoholic."

"Give me a break, kiddo," Billy said. "These are baby shots. We only fill them up about a quarter of an ounce, so if you do nine shots, you've actually only had about two. Plus you're on your feet all night burning them off quick."

That made me feel a lot better. I'd never been a shot girl—even when my college friends had been fans of the $2 Kamikaze specials at happy hour hosted by Night Café, our college dive. I could chug Bud Lights with the most notorious of frat guys and would indulge in the occasional rum and Coke or vodka tonic, but for the most part, I didn't do well with hard liquor.

When my friends came into Finton's, they too took full advantage of staff shots. That night was no different. "Cassie!" I heard Alexis bellow from amid a pack of young trader types in suits.

I looked up from the paying customers I was busy serving.

"Give us another round of *shots!*" she yelled from across the bar.

I smiled at her through clenched teeth as I mixed her eighth round of shots, which she'd long ago stopped offering to pay for. I'd only been working in the service industry for a few weeks, but had already been indoctrinated to the importance of always offering to pay for your drinks and, more important, tipping the bartender—even when that bartender is your best friend. I of all people knew how much disposable money Alexis had, but she never left me a tip, and I felt too uncomfortable to say anything.

I'd taken to keeping my notebook behind the bar, as each person I talked to—mainly the Finton's regulars, but also my friends and their drunken alter egos—were providing plenty of good script material.

I was learning that a lot of people came to Finton's because they needed somebody to talk to, but I didn't feel qualified to offer advice when my own life was still so unsettled. In many cases, I found, drunks just wanted to hear themselves talk and have someone else absorb their problems. Even if I'd been Dr. Phil, they wouldn't have taken my words of wisdom. It could get depressing watching the same person come in night after night and drink twelve Ketels— on the rocks—one after the other while telling me the same sob story.

Steve Mitchell, one of the regulars, always came in at

around 2:30 A.M. on weeknights, precisely when Billy and I were closing up the bar. We couldn't lock the door on him because we felt guilty, but it was also more than that. I hated to admit it, but we knew that Steve, without fail, always left a huge tip: $50 or more. And at the end of a slow night, the difference between making $100 or $125 each had a real impact on our finances. Bartending was a quid pro quo.

"Hi, Cassie," Steve would say dejectedly. He was a tall, gaunt man with sunken eyes rimmed in black circles and the worst comb-over since Donald Trump. Every night he wore a battered T-shirt tucked into jeans that should have been retired along with Debbie Gibson in the late 1980s.

"Hi, Steve," I said. I tried not to cringe, but I always suspected that my annoyance was noticeable. "How are you?" I asked dutifully.

"Not so great," he said, looking at me expectantly.

"What's the matter?"

"Things at work aren't going so well—my pension hasn't gone through yet—Dawn isn't returning my calls. She just doesn't appreciate me . . ." He sat, slumped and forlorn, as I mixed his usual, Tanqueray and tonic.

Another night a short, overweight man with a reddish beard that matched the color of his cratered nose approached the bar and ordered a martini up with olives. After I made the drink he said, "I'll give you a hundred dollars if you suck on those olives and then spit them into my glass."

For a moment I'd actually entertained the idea, mesmerized by his hundred-dollar bill. I hated needing money that badly. When I hungrily gathered all the singles thrown on the bar to stash in my tip jar, I felt like the stripper I'd seen on Howard Stern, who, when her song was over, had to clamor on her hands and knees picking up the crumpled bills that had been thrown at her. When I reflected on all of this, I realized that, bizarrely, I was relating more and more to the heroine of my screenplay.

"What's your name?" the crater-nosed man had asked.

Still feeling like I had to be polite to everyone, I responded, "Cassie," and gave him a neutral smile, but I inched farther down the bar and farther away from him.

He stayed at the bar all night watching me. I became hyperconscious of my movements. I tried my best to ignore him, but every time I looked up I seemed to catch his eye. It was disturbing. You never know what kind of person you might come across in New York City, and I didn't know if he was just a harmless, lonely man or a potentially dangerous stalker. Sometimes I felt trapped behind the bar—anyone who wanted to could come in, order a drink, and sit and stare at me all night, and there was nothing I could really do about it.

Edward was another regular who felt it was his duty to pay me a visit every time I worked. He drank Jack Daniel's neat with a Carlsberg back (which meant he ordered the beer to soften the blow of the whiskey) and was tolerable compared to the rest of my needy coterie. He seemed to have his act together, and he usually didn't monopolize my time with mundane drivel, preferring instead to try his best to worm his way into Annie's skintight pants.

All that changed one Saturday night when he trudged into Finton's at 4:30 A.M., just as Billy, José, and I had finally finished our cleanup after a long night of work. His drawn face bore the telltale signs of recent crisis coupled with too much booze and a need to talk to someone.

"Sorry, Edward," Billy said. "We're about to walk out the door."

"Please don't close," he pleaded. "My wife just left me, and I have nowhere else to go."

Hours later, when I was tucked safely into bed, my mind still awake and racing from the night's activities, I fumbled for a pen on my nightstand and reached for my notebook.

There are so many lost souls drifting around Manhattan, and they all seem to gravitate toward bars. It's a lot to deal with at 4:30 in the morning.

Martin Pritchard, Dan Finton's art dealer friend whom I'd met my first night, returned often, and before he could order, I was always ready with his gently stirred manhattan.

"Another perfect manhattan," he said one night after savoring his first sip. "Billy, I think Cassie's a keeper."

"You know, you might be right. Surprisingly, she's turning out okay," Billy said, smiling at me.

"Dan and I were just talking about how great the two of you look together behind the bar," Martin went on.

As my skills had improved and Billy and I were both able to relax, it had become clear we had great chemistry. But I didn't have any delusions about it translating to the other side of the bar. There was something about the environment of a bar as a workplace—everything became concentrated in such a small space and, as a result, somehow intensified. Within just a few weeks, Annie had become one of my best friends, I had become a shrink to regulars (privy to secrets they wouldn't tell their own spouses), and Billy and I had developed a public flirtation that was all at once a calculated performance yielding bigger tips and sales and a reflection of what happens when you stick two red-blooded people in a confined space together for an extended period of time—and add a little alcohol into the mix.

"Thanks," I said, regarding Billy with a smile. "How are you, Martin?"

"Fine, dear. Getting ready to head out east in the morning."

"Where're you going?"

"I have a house in Southampton."

My ears perked up. The Hamptons—the exclusive Long Island retreat for every New Yorker who "was somebody." I'd been hearing about it since my first days at Columbia. From the details I'd consumed from *New York* magazine, I had conjured up images of a mythical Avalon in my mind.

"The Hamptons" is the general term used to describe the towns encompassing the stretch along the Atlantic Ocean on the "south fork" of Long Island, starting about a hundred miles east of New York City. They were named after Hampton Court, the summer retreat of the British Royal Family. Hampton Bays and Westhampton were the farthest west and, according to Alexis, the least exclusive. However, she'd reluctantly admitted, "If that's all you can afford, at least it's better than the Jersey shore." Just a little farther east on Route 27, Southampton started the string of towns that housed those with money, both old and new.

Martin's cigarette smoke burned my eyes (pesky rules like "No Smoking in New York City Bars" apparently didn't pertain to him). I blinked, reaching for a bev nap to take some of the sting away.

"Ever think about bartending out in the Hamptons?" he asked.

"Not really," I said. "I'm still trying to get on my feet after graduation." Plus, I'd only been at Finton's a couple of weeks. How could I already jump ship?

"I'm sure you could make a lot more money out there. Finton's really slows down during the summer months, as does everything in Manhattan. But the bars and clubs in the Hamptons are always packed in the summer. The season's so short, no one wants to miss a chance to go out. Furthermore, all the sophisticated young people in New York get shares in the Hamptons nowadays. You'd have a marvelous time."

"That sounds great, but I'm sure it's impossible to get a job."

"You should come out with me this weekend," Martin suggested. "I can take you around to some of my haunts. I know a couple of people who owe me some favors."

"Maybe." I contemplated his offer. I definitely wasn't making the money I'd anticipated at Finton's and was spending more time listening to sob stories than making drinks. If I'd gone to grad school for psychology, I'd be making $500 an hour for what I was already doing basically for free. In the Hamptons I could probably make fistfuls of cash, go for runs every morning along a stretch of white sandy beach—and maybe even spot Clive Owen. It was unavoidably appealing, even though part of me wondered how I'd fit in with such a wealthy scene. Was it crazy to even think about trying to take on another job when I was just getting the hang of things here? Still, I could hear the song of the Hamptons Sirens luring me away from the monotonous din of Finton's.

"I'm leaving tomorrow morning if you'd like to join me. My house has more than its share of guest rooms, and you can take the train back the next morning if you have to work at night," Martin offered.

"Okay, maybe I will," I said. After all, what harm could

it do to check it out? At the very least, I'd be able to get out of the city for a few days.

I returned to the stack of lipstick-smeared champagne flutes that had piled up around the grimy sink. As I watched Martin savor *his* "perfect" manhattan, I wondered if the Hamptons might be a necessary ingredient in mine.

Four

SALTY DOG

 "Why do you need *another* bartending job?"

My mother's concern had been palpable, even over the phone, when I told her I was going job-hunting in Southampton.

"You're going to get run down and sick, and you don't even have health insurance," she continued.

The truth was that my previous summers in New York had taught me that from Memorial Day to Labor Day the city underwent an unpleasant transformation unlike any other major metropolitan area in America. Hundred-degree heat coupled with stifling humidity, a seeming boom in the rat and roach populations, and the proliferation of all kinds of unique bodily odors engendered a mass exodus of New Yorkers to second homes in Connecticut, the Catskills, Fire Island, and, of course, the Hamptons, the crown jewel of summer retreats. The paved streets and sidewalks soaked up the sun's rays and trapped the brutal heat so that even after sunset, they radiated oven temperatures, filling the atmosphere with a sticky, tarry taste. Pollution cloaked the island in a thick layer of smog, and entering the subway system was like hitting an unbearably oppressive wall of heat saturated with the stench of urine. The sweltering temperatures forced you to wear as little as possible, and the resultant catcalls made walking down the street a study in sexual harassment. Alexis had installed an air-conditioner in her bedroom, but I—typically—couldn't afford one. My room was already a sweat lodge, and it was only the third week of May. In short, New York City was the single worst place to be in the summer, and if you had any means of escape you'd be a fool not to take it—especially if it meant hobnobbing on the beach and in five-star restaurants with heiresses and rock stars.

"Mom, I promise I'll be fine," I assured her. "And I'll be able to make a lot more money."

"But, honey, I thought you said that if you went to bartending school, you'd be making more money than you'd possibly need."

At this point, I still hadn't told my parents that Martini Mike's promises of $1,000 a night hadn't come remotely close to meeting reality. And it would be a cold day in hell before I told them I'd never even passed the class in the first place. They kept pressing me to log onto ehealthinsurance.com, a website devoted to helping freelancers and other "nontraditional" workers find health insurance and avoid "middle-class poverty." Even though the site offered a good service, I couldn't see how another monthly bill of $307 would keep me any healthier. I decided I'd have to get by with the vitamin C and multivitamins I bought at Duane Reade.

I'd also decided that the best way to get ahead was to go bartend where money was growing on the white poplar trees. "I spent a couple of summers out there in the eighties, working at this gay bar in Wainscott called the Swamp," Billy had told me when he overheard Martin mention the Hamptons. "We were walking with $600 a night, easily, and sometimes we'd bank a grand—and that was over ten years ago. There's no limit to the amount of money people throw at you out there."

You're going to bartend in the Hamptons? That's amazing!"

It was seven o'clock on a Thursday morning, and Alexis was shocked to find me awake and dressed at such an early hour. "So this guy you met at Finton's—what's his name again?"

"Martin Pritchard," I told her.

"Right, Martin. And he's taking you out there today?" She was standing in a raw silk crimson kimono, her blond hair swept back in a perfect knot at the nape of her neck, steaming her first espresso of the day in the $5,000 Boden espresso and cappuccino machine her mother had bought us.

"Yeah, he knows the owner of a bar out there called Saracen. It's in Wainscott, I think. Do you know where that is?"

"Yeah," Alexis mused, while inspecting the flawless French manicure she got at Rescue Beauty Lounge every

Tuesday evening. "It's a tiny town somewhere between Bridge and East Hampton."

"Bridge?"

"Bridge*hampton*," she sniffed.

"Oh," I said. I stuffed my headphones and a copy of the *New Yorker* into my backpack and zipped it shut. "Lex, you don't think it's weird that I'm going out there with Martin, do you? I mean, I hardly know him."

"He's a friend of Dan Finton's, right?"

I nodded.

"Has he ever hit on you?"

"No!"

"Besides him asking you out for a romantic weekend getaway in the Hamptons, that is." Alexis smirked.

"Honestly, it's not like that," I protested.

"Has he ever asked you out or anything?"

"No. Nothing like that at all."

"Does he check you out when you're behind the bar?"

"No," I said, wracking my brain for any instance where he'd made me feel uncomfortable. "He's actually always been a gentleman."

"Then, no, I don't think it's weird. He's probably just trying to help you out. Didn't you say he went to Columbia?"

"Yeah, he went to Columbia for undergrad and got his master's at Harvard. Dan says he's one of the most successful art dealers in New York."

She nodded approvingly as she emptied a blue Equal packet into her scalding espresso. "I swear to God, I drink so much Equal, that I'm going to wake up one day to find a third eye growing in the middle of my forehead." She stirred the espresso with her finger. "Do you want some?"

"No, thanks. I feel so sick. I'm never drinking again."

I'd had fifteen baby shots of Jameson at work the night before, and even though under Billy's calculation that only amounted to four actual shots, I'd woken up that morning with a toxic hangover. In addition to the hundreds of calories in each shot, beer, or glass of wine I imbibed, I couldn't even begin to calculate the infinite calories I was ingesting in food. I'd taken to eating full breakfasts at 7A with Annie at five every morning on my way home *after* our after-work drink(s). Not to mention the fact that working at a restaurant didn't do much to combat an expanding waistline—white bread, fried calamari, French fries, and chocolate cake were readily available for me to pick at all night long in the kitchen. I vowed right then and there that I wouldn't drink for at least a week and would try to incorporate more vegetables into my diet.

"But, seriously, Lex," I went on, banishing my hangover guilt and anxiety, "you don't think I should worry about . . . I don't know, being alone with him. I've never been anywhere with him besides Finton's, and then there's always the bar between us, you know?"

"You're definitely overthinking this. What is he like, seventy? He probably just wants to help out a fellow Columbia alum. Besides, I go out for drinks with my boss all the time, and he's like a hundred years older than me. Just think of Martin as a work colleague. This could be great for you. Maybe you'll finally be able to stop worrying about money."

For Alexis, my constant fretting over bills was akin to worrying about a bad dye job from Bumble and Bumble—it was never as bad as you thought it was, and if you just decided not to focus on it, you'd be much better off.

I grabbed my backpack and headed for the door as she downed her double espresso in a single shot.

A half hour later I arrived at Martin's building, still nursing my hangover but excited for the journey. Martin lived uptown in the Pierre on Fifth Avenue, amid the extravagant structures of Museum Mile—the stretch of Fifth Avenue that hugs the idyllic east side of Central Park and houses the paramount New York museums including the Metropolitan Museum of Art and the Frick. I paid the cab driver with my last $20 bill, which was supposed to tide me over until my next shift at Finton's, and stepped out in front of the Pierre. The doorman, wearing the standard emerald green uniform complete with large brass buttons and military-style cap, looked me up and down, eyeing my Old Navy ensemble and battered backpack.

"Can I help you?" he asked.

"Hi." I smiled. "My name's Cassie Ellis. I'm here to see Martin Pritchard."

His face softened. "Hello, Miss Ellis." He opened the heavy glass door with his gloved hands. "Please have a seat while I notify him of your arrival."

Gazing around the opulent lobby, complete with a grand marble staircase and crystal chandeliers accenting the plush ivory and gold rug that looked like an heirloom from a Persian monarch, I felt like Little Orphan Annie at Daddy Warbuck's mansion. I got a shiver of excitement (and a tinge of jealousy) looking around at all the perfectly coiffed residents sailing in and out of the lobby, carrying shopping bags from Takashimaya, Gucci, and Henri Bendel. I sat down on a luxurious red velvet couch that looked like it had once belonged to Cleopatra.

"Hello, dear," Martin said, emerging from the elevator, cane in hand, and trailed by a valet with five Louis Vuitton suitcases neatly stacked on a luggage cart. He leaned in to plant a wet kiss on my cheek. His breath was acrid—reeking of nicotine and tomato juice, as if he'd polished off a few Bloody Marys with breakfast. Without a bar between us, I realized he was a good five inches shorter than I was.

"Hi, Martin," I said, trying not to blanch at his sour smell. "Sorry I'm late."

"Don't worry. I'm still waiting for them to pull the car out of the garage so the doorman can load it for us." He walked over to the doorman and asked him, "Has Lily arrived?"

"Yes, sir," the doorman said.

"Who's Lily?" I asked.

"She's the woman I'm seeing. She's coming with us to Southampton," Martin answered.

I inwardly breathed a sigh of relief. I hadn't known Martin was seeing anyone, but I was glad it wouldn't be the two of us alone all day. What kind of woman, I wondered, did a man like Martin date? I envisioned Lily as a curator from the Louvre, a distinguished professor of anthropology, or maybe an auctioneer from Christie's who shared his passion for art.

While waiting for Martin, I'd noticed quite a few younger women of the Plum Sykes's *Bergdorf Blondes* variety swarming about, armed with chihuahas in pink sweaters that peeked curiously out of Bottega Venetta woven bags. Now I scanned the other faces in the lobby, looking for Lily, and spotted an attractive fair-haired woman of about fifty-five, in an eggshell Chanel suit and tasteful black Manolo Blahnik pumps. She seemed to be looking in our direction but then walked right past us, and Martin revealed not a flutter of recognition. There was another older woman with chestnut hair tied elegantly in a bun, who was sitting on a couch reading *The Economist*, but Martin didn't so much as glance her way. Then I noticed a slight young woman, about my age, sitting on a Victorian armchair in the center of the lobby. She was likely the daughter of some wealthy real estate mogul, who'd had the privilege of growing up in this luxurious building or others like it.

"Good morning, Lily, dear!" Martin called out to her.

"Marty, darling!" she said, as she leapt to her feet and threw her graceful arms around his neck, giving him a lingering kiss on the mouth. Stunned, I watched as he placed a liver-spotted hand on her porcelain shoulder and briefly considered abandoning the trip. When a good-looking, forty-year-old businessman picked up the check for a twenty-two-year-old girl at Spice Market—that was one thing. When a portly septuagenarian made out with a girl fifty years his junior—that was crossing the line in my book.

Then again, Lily wasn't the stereotypical blond, big-breasted bombshell for whom most wealthy men, especially in New York, traded in their first wives when they got older. Lily was delicate, dressed all in white, with a cashmere sweater tied loosely around her narrow shoulders. Her auburn hair complemented her hazel eyes, and she was taller than Martin by about a foot and very thin—ninety pounds soaking wet, as my grandmother used to say. She had been reading *Town & Country*, her black-rimmed glasses balanced carefully on her diminutive nose.

"Lily, this is Cassie," Martin said.

"Hello, dear," Lily purred, "It's lovely to finally meet you. Martin's told me all about you." She tucked the magazine in her monogrammed Goyard bag and flashed a smile, revealing teeth that rivaled the whiteness of her pants.

"It's nice to meet you too," I said, leaving out the fact

that Martin had never even mentioned her. I offered one of my sweaty hands to shake the dainty, manicured one she held toward me.

"Well, are we ready?" Martin asked.

Lily and I nodded in unison. Martin snapped his fingers and the valet immediately rushed forward to add Lily's own collection of Louis Vuitton suitcases to our pile of luggage. We followed him to the street, where Martin's Bentley stood idling. Before Martin and Lily even buckled their seat belts, they each lit up a cigarette. I'd always detested cigarette smoke, and as clouds of fumes circled my head, I almost passed out.

Driving down Fifth Avenue en route to the tunnel, we passed a series of pricey doorman buildings with green awnings draped across brass poles, glinting in the morning sun. As we passed Bergdorf Goodman, the single most expensive, and most intimidating, department store in all of Manhattan, Lily piped up, "Darling, we have to stop into Bergdorf's and look at the new Celine line. I hear it's fabulous."

"I'm sure it is. And knowing you, you'll have me buying all of it for you before the summer's out," Martin replied archly, and Lily giggled with an air of guilty glee.

I reflected that the benefits of a May–December romance in New York City ran both ways. Martin got arm candy out of it, and Lily got Bergdorf's. I wondered if Martin was still capable of having sex. Even though I'd love a pair of Sigerson Morrison shoes, an Anthony Nak necklace, and the run of a house in Southampton, I still wouldn't have sex with Martin Pritchard for all the Bulgari jewels in the world.

What seemed like days after leaving the Upper East Side, we arrived in Southampton. Right away I saw that the Hamptons were a serene blend of green pastures, corn and strawberry fields, deciduous trees, country cottages converted to designer shops dotting quaint little villages, and a seemingly endless stretch of the roaring Atlantic. Martin parked the car in the heart of Southampton Village and took us on a brief walking tour. With relief, I breathed in my first gulp of fresh Hamptons air—Martin and Lily had chain-smoked Dunhill's and Silk Cuts the entire ride out with the windows shut, and I'd spent the last few hours trapped in the backseat feeling more nauseated and hungover than ever.

Main Street was impeccably clean and lined with old brick buildings that housed high-end stores like Saks Fifth Avenue and Theory. Winding side streets with flagstone walkways and canopies of trees branched off into a blur of picturesque cafés, boutiques, and antique shops, and it felt more like New England than New York.

"The shopping in East Hampton is much better," Lily remarked as she studied a pair of Jimmy Choo stilettos displayed in the window of the Shoe Inn.

"Let's stop at Barefoot Contessa," Martin suggested. The Barefoot Contessa was apparently a small chain of gourmet grocery stores limited to the Hamptons—but, as Martin and Lily explained, famous throughout the country.

"We have to get that pâté. It's to *die* for," Lily gushed with pseudosophistication. "Cassie, whenever Martin and I entertain, our first stop is always the Contessa. Their imported sheep's milk cheeses are divine."

Entertain? She didn't even live with him, and her airs rang completely false—at least to my ears. I'd already noted that Lily sprinkled her speech with so many sugar-coated "darlings," "dears," and superlatives that she could give you a toothache. She seemed to be playing the role of a spoiled 1950s housewife, but she couldn't have been more than a few years older than me. She was clearly doing her best to behave like one of the middle-aged Hamptons "ladies who lunch." I wondered what she did and how she spoke when she wasn't sitting beside her seventy-year-old boyfriend. Did she giggle about former college flames and fashion victims she passed on the street like Alexis and I did?

"Of course, darling," Martin said. "We can get the pâté. And Cassie also needs to sample that Beluga caviar and the Stilton—it goes so nicely with the Petrus. I wonder if they have those glorious yellow tomatoes."

We arrived at the Barefoot Contessa, and I stared in awe at picture-perfect cupcakes draped in chocolate ganache, apple galettes framed in puffed pastry, and flaky chocolate croissants. Lily selected cheeses I had never heard of, along with caviars imported from Scandinavia, pâtés shipped daily from France, and tiny pear-shaped tomatoes. Martin stood up front by the cash register, flipping through *Dan's Papers* and the *Southampton Independent*, two of the Hamptons' weeklies.

After our items had been bagged, the cashier read the total: $334.09. I looked at the twelve items on the belt—all of which couldn't really qualify as anything more than snacks (or maybe hors d'oeuvres if you wanted to get fancy about it)—positive that the amount had resulted from a major error in the store's computer system. Martin reached for his wallet without so much as a blink. He produced a black American Express card and paid for the items. I'd never seen a black AmEx before, and I wondered where it fit in the hierarchy of plastic. Lily leaned in to nuzzle his ear while he signed the receipt.

Unless they expected me to starve, Martin was apparently paying for me too. I'd thought about taking out my wallet, but I knew my last $10 wouldn't make a dent in the grocery tab. I just hoped Martin wasn't expecting the same payback from me that he was getting from Lily.

On the way to the car, he put his hand around her tapered waist and then casually let it drop to fondle her rear end. "Darling! You need to behave!" she chastised him coyly, freeing herself from his grasp.

I felt so uncomfortable, like I'd just walked in on my parents having sex. I quickly walked toward the car and pretended to admire the landscaping of Main Street. It was like I was babysitting two horny fifteen-year-olds, a situation made all the worse by the fact that at least one of them was my grandfather's age.

We got back in the car and traveled south on Mecox Lane away from town and toward the ocean. The houses grew more and more impressive—expansive rolling lawns spotted with rose gardens and tennis courts gave way to enormous residences with commanding white columns and elegant verandas. Most of them appeared vacant. It was still a week before Memorial Day, and the summer season hadn't officially begun. Dozens of landscapers busied themselves in the yards, pruning lilac bushes, trimming hedges, and cleaning pools in preparation for the owner's arrival.

"There's a large Hispanic population here during the off months," Martin said when he noticed me looking at the workers.

"Where do they put them all during the summer season?" Lily asked.

"Damned if I know." Martin harrumphed. "As long as they're not on my beach, I don't care where they go."

I looked out my window and lost myself in Walter Mitty–like daydreams, simultaneously trying to peer between colossal hedges to get a look at the homes that lay hidden behind them and to set aside my embarrassment at having been privy to such an appalling comment on Martin's part. I was liking these people less and less with every passing minute and beginning to dread what the rest of the trip would bring. What on earth had I gotten myself into? Still, I was determined to see it through and at least try to secure a bartending job since I'd come all this way. It was only twenty-four hours, and if the Saracen opportunity worked out, I'd just get my own place out here for the summer and avoid these two cretins.

A few minutes later we turned onto a road marked PRIVATE. We drove down a long winding, wooded path, slowing down just as I noticed a sign that read PRITCHARD SERVICE.

"What's 'Pritchard Service'?" I asked.

Lily laughed.

"It's the service entrance," Martin said. "The driveway used by my cook, maids, and groundskeepers. And that cottage you see is where my three main workers live year-round, so they can take care of the property and also prepare the house at a moment's notice if I decide to come out for a weekend."

We drove a few yards farther and pulled up to immense wrought-iron gates. Martin punched a code into some sort of security device, and we were granted access to his long driveway. My breath caught as we approached the house; I felt like we'd driven into the first panel of Bosch's "Garden of Earthly Delights." Vibrantly colored flowers complemented the green rambling hills, and ponds, fountains, and gardens adorned the property. In addition to the sprawling Manor House on the south side of the estate and the small service cottage on the north side, a deluxe pool house and horse stables loomed in the distance. Martin pulled the Bentley into an eight-car garage, sandwiching it between a fire-engine-red Porsche 911 Carrera and a midnight blue Tahoe. Despite the bitter taste in my mouth from Martin and Lily's earlier behavior, I had to admit that all of it took my breath away. After all, I'd grown up in a tiny three-bedroom ranch with fifty square feet of dry yellowed grass for a backyard.

Martin spanked Lily playfully on her butt as she got out of the car.

"Martin, not in front of Cassie!" she squealed.

I forced a smile and stepped out into the driveway. The salty sea air alerted me that the ocean was nearby. And whereas the sky had been gray and overcast for much of the drive, the sun was now shining brightly.

"It's splendid outside!" Martin exclaimed. "The sun finally looks like it's here to stay. Let's drop off our bags and head to the club, shall we?"

"Sound good," I said, although the last thing I felt like doing was getting back inside the cigarette smoke–filled car. I watched as several of Martin's servants scurried out of the mammoth pillared house to collect our bags and deposit them inside.

Martin had been a member of the Southampton Country Club for over thirty years. The club was incredibly exclusive—fewer than fifty members, he informed me—and I suddenly wished I'd chosen something different to wear. Lily looked pristine in her tennis whites; meanwhile, I'd discovered a stain on my faded pale blue top.

By the time we arrived, my appetite had returned full force, especially after our tempting sojourn through the Barefoot Contessa. As we passed the club's English gardens overrun by a rainbow of climbing roses and poppies, all I could think about was eating. We entered the dining room to find every imaginable variety of food laid out in a gourmet buffet: omelets made to order, bacon, sausage, fresh fruit, salads, pasta, vegetables, filet mignon, beef brisket, and desserts. Giant ice sculptures of swans and mermaids graced the tables, and the cheese platter lined with grapes and figs looked like a still life by Velasquez. There was an entire ten-foot table devoted solely to bread—baguettes, croissants, brioches, chocolate bread, rhubarb bread, seven-grain bread—it was an Atkins follower's worst nightmare. There was a raw bar piled high with lobster, clams, oysters, shrimp, and caviar, and another station housed two chefs who would create virtually any salad you could envision, out of the thousands of fresh ingredients spread out in front of them. I spent a full twenty minutes deliberating, picking and choosing, and circling around until I finally struggled back to our table, my arms balancing heaping plates of salmon, New York strip steak, and potatoes au gratin—as well as glasses of orange juice, water, and red wine.

My few weeks at Finton's had already taught me how to carry loads of plates and glasses at a time, so when a waitress asked, "Do you need some help with that, miss?" in a lilting Irish accent, I smiled at her in a manner I hoped communicated that I too was a veteran of the service industry and said, "No, thanks, I think I've got it."

As I tried to set everything down on the table, my Nutella tartine, a handful of champagne grapes, and a tiny ramekin of cocktail sauce slopped off the plate and onto the floor, almost landing in Lily's lap.

"Oh, I'm so sorry," I said, bending down immediately to pick up the fallen items and mop up the mess with my napkin.

"Cassie, don't trouble yourself." Martin laughed, expelling cigarette smoke. His laughter sounded more like a smoker's cough. "They have staff here for that sort of thing. Besides, you can go up again and get more food, you know."

"Though it looks like you cleared everything out the first time," Lily sniffed, eyeing my heaping plate of selections. I looked at hers: it held exactly five lettuce leaves and two pieces of grilled shrimp.

"I skipped breakfast this morning," I said apologetically. But a small part of me was actually beginning to feel sorry for Lily. It was clear that she not only denied herself an attractive, age-appropriate boyfriend, but the pleasures of food as well.

"Martin, I see you're not drinking your usual," I commented, eager to take the attention off of me.

"Ketel and tonic is my summer drink—I just switched from salty dogs, because the grapefruit was too acidic. Now that the weather's warming up, I'm ready to abandon manhattans for the next few months," he explained, snapping his fingers for the waiter's attention, so that he could order another one before his current drink ran out. Martin was the type of person who hated to have an empty glass in front of him.

We were sitting at an ocean-side table on the deck of the Victorian mansion that housed the club. Silverware tinkled, ice rattled in glasses, and quiet conversation ebbed and flowed with the tide. All of the other members were older WASPy types like Martin, dressed in white golf shirts or dress shirts with the sleeves rolled up and the top buttons undone, sans ties. A handful of them were sporting navy-blue blazers with their family crests engraved on the shiny brass buttons. I noted that there was a disproportionately high number of much older men with young, attractive women on their arms.

As I observed the boats tossing in the waves and the sloping sand dunes, I relaxed a little and began to enjoy the delectable spread in front of me. My worries receded amid the sunshine and ocean air, as I came to my pièce de résistance— chocolate soufflé.

The warm chocolate tasted like sweet dark satin melting on my tongue. "You guys *have* to try this chocolate soufflé, it's the best dessert I've ever tasted," I said, eagerly dipping in for a second bite. I'd read somewhere that chocolate makes your brain release the same endorphins your body produces during an orgasm—not too far off from what I was experiencing at that very moment.

"I feel like I'll get fat if I even let myself *smell* that," Lily huffed. She then fixed me with an irritated look. "Cassie, you have chocolate on your *teeth.*"

Just then Martin bellowed, "Well, hello, James!"

I turned around expecting to see another gray-haired, gray-skinned, middle-aged playboy out to lunch with his twenty-year-old girlfriend. Instead, my jaw almost hit the deck when I saw the stunningly gorgeous young man standing in front of me. He had wind-tossed, light brown hair that fell charmingly over his forehead, and his cheeks and nose were slightly rosy in a way that suggested he'd spent the morning outdoors. I guessed that he stood at least six two—perfect for my five feet eight—and my heart jumped as I took in the copy of F. Scott Fitzgerald's *This Side of Paradise* and the *New York Times* tucked under his tanned, toned arm. I hurriedly wiped my mouth and ran my tongue over my teeth before attempting a smile.

"Martin! How are you?" James asked.

"How could I be anything but wonderful on such a glorious day?" Martin said as his eyes swept our panoramic ocean view.

"I know. Dad and I were fishing all morning," James said.

"How is your father?" Martin asked.

"He's doing great," James said. "Looking forward to beating you at golf on Sunday, from what I hear."

Martin laughed raucously while grasping his protruding midsection. "Ladies, this young man's father, James Edmonton *the Second*, is one of my best clients and also one of the most skilled golfers I know. The Edmontons are tremendously fond of ridiculing my very high handicap."

"Hi, I'm James," he said, suddenly turning to me with a radiant smile. I snapped to attention and did my best to offer him an equally fetching gaze, while desperately wishing I had reapplied lip gloss.

"Where are my manners?" Martin tsked. "Cassie, allow me to present James Richard Edmonton the Third, graduate of Yale University, vice president at Goldman Sachs, and master boatman and golfer. James, this is Cassie. She's a bartender at Dan Finton's place downtown. And you already know Lily."

"It's nice to meet you," I said, discreetly wiping my clammy hand on my pants before shaking his. Why the hell did Martin have to introduce me as a bartender? "What year did you graduate from Yale?"

"Nineteen ninety-eight," he replied.

"Do you know Matt Riordan?" I asked. "He's from my

hometown and graduated that year." I was barely even aware of the words as they came out, just watching his mouth as he responded.

"Sure, I know Riordan. A good friend of mine actually dated his younger sister. She went to Columbia, I think."

"Yeah, Amanda!" I said. "I know her pretty well. She graduated this year with me."

"So you went to Columbia, huh?" he asked. "We killed you guys at the Yale Bowl."

"Well, we have a young football team—all eleven starters are coming back next year, and if I remember correctly, none of Yale's are. So I think you're going to have some competition over the next couple of seasons." I smiled, amazed that the one article I'd ever read about the Columbia football team had remained tucked away somewhere in my brain.

"Pretty impressive," he said, nodding. "So what days do you work at Finton's? That's a great bar."

"Well, hopefully I'm going to be working out here this summer on the weekends, and I'll keep some shifts at Finton's during the week. I'll probably be working Tuesday during the day and Wednesday and Thursday nights," I replied, conscious of Lily's disdainful eyes on me and hoping I didn't sound as eager as I felt.

"Cool. Well, maybe I'll see you there sometime." He turned back to Martin. "I'll let you guys get back to lunch. It was nice to see you again, Lily. And Cassie, it was great meeting you."

I watched him vanish into the country club where he was immediately camouflaged by a sea of white Polo shirts and khakis, and I was overcome with the delicious sense of giddiness that comes from meeting someone you're instantly attracted to. I felt like Ingrid Bergman in *Casablanca* when she sees Humphrey Bogart and the world momentarily stops turning. My mind momentarily flashed to my screenplay. Perhaps I had a new model for my Prince Charming.

"Is James dating anyone?" Lily asked, reading my mind. "He's so handsome." Handsome doesn't begin to describe it, I thought.

"I don't really know," Martin mused. "I heard he ran around with Amanda Hearst quite a bit last summer."

I knew from *Gotham Magazine* that Amanda Hearst was a socialite, and my heart sunk at the thought of all the wafer-thin, platinum blond, unbelievably rich, "aspiring actresses, models, and recording artists" that James must know and who I could never in a million years compete with. A guy like that—who was I kidding? He obviously had women—heiresses, even—lined up around the block. My brief visions of striking up a summer romance floated away on the same salty breeze that kept the yachts tossing on their moorings only a few hundred yards away.

I quickly changed the subject and turned toward Lily, just as a waiter was bringing her another glass of wine. She had easily consumed twice the amount of alcohol that I had since we'd arrived at the club, and she was half my size. Her eyelids were noticeably heavier and her regal posture had softened. I felt like I might finally be able to have a genuine conversation with her—if there was one thing bartending had taught me, it was that alcohol was a truth serum. "So, Lily, what do you do?"

"Lily is a personal trainer," Martin answered for her. "She just opened her own boutique fitness studio on the Upper East Side."

"It's really picking up," she boasted. "I have twice as many clients now than I did last month. Most of them are women who are trying to shape up their rear end—it's the first thing to go on women over twenty-five. It starts to sag."

"I don't notice that problem on you, darling," Martin said as he took a big gulp of his Ketel and tonic. "You just turned twenty-seven and your ass looks better than ever."

"Well, that's because I work on it practically every day," Lily said, smiling at him and tossing her glossy hair.

"I like to go to work on your ass every day too," Martin growled, leaning in toward her. I cringed. This time even Lily blushed.

"Cassie, darling, I apologize," she said with an embarrassed laugh. "Martin is exceptionally frisky today."

"Oh, now, that's not true, darling. I'm always like this when I'm around you. I'm sure Cassie doesn't mind, do you, Cassie?"

"Uh . . . no," I stammered.

"Of course you don't," Martin said. "You're a bartender. I'm sure you've heard worse."

This was a new one. It hadn't occurred to me that my profession might give people license to do or say things they wouldn't do or say in other company. It was possible, I realized, that Martin and Lily didn't carry on like this around everyone and that their behavior was a function of how they perceived me. I was a bartender—I came from a world of decadence and debauchery. I was also working class and thus not in a position to have my judgments of them matter.

Martin turned toward the ocean, gazing over my head at the clusters of people on the beach. Flocks of mothers in Juicy sweat suits sheltered by the official blue-and-white beach umbrellas of the country club were keeping vigilant watch over children in Vilebrequin swimwear. "Speaking of asses," he went on, "that girl's got an ass on her that's going to break hearts."

I followed his gaze down to where a four-year-old girl was playing in the sand with brightly colored shovels and buckets. Her blond curls were captured in two pigtails with matching pink bows, and she wore a tiny bikini covered in little yellow ducks. She was bent over filling pails with water for her sandcastle.

"You mean *that* little girl?" I asked incredulously. "She's only about four years old!"

"I can tell a good ass when I see one." He chuckled. "I've noticed from my vantage point at Finton's that you have a nice one yourself."

"Marty!" Lily said, feigning astonishment. "Behave yourself, darling."

I was now feeling downright disgusted. Martin's behavior toward Lily was one thing—many older men coveted the bodies of younger women. It might not have been pleasant to think about what Lily and Martin did behind closed doors, but they were both consenting adults. But a four-year-old girl? Was he a child molester? At the very least he was a pervert, which made me even less thrilled at the revelation that he'd been secretly eyeing me. At Finton's there was always a bar between us, but in this sort of social setting I felt uncomfortable and exposed. I looked at Lily, who was so drunk at this point that I wondered if Martin's comment had really registered. She was smart, I reflected. If she had to deal with Martin's company in exchange for a lavish lifestyle, she might as well spend her time with him drunk and clueless.

I was weak with relief when Martin asked for the check and we prepared to leave. When the waitress brought the bill, I started leafing through my credit cards to find the only one that wasn't maxed out. I hoped they took Discover. Even though I had no money, I wanted to pay for my own lunch. I didn't want anything else from Martin.

"Cassie, what are you doing, dear?" Martin asked.

"I just wanted to give you some money toward my lunch . . ." I began.

"Darling, here at the club, no cash is exchanged. Every member has a standing account, so each time I eat here, I just sign for it and then pay one bill at the end of the year."

"Oh, I'm sorry, I didn't realize. Well, thank you very much," I said. Lily smiled indulgently as I quickly stuffed my wallet back into my bag.

The three of us piled into the Bentley again, and before Martin had even started the car, he lit a cigarette. Lily did the same, and clouds of smoke formed circles around my head. I wondered how Martin could even see out the windows of the car. The two of them smoked so much that I was surprised everything around them wasn't fogged by a sticky, grayish glaze of tar and nicotine.

"Shall we head over to Saracen?" Martin asked. "Joseph said I should bring you by any time after four."

"Sure. That'd be great." I was starting to question whether I could stomach spending my summer working out here. What if everyone was like Martin and Lily? Then again, James Edmonton had seemed like a great guy in addition to being unbelievably attractive. I'd just have to make sure I found a share house with normal people my own age. Besides, I was determined to get out of debt—and from everything I kept hearing—and from everything I'd already witnessed—money flowed freely in the Hamptons. "Do you really think I could get the job?"

"I don't see why not. I spoke at length with Joseph about you. He was the one that suggested you come in for an interview."

G ive us a call when you're done and we'll come pick you up," Martin called as I climbed out of the Bentley. It was a quarter to five when we arrived at Saracen, and the temperature had already dropped another five degrees. "Lily needs a few items from Henry Lehr in East Hampton, so we'll be nearby. Call my cell."

Martin had explained earlier that Saracen was one of his favorite watering holes in the Hamptons. It was an upscale Italian restaurant that let its hair down after the dinner crowd faded and transformed to a disco of sorts for the older Hamptons set who still liked to swing, but wanted to avoid the official velvet-rope-madness of the club scene. Typical of the Hamptons, it was an old estate house on Georgica Pond converted to a restaurant. It had whitewashed shingles and a grand doorway that in its heyday could have been the reception hall for a debutante ball.

"Hello?" I called as I entered the empty restaurant. Tables and chairs were stacked haphazardly in the entranceway, and the place looked nowhere near ready for the upcoming Memorial Day weekend.

"What do you want?" an irritated voice shouted from somewhere in the back.

"Hi . . . I'm Cassie Ellis . . . Martin Pritchard recommended that I meet Joseph about a possible bartending job and—"

"Hold on, I'll be right there," the voice yelled.

Moments later a squat, portly guy of about thirty-five strolled out of what I assumed was the kitchen. His black hair was slick-backed like the Fonz, and he was wearing a turquoise silk shirt tucked into black Cavariccis and a thick black leather belt with a shiny silver buckle. He reeked of Drakkar Noir, and he was the kind of guy who gave Long

Island a bad rap. I was sure he had a can of Binaca in his back pocket.

"Hi," I said, "Are you Joseph?"

"No, I'm Tony, Joey's better-looking younger brother," he chortled. "Joey couldn't make it today because he's stuck at our other restaurant in Brooklyn."

"Oh," I said. "Well, Martin Pritchard said I should stop by because I'm looking for a bartending job. I brought along my résumé and . . ."

"I wish I could help you out, sweetheart," he said, his eyes lingering on my breasts. "We definitely owe Martin a favor or two, but we're overstaffed as it is. Joey and I usually have our staff all set by late February. It's going to be tough to find a job this late in the game."

"Oh. I had no idea," I said hollowly. "Thanks."

"Sorry, sweetheart," he said. "Good luck, and tell Martin we're sorry we couldn't come through."

Trying to shrug off my disappointment, I walked outside and hovered in the empty parking lot, watching the evening traffic on Montauk Highway. I took out my cell phone and dialed Martin's number, but the call wasn't going through. I looked down at my phone and saw the ominous message, "No Service," blinking on the tiny charcoal screen.

"Cell service in the Hamptons sucks," Alexis had warned. I took a deep breath and tried the call again. No luck.

I kept on trying, but the call wouldn't connect. As I shifted from one foot to the other, I looked across the road and saw a sign for a place called Spark about a hundred yards down the street. Rather than bother Tony again, I decided to go there, sit down, regroup, use their phone, and maybe have a drink.

The neon lights emblazoning the bar's sign were incongruous with its weatherbeaten paint-chipped exterior. It looked like a large dingy shore house. But despite its tacky facade, the inside was bright and tasteful. The main room had been converted from an old barn, so the ceilings were lofted and gaping windows had been installed on all of the walls. In contrast with the dusty emptiness of Saracen, there were at least a dozen people running around frantically trying to get the place ready for the holiday weekend that would kick off the summer season.

"Can I help you?" a man behind the bar asked. He wore a grungy red bandanna knotted around his sweating head and an oversized T-shirt with the sleeves ripped off. On his arms were thick Pony sweatbands. His bloodshot eyes were deeply set, highlighted by his pasty skin. He held nine wineglasses in one hand and four liquor bottles in the other as he swiftly stocked the desolate bar.

"Uh . . . yeah," I ventured. "I just came out from the city for the day, and I was wondering if you guys were hiring."

"Cocktail waitress?" he said, as he blatantly checked out my body. I suddenly wished I hadn't eaten that chocolate soufflé. But on some level, it was a flattering question. Cocktail waitresses in Manhattan and the Hamptons were usually aspiring models, dancers, and actresses—incredibly tall, thin, and attractive. It was a compliment to be mistaken for one.

"No—bartender."

"Our bar staff is full," he said. "You want a drink?"

I accepted and sat on a bar stool sipping a Bud Light and watching him prepare the bar.

"Where'd you go to school?" I asked, after we'd introduced ourselves.

"Deer Park High School," he replied.

"Is that in Long Island?" I asked.

"Yup. How about you?" he asked.

"I grew up in Albany and went to high school up there, and then moved to the city and went to Columbia."

"That's cool. I went to Southampton College for a year, but all I did was smoke pot, so my parents were like 'I'm not paying thousands of dollars for you to get stoned all day,' so I just dropped out. I started bartending at Blue Collar Bar when I was nineteen. I've worked at just about every single bar in the Hamptons," he explained as he expertly layered bottles of triple sec in a storage cabinet. "It's crazy out here—you start work at one place, then you pick up some shifts somewhere else, and the next thing you know, you're all over the place. If you meet the right people, you can start working at the nicer clubs where people really drop money. Last summer I worked at NV on Thursday, Jet East on Friday and Saturdays, Sunset Beach on Sundays. It was insane."

"Do you have another job besides bartending?" I asked.

"What do you mean?" he asked.

"Like a day job or something," I said, regretting the question. I was learning that even in a city like New York, where a lot of the bartenders were doing other things like acting or writing, there were still a lot of career bartenders like Billy. If the money was good, it was easy to get sucked in.

"Nope, I make enough money bartending out here in the summers to take the winters off. I usually head down to Miami, and if I run out of cash I can always bartend in South Beach. I've been thinking about going to Hawaii this coming fall after the season's over. I hear they got a bartender's union down there, where you get health insurance and something like twenty bucks an hour plus you make sick tips."

"God, I wish they had that here. I could really use it," I

said, thinking that I could probably finish my screenplay in one winter in Hawaii.

"Are you a good bartender?" he asked suddenly.

"Yeah," I said with bravado I wasn't sure I deserved to use. I guessed I was a good bartender. I seemed to be holding my own at Finton's. But I didn't really know.

"Can you handle volume? Because this is gonna be slammed this summer. I'm talking twenty deep at the bar."

"I can handle anything," I said, more firmly than I felt.

"Hold on a sec." He climbed over the bar and vanished out the front door.

Moments later he returned with a six-foot-five man in a flashy double-breasted white suit.

"This is Teddy," Jake said. "He's one of the promoters here, and he's in charge of hiring."

Promoters, like publicists, were minor celebrities who jockeyed for fame and publicity and were yet another notch to contend with in the hierarchy of a bar or club. At smaller bars and restaurants like Finton's, the general manager ran the show with occasional help or input from the owner. At big clubs in the Hamptons, owners hired a team of promoters to make their place "the" spot for that summer. Often promoters have Rolodexes containing numbers of celebrities and other beautiful people they can always count on to decorate their club, and get mentions in Page Six, *DailyCandy*, and on *Access Hollywood*. Promoters have a lot of power, and are often put in charge of a lot of operational duties like the hiring and firing of the bar staff.

"Hey. I'm Cassie," I said, straightening up on my bar stool.

"So I hear you're fast," he said.

"What?" I asked, alarmed.

"Jake said you're a fast bartender . . . you can handle heavy volume," he said. "Because this is going to be *the* spot out here this summer, and we need bartenders who can really bang it out. I'm talking tons of celebrities—everyone from Donald Trump to P. Diddy, and we already have parties booked for thousand of people. You need to make them want to stay and make them want to *pay*."

"Of course," I said, wondering exactly what he meant by "heavy volume."

"What's your highest ring?" he asked. A "ring" is bartender jargon for sales.

"Ah, well, um . . ." I stammered, trying to think of a number. I had no idea how much I rang at Finton's, because we did what's called a "blind drop." Laurel always did our register reports the day after we worked, so we never saw how much money exchanged hands or went into our register. I took a stab in the dark. "Probably about eight thousand?"

"Wow," he said, visibly impressed. "We'll definitely try you out."

"Great!" I said, letting out the breath I'd been holding and breaking into a smile.

"You talk a lot of shit, sweetie," he said. "I like that. Be here nine-thirty on Friday night."

I was both thrilled and relieved. This bizarre day and all the awkwardness with Martin and Lily had very nearly amounted to nothing. Now I suddenly had a job at what promised to be the hottest spot in the Hamptons. I shook Teddy's hand and thanked both him and Jake profusely. I could hardly wait to tell Alexis.

As I walked out the door, Teddy called after me, "And remember—dress sexy, but not slutty. This is a classy place, but they still want to see some skin."

Outside, I pulled out my cell phone to check the time: 7:18. I'd forgotten to ask Jake if I could use the phone, and I felt funny going back inside. Teddy's parting comment had left me with a vague sense of sleaziness that I tried hard to let roll off my back. Clearly I was going to have to let go of a lot of my more feminist notions if I wanted to be successful in this industry. I wasn't sure whose yardstick of success I was measuring myself against these days—certainly not my mother's! I looked at my cell: still no signal. But a cab idled in the parking lot.

"How much to Southampton?" I asked the driver.

"Just you?" he asked.

I nodded.

"Twenty."

"I only have ten," I said, which wasn't a lie.

"All right, get in. It's been a really slow night anyway. Where you going?"

"The Pritchard estate on Mecox Lane."

I climbed in the car, and we careened west on Montauk Highway. Twenty minutes later I saw the familiar PRIVATE sign emerge from the wall of impeccably manicured hedges. The driver let me off right in front of Martin's security apparatus. I wondered if someone inside was watching me on a television screen.

"Here's my card," the cabdriver said as I slid across the cracked black leather seat, opened the door, and slung my backpack over my tired right shoulder. "Call me if you ever need a ride."

"Thanks," I said, handing him the battered $10 bill and stowing the card safely in my wallet.

By now it was almost eight o'clock and the sun had set,

dipping below the weeping willow trees on the horizon and leaving an unnatural purple glow in its wake. I pulled on my jean jacket and fastened the buttons as a cool breeze wafted off the water and across the grounds of Martin's estate. I wasn't sure how I should deal with the security system. After studying the device more closely, I realized there was a tiny red call button. I pushed it.

"Yes? Who is it?" A woman's voice crackled like a rifle shot out of the speaker box. I jumped, startled. From her thick Spanish accent, I assumed it was one of the maids.

"Hi, it's Cassie, Martin's friend. I'm outside," I said, my voice echoing throughout the empty grounds. A buzzing sound followed and the gates slowly opened. Passing by the servants' cottage, I tried to get my bearings as sensor lights eerily illuminated my path. I broke into a run, sprinting the quarter mile to the Manor House.

I knocked on the massive door, but there was no answer. I had expected at least the maid to be waiting for me, but the house appeared vacant. With trepidation, I pushed open the door and walked inside.

"Cassie, dear?" Martin's voice echoed somewhere off to my left.

I relaxed. "Hi, Martin," I called. "I'm back."

"We'd all but given up on you. Come join us. We're in the sitting room."

I followed his voice down the hall to find him and Lily sitting next to another couple on a gold-upholstered couch in a candlelit room. They were murmuring softly, and I noticed two open bottles of red wine and half-filled, lipstick-smudged glasses spread out before them, along with a half-empty bottle of Ketel One, more used glasses, plates with remnants of food, and four ashtrays overflowing with still-smoking cigarette butts and cigars. In his red velvet bathrobe, Martin gave the appearance of a stubbier Hugh Hefner. Lily wore a lacy, very short white negligee. I stopped in the doorway.

"Hello, Cassie, darling," Lily said with a graceful tilt of her head. "Come meet Denise and Bill."

"Hi," I said cautiously, moving slowly toward them, not wanting to seem rude. Denise was a striking Asian woman no older than thirty. Dressed in a black bustier and a Russian sable coat, seductively sucking on her long cigarette, she looked like one of the women you saw advertised as escorts in the back of the *Village Voice*. Bill, on the other hand, was a mirror image of Martin—short and plump, with an expensive robe and a hand that groped at Denise's inner thigh.

They all sat there smiling mutely at me. What the hell was going on here? My mind raced, and I felt a surge of fight-or-flight adrenaline hit my nervous system, urging me to turn around and bolt. Martin in his bathrobe, Lily in lingerie, both of them sitting there with another scantily dressed couple. This can't be what it looks like, I thought.

"Well," I fumbled, "I guess I should start getting my things together if I'm going to make the nine o'clock train." There was no way I'd feel comfortable staying there overnight.

"You can't just scurry away without telling us how it went at Saracen," Martin slurred, his eyes half-mast. As a bartender, I'd already become highly sensitive to the nuances of drunken behavior, but any idiot could tell that Martin was wasted out of his skull. My eyes fell to rest on several prescription pill bottles spilling their contents onto the glass table, jumbled in between the liquor bottles and cigarettes. "Sit down and have a glass of wine," he urged.

Ever since she'd put the book *The Gift of Fear* by Gavin de Becker in my Easter basket one year, my mom had instilled in me the importance of following my instincts—which I'd now been ignoring long enough. These people were certifiable. I needed to get out of this house, get on the train, and get back to my safe little converted two-bedroom where my worries about bills and Alexis's dirty dishes now seemed comfortably benign. But as soon as I turned to go, Martin blocked my path. He placed a wrinkled paw on my shoulder. "Why don't you slip into something more comfortable and come and join us?"

My words tumbled out, as I flinched and pulled away. "My roommate actually just called, and she's really upset about . . . I have to get on the nine o'clock train. My cab's still waiting outside."

I backed out of the room and quickly started making my way down the hallway and toward the front door. "I got a job at that new club, Spark, so that's actually great," I called in their general direction without looking back. "Thanks again!"

I clicked the door shut over their protests, and, fearful that Martin might actually follow me and try to entice me to stay, I hurried down the long, spooky driveway. Crickets and tree frogs croaked a dirge in the dark. Once I'd arrived at the street, I sat down on my backpack, pulled the cabdriver's number out of my wallet, and opened my cell phone. For the first time since I'd arrived in the Hamptons, I was getting a clear signal.

Five

PABST
BLUE RIBBON

Fluorescent orange Cheez Doodle crumbs illuminated the soiled rug as I stepped over the threshold of III Montauk Highway in Amagansett. Mold and mildew stains were spread across every cushion on the grimy couches, and beer cans, cigarette butts, and empty pizza boxes littered the floors. I ran around the house opening as many windows as I could to let in some fresh air before the stench of mothballs, sweaty gym socks, and stale beer made me faint. My visions of a grand summer hideaway with crisp white linens and oceanfront property were dissolving as quickly as my hair was curling in the muggy heat. I cursed to myself as an hour of work with my hot iron went down the drain.

After my roller-coaster ride through the Hamptons with Martin and Lily, I'd decided I needed a wingman if I was going to survive the scandalous life of an East End bartender. The minute I was safely back in my apartment on Jones Street, I'd called Annie. I was all set with a pitch about how we'd make millions and spend our days luxuriating on the beach, but Annie didn't need the hard sell.

"Why not?" she laughed. "I always prefer my men with a tan." I'd given her Teddy's number, and in less than twenty-four hours she'd worked her charms and secured a job as a server in Spark's restaurant, with the possibility of being promoted to cocktail waitress if a position opened up.

I'd also recruited Alexis to help us find a place to stay for the duration of the summer. She'd spent the better part of her hundred-hour workweek trolling through her high-society Long Island Rolodex to come up with a spot for us in a summer share house. Initially she'd suggested I take a spot in a house in Bridgehampton with a couple of her Alberta Ferretti–clad girlfriends from high school who all worked for Bragman Nyman Cafarelli PR firm. But it was $7,000 a share for the summer, which we clearly could not afford. So I'd sent out a mass e-mail to all of my friends from Columbia, subject: Homeless in the Hamptons.

The politics of a Hamptons share were as convoluted as the current condition of partisan politics in the United States. Just as politicians start campaigning years in advance for an election, Hamptons share-housers start lobbying for a choice spot for the following summer as early as two weeks after Labor Day. Typically the life cycle of a share-houser in the Hamptons is as follows: the first summer is spent crammed in tenementlike conditions in a house located as far as possible from the beach and town. While you might have spent $2,000 on a full share (which allows you to have access to the house every single weekend), you'll most likely still be competing with the half shares and quarter shares (who tend to come out to the house more than their allotted weekends) for bedroom and bathroom space. The second summer you graduate to a house with a pool—though you're still squeezing twenty-plus people into a three-bedroom ranch. Finally, after three consecutive bonuses from Merrill Lynch, you might be lucky enough to land yourself a house on Egypt Lane in East Hampton with beachfront property, tennis courts, and your very own bedroom for the bargain summer rental price of $180,000 per house (which, by the way, is the asking price for an eight-bedroom residence back home in Albany).

It turned out that Alexis's ex-boyfriend, Walker, had a bunch of friends from high school who had a cheap share house in Amagansett and still needed to fill two of the slots. Walker was a Jack and Coke, blue-button-down-shirt, banker type who'd majored in finance and now only a month out of school was well on his way to making his first million. But I liked him—he was laid-back and generous, with a gift for managing Alexis's more high-maintenance attributes—so spending a summer with his friends sounded good to me. I picked up the phone to call Travis, his friend who was in charge of managing the shares in the house.

"Hello?" a groggy male voice answered on the eighth ring.

"Hi," I began. "My name is Cassie. Walker gave me your number. I'm calling about possibly getting a share in your house in Amagansett—"

"What?" The voice on the other end was muffled.

"I'm sorry, maybe I have the wrong number. Is this . . . Travis?"

"Yeah, who did you say you were?"

"My name's Cassie. I'm a friend of Alexis Levkoff's. Walker Burke gave me your number. I need a place to stay in the Hamptons."

"Oh . . . Cassie, right. Walker said you were going to call."

"Yeah. Is this a bad time?"

"No, not at all. So you're interested in a share?"

"Yeah, my friend Annie and I are going to be spending the weekends out there bartending and we need a place to stay."

"Okay. Well, here's the deal. The house is on 111 Montauk Highway right in the village of Amagansett. We rented the same house last year. It's awesome. It's walking distance from the train station and McKendry's and the Talkhouse—our favorite bars out there. Most of the guys in the house are my buddies from college, but there's gonna be less people this year because last year it got a little out of hand. We're trying to keep it pretty mellow."

"How far is it from the beach?"

"Really close. Maybe a ten-minute walk."

"Perfect! How much?"

"A thousand."

"For the whole summer?"

"Yup."

"That's not bad at all."

"So, you're in?"

"Definitely."

"Sweet. So why don't you and your friend just write your

checks out to me, Travis Whitter, that's W-H-I-T-T-E-R, and bring them with you this weekend."

"Sounds good," I said.

"What time are you planning on coming out?"

"Probably early on Friday. I have a bar meeting at noon for my new job."

"You'll be the first one there. But don't worry, a couple of us went out there last weekend to set the place up. So it's all ready. Sheets and towels are in the closet at the top of the stairs, and help yourself to the beers in the fridge."

"Thanks."

"No problem. See you Friday."

Alexis had walked in the door just minutes later, and I'd trilled with excitement, "I just got off the phone with Walker's friend—I found a house in the Hamptons!"

"That's great! Which friend?"

"Travis. I guess Walker knows him from high school."

"Travis? Travis *Whitter*?"

"Yeah. I feel bad, I think I might have woken him up from a nap. He was kind of out of it."

"He was probably stoned. Those guys are *always* stoned. Why do you think I broke up with Walker? He was always half-baked. His friends from high school are even worse."

"But I thought you said you liked his friends," I protested.

"Yeah, they're nice guys—when they're sober, which is never. You'll have fun with them, but I'm just warning you: they're all total meatheads. The amount of beer they can drink is inhuman."

Alexis seemed to have selective memory about all the times *she* had overindulged in booze. "You seem to have forgotten that I'm a bartender," I reminded her. "If there's one thing I'm used to, it's drunk people. Where'd Travis go to school?"

"Boulder, just like all the rest of the frat guys who'll probably be in your house. Biggest party school in the country. But don't worry, I'm sure you'll be very impressed with their keg stands. And Rickman, Travis's roommate, can shotgun a beer in less than two seconds. Truly an accomplishment."

"Well, Annie can guzzle an entire bottle of champagne in ten." I wasn't going to let her warnings put a dent in my optimism.

"How many people are in this house?" Alexis asked, pulling a bag of ground espresso beans from the freezer.

"I didn't ask."

"Oh God," she groaned. "Last summer Walker went out to visit Travis, and he said there were like a *thousand people*—mostly Fiji frat guys—passed out everywhere. It was a nightmare."

"Well," I said, trying my best to sound dismissive, "Travis explicitly said that last year got out of hand and that this year they were keeping it mellow."

Alexis raised an eyebrow in a way that let me know I'd been incredibly naïve. "Mellow to Travis Whitter is a night at the Hog Pit with a forty of Pabst Blue Ribbon and a half-dressed stripper on his lap."

The final obstacle between me and the Hamptons had been perhaps the most daunting of all: I still had to convince Laurel to let me keep my weekday shifts at Finton's while I spent my weekends working elsewhere. Giving up a weekend shift was a cardinal sin in the bartending world, and I certainly didn't want to leave Dan in the lurch—especially since I knew all too well that if it wasn't for him, my unlikely hero, I'd be living at home with my parents in

Albany. My fear of being outright fired had caused me to bury my head in the sand, and I put off approaching Laurel even though I was set to start at Spark that weekend. Alexis found me stressing in the kitchen over a bowl of ramen noodles.

"What's the matter?" she'd asked, sitting down beside me. Over her shoulder, I could see the headline in her *In Touch* magazine: "Body Language Expert Willow Estrella Says Britney and Kevin's Body Language Indicates She's Pregnant with Another Man's Baby."

"I have to tell Laurel about the Hamptons," I said. "And I'm scared she's going to fire me. I should have told her as soon as I got back, but I've been putting it off, and now . . ." I trailed off, my voice wavering.

"Cassie, why are you even thinking about Laurel? You need to call Dan Finton," Alexis said matter-of-factly.

I rolled my eyes. "What good would that do?"

"*Please*, Cassie, that man loves you and you know it. I've seen the way he looks at you. Why do you think you got the job in the first place?" She looked at me pointedly. "Certainly not because of your experience."

I chewed my bottom lip sullenly. "I don't know. I feel weird calling Dan."

"Why?"

"Because as a bartender, I'm supposed to deal with Laurel. That's the way it goes. Laurel is my boss, and Dan is Laurel's boss."

"Oh, give me a break," she said, cracking open a can of Diet Coke. "You'll never get anywhere in this world with that kind of attitude. It's eight-thirty, and I'm the only analyst at Morgan Stanley who's already at home. Why do you think that is?"

"I don't know." I sighed.

"Because my hairy old managing director fucking loves me, and I mentioned I had a little tension headache. And the next thing I know, he's sending me home at seven-thirty. I can do no wrong in that office as long as I deal with him. Is he directly over my head? Is he technically the one I'm supposed to answer to? NO! I'm supposed to answer to my VP, Barbara, a fat, gross old woman who wears tacky Liz Claiborne suits and hasn't gotten laid *since before I was born!* Now, call Dan."

However much I hated to admit it, I suspected she was right—and that at the very least, I stood a better chance of winning over Dan than Laurel. I picked up my phone and dialed his number.

"Well, if it isn't my star bartender!" Dan said when he answered. "Remember last Saturday night when Baby Carmine brought in all of those people to celebrate his birthday?"

"Yeah . . ."

"Well, he called me today to tell me what a great party it was, and it was all thanks to you. He said you played great music, took care of everyone, had infectious energy, and just made the whole night! And I told him, 'I'm not surprised—Cassie's my star!' "

"Wow," I said, dumbfounded. "Thanks."

"So what's going on?"

"Well," I began, "I wanted to talk to you about something. I've been offered a bartending job in the Hamptons for the summer, and it's on Friday and Saturday nights. I love working at Finton's but—"

"The Hamptons? Which bar?"

"Um, it's a new club called Spark. I know it's last minute—"

"Listen, Cass. I know how it is, and to tell you the truth,

I think it's a great opportunity for all of us. It'll be a chance for you to meet a whole new base of customers and lure them into Finton's. You'll still keep some shifts here during the week, right?"

"Yeah," I said, the weight lifting off my shoulders in one fell swoop. "I'd love to keep my shifts during the week, if that's possible—"

"Of course it's possible!" he'd exclaimed. "As long as you promise to come back to me full time in the fall."

I gingerly climbed the rickety stairs of my new share house, stepping over damp beach towels, an oozing bottle of suntan lotion, a chewed-up Frisbee, and a Pro-Kadima set. When I arrived at the top I peeked inside the first room to my right and saw a sunny window looking out into the yard and two small beds.

"As soon as you get out there, Cass, make sure you reserve us some beds so we actually have somewhere to sleep when we get home from work," Annie had made me promise as we planned the first leg of our adventure over the phone the night before. "Everyone I know who's done a share house has ended up sleeping on the lawn or something, and that's the last thing we need after working all night." As I investigated the rest of the upstairs, which looked like it could comfortably sleep no more than a family of four, I was doubly glad I'd gotten there early.

I dropped one bag on each bed to stake our claim and walked back toward the staircase. My mother's influence reared its head, and I found a box of garbage bags in the shed and began picking up my housemates' trash. I harangued them in my head (though I hadn't even met them yet) as I held my nose against the sour smell of garbage, mold, and the all-too-familiar stench of stale Jack Daniel's. Clearly Alexis had been right. What kind of people didn't mind spending the weekend in this kind of filth? Evidently, this was what a grand got you in the Hamptons.

I looked at my watch, which read 11:20, and realized I couldn't spend any more time trying to clean up the house or I'd miss my bar meeting. In a final effort to make the place presentable, I shoved a damp phone book underneath one of the legs of the dining room table to keep it from wobbling. Then I fished around in my backpack and pulled out the card the cabdriver had given me the weekend before when he'd taken me to—and quickly back from—Martin's den of iniquity.

I was still trying to fully process what had transpired with Martin and Lily the previous weekend. I'd arrived back in New York half convinced that it had all been a misunderstanding and that the whole scenario hadn't really been as weird or scandalous as it had seemed. One conversation with Annie, however, convinced me otherwise.

"So you know how I went out to Southampton with Martin Pritchard last weekend to go job hunting?" I'd asked her.

"Yeah . . ."

"Well, after I got the job at Spark, I took a cab back to his house and he was sitting in the living room practically naked with his girlfriend, Lily—who's like our age by the way—and this other weird couple that they 'hang out' with. And I think—and I'm not a hundred percent sure about this—but I *think* Martin was propositioning me to join them in some kind of group sex thing. I was so creeped out!"

Annie chuckled. "I'm not surprised. He's a total perv. A couple of months ago he had front-row tickets to see the Alvin Ailey dance company, and he asked me to come with him. I was dying to see the show, so I said yes, and afterward he invited me to go up to his apartment for a nightcap, which I didn't think was a big deal. I figured, I can handle myself. So, I get up to his penthouse and pour myself a scotch while he goes to the bathroom. Anyway, I'm sitting in his library when he comes back *completely naked* and then comes over to kiss me! I was so revolted that the scotch came flying out of my nose, which burned like hell by the way, but I hardly noticed because I was so grossed out by his saggy ass. I was like 'Martin, I think you have the wrong idea here,' and he was like 'No woman has ever said no to me before.' Obviously *I* said no, and made a beeline for the elevator! The next day when he came into Finton's, he acted like nothing had happened, even though I was practically scarred for life."

"You saw him *naked*?" I'd gasped.

"In all his liver-spotted glory."

"Well, you could have *warned* me, for God's sake!"

"Hey, you're a big girl, I figured you could hold your own with Grandpa," she smirked, adding, "you never know who you'll meet at this job."

L   arry's Taxi!" mumbled a gruff voice on the other end.
    "Hi," I said, "I was wondering if I could get a taxi to pick me up in Amagansett at 111 Montauk Highway and take me to Spark in Wainscott."

"Animal House?" the voice asked.

"Excuse me?"

"111 Montauk Highway . . . we call it Animal House because there's always someone throwing up on the front lawn or passed out in the bushes," he replied.

"Oh."

"What time do you need the pickup?" he asked.

"I have to be at Spark by noon."

"I'll be there at twenty of."

I had seventeen minutes to pull myself together. Last night's makeup remained caked on my eyelids. My eyes looked like two burned holes in a blanket. I tried to shake off my exhaustion, and grabbed some face wash out of my bag. My new summer schedule of working Thursday nights at Finton's until four in the morning and then rushing to make the 7:25 train to the Hamptons didn't allow much time for sleeping. I consoled myself with the familiar mantra: I'll sleep when I'm dead.

The same plump middle-aged cabdriver picked me up right on time. I could see him better in the daylight. He had untamed gray hair that curled around his ears and a balding spot on the top of his head that revealed a shiny pink scalp.

"Hi," I said, climbing into the backseat. "How's it going?"

"Make sure the door is closed," he ordered, pulling out of the driveway. He didn't seem to remember me.

As we traveled west on Montauk Highway, I tried to forget about my small "register ring" problem. On Wednesday night I'd asked Laurel what my average nightly sales at Finton's were, and it turned out that on my busiest nights I rang somewhere between $1,000 and $1,200. With a sinking feeling, I'd realized that I'd exaggerated my ring to Teddy eight times over. No wonder he'd hired me on the spot without so much as glancing at my résumé: he thought I was the highest-ringing bartender in history. I thanked God Annie was coming out to the Hamptons with me. Things were always easier with a partner in crime.

As if on cue, my cell phone rang. "Cass!" Annie shouted. "I just got off the phone with Teddy, and he said there might be an opening for a cocktail waitress sooner than he thought, which would be sooooooooooooo much better than waitressing in the restaurant. He asked me to e-mail him a picture of me, so he can decide if I 'have what it takes' to be promoted to cocktail waitstaff. Should I send him one of my headshots? Or I have this really cute shot of me in a bikini in Rio. What do you think?"

"He asked you to e-mail him a picture?" I asked. With every passing day I was developing a thicker skin with regard to the bar industry's blatantly misogynistic practices. Still, a big part of me was rankled by men like Teddy who didn't even bother to try to hide it. At least Dan Finton's preferences masqueraded as flattery.

"Yup, so what do think—headshot or cleavage shot?"

"I don't know. I think it's weird that you have to do this."

"He just wants to make sure I'm not a total dog, you know? That's how these big clubs are. Maybe I'll just send him both. Couldn't hurt, right?"

"I guess not." I sighed. I was too tired to get on my soapbox and start preaching to her about resisting sexual exploitation. Besides, I'd begun to feel like I was walking a fine line myself. "Are you on your way out here for the meeting?"

"Yeah. I have a separate server meeting, but Teddy told me to swing by the bar meeting afterward, just in case I end up cocktailing."

Annie had decided not to take the train with me, because she always took a modern dance class at eight on Friday mornings. Instead, she was taking the 10:00 A.M. Jitney—the ubiquitous green tour bus that ran back and forth between Manhattan and all of the Hamptons—which would drop her off in Wainscott right in front of Spark a little after twelve. I hoped she would be on time since her laid-back Brazilian sensibility always provided room for being "fashionably late." Though after seeing her in a bikini, Teddy would likely let her skip the meeting all together if she wanted.

"So how long have you been coming out to the Hamptons?" my cabdriver asked after I'd hung up.

"Actually this is my first summer out here," I told him. "I'm going to be bartending at Spark. How about you?"

"I've lived here all my life. I was born and raised in the Springs."

Martin had told me that the Springs was the name given to the northern part of East Hampton, known to the elite as "the other side of the tracks." The real estate was a lot cheaper there and was considered to be a sizable step down from the rest of East Hampton—south of the highway—which was closer to the ocean and where most Manhattanites had their summer homes.

"So you live here year-round?" I asked, trying to imagine what it was like in February when all of the restaurants and boutiques were closed and the towns were nearly deserted.

"I do," he said. "I love it out here in the winter. It's so quiet and peaceful when all you New Yorkers finally go home."

He said the last part with a playful smile, but I could tell he really meant it. The New York magazines and papers loved to expound on the tension—imagined or otherwise—between the Hamptons locals and the city people. Which is not to say it wasn't a mutually beneficial relationship. After all, the entire economy of the Hamptons would go under if it wasn't for the crowd of New Yorkers who flocked to the

East End during the three short summer months. But I could understand why he and the rest of the residents who lived out there year-round might get sick of the pushy, Hummer-driving housewives and hordes of drug-addled, drunk-driving nightlifers. The minute Labor Day faded into the first unofficial day of fall, the traffic disappeared, the beaches were no longer crowded, and instead of being Manhattan transported to the ocean, the Hamptons were just a constellation of quaint coastal towns.

We pulled up in front of Spark. "Thanks for the lift," I said, prolonging my exit by fishing in my bag for an extralarge tip. "I'm sure I'll see you soon."

"I am so fucking tired."

"This meeting better not last too fucking long."

"I didn't get any sleep last night, and I'm so fucking hungover I feel like I'm going to die," bemoaned a chorus of twenty-something girls clustered in one corner of the cavernous main room.

"I know, I never even slept. I got so fucked up blowing lines after-hours at Green Room that I didn't leave until it was time to start driving out here at around nine," confided one, a petite blond with a spiky, pixie haircut.

"Well, I was blowing Marcus for what seemed like hours, so I didn't sleep either," crowed another. She was tall and skinny without being at all lithe, and had ashy skin and black circles under her eyes. Her stringy blond hair looked like it had fallen victim to too much peroxide, and she wore a microminiskirt, high clunky gold sandals, and a tattered sweatshirt that slid off her shoulder revealing a hot-pink sequined bra strap.

I stood on the periphery of the group, trying to look nonchalant. Annie hadn't arrived yet. I looked around hoping I would see Jake or Teddy or someone I recognized, but apparently the only people who'd arrived on time were a ragtag herd of strung-out cocktail waitresses with bloodshot eyes and colorless cheeks, shrilly advertising their drinking, drug, and sex habits. They smelled collectively of smoke, stale booze, and dirty hair.

"You are such a fucking slut!" the same skinny blond with the sequined bra strap yelled at one of the other girls. Her voice had a gravelly quality, like she'd just smoked sixty cigarettes in quick succession. "I saw you flirting with that guy Jason last night when his girlfriend went home. You practically gave him a lap dance when he ordered that third bottle of Louis XIII!"

"Whatever, bitch, you do it too!" the other girl replied sleepily, her huge black sunglasses obscuring half of her face. She sat slumped on one of the dining room chairs, wearing jeans so low-cut that they exposed her glaring red thong.

I searched the group, trying to ascertain which one was the least crazy, and if there was anyone I might actually be able to talk to about what to expect from Spark.

"Who are you?" asked the skinny blond with the sequined bra strap, who was obviously their leader, as I warily approached.

"I'm Cassie," I said, forcing a smile. I felt like the new kid in the lunchroom in junior high.

"I hope you're not here to cocktail waitress because there are too many of us as it is," she said defensively.

"No . . . I'm a bartender."

"Oh!" she said, her tone dramatically brighter. "I'm Elsie."

"Nice to meet you," I said, stepping forward. A split second later Elsie pulled off her worn blue sweatshirt to reveal nothing more than her hot-pink sequined bra. "It's so fucking hot in here," she breathed impatiently. "I can't wear this."

Her only other "coverage" besides the outrageous undergarment was a shimmering belly-button ring that glinted in the sunlight.

A few of the girls laughed. "Elsie, put your clothes back on," one of them groaned.

"Fuck you!" She laughed, throwing her sweatshirt at the girls. "I can do whatever I want, and I'm too hot to wear that fucking thing."

One by one the girls introduced themselves, but I knew there was no way in hell I'd ever be able to tell them apart. They all looked exactly the same: tall and blond with killer bodies and attractive faces, but they wore too much makeup and were generally overprocessed—as though they'd spent all their hard-earned tips on too much plastic surgery, Garnier hair bleach, and Wet 'n' Wild makeup. They looked tired and used. Most were wearing tight, cut-off shirts that showed off their chiseled abs and Pam Anderson—size breasts. Their legs seemed to go on forever under their tiny micro-miniskirts, exposing brightly colored tattoos on their ankles and inner thighs. One of the girls, the only brunette among them, had blue streaks woven through her hair and a pink studded nose ring.

"I hope you didn't think the meeting was going to start on time," Elsie said. "Teddy's always late. He doesn't give a fuck about wasting our time."

"Oh," I said, as one of the girls pulled a pack of cigarettes from her bag and walked outside.

"Hey, speaking of Teddy." Elsie leaned in and dropped her voice to a whisper. "How about Meg's ass-licking last night?" She threw a glance over her shoulder that suggested Meg was the girl by the door with a cigarette. "Yeah, Meg has a little problem with licking the asses of our asshole bosses. She wasn't even supposed to come out to work in the Hamptons because she doesn't sell enough bottles in the city, but she went up to Teddy and got down on her hands and knees right in the middle of the club, in front of all the customers and everything, and licked his butt so he couldn't say no," Elsie said as she got down on her hands and knees behind one of the girls to mimic the "butt-licking" and started making wild lapping motions like a dog in heat. The rest of the girls all broke into hysterical laughter.

I stood there silently, wondering what I'd gotten myself into. These girls made Annie's risqué banter look tame. Two of the girls started talking about their shift the previous night back in New York.

". . . yeah, I did so much blow with those guys at table seven from Croatia, or wherever the fuck they were from, that I thought I was gonna wake up and half my face would be melted off," one of the girls was reporting to Elsie. "I almost had a fuckin' heart attack."

"You should have done some shots then." Elsie shrugged.

"I couldn't even fucking see straight," the girl complained. "How was I supposed to get to the bar?"

"Those guys were drinking Grey Goose. You should've fucking taken some. It's the only way to bring you back down," Elsie said. "How much did you girls end up making last night, by the way?"

"We walked with about nine."

"Walked" was a term used to convey how much money the

cocktail waitresses ended up with after tipping out the bartender and busboy. Bartenders made all of the drinks for the cocktail waitresses and customarily got 10 percent of what the waitresses made in tips; the bus boys got their own 10 percent for bussing tables and bringing ice, glasses, and mixers.

"*Nine hundred dollars?*" I asked, dumbfounded.

"That's nothing," Elsie said. "At Jet last summer we were walking with at least twelve every Saturday night."

"Jet East?" I asked, proud of myself for having remembered the name of the Southampton hot spot from one of Alexis's Hamptons tutorials.

"Yup. Where'd you work last summer?"

I wasn't about to tell her that last summer I'd been interning for a senior editor at *New York* magazine, while living in a dorm and going home to Albany most weekends. "I actually didn't work out here last summer. I stayed in the city."

"Where do you work in the city?" she asked, twirling her fluorescent green gum around her taloned finger.

"I work at a bar called Finton's. It's downtown."

"Is it a club?"

"No. It's a restaurant and a bar. But it gets pretty crowded."

"I've never heard of it," she said, popping her gum back in her truck-driver mouth with a loud smack.

"Where do you work in the city?" I asked, hoping to shift the limelight away from me, which wasn't too hard with this group of attention-grabbing girls.

"Pink Elephant, Bungalow, Crobar, Ruby Falls, Marquee, Duvet, Gypsy Tea . . . wherever Teddy and his crew are. We follow them to the different clubs they open up either in the

Hamptons or in the city. Wherever there's Teddy, there's a lot of fucking money. I won't work anywhere unless I'm making a grand a night."

I hid my amazement with the most disinterested expression I could muster, but inside I was turning somersaults. I'd thought I was doing well when I made $200 at Finton's. And now I'd lucked into a gig run by one of the hottest promoters in the area. Just as I was starting to get depressed about wasting a month of my time at a slow downtown bar no one had ever heard of, Annie walked through the door.

"Hey!" I shouted, jumping up and heading over to the door to give her a big hug. Relief coursed through me just at the sight of her. "How was the Jitney?"

"Not bad at all," she enthused, dropping her bags. "They give you coffee, juice, the paper, and snacks!" She looked around. "This place is amazing. It's like ten times the size of Finton's!"

"And this is only *half* of it, Annie. The VIP room is up those stairs, and then there's a lot of outdoor seating, and the Club is across the walkway. The dance floor is over there."

"Ooo, I can't wait!" she squealed.

Teddy arrived at twelve fifty-seven with an army of other promoters all wearing dark sunglasses and diamond stud earrings. Before he convened the meeting, I whispered to Annie, "Wait until you get a chance to talk to these girls. They're *crazy*." I slid my eyes toward the group, which had descended on Teddy like a flock of seagulls on an abandoned sandwich. Elsie had literally jumped on him, wrapping her spindly legs around his midsection.

"That's Teddy." I gestured to Annie.

"Just as I suspected." She grinned. "Hot as hell. I've found my first summer conquest."

"Hey, everyone," Teddy began after Jake appeared on the periphery of the group. "As you can see there are a lot of you here. On any given night we're only going to be able to use six bartenders—maybe seven on holiday weekends or if it gets really slammed—and eight cocktail waitresses. Tonight and tomorrow you'll all get to work, because we're setting up extra bars outside on the patio and service bars throughout the club for the cocktail waitresses. This weekend only, you'll all get a chance, and we'll decide who we want to keep and who we don't. If you're picked, you should consider yourself extremely lucky to have a job here. This place is going to be sick."

A wave of anxiety washed over me. I hadn't even entertained the thought that this was an audition and not a done deal.

"I want to introduce you to Shalina," Teddy continued. "She's a consultant here and in charge of PR."

I was debating whether it would be appropriate to ask exactly why a bar needed a consultant, when an attractive brunette in her early thirties, with a slim body strategically peppered with silicone and collagen, appeared at Teddy's side.

"Hello, everyone," she addressed the group in a clipped British accent. "Welcome. We all want to make a lot of money this summer, and by following a few simple rules, this can all go smoothly." She spoke rapidly, glancing down from time to time at the list attached to a clipboard in front of her. "First, there will be no smoking by employees on the premises. There will be no use of profanity. There will be no drinking by the employees. Even if a customer should offer to buy you a drink, I expect you to turn them down politely. You will all be handling a lot of money and holding on to clients' credit cards. And it's unacceptable to manage such things while intoxicated. Also, if I see any of you eating behind the bar, you will be immediately dismissed. Obviously, there will be no drug use by employees, and if I hear that anything of that nature is going on, you'll be fired on the spot. Make sure you don't drink the bottled water, the tap is perfectly fine for you people. And don't even think about drinking the Red Bull. We switch from restaurant to nightclub promptly at ten-thirty. Bartenders and cocktail waitresses need to get here at exactly nine-thirty. Do we understand each other?"

We all nodded dumbly. I thought of Laurel and wondered if it was an unwritten rule that all women in charge of managing a bar or restaurant had to behave like drill sergeants. Then I immediately chastised myself for falling into the trap of thinking all women in positions of power were bitches.

"Additionally," Shalina went on, "we want to let you know that we'll have spotters here every night."

"What's a spotter?" I asked Annie.

Elsie, who had dug a nail file out of her ragged Dior bag and was busy shaping her clawlike nails into perfect ovals, answered me. "Basically a guy who comes up to the bar and acts like a customer, but really he's a fucking asshole who's making sure you're ringing in all your drinks and not stealing money. Usually you can see them a mile away—they stand at the bar by themselves nursing one drink the whole fucking night."

"Oh." I wondered if Dan Finton ever hired spotters.

"Don't plan on giving away any free drinks at all," Shalina warned. "The cameras are hooked up to the Internet so we can watch you whether we're at the bar or not, and the spotters will catch everything. We will immediately fire anyone who doesn't account for every single drink."

As she continued talking, it occurred to me that no one ever gave their last names in the bartending world: Teddy, Elsie, Shalina—through all of their introductions, not one of them had offered a last name. I felt a strange disconnect from all the people around me as I contemplated the mystery-cloaked bar world. I wracked my brain and couldn't even think of Billy or Annie's last names. I wondered if they knew mine.

"Now for the great news," Shalina said, her perfectly puffed lips breaking into a smile for the first time. "Catherine Malandrino has designed uniforms for you to wear!" All the cocktail waitresses ooooooohed and ahhhhhed.

"Who's Catherine Malandrino?" I asked Annie, whose eyes had lit up just like the rest.

"She's a designer," Annie gushed. "She's amazing. She has a store in Soho and one in the meatpacking district."

"Catherine is a very dear friend of mine," Shalina explained. "She's been working for months designing your outfits. Going with a summer resort theme, she's created an adorable little miniskirt, all white, with a delicate ruffle along the bottom, and a pastel satin halter top that cuts off a few inches above your belly button."

Miniskirt? Halter top? Panic gripped my heart. My thighs and lower butt would be exposed, as well as most of my midriff, for all of the Hamptons to see. Scenes of bending down to grab a beer hidden low in a cooler while drunken customers heckled me flashed through my head. Needless to say, I hadn't gotten around to expanding my workout routine to include five hundred crunches a day. Not to mention that it seemed completely absurd for us to bartend in white satin, when cranberry juice, José Cuervo, and red wine inevitably saturated my clothes by the end of a shift.

"I managed to work out a great deal with Catherine," Shalina continued, "so your uniforms are very affordable. The skirt is a hundred and eight dollars and the top is ninety-six. Please bring the money tonight when you come in to work. I'd prefer cash."

"We have to *pay* for the uniforms?" I asked Annie incredulously.

"Guess so," Annie said with a shrug. As long as she remained working in the restaurant, she didn't have to worry—the dinner servers all wore the same black pants and Polo shirt. At first I'd thought they looked dowdy, but after Shalina's announcement and its $204 price tag, I would've given my eyeteeth to wear them.

"I hope I get promoted to cocktail waitress," Annie said fervently. "I don't even care about paying for the uniform. I'll never see any celebrities in the dining room, and Teddy'll never notice me in that frumpy Polo shirt."

"Are you crazy? I'd rather die than work with my whole body exposed. These other girls are all like a size negative two."

Of course, I was in no position to argue. A quick head count showed that there were nine bartenders at the meeting, and as Teddy had pointed out earlier, they only needed six per shift. By my calculations, I had eight and a half hours to figure out a way to ring $8,000 a night. Shalina's voice interrupted my neuroses.

"This is Chris, the bar manager," she said unceremoniously, gesturing toward an awkward man with skin so pale it looked liked he had never seen the sun. His beanpole body was at least as tall as Teddy's, but probably half the weight. "He'll be in charge of all bartenders, bar backs, and cocktail waitresses. The restaurant has a different manager entirely, but most of you here won't have to worry about that. You'll all answer to Chris."

I thought the chain of command sounded a little convoluted. Annie looked confused as well, so I turned to Elsie.

"I don't understand," I whispered. "Is he our boss, or is Teddy or Shalina?"

"Don't worry, it's always a fucking nightmare when a million people are involved with opening a new club," she said. "Don't bother trying to figure everyone out. Half of these people will be fired after Memorial Day."

I nodded and smiled grimly, worried that I would be one of those getting the ax after only one weekend. It would be the worst kind of humiliation if I had to crawl back to Laurel and beg her for my weekend shifts.

"Why do so many people get fired?" I ventured.

"Quiet down, girls!" Shalina snarled. "Listen to your manager!"

My face turned red, and I heard Annie stifle a giggle as I turned my attention toward Chris. He looked uncomfortable, and Shalina practically had to give him a push to speak.

"Hi," he began, almost inaudibly. "Basically, I just need everyone to keep the bar clean. The bar backs need to help with that. If you guys have any questions about where anything is, you can always ask Jake. He helped us open up and he knows what he's doing. He's the head bartender for the summer, so you can get help from him." I strained to hear him. When he finished, he smiled halfheartedly and quickly stepped back behind Shalina.

The meeting finally wrapped up at a little after two o'clock. Since I didn't have to be back for work until nine-thirty that night, I had the afternoon free. I turned to Annie, who was busily applying Lancôme's Juicy Tubes in

Berry Bold. She was visibly glowing from the brief conversation I saw her have with Teddy.

"Annie, what's your last name?" I asked.

"Borolo. Why?"

"Just wondering," I said. "What time do you have to be back?"

"Well, I have to be back at four tonight, because I'm working in the restaurant, which totally sucks. But Teddy said I can start cocktailing as early as tomorrow!"

"That's great," I said happily. "That means we'll be working together."

"*And* Teddy told me to call his cell tomorrow afternoon so we can meet at the beach." She gave a dreamy sigh. "I *love* the Hamptons!"

"Fast work," I teased her. "I'm impressed."

We were about to say good-bye to the girls, who were busy gathering up their things, when I overheard Elsie say to one of them, "I hope I see that guy James again. He was the best fuck I ever had."

My stomach lurched. "James Edmonton?" I interjected before I could stop myself, my voice sounding like a coloratura soprano's. Please, please, please, I thought, don't let James have slept with this raunchy girl. The very thought of having to share him with anyone made me feel nauseated.

"James Edmonton?" Elsie stared at me, confused. "Who the fuck is that?"

"Oh, sorry," I said, relieved. "I thought I heard you mention a friend of mine."

"No, I was talking about James Elliot, that actor from that show on the WB. I hooked up with him the other night."

"Oh, cool. Well, anyway, nice meeting you guys." I slung my backpack over my shoulder. "We'll see you tonight."

"A little paranoid?" Annie joked as we stepped outside into the brilliant sunshine. I ignored her and flipped open my cell phone to call a cab. Within minutes my favorite driver was pulling into the gravel parking lot.

"Going back to Animal House?" he asked cheerily as we made a left on Montauk Highway.

I forced myself to laugh.

"What's he talking about?" Annie asked, puzzled.

"Don't worry," I said. "You'll see." I'd decided against telling her about the hellhole that was to be our summer residence. I didn't want to ruin her mood.

The whole ride home I fantasized about the nap I was going to take before work, knowing full well that I wouldn't survive an intense night of bartending on just three hours of broken sleep on an overly air-conditioned train. But when we pulled into the driveway, I saw that nine of my housemates had already arrived to start the holiday weekend a little early. They were shotgunning Pabst Blue Ribbon, most of them shirtless, on the porch.

"Is this it?" Annie asked, her eyes wide.

"Um . . . yeah," I said, cringing. The front lawn was already a disaster with empty beer cans and plastic cups strewn among the overgrown grass and weeds, and a half-assembled volleyball net lay drooping in the middle. It was a frat house, plain and simple, and I felt wholly responsible for getting us involved.

"Oh my God!" Annie gasped. I braced myself. "Those guys are *so cute!*" she exclaimed, hopping out of the cab. I stared after her, amazed. A cute guy was enough to make Annie see the positive side of every situation.

"Hey, ladies!" one guy called out before stabbing a hole in the side of a PBR can with a key, popping the top, and sucking all the beer out in one gulp.

"Hey, boys!" Annie waved as she sashayed across the lawn toward the house. I paid the driver, then stepped out of the cab to join her.

One of them, an attractive, tall guy with disheveled curly brown hair, came down off the porch and said, "You must be Cassie."

"No." Annie giggled. "I'm Annie. This is Cassie."

"Hi," I said, coming up behind her. He was wearing a vintage red Coca-Cola T-shirt and worn-in jeans with Reef flip-flops.

"I'm Travis. We spoke on the phone."

"It's nice to meet you," I said. "We have our checks. I left mine in my bag upstairs. I'll go get it now."

"No rush. You can give them to me whenever. So you went to Columbia with Alexis?"

"Yeah," I said.

"That's a great school. I wanted to go there, but the tuition was a little steep. When Boulder offered me a full ride for lax, my parents were pretty excited to save the money, so I went there with the rest of these clowns." He gestured toward the guys behind him slamming beers on the porch.

"I hear you," I said sympathetically. "I have so many student loans—that's why I'm bartending."

"Yeah, it's rough. Well, come and have a beer and meet everybody," he said.

"I was actually thinking about going upstairs to take a quick nap," I began, trying to telepathize with Annie not to trap us down here.

"Oh, come on, Cassie," Annie pleaded, "it's the start of the summer. One beer wouldn't *kill* us!"

"Yeah, come on Cassie, one beer won't *kill* you!" Travis laughed. He motioned with the football in his hand that I should go out for a pass, and I reluctantly ran backward into the yard, catching the ball easily. I wasn't about to let a house full of frat boys think I was a wimpy, unathletic girl.

"Nice catch, Jerry Rice," Travis said, smiling. I couldn't help but think Alexis's unflattering summation of him had been unfair at best.

Several hours and ten PBRs later, I was running around the yard playing a rousing game of touch football. Annie had left hours before to make it to Spark for the dinner shift.

"Come on, you loser, catch the ball!" I roared when one of my teammates dropped a pass.

"Um, Cass?" Travis called from his place at the fifty-yard line.

"Yeah?" I yelled, taking a gulp of beer.

"When do you have to be at work?"

"Oh, shit!" I said, looking at my watch. I'd almost entirely blocked out work. "I gotta get going." I passed the ball nonchalantly one last time with a perfect spiral. "I'll see you guys when I get home later. Good game!"

Two Stoli tonics, a cosmo, three Jack and Cokes, two Bud Lights, a bottle of water, and do you have champagne by the glass?" an impatient woman barked.

It was only ten-fifteen, and I was already in the weeds. I hadn't had enough time to acclimate myself to the layout of the bar or the enigmatic computer system, and I was having trouble keeping up with the demands of the insistent, and very thirsty, customers.

Due to my bragging about my imaginary bartending expertise, Teddy had placed me where most of the volume was concentrated, behind the front bar with Jake, who was the fastest and most efficient bartender I'd ever seen in my life. Flustered, I couldn't remember the ingredients to any drinks. Jake, on the other hand, probably made about twenty drinks, including martinis and cosmos, for every one drink I made. Sweat was pouring out of me, leaving my hair plastered to my face, and I had only been at work for forty-five minutes.

My initial mortification about wearing the designer crop top and miniskirt had disappeared around the same time my sanity and coordination vanished behind the bar. Earlier that night I'd stood in the girls' bathroom retying the shirt lower and lower in an attempt to cover at least some of my stomach. The problem was, the lower I tied it on the bottom, the lower it fell on top. There just wasn't enough material to go around. The skirt, I'd already decided, was a lost cause. It was too damn short, and I felt like a trashy cheerleader.

"I can't wear this!" I'd wailed to Annie, who was busy applying a new coat of mascara in anticipation of the restaurant's switch to nightclub mode.

"Yes you can. You look amazing."

"Annie, I'm naked."

"No you're not. Now calm down. Maybe if we pull the shirt down a little lower, it will give you a little more coverage." She slid her fingers under the tiny halter searching for a hem, and with a nail clipper and a pair of tweezers managed to let it down, giving me an extra one and a half inches of iridescent baby blue material.

"Wow," I'd said. "You're a genius!"

"I'm not done yet," she said, stepping back to take critical stock. The bottom of my $96 top was a little frayed, but in the dark of the bar no one would notice. "Okay, now that your stomach is a little more covered, try pulling your skirt down on to your hips so it at least covers your ass. There. Do you feel more comfortable?"

I looked at myself in the full-length mirror. I was still horrified, but it was a vast improvement. I started to laugh.

"What's so funny?" Annie had asked.

"I was just thinking. This is the most expensive top I've ever owned, and we just butchered it with a nail clipper."

Now, officially stationed behind the bar, I couldn't remember any of the drink prices because I kept mixing them up with Finton's, which were considerably cheaper, and if I kept up like that all night, my ring would be even lower. The computer froze every time I used it, and I couldn't find the bottle of Ketel One anywhere, which seemed to be the liquor every single person wanted. I kept mixing up which coolers held domestic beers and which ones housed the imports. And to make matters worse, Jake kept abandoning me to go to the bathroom, leaving me alone for a good five minutes every half hour—which behind a slammed bar felt like a lifetime.

"Where are all the bottle openers?" I called to Jake with two unopened Bud Lights in my hand.

He bounded over and twisted the caps off with his bare hands. "The Bud and Bud Lights are twist-offs, babycakes!"

"Oh," I said sheepishly. "Well, what about the rest of the beer?"

"You didn't bring a bottle opener?"

"No," I said. "I didn't know I had to. At my job in the city they have them for us and—"

"Rookie!" he chastised, tossing me an extra bottle opener that he just happened to have in his back pocket. Apparently, Jake was the MacGyver of bartending. I stuck my new tool into the waistband of my nearly nonexistent skirt, which I had to keep pulling down every few minutes to keep it from exposing my pink thong.

At Spark things seemed needlessly difficult. Every time you rang in a drink you were first confronted with a sign-in screen where you had to enter your employee number (a four-digit code I kept forgetting). Then you had to choose from a long list of drink genres including liquor, red wine by the glass, white wine by the glass, champagne by the glass, wine and champagne by the bottle, domestic beer, imported beer, ports, shots, miscellaneous. If you picked liquor, you were then presented with a screen that read vodka, gin, rum, tequila, and so on.

Your selection on this screen led to another more specific screen. For example, if you selected vodka, you would then be faced with a screen that listed the most popular brands: Grey Goose, Ketel One, Stoli Raspberry . . . If the vodka you were looking for did not appear on the list, you had to find it alphabetically using the lettered icons on the left of the screen. Once you made that selection, you had to enter in the mixer as well. When you finally selected all of your ingredients, you had to reckon with the payment screen, which to me seemed as cryptic as hieroglyphics—even cash transactions were tedious. By the time I was ready for another customer, the annoyed crowd was ready to hop over the bar and serve themselves.

Jake was like Billy on speed. He bartended with the same ease and grace, only on a much larger scale. His arms seemed to be able to reach any cooler or liquor bottle from wherever he happened to be standing. It was as though he made the cups appear out of nowhere, ten in a row on his bar mat, already filled with ice and a straw. And even though he kept leaving the bar, he always got right back in the mix and caught up immediately. I, on the other hand, had trouble coordinating even the simplest things and kept dropping my bottle opener and knocking over cocktails. My side of the bar looked like a tornado had ripped through it, while Jake's was still impressively neat and clean. I marveled at his speed, wondering how he managed to turn out what seemed like ten drinks per second. His skillful fingers danced effortlessly across the computer screen pressing all the right icons as he served the masses. Nothing seemed to wear him down, and he didn't ever lose steam. He was hyper and amped up throughout the entire night. I imagined he must have chugged thirty forbidden Red Bulls.

I watched Jake intently. At Spark, I was learning, it wasn't enough to ask a customer what they needed, make the drinks, collect money, give change, and then move on to the next person. You needed to ask someone what he wanted, start making his drinks, ask another person what she wanted, start making her drinks, collect money from the first guy, ask a third person what he wanted, give change to the first guy, get money from the girl, start making the third guy's drinks, open a new bottle of vodka, give change to the girl, give the manager a payout for the door guy, ask the bar back for more ice, and get money from the third guy. In short, bartenders at Spark had to be the ultimate multitaskers.

"Can I buy a bottle at the bar?" a customer asked. He was a short, stocky man with too much gel in his hair, wearing a button-down shirt covered ostentatiously in Burberry plaid. He was surrounded by a throng of attractive platinum blonds who—like me—were wearing next to nothing.

"I don't know," I said, taking a deep breath. "Let me ask."

I hurried over to Jake, leaving hundreds of customers screaming drink orders and waving cash. Even though it was only eleven-thirty, the floor behind the bar was already filthy with grubby bev naps, bent stirrers, smashed plastic cups, and discarded beer caps.

"Jake!" I called out. "Is it all right for me to sell a bottle at the bar?"

He wheeled around so fast it startled me. He was sweating, and his eyes looked red and wild. "Are you crazy?" he shouted. "Of course it's okay. The rule is: SELL AS MUCH AS YOU CAN! Just remember to tell him there's a mandatory gratuity charge of twenty percent on bottles. And don't forget the owners are watching the bar, so don't just hand the bottle over to him, make sure you *ring it in first*, because they synced up the registers with the surveillance. The cameras are right there." He pointed discreetly to the front of the bar where two small red lights were blinking. I felt naked and watched, like I was in one of those glass snow globes, being shaken up by the invisible hands that owned and operated Spark.

I scampered back over to the Burberry Plaid Man, much faster this time. "Sure," I said. "What would you like?"

"Give me a bottle of Goose," he said.

At clubs and lounges in New York City and the Hamptons, people had the option of buying entire bottles of liquor, instead of ordering separate drinks. Each bottle ranged from $200 to $800 or more, and was usually shared by a group of people sitting at a table. (In certain hot spots, agreeing to buy two or three bottles was the only way for some people to make it past the velvet ropes.) The setup came with glasses, ice, mixers, lemons, limes, and stirrer straws—a be-your-own-bartender extravaganza. Usually bottles were ordered through a cocktail waitress, but that night all of the tables were occupied. The great thing about selling a bottle at the bar was it was an easy way to bring up low rings. Tonight it was just what I needed.

After a few torturous seconds staring at the computer screen looking for the price of a bottle of Grey Goose, I rang it in and returned to the man, wiping a sweaty strand of hair from my brow. "It's $350 plus twenty percent gratuity, so the total is $420."

He leaned over and handed me a wad of cash.

"Keep the change," he said with a wink, eyeing my bare midriff. "Just make sure you take care of us."

I turned around to count the folded bills and was shocked to find he had given me $600—a $250 tip for doing next to nothing! I walked over to the Moët Chandon champagne bucket that we used as a communal tip jar and tossed the bills inside, pressing them down to the bottom of the bucket to make room for more bills, just like I did to the garbage bin in our kitchen when Alexis forgot to take it out. I immediately felt a lot better and, for the first time that night, turned around to face the angry mob of screaming patrons with a confident smile.

At around midnight, I was busy filling glasses with ice trying to keep track of all seven of the drinks I was working on, when I suddenly felt a sharp pain as my head was jerked over the bar. I looked up and realized to my horror that an angry woman wearing a Proenza Schouler top and Paper Denim jeans that looked painted on had climbed halfway over the bar and was pulling my hair.

"Stop it!" I yelled, trying to pry her hand from my head.

"I've been trying to get your attention for the last twenty minutes!" she screamed. "And you've been ignoring me. I need a drink!"

I succeeded in getting her to release her grip and frantically looked around for a bouncer to help me throw this psychopath out. Jake laughed from his side of the bar. "Are you okay?"

"I think so," I said, rubbing the sore spot on my head. "This is insane! I don't even know what I'm doing. I'm just grabbing the nearest bottle I can get my hands on."

"That's the way to do it." He grinned. "I call it guerrilla bartending."

During this brief exchange, while I caught my breath, Jake managed to take care of two different customers. He was also talking to two men dressed in dark, expensive-looking suits and open-collared silk shirts. He deftly reached down and pulled out a bottle of Chopin, which he handed to them to go along with a carafe of cranberry juice already sitting on the bar.

I glanced reflexively at the cameras mounted in plain sight above the bar. He had just warned me not to pass a bottle over the bar without ringing it up, yet he himself had done just that. I wondered if, as head bartender, he had some sort of comp privileges.

"Get over here," he beckoned.

Hesitant to leave my side of the bar and the throngs of thirsty customers, I walked over and saw that he had two shots of Patrón Silver tequila lined up and ready for us.

"But I thought Shalina said we couldn't drink."

"Who are you? The fucking Virgin Mary? What's the point of working at a bar if we can't do shots?"

The last thing I wanted to do was piss off Shalina, but I knew I had to take the shot—my rite of passage into the Hamptons bartending world. Before doing so, I quickly looked around for any customers who looked like spotters— or what I guessed spotters would look like—and turned my back to the cameras. The coast seemed clear.

"I don't usually drink tequila, just Jameson," I said.

"Just shut up and drink it, prima donna."

"Can I at least have a lime?"

"No training wheels. You're a bartender. Learn to drink your tequila straight. Salud."

"Salud." I slammed the shot, which scorched the entire length of my esophagus.

"Now get back to work." Jake waved me off.

For the rest of the night, every half hour or so, Jake would call me over and we would do a shot. I was grateful for the five-second break, but I didn't know how I was going to make it until four in the morning if we kept doing shots so frequently. I'd only just gotten used to Jameson, and tequila was a whole new ball game. It was hard to imagine I had room in my system for tolerance to another type of hard liquor.

By one o'clock we were running out of everything. Like me, the bar was not equipped to handle such heavy volume, and all of the lemons and limes were used up, and we were running dangerously low on ice and cups. My hands were frozen from scraping the corners of the ice bin for slushy remains.

"That'll be twelve dollars, please," I said to a guy in a metallic blue Dolce & Gabbana button-down, who had just ordered a vodka tonic.

"How the hell can you charge me twelve dollars when there's hardly any ice, and no lime—not to mention that I ordered Ketel One, which you don't have, so you're using your shitty house vodka?"

"I'm really sorry. It's not my fault," I said miserably.

"Forget it," he said, and walked away from the bar, leaving the drink behind.

I was exhausted. My expensive uniform, once baby blue

and white, was now a sickly shade of puke brown. My shoes were soaked in bar muck, and my lower back ached. All the tequila combined with my compulsive water drinking made me desperately need a bathroom break.

"Jake! I have to pee so badly but the line for the bathroom goes all the way around the club," I said, hopping from foot to foot like a little kid. "What should I do?"

"Relax, rookie, there's a bathroom upstairs through the VIP room for employees. Go ahead. I got this bar covered."

On my way to the secret employee bathroom, I pushed through the wall-to-wall crowd of Beautiful People in VIP, all of whom were either dressed to the nines in Rebecca Taylor and Foley & Corrina or purposefully dressed down in the style known as "Hamptons cute"—hundred-dollar glorified metallic flip-flops from Calypso, with ripped-up Juicy Couture jeans skirts. (I'd been in New York long enough to be able to identify designer clothes, even if I couldn't afford them.) The music pumped at a dangerous decibel level and I could feel the bass thumping in my chest cavity. The room was vibrating with hot, sweaty, drunken revelers. Someone bumped into me and nearly knocked me over.

I was just about to yell "Watch it!" when the words died in my throat. It was James Edmonton.

"Hi," I said, flustered, self-consciously pulling down on my tiny top. Even in my tequila haze, I was immediately aware of the shortness of my skirt.

"Cassie!" he said, breaking into a smile, his green eyes lighting up. His cheeks were flushed from the heat generated from all the bodies packed into the room, but he looked relaxed, like a polo player who'd just won the world title. "I told you we'd run into each other this weekend," he said, raising his voice over the volume of the crowd.

Barely twenty-four hours had passed since I'd last seen

James. He'd shocked me by suddenly appearing at Finton's with his father and Martin Pritchard. As soon as I'd spotted him walking in the door, I'd felt like I did in junior high school when my very first crush, Ricky Davy, passed my locker on his way to class—all butterflies and so stupefied by his presence that I barely even managed to get out as much as a "Hello." I'd never entertained the fantasy that I would actually see James again. I quickly ran my hands through my hair to make sure it was laying straight and glanced at my reflection in the mirrors behind the bar in hopes that my Benefit lip gloss had some staying power. When Martin waved me over, I hurriedly thought of what I could say. What if he didn't remember me? I didn't know whether to ask James if he'd finished *This Side of Paradise*, conjure up another Ivy League football fact, or just say what I normally would to any customer: "Hi, what can I get you to drink?" Thankfully he'd saved me from my decision-making angst.

"Hey, Cassie."

He remembered my name!

"Hey," I'd said, with a smile I hoped was both flirtatious and casual.

"Cassie, this is my father. Dad, this is Cassie. I met her last weekend at the Southampton Club."

"It's a pleasure to meet you, Mr. Edmonton," I'd said, offering my hand over the bar.

"Macallan 25. Neat," was his only response.

"Coming right up," I said, flustered. Had he really just dismissed me as rudely as I thought? Maybe he hadn't heard his son's introduction. Or was it because I was a bartender? How humiliating. I stretched up on my tiptoes to reach the highest shelf, where the expensive single-malt scotches lived, and tried as hard as I could to avoid letting it get to me.

"Dad, what's your problem?" I'd heard James admonish him.

"I need a drink," his father had replied gruffly.

I returned bearing Mr. Edmonton's scotch. He didn't say a word.

"Sorry about my dad," James said with an apologetic smile. "He doesn't get out much." I decided to set the father's rude behavior aside and focus on the son.

I took a deep breath, smiled back, and asked, "Can I get you a drink?"

"That would be great. I'll have a Jack and Coke, please."

Just then James's cell phone rang. He grimaced when he saw the number on the screen. "I have to take this. Excuse me," he said, stepping away from the bar and making his way toward the door.

I made his cocktail, and took advantage of the moments he was gone to apply another coat of lip gloss and force my eyelashes upward with my fingers. Just like Vivien Leigh in *Gone with the Wind*, I fiercely pinched my cheeks to give my face a healthy glow. I did this more for dramatic effect than necessity, since I was pretty sure I blushed naturally when James was near.

He'd walked back into the bar shaking his head. "They need me back at the office," he said. "I have to work on a model for a presentation on Friday." He looked down mournfully at the Jack and Coke. "Sorry, Cassie. It was great seeing you again. I'm sure I'll see you this weekend. You'll be out in the Hamptons, right?"

"Um . . . yeah."

"Perfect. Good-bye, Martin. Dad." And then he was off, more quickly than he'd arrived.

I'd wanted to scream after him "How will I find you?! The Hamptons are a really big place!" It seemed impossible that we'd actually cross paths. And yet now here he was at Spark, right in front of me.

"How are you?" he shouted over the chaos of the club.

"Great!" I shouted back. "How did that presentation end up going?"

"What?"

"Your *presentation*," I yelled, making good use of the pauses between the throbbing bass of the hip-hop music.

"Oh, *that*. Good memory!" He smiled and leaned in closer so his shoulder was almost touching mine. "It went well. Are you having a fun night? This place is insane!"

I wished more than anything that, like him, I was drinking and socializing with my friends in the VIP section of the newest and hottest club around. "Actually," I said, "I'm bartending here tonight."

"Oh, that's awesome! Which bar?"

"I'm at the front bar downstairs in the main room."

"Well, I'll have to come down and visit you."

"I wouldn't want you to have to leave the security of the VIP scene," I teased with what I hoped was a sexy smirk.

"Listen, I can hold my own both upstairs *and* downstairs," he assured me. "Besides, this whole club is practically VIP. You should see the line to get in."

My bladder felt like it was about to explode.

"Well, I gotta get back to work," I said, trying not to hop from one foot to another like a little kid.

"Okay," he said. "I'll see you downstairs." And like that, he dissolved into the mob of elite patrons. I fought the urge to turn around and watch him walk away, and instead made a beeline for the secret bathroom.

When I returned to the bar, my head was spinning, and I couldn't decide if it was from the shots, the stressful labor, or the fact that I had just run into James. I glanced over at

Jake's end and saw him pouring a round of shots for all of the promoters and cocktail waitresses.

"Cass," Jake called, "this one's got your name on it. Try not to gag this time."

Everyone was there—Teddy, Elsie and the girls, even Annie had stuck around after the dinner shift to soak up the scene. I hardly recognized the cocktail waitresses. They had completely transformed from straggly, strung-out, sleep-deprived girls in sweatpants to glamorous made-up Vegas showgirls in six-inch stilettos.

"To making a shitload of fucking money!" Elsie shrilled. The rest of the girls answered with rounds of high-pitched "woo-hoos!"

The shot didn't go down easily. It got stuck somewhere in my throat, and I started to gag. I looked up to see Jake laughing at me.

"Jesus Christ, Cassie! Do you realize this is top-shelf tequila? I can't imagine what would happen if I gave you Cuervo." He chuckled. "Are you gonna make it, or should I do some mouth-to-mouth on you?"

"I'm fine," I said, but I was sure my bloodshot eyes told a different story.

I turned my back to Jake and sucked greedily on a lime, which eased the sting of the tequila. I started bartending with a renewed vigor, hoping to look impressive and seasoned when James came down to visit me, and stashed a bottle of Jack, which I knew he liked, under my well. I couldn't stop myself from smiling when I reflected on our conversation, and I furtively scanned the bar for his arrival.

I was still scanning hopefully at four o'clock in the morning, when, despite the crowd's objections, Jake yelled, "Last call!" and the bouncers immediately started ushering everyone toward the door. I finally reconciled myself to the fact that James wouldn't be coming by to see me. I pulled my Columbia sweatshirt over my tequila-stained halter top and stepped into my favorite pair of American Apparel black drawstring pants. As I tried to swallow my disappointment, a very intoxicated Annie staggered toward the bar.

"Cassie, I owe my life to you," she gushed, slamming both hands on the bar. "I *love* the Hamptons. I just danced with Fab Moretti of the *Strokes*! He's so hot! What time is it in Rio? I'm calling my sister!"

I smiled in spite of myself. "Sounds like you had a pretty fun night."

"I love this place. I love the Hamptons. I love our share house. I love our housemates. I love Amagansett. I love Spark. Anyway, Jake's driving us home, right?"

"Yeah, but we have at least another hour of work to do. So you might as well go find Teddy or Fab. I have to clean up and close out my register. I'll find you when I'm done."

At least my first night of madness was over. The bar was a war zone of empty bottles, sopping bar rags, and overflowing garbage cans. Jake was nowhere to be seen.

After I'd bundled up all of my money, credit card slips, and tips, I was escorted by a three-hundred-pound bouncer to a locked cinder-block room where I joined the rest of the staff in counting out the money from the registers, filling out the night's register reports, adjusting credit card tips, and counting out the cash tips. I couldn't believe how tight the security was at Spark. At Finton's we didn't have a bouncer, and we counted our money behind the bar—right in front of the windows for all to see.

The snap of Jake's lighter set off a chain reaction, and in quick succession every staff member except for me had a lit cigarette dangling between their lips. Quickly the room became hazy with smoke. We spread out our cash on the desk and started counting how many hundreds, fifties, twenties, tens, fives, and ones we had, putting them into piles all facing the same way "like little soldiers," as Shalina had instructed, and then noting how many of each bill we had on our close-out sheet. I tabulated our credit card tips while Jake wandered off to talk to Elsie. Chris shuffled by, looking sweaty and harried. His eyes were so red they almost looked like they were bleeding.

Jake and I finished closing out quickly. We bundled our money up into two respective piles and sat at a table in the dining room, where we waited for the waitresses to figure out their money so we could get our tip-out and go home. Jake cracked open two Bud Lights and poured out two more shots of Patrón, and handed me one of each.

"How much did you ring?" Jake asked me. We clinked our shot glasses together and simultaneously downed them.

"I don't know," I said, chasing the tequila with a swig of beer. The burn wasn't as bad as it had been earlier that night.

"It's on the printout from the computer. Next to where it says 'Sales.' "

I unrolled the long, narrow sheet of paper. "Two thousand eight hundred and seven dollars," I said proudly. According to Laurel's information, that was almost three times as much as I usually rang at Finton's.

"That can't be right," he said, snatching the paper from me.

"Why? How much did you ring?"

"Six thousand and eighty-two."

"No way," I said. He tossed his report over to me, and sure enough, next to 'Sales' read the number 6,082. He had more than doubled my sales.

I felt a tinge of fear. Would I be fired for this? So far I'd been proud of myself for my high bartending learning curve—I was ten times the bartender I was when I'd first arrived at Finton's—but like everything in the Hamptons (money, houses, cars, the "scene"), the bartending was hyperintensified. How could I think I could compete with a career bartender who'd been slinging drinks on the Hamptons club circuit for years?

Two hours later the cocktail waitresses were still counting. Strung out on all kinds of drugs, they were too fried to do even the simplest math.

"If I made two hundred from table seven and three-fifty from table nine, then how much did I make?" one of them asked.

"Five-fifty," I said.

"Okay, and what's ten percent of that? I don't have a calculator."

"Fifty-five dollars."

I tried to find Chris, the so-called manager, to help them so we could speed up the process, but he was out back smoking a blunt with a flock of bar backs. The sky was slowly starting to lighten and my eyes were beginning to droop. For the first time I could understand what being "bone-tired" meant. I had already passed the drunk stage and was well on my way to hungover, even though I was still nursing a Light.

I put down my beer and arranged two chairs side by side in the dining room so I could lie down. The sun was now rising, and it peeked through the skylights of Spark's high ceilings. I closed my eyes to block out the rays that filtered through the cigarette smoke clouding the room. Another day was beginning, and I hadn't slept in almost forty-eight hours.

"Here you go," Elsie finally croaked as she handed me a

stack of bills. In her late-night sweatpants, she had once again morphed into the raggedy girl with a hacking smoker's cough I'd met earlier that day. The waitresses had tipped us out $300—$150 each for Jake and me. In total we had made $487, more than double what I'd made on my busiest night at Finton's.

"Jake!" I called out. "We made almost *five hundred dollars!*"

"So what?" he snapped back. He was no longer hyper and fun; he was tired and irritable. "Come on, let's get out of here," he grumbled. "Where's your little blond friend?"

"I don't know," I said. "I haven't seen her in hours." I turned to the throng of cocktail waitresses. "Have any of you guys seen my friend Annie?"

"She fucking left with Teddy," Elsie answered, not bothering to cover up the note of jealousy in her voice.

"Oh," I said. "Well, I guess I'll see you girls tomorrow night then."

I followed Jake into the nearly empty parking lot, but before we reached his '81 Toyota Camry, I heard a familiar voice call out, "Cassie!"

I turned around to see James Edmonton climbing out of a black Range Rover—a white knight descending from his horse. Suddenly I got my fifth wind.

"Hey," he said, approaching me, his buttery brown Lobb shoes crunching on the gravel in the parking lot. "I realized I'd left my credit card here with one of the waitresses. I was hoping I'd still be able to pick it up."

"I'll get it for you," I volunteered, turning to head back into the bar. Once inside, I seized his black AmEx from Elsie's hands and hurried back across the parking lot, my J. Crew flip-flops clopping loudly in the early-morning silence. Various customers had been giving me black AmExes all night long to pay their tabs, and I was intrigued because

I'd never seen one before I came out to the Hamptons. I made a mental note to ask Alexis, my informant on how the other half lives, what the card was all about.

"You're the best," he said. "Do you need a ride home?"

Jake or James? I didn't need time to think about this one.

"Sure," I said. "Jake, I'm gonna get a ride home from—"

"Whatever," Jake mumbled, turning up the Buju Banton on his antiquated stereo system before peeling out of the parking lot.

James opened the passenger door, and helped me into his mammoth vehicle. Maybe chivalry wasn't dead after all, I mused happily. It had just been hibernating in the Hamptons.

"So, where's your house?" he asked, after he'd settled himself in the driver's seat.

"In Amagansett, right on Montauk Highway—III Main Street," I answered.

We pulled out of the parking lot and onto Montauk Highway, and the early-morning light dappling through the canopy of pink dogwood trees gave the thoroughfare a dreamy quality that perfectly complemented the way I was feeling inside.

"I live in East Hampton," he said, "so we're neighbors."

"That's right. Martin mentioned something about that." The scenery with its vast cornfields and old rambling farmhouses whizzed by my open window. As we passed Jean-Luc and Bamboo—East Hampton dinner staples for the well heeled—I inhaled the blissfully smoke-free seaside air and briefly closed my eyes in contentment. I felt like the whole world was still asleep, a feeling I could never capture in Manhattan.

"He was probably talking about my father's house,"

James said. "I don't stay with him. He drives me crazy, as you may have gathered from our little exchange at Finton's the other night."

"So where do you stay?"

"Last year I bought a house on Further Lane with a couple of buddies of mine from Yale."

"You *own* the house?"

"Yeah. We thought it was a good investment. Plus it's just the three of us, me and my two friends, and we can come out year-round. It's really beautiful out here in the fall. You'd love it."

I hoped that was an invitation. I reached across my torso to fasten my seat belt and noticed a Yankee baseball hat on the backseat.

"Are you a Yankee fan?" I asked hopefully.

"Diehard. You?"

"I'm obsessed." I laughed. "I went to thirty games this year. I'm their biggest fan."

"You might have some competition in that department," he challenged with a smile. "I go to Tampa every year for spring training. Have you ever been to Legends Field?"

"No." I sighed. "But when I was little we had a dog named 'the Babe,' and all of our family vacations were trips to the Bronx to see the Yankees."

"Okay, you win," he conceded with another winsome smile. "So where'd you grow up?"

"Albany," I replied. "Did you grow up in the city?"

"Yep, born and bred on the Upper East Side." He turned on the surround-sound stereo system and Led Zeppelin's "Going to California" wafted through the speakers.

"I love this song," I commented, resting my head on the supple black leather headrest.

He reached over the console and briefly stroked the top of my hand. "Did you have an okay night?" he asked. My stomach flipped, and I felt the same spark that had shot through me when he leaned in close to me in the VIP room earlier that night.

"Yeah, but I'm a little tired," I managed. The spot on my hand he'd just touched still tingled. "I couldn't keep up. Everyone was screaming at me. I don't think I can ever go back there again."

He laughed. "I hear you. I've been working hundred-hour weeks at Goldman. I'm starting to get burned out."

"That sucks. A lot of my friends are in banking, so I know how bad the hours can be. But you can't beat the money, right?"

"Yeah, but money isn't everything. I'm ready for something else. I'm actually trying to start up my own production company."

"What do you want to produce?" I asked.

"I'm really interested in independent films." That was it. I was in love. "I produced my first film when I was a junior at Choate, and then I worked on a couple of documentaries at Yale," he went on. "It was just a hobby, though. I majored in finance. I'm pretty sure my dad would've killed me if I told him I was changing majors to study film. But the problem is, I'm always at work. I don't have much time for anything else."

"I know exactly what you mean," I sympathized. "I'm working on a screenplay right now, but by the time I get home from bartending at five in the morning, get some sleep, go to the gym, or run a few errands, it's already time to go back to work again. I feel so guilty, because I originally decided on bartending so I could free up my days for writing. But truth be told, I haven't been getting any writing done at all lately. Especially after nights like this."

"I think you just need to make yourself sit down and do it," he said. "At least that's what I try to tell myself—not that I always follow my own advice." He glanced over at me and smiled. "You should just try to write a little every day, even if you're not always feeling inspired, you know?" At that moment, as I watched his profile glowing in the amber light of the Hamptons sunrise, I was *very* inspired indeed.

"I know." I sighed. "It's just so hard to force it, so I end up reading the paper or checking my e-mail."

He laughed and then, in the blink of a moment, reached over and tucked a strand of my hair behind my ear. I wanted to turn my head and press my lips into his palm. I could feel the electric current humming between us. I'd never felt so violently attracted to anyone in my life.

We drove on through the town of East Hampton past the Windmill, and, all too soon, we were pulling into my drive-way. He put the car in park and turned off the engine. We sat in silence for a moment, and I could hear the seagulls crying in the distance. "What are you doing tomorrow night?" he asked.

"Working," I said. "I work Friday and Saturday nights out here."

"Oh. I was going to ask you if you wanted to have dinner with me at Pacific East. Have you ever been there?"

I shook my head, raw disappointment coursing through me.

"Well, another time then. Come on, I'll walk you to your door. Amagansett's a pretty rough neighborhood," he joked. "I have to make sure you get there safely."

"Yeah, I'm sure it's very dangerous." I laughed as I climbed out of the Range Rover. "I could get mugged by a socialite."

He offered me his hand, which I readily accepted, and we walked up to the old wrap-around porch of Animal House. In the early-morning quiet, without the added decoration of nine frat guys grunting on the porch, I saw the house with new eyes. It had a lot of character and with a little work could be a beautiful historic hideaway.

When we reached the door, James released my hand and turned to face me. "Good night, Cassie," he said, cupping my face in his hands and kissing me softly on the lips. I felt my heart slide down into my toes and a whole flock of butterflies fluttered inside me. He brushed the hair away from my eyes and kissed me one more time before turning to walk back to his car.

When I saw that his Range Rover was a safe distance away, I let out a giddy squeal and pounded my feet on the old wooden planks of the porch. I loved this porch. I loved this house. I loved the Hamptons, just like Annie did. I didn't care if I had to bartend for the rest of my life. I had kissed James Edmonton.

Once inside, I looked around and was shocked to find people I'd never met strewn across every imaginable surface. Someone was sprawled in the bathtub, a couple was passed out in the kitchen curled up under the table, and the hallways were littered with sleeping bodies, many of whom were still holding their beer cans. One guy I didn't recognize had passed out with his face halfway into a bag of Doritos. Worried he would die of asphyxiation, I removed the bag and placed it beside his limp body. I climbed the stairs one by one, trying to be as quiet as I could. Relieved, and ready to crawl into bed, I opened the door to my room.

I blinked, then almost had a heart attack. There was a naked guy sprawled out on top of the covers on *my* bed and a couple entwined on Annie's bed. I looked around frantically and saw my bag tossed into the corner, my clothes scattered around the room. I debated what to do; clearly I couldn't move the ogre on my bed—the guy was at least two hundred pounds. My lower back aching, I gathered up all of my belongings and shoved them back into my bag, all the while cursing the ugly, sweaty shape on the bed. I then yanked the room's only blanket and pillow out from underneath his snoring mass; the idiot didn't even stir. I crept out of the room and wandered down the hall, looking for a place to lie down.

I finally walked outside into the cool ocean breeze and settled uncomfortably into one of the chaise lounges on the porch, but not before first spreading the blanket over its dirty surface. I pulled the sleeves of my hooded sweatshirt over my hands and curled up into a ball on my side, shivering. As I finally drifted off to sleep, visions of James's kisses dancing in my head, I felt another blanket being placed over me. I cracked my eyes open, expecting to see Annie, and was surprised to see a sleepy, smiling Travis covering my cold feet.

Six

SOUR APPLE MARTINI

"Cassie, get over here and drink this before I have you fired!" Jake ordered, gesturing toward the mind eraser—a potent mix of Kahlua, vodka, and soda water, meant to be chugged through a straw—that was idling on the bar. "You call yourself a bartender!" he scoffed, after I'd obliged. "It took you twenty minutes to suck that down." He was furiously banging his head along to Nirvana's "Smells Like Teen Spirit," as he perfectly layered twelve shots of B-52s. "I know what you need," he said, slamming his register drawer shut with his hip. He leaned down and pulled a bottle of Jameson out from under the speed rack and handed it to me. "By the end of the night," he warned, "there'd better be a serious dent in this bottle."

"I thought we only had Bushmills," I said, thankful my old friend Jameson had made an appearance at Spark.

"I brought this from the liquor store on the way here, especially for you. I couldn't handle seeing you gag on Patrón again."

"Thanks," I said, taking two disposable shot glasses out of a long plastic sleeve.

It was already after midnight and the night seemed to be flying by. Mind erasers had a way of distorting time, as did the endless stream of drink orders from our demanding clientele. Despite Jake's ever-constant excursions away from the bar, I'd finally gotten myself into a bartending rhythm, smoothly transitioning from customer to customer and handling his absences better and better. On the way to Spark that night, I'd had my favorite cabdriver stop at Brent's Deli in Amagansett, where I picked up my very own bottle opener and wine key. Armed and ready, this time I made sure to set up my own side of the bar so I knew exactly where everything was.

"Who puts Jack and Ketel in the speed rack?" Jake had criticized when he arrived on the scene.

"I do," I retorted.

"Where the fuck did you learn how to bartend?" he asked.

Thankfully, it was a rhetorical question.

It was only my second night at Spark, but I was learning to hold my own. Earlier, when I'd walked in with Annie, who was newly promoted to cocktail waitress, we ran into Teddy at the entrance. I managed to impress him by mentioning that I was working on a screenplay—it turned out that Teddy was interested in film production as well. It seemed like a lot of people in the service industry had other irons in the fire.

"Can't wait to read it," he said. "And by the way, great job last night. You and Jake rocked it out." His compliment buoyed my self-esteem for the rest of the night. Bartending, I was learning, was all about confidence. I invented drinks all night long. When anyone asked for a red devil or a mai tai, I winged it. As long as it turned out pink, I was in the clear.

As soon as the doors opened and people started streaming in, my antennas rose, hoping that James was among them. I kept one eye on the door so I wouldn't miss him, wondering if he was still having dinner at Pacific East, and who had taken my place at his table.

"Two glasses of champagne," a customer instructed just as I finished my first shot of Jameson in the Hamptons. He was an older man, with a Pierce Brosnan air and silver hair that matched the pinstripes on his Armani suit. On his arm was a girl half his age with jet-black hair and the biggest breast implants I'd ever seen. She was advertising them with an extremely low-cut halter top that made my skimpy uniform look conservative.

I dove my hand into the ice bin, pulled out a bottle of champagne, and filled two glasses. "That'll be thirty dollars, please," I said. He handed me a black American Express card. "Keep it open?" I asked.

"No. Close it."

"I'm sorry, sir. There's a fifty-dollar minimum on all credit cards."

"We're just staying for one drink. Do me a favor. I'm low on cash. Just charge these two glasses for me, and I promise I'll take care of you."

Ever since Baby Carmine had given me that $100 tip on

my first shift, I'd been aware that taking care of the right customers could have surprising benefits. I returned a moment later with his credit card and receipt tucked neatly into a leather folder.

"Thank you," he said. His girlfriend leaned over the bar as she took her first sip of champagne, resting her breasts on her arm. Glancing sideways, I saw Jake's eyes almost pop out of his head.

The man signed and handed me the receipt. Next to tip, it read $150.

"Jake!" I called out, after making sure the man had disappeared into the crowd. "That guy left me *a hundred-and-fifty-dollar* tip on a *thirty-dollar* bill!"

"Did you see her *tits*?" he shouted back.

I ignored his Neanderthal remark and started rooting around in the tip jar to gather singles to make change. We had almost instantaneously run out of small bills in the register, since everyone in the Hamptons seemed to pay with hundred-dollar bills. When I turned back around to face the bar, I noticed two attractive guys in matching mint-green Lacoste shirts smiling at me, waiting for drinks. They had identical athletic-looking physiques and neatly groomed sandy-blond hair.

"Hi," I said, smiling back at them. "What can I get for you?"

"Two Jack and Cokes," one of them requested.

"And your phone number," the other one added with a huge grin.

Between the shots and the frantic physical activity of the night, I'd lost my ability to muster any sort of passable retort. I grabbed the Jack from the well and swiftly made their drinks, wondering if there was a class at Wharton or Harvard Business School where all future bankers and brokers were instructed to drink Jack and Coke.

"Seriously, sweetheart, what's your name?" one of them went on.

"Cassie," I said. "What's yours, *sweetheart*?"

"Ha-ha, I like this one," he said with a laugh. "She's feisty." Then he added, "I'm Glen. And this handsome man is Tom."

"Nice to meet you," I said. "So tell me, did you two get together before you went out tonight to plan your matching outfits?"

They both laughed. "No way!" Tom protested. "I was wearing this shirt all day, and I came straight from Cyril's. Then Glen over here shows up an hour later in the same damn thing. Not that I mind—imitation is the sincerest form of flattery."

"That's bullshit!" Glen refuted. "I've had this shirt since freshman year."

"Hey, Cassie, what are you doing tomorrow?" Tom asked. His cheeks were flushed and his expression hovered somewhere between a genuine smile and a drunken leer.

"Recovering from tonight," I said.

"Well, we're having a barbeque at our house. You can recover there. It should be fun. We've got a ton of liquor and steak and lobster."

"Where do you live?"

"In East Hampton on Further Lane," Glen chimed in.

The minute James had told me he owned a house on Further Lane, it had been imprinted on my memory like branding on the side of a cow. And that afternoon, when I'd finally awoken from a fitful sleep on the front porch, I'd called Alexis. Since my first weekend in the Hamptons, I'd been boring her with musings about James. As far as she was concerned, "marrying up" was exactly what I needed to put an end to my worries about money, and she'd encouraged my every rumination in the hopes that they would turn into reality.

"Lex!" I'd squealed. "I kissed James Edmonton and I'm in love! He's amazing. *Amazing*. And you'll never believe this—he wants to start his own production company. And he's the best kisser *ever*!"

"Oh my God!" she cried. "That's great! How did you find him?"

"He came into Spark. He lives somewhere in East Hampton. He told me where, but I can't remember, Far Away Lane, or Furthest Lane, or something like that."

"Further Lane?" she asked excitedly.

"Yeah, that sounds right."

"Oh my God, that's one of the most exclusive streets *in the world*," she moaned enviously. "Seinfeld has a house there, and so do Steven Spielberg and Kate Capshaw . . . It's like the Park Avenue of East Hampton. Further Lane and Lily Pond Lane are the *only* addresses worth having in the Hamptons. He must be loaded."

While this detail about James thrilled Alexis, it seriously intimidated me. I thought about my summer getaway, which was not only on the wrong side of Montauk Highway, but was also serving as the Hamptons chapter of the Fiji Fraternity. James, on the other hand, was not only living south of the highway in a house that he *owned*, but I imagined he also had the Hilton sisters over for cocktails on a regular basis. I thought back to his father's tasteful custom-tailored suit, Chopard watch, and brutal brush-off. Anyone could see that I was playing way out of my league. I wondered if I'd even really registered on James's emotional radar screen— maybe I hadn't affected him at all.

"You got a pen, Cassie?" Glen asked, interrupting my wandering thoughts.

"I got one," Tom said, producing a platinum-plated Mont Blanc.

"Great," Glen said as he smoothed out a bev nap and carefully wrote down their address and cell phone numbers, the ink bleeding into the tiny folds of the absorbent material. Bev naps were the papyrus of the bartending world. Soon after I'd first started working at Finton's, my day planner had been rapidly replaced by reams of cocktail napkins that accounted for my grocery lists, to-do lists, attempts at budgeting, addresses and phone numbers of the people I was meeting, and screenplay ideas. "You can bring some friends if you want," he added.

"As long as they're hot girls," Tom qualified.

"I'll see what I can do," I said, folding the napkin and sticking it in my LeSportsac makeup case.

"So, say around three?" Glen asked.

"Sounds good," I said, giving them a noncommittal smile and turning to take an order from another customer. The two of them continued to hover near the bar and soon started hitting on two "fake-and-bake" local girls who looked like they were about sixteen.

I made what seemed like thousands of white chocolate martinis and Kir royales for a group of high-maintenance "desperate housewives," and was pushing the hair back from my face when my heart suddenly stopped: James Edmonton had materialized a few feet down the bar. He looked like he'd stepped right out of the Ralph Lauren showroom, and I was nearly knocked off my feet by a surge of attraction. Still, I pretended not to see him, determined to show off my bartending finesse as I flirted with customers and skillfully shook martinis.

After a few minutes, I glanced over and feigned surprise. "Jimmy! I didn't even see you there."

"Jimmy?" He smiled as he leaned over across the bar to kiss my cheek. "No one's called me that since the third grade." As his chiseled cheek brushed mine, I caught the faintest whiff of his Bulgari aftershave. He smelled good enough to eat. "How's your night going?" he asked.

"Great!" I exclaimed. "Much better than last night. Can I get you a drink?"

"Sure, I'll have a—"

"Jack and Coke," I supplied. He smiled, flashing perfectly white teeth worthy of a Crest Whitestrips commercial. I didn't usually obsess over a man's teeth, but James's really were *that* perfect—and like everything else about him, they added to his magnetic allure.

As I started making his drink, the Burberry Plaid Man from the night before appeared at the bar, accompanied by the same group of scantily clad blonds.

"What can I get for you?" Jake asked him.

"If you don't mind I'd like to order from her," he said, pointing in my direction.

"By all means," Jake said.

I walked over to the man after delivering James's drink, hating that I couldn't linger with him longer. "Hi, what can I do for you?"

"Honey, there are a lot of things you can do for me." He smirked, scanning my body up and down, even as his right arm twined around the girl at his side.

"What can I *get* for you to *drink*?" I clarified.

"Bottle of Goose."

I rang it into the computer and handed it over to him. "Three hundred fifty dollars."

"Wait . . . that's not all," he said, leaning in to confer with his fair-haired entourage. "Do you sell bottles of champagne?"

I nodded.

"Veuve?" he asked.

"Yellow Label or Grande Damme?"

"Grande Damme, of course."

I rang it in and sent a bar back to grab a bottle out of the walk-in cooler. "Okay, your total's six-fifty."

He pulled out a wad of hundreds and counted out ten. "Here you go, blue eyes," he said with a wink. "Keep the change."

I did the math in my head. "Jake!" I shouted. "I just made a *three-hundred-and-fifty-dollar* tip!" That was $500 in the last twenty minutes. I wanted to be sure James heard how much my customers loved me.

"You're on a roll tonight!" Jake hollered back.

"Looks like we need another round of Jameson to celebrate!" I turned to James. "Are you interested?"

"If you can handle it, so can I," he laughed. I grabbed our hidden contraband and poured three shots.

"Jake, this is James. James, Jake," I said.

"Salud," Jake said, raising his shot.

"Salud," James and I said in unison. As I downed the shot, I reflected that Jake didn't seem to mind switching from Patrón, to mind erasers, to Irish whiskey. He could knock back anything equally fast and without a problem. His system probably could have tolerated isopropyl rubbing alcohol.

After slamming the shot like a pro, James turned around and summoned a bunch of guys over to the bar. "Cassie, these are some of my friends," he said as he rattled off a laundry list of first names like Taylor, Christian, and Landon paired with last names like Duke, von Furstenberg, and Lauren. They were all handsome, WASPish, Thomas Pink button-down-wearing guys who looked like they had just finished eighteen holes of golf at Shinnecock Hills. "And these two—"

"Are Glen and Tom," I finished for him.

"You know each other?" James asked.

"We go way back," Glen said, grasping my hand and kissing it. "Jealous, Edmonton?" James shot him a smirk.

"We actually just met," I said. "They were trying to convince me to come to their barbeque tomorrow."

"We figured we'd invite as many pretty girls as possible," Tom explained. "I should've known this one belonged to you. How is it you know every single hot girl in the Hamptons?"

"It'd be great if you came," James said to me, ignoring Tom. "I was going to invite you myself when I saw you tonight."

"Cassie!" Jake called from the other end of the bar. "What the fuck are you doing? Get back to work!" I looked up and was terrified to see that an angry mob of thirsty patrons had formed, all of them wildly waving cash.

"I'll see you guys later," I said hastily, returning to my station and taking as many orders as I thought I stood a chance of remembering.

The night rolled on in a mad rush of drink-making, Jameson-shooting, and a series of quick interrupted conversations with James. Finally, a little after three, Annie came bounding up to the bar and held on to it for dear life. The magenta staining her lips and tongue indicated she'd been indulging in her favorite shot—a mix of So Co, Jäger, and cranberry juice, called a redheaded slut.

"Hey, Cass," she slurred slightly, "I just closed out my last table, so I'm running over to Southampton with Teddy. He wants to check out the scene at Jet and Tavern and make sure ours is hotter. And if they have any celebs there, he's going to try to lure them out to us next weekend—even though Liv Tyler, Kirsten Dunst, Jake and Maggie Gyllenhaal, and Uma Thurman were all sitting upstairs in VIP tonight! Can you believe it?"

"I'm so jealous," I groaned, wiping sweat from my brow, and ignoring the Pucci-clad woman to my right who was angling for a drink. "There's no way in hell I'm getting out of here for at least another four hours."

I was in the middle of making my four-hundredth key lime martini when I heard Jake announce, "Last call!" Immediately afterward, he sprang up and over the bar and disappeared up the stairs toward the employee bathroom, getting lost in the sea of people trickling toward the door. I couldn't believe twenty-four hours had catapulted by and my second night of bartending at Spark was almost over.

"Do you want me to wait with you and give you a ride home?" James asked as one of the bouncers, a three-hundred-pound man in a cheap black suit with a face like a cartoon bulldog, loomed over his shoulder.

"It's okay," I said to the bouncer. "He can stay. He's with me." I turned to James. "You really don't have to wait. I'm going to be here forever. I have to clean up, cash out, and then wait for the waitresses, who are mentally impaired even when they're sober. You'll end up being here all night."

"Then I guess I'll have another Jack and Coke, please."

"Seriously, you don't have to wait with me."

He shook his head and smiled. "Somebody's gotta drive you home."

"I can call a cab."

"I'm not letting you take a cab. Can I do anything to help?"

I laughed. "I don't think so."

"You look so beautiful, tonight," he said, leaning over the bar to kiss me. I could feel my face getting hot; the thrill of kissing him seemed to produce more energy than cold fusion. The surrounding bedlam of busboys mopping the mélange of liquids on the floor, waitresses prattling over credit card receipts, and drunk stragglers being forcibly removed by the bouncers faded into the distance.

"Get a room!" Jake called from the balcony of VIP.

I quickly pulled away from James and started randomly wiping down bottles of liquor and the coolers—anything to look busy. Jake returned and we bundled up our cash and adjusted our credit card tips. Just like the night before, Jake and I were cleaned up and closed out hours before the cocktail waitresses. So James and I settled into a quiet corner in the back of the dining room where we sipped Bud Lights as I waited for the waitress tip-out.

"So tell me about this screenplay of yours," he said, offering me the Yale sweatshirt that he'd grabbed out of the back of his Range Rover.

"It's kind of a long story," I said.

He gestured toward the group of waitresses struggling with basic math. "I think we've got some time to kill."

I glanced ruefully over at the girls. "Well, I was on my way home from a party a couple of years ago, and I saw this girl who I'm pretty sure was a prostitute get picked up by a Lincoln Town Car."

"Uh-huh," he nodded, listening intently.

"Anyway, it made me think," I went on. "I complain about money or other stupid problems all the time, but relatively speaking, my life is pretty damn good. I mean, I'm sure I've had a million more opportunities than this girl. So on the train home to Albany, I just started outlining her story."

"So what happens to her?" James asked. His sincere interest made me feel like I was the most fascinating woman in the world.

"That remains to be seen. I had my initial draft produced as a short by some film students at Tisch, but I want to work on how the story plays out and then expand the original script into a feature-length version. The problem is, lately I've been spending a lot more of my time making drinks than writing." I shrugged.

"Well, it sounds like a great idea. I'd love to take a look at it when you finish."

It was a beautiful morning when we finally stepped outside. The sun was rising clear and bright over Montauk Point, and I tasted a soft salty breeze as James opened the passenger door of his Range Rover.

"It's gorgeous out," I said, gazing out the window at the slightly hazy air. It was going to be the first really hot day of summer. "I feel like skipping bed and going straight to the beach."

James smiled and, without saying a word, took the next right onto a rustic country road dappled with white picket fences and monstrous houses—the American dream filtered through the lens of the Hamptons—and we started driving southbound toward the ocean.

"Where are we going?"

"To the beach," he said. "My dad lives down there." He pointed to an old carriage road that ran parallel to the shore. "That's Lily Pond Lane." I craned my neck to see if I could glimpse the historic mansions that lined the shore, but each estate had manicured hedges a mile high that concealed their grounds.

Moments later we arrived at Main Beach in East Hampton. Cascading dunes sprinkled with tall spiky greenery impeded our view of the ocean as we pulled into the tiny parking lot—I wondered how the thousands of beachgoers managed to squeeze their Denalis into such a confined space. Maybe Hamptons beaches were like Hamptons nightclubs—entry was limited to rich, beautiful people who owned waterfront property.

We walked clumsily across the dunes, and suddenly the ocean roared into view. As I idled near the surf, burrowing my toes into the cool wet sand, I felt like I was standing on the edge of the earth. James spread out the blue wool blanket he'd pulled from the back of his car while I opened the two Bud Lights that I'd embezzled from Spark on my way out. There was a slight chill in the air down by the water, and I pulled my arms inside his sweatshirt. James sat behind me and wrapped his arms around me, and I snuggled back into his chest.

"Who knows, Cassie," he said, pausing to take a sip of beer. "Maybe once my production company's on its feet, *I'll* end up producing your screenplay."

I turned around to smile up at him. "Sound good to me."

As the waves thundered at the shoreline, he leaned down and kissed me. I didn't protest when he slid his hands up under the sweatshirt and lifted it up over my head, revealing my tiny halter top, which only twenty-four hours ago had made me feel embarrassed and self-conscious. But now, lying in James's arms, my legs intertwined with his while the morning light crept across the empty beach, I felt amazingly sexy. He started kissing my neck and then began moving down to my shoulders. I ran my hands through his hair and held him to me, losing myself in the cyclone of our chemistry. But when he started to unbutton and ease off my skirt, I snapped to attention.

"Wait," I said reluctantly, caught off guard by a sudden surge of Catholic guilt. "We shouldn't."

"It's okay," he said. "We don't have to."

"It's just . . . I don't know . . . we just . . ." My body literally ached with wanting him. But I also didn't want to open myself up to someone I hardly knew. Deep down, I worried that flash-in-the-pan romances might be part-and-parcel of James's M.O. I was conflicted. I wanted him, but I also wanted him to respect me.

"Shhhh," he said, kissing me gently on the forehead and enveloping me in the blanket. He carefully pulled the sweatshirt back over my head.

My confusion over how far and how fast to go with James continued to rattle around in my mind as Annie and I got ready for the barbeque the next afternoon. I'd arrived back from the beach around nine, giddy and exhausted, and collapsed into bed. The previous night, before we left for work, Annie had figured out that if she locked the door to our bedroom from the inside, she could open it later with a butter knife. This solved the problem of coming home at seven in the morning and finding a naked inebriated jock snoring in our beds. But even as I drifted off to sleep, my brain was awash in a sea of images: James kissing me while the sun came up; James's father brushing me off at Finton's; James mingling up in VIP with the rest of the

Hamptons elite. There was no question that I was smitten, but I worried about falling for someone whose life was so different from my own.

". . . so Teddy has a huge cock," Annie babbled as she scrunched L'Oreal Volumatic Full-Up Mousse into her hair. "I mean, I didn't know what to do with it! We were in the backseat of his Jeep, and I was trying to give him head, but I kept gagging and . . ."

"Mmm-hmm." I nodded distractedly. Annie's sexual play-by-plays usually shocked me into incredulous laughter, but I was too busy obsessing over which skirt would look the cutest with my brand-new bright turquoise Juicy Couture tank top—hastily purchased at Scoop Beach earlier that day for a mere $98—to pay her any attention.

"You're not even listening to me," she complained.

"I'm sorry," I said. "For some reason I'm really nervous about going over to James's house."

"Oh, come on. You have nothing to worry about. It's gonna be so much fun. And you look adorable. I love that top."

A half hour later, though, even Annie was awed into silence as we stood outside James's massive front door on Further Lane, which looked like the portal to a medieval fortress. I felt like Jay Gatsby staring longingly at Tom and Daisy's East Egg estate. Despite my nerves, though, I was determined to play it cool. I glanced down again at my new tank top—even though it had set me back almost $100, its flattering shape gave me a necessary boost of confidence.

"Cassie. Hey!" Tom said, Heineken in hand, as he opened the double doors. "So glad you could make it."

"Hi," I said, stepping into the foyer and discreetly looking around for any sign of James. "This is my friend Annie."

"Nice to meet you," Tom said. "I see Cassie follows instructions very well."

"Excuse me?" Annie asked.

"I told her to bring her cutest friend, and here you are."

Annie's pouty lips spread into a big, gleaming smile. She was, by her own admission, a complete sucker for cheesy one-liners. Meanwhile, I took a deep breath and purposefully directed my eyes right at Tom.

"This is an amazing house," Annie gushed, tilting her head back to scan our surroundings, which included a lofty entrance hall that stretched up to reveal the second floor. I followed her gaze, and for a moment the grandeur of the house distracted me. I couldn't believe that three guys only a few years older than us could own something this lavish.

Tom led us into the dining room. "Wow, this table is incredible," Annie said, tracing her fingers across the glass pane that protected what looked like an ancient artifact resurrected from a dig in western Europe.

"It's actually from a castle in Scotland," Tom replied. "James got it at an auction on one of his golf trips."

I was trying hard to stop my mind from racing ahead and feeding me images of James sitting across from me at that very table while the two of us clinked wineglasses over a dinner we'd cooked together in his stainless steel kitchen, or of me wearing his bathrobe and making him pancakes in the morning. My eyes caught the reflected light off a wall of picture frames, and I walked over to take a closer look. The first photograph was of Tom and an older man flanked by Bill and Hillary Clinton.

"How'd you get to meet Hill and Bill?" I asked him, impressed.

"My dad's a senator."

"What's your last name?"

"Pendergast. My dad's Charles William Pendergast of Rhode Island."

There were also photos of James and his dad posing beside George Steinbrenner, the principal owner of the New York Yankees, Tom next to Rande Gerber and Cindy Crawford, and Glen with Keith Richards.

Just when I thought I could no longer be impressed, Tom led us outside onto the marble patio where people were mingling, sipping cocktails. Beyond the patio lay an Olympic-size pool, two Jacuzzis, tennis courts, and an expansive lawn that stretched down toward the beach. On the horizon, past the perfectly landscaped flower beds and hedgerows, I could see the ocean.

"Wow, this is just a *little* different from our backyard," Annie whispered. Both of us were trying hard not to look too obviously awestruck.

"Yeah, not nearly enough empty PBR cans," I joked.

Glen spotted us and waved hello. He was flipping filet mignon and lobster tails on what Tom cheerfully pointed out was "the Cadillac of grills"—a $10,000 apparatus complete with refrigerators and separate cooking surfaces designed for seafood, red meat, chicken, vegetables, and anything else you might want to prepare. Back home in Albany, we still barbecued on an old charcoal-and-lighter-fluid camping grill we'd had since I was six. James was nowhere in sight.

"Can I offer you a martini?" Tom asked.

"I'll just have a beer," I said.

"Me too," Annie agreed.

"Heineken, Stella, Corona, or Budweiser?"

"Budweiser," we said in unison.

"King of beers," Tom agreed. "Okay, ladies, these

are some of our buddies from college—this is Taylor, Christian . . ."

As I was being reintroduced to James's friends, I noticed a cluster of highly manicured women conspiring in one corner of the patio over glasses of white wine. They were all slender with expertly (and presumably expensively) styled blond hair. Each one of them had perfect posture and perfectly smooth, creamy skin. Their clothes were a tasteful mix of soft pastel cashmere sweater sets, Lily Pulitzer dresses, and shahtoosh shawls that draped over their narrow shoulders, revealing toned arms. Their nails were all meticulously painted a sheer pink, and the toes I saw peeking out of their Sigerson Morrison sandals matched perfectly. A strand of pearls lay elegantly around each of their swanlike necks. With dismay, I reflected on my own generic jeans skirt, dark, windblown hair, and chipped coral nail polish. My new top, which only moments earlier had seemed like sexy summer fun, now seemed unrefined and loud.

"What's up with the Pearls Girls?" Annie whispered, shooting me a devilish look.

"Sssh," I hissed, hoping Tom hadn't heard.

"And this is Buffy, Abigail, Charlotte, and Rosalind," he continued, apparently unaware of our whisperings. "They have houses over on Middle Lane, a couple of blocks from here. James's family is really close with Rosalind's, and Charlotte's father and my father have worked and summered together since we were little kids. Buffy and Abigail winter in Telluride next door to Christian's family's chalet. It's all a little incestuous." He laughed.

I forced a smile at the girls. "Hi, I'm Cassie," I said. "It's nice to meet you."

"It's nice to meet you too," they responded coolly, surveying me with their pale blue eyes. I caught a hint of a southern accent from at least one of them.

"You didn't go to Yale with the boys, did you?" Buffy sniffed. "I've never met you before." As if to imply that if I was "somebody" she would certainly have met me ages ago. She had champagne-colored hair that curled upward at her shoulders and made her look like a country club mom.

"No, I actually went to Columbia," I said, hoping to at least impress them with my educational pedigree. "I met Tom and Glen last night."

Rosalind arched a perfectly threaded eyebrow at Charlotte as if to imply that Tom and Glen had picked me up on a street corner. I floundered to correct the situation. "But I met James a couple of weeks ago in Southampton."

"At the Southampton Country Club?" Charlotte asked, suddenly interested. She had caramel blond hair neatly combed back and fastened with a white headband.

"Yes, actually," I said.

"Oh, how long has your family belonged there?" Abigail asked, wrapping her pink shawl around her slim frame in the same manner Cruella De Vil donned her dalmation-fur stoles. She was the tallest of the girls and had the lithe figure of a ballerina. Her strawberry blond hair was tidily swept up into a flowing ponytail.

"Actually, I was with a friend, who's a member."

"Oh," Rosalind said somewhat reprovingly. She caressed the delicate strand of pearls around her neck, which reflected the translucence of her flawless skin. "Well, is your family's house in Southampton?" she continued. Her hair was the fairest of all and tumbled in soft flaxen waves onto her shoulders.

"Uh . . . no. I have a place with some friends in Amagansett. So, where did you all go to school?" I asked, eager to shift the attention away from me before I was forced to confess that I was from upstate New York.

"UVA," Buffy, Abigail, and Charlotte sang in unison.

"Harvard," Rosalind declared.

Shit, I thought.

"But Abigail and I grew up together in Charleston. And Rosalind and Charlotte grew up together in Greenwich. It's such a small world," Buffy explained. "The three of us ended up Kappa Kappa Gammas together in college. I think they have a chapter at Columbia. What sorority were you a member of?"

I gnawed nervously on my thumbnail—a habit I was desperately trying to break. "I actually never pledged—I couldn't get time off from my job during rush."

Rosalind gasped. "You *worked* while you were in college?"

I ripped my whole thumbnail off with my incisors and felt like crawling in a hole. Who were these girls, and why did I suddenly feel so inadequate? I needed to change the subject. "So, what do you girls do?"

"Charlotte, Buffy, and I work at Cheban/Grubman PR," Abigail told me proudly.

"Cool," I responded. "Rosalind, what do you do?"

Before she could answer, Charlotte volunteered excitedly, "Rosalind's the newest muse for Calvin Klein!"

A satisfied smile played at the corners of Rosalind's mouth as her minions chattered excitedly about her new "job," which I couldn't begin to wrap my head around. What exactly was a *muse*?

"Oh my God, Rosalind! You're following in the exact footsteps of Caroline Bissett Kennedy, God rest her soul," Buffy continued amorously.

I longed desperately to get away from these women and join Annie, who had wandered over to where Tom, Taylor, and Christian were tossing a football around on the impossibly green expansive yard. She was perched on the long stone wall that ran alongside the hedges, sipping her beer and swinging her long shapely legs.

"Tom, I'll go out for the pass!" I yelled. But as soon as the words escaped my throat, it was as though the proverbial record had screeched to a stop at a crowded dance. The guys just stood there uncertainly holding the football, and I heard the Pearls Girls tittering behind me.

"Is she *serious*?" Rosalind's voice carried over the others. My knees nearly buckled with mortification, and I stood there paralyzed for a few agonizing seconds until Annie saved me.

"Come on, Tom, what are you, afraid to play with a *girl*?" she called out. He laughed and lobbed the ball to me, which I caught easily, and threw back to Christian. I decided right then and there I was not going to let these girls get to me. Tom, Glen, and James had invited me, and I belonged there just as much as they did. I looked around hoping James had witnessed my nice pass, but he was still nowhere to be seen. I was determined to look like I was having a good time should he emerge. "Any of you guys up for a game of touch football?" I asked.

Tom pretended to chuck the ball at Buffy. She squealed with fright, ducking behind Rosalind.

"Tom, you're such a brute!" she protested.

"What's the matter, Buffy, you don't like football?" he said with a wink in my direction.

"Why on earth would I play a man's sport?" she sniffed à la Scarlett O'Hara. She turned to Rosalind, and the two shared a hushed exchange, eyeing me disdainfully the whole time. I didn't want to be paranoid, but something told me I was the topic of conversation.

"I think it's time for another beer," Taylor said, spiking the football. Annie and I followed the boys back to the patio where Glen was taking orders for dinner. The Pearls Girls strolled behind us.

"I'll have a small chicken breast—no skin, no sauce, no potatoes, no corn. And a little salad—dressing on the side," Rosalind said.

"Me too," Abigail said. Charlotte and Buffy nodded in agreement. Annie rolled her eyes.

"What can I get for you, Cassie?" Glen asked.

"I'll try some of the filet mignon, and the lobster, and I'll have some corn and a potato," I said quietly, hoping to avoid further condemnation from the Pearls Girls—given how they felt about football, I was pretty sure I could guess how they felt about eating—but no such luck.

"A little hungry?" Rosalind frowned, her eyes concentrating on my heaping plate.

I ignored her barb. I could easily guess what had triggered their vicious behavior. Annie and I were outsiders—different from them—and had clearly captured the attention of their male friends. It was a classic case of girls being bitchy to defend their territory. I felt impotent, though, because they were James's friends and I didn't want to ruffle feathers.

Rosalind turned away and joined the other girls, who were now absorbed in a heated debate over the merits of cushion versus brilliant-cut diamond engagement rings—a distinction that had about as much meaning to me as quantum physics.

"Well, when Andrea got engaged to Graydon, she got a three-point-five-carat cushion cut from Harry Winston," Abigail was saying.

"But the five-carat classic brilliant-cut ring from Tiffany that Allison got was so much more timeless," Charlotte disputed. I looked around to Annie for support, but she had long since left to get a lesson at the grill from Tom. He had his arm around her as he explained how Wolfgang Puck handled a lobster tail. I was on my own.

I felt awkward hovering on the periphery of their group so I made one last stab at amicability. "So what brings you to the Hamptons all the way from Charleston?" I asked Buffy and Abigail.

"Well, my daddy's always kept a place up here," Buffy said. "He's from Manhattan originally, and he just adores the Hamptons. I've been coming here since I was a baby."

"We all live in Manhattan now, on the Upper East Side, and we come out on weekends," Abigail added. "Where do you live in Manhattan?"

"I live in the Village and Annie lives on the Lower East Side."

"Oh," they said, looking bemused that anyone might actually choose to live in those neighborhoods. I cut off several small pieces of my filet hoping to eat in as delicate a manner as possible.

"You look really familiar," Rosalind went on, scrutinizing my face. "Have we met before?"

I met her gaze. She looked familiar to me as well, but I couldn't place her. It was hard to imagine we ran in the same circles. "I don't think so," I said, taking an uncomfortable gulp of Budweiser.

"I know!" she finally exclaimed, careful not to upset her brimming glass of Sancerre. "You're a bartender at Spark. I saw you there on Friday night."

"Yeah. That must be it." I smiled awkwardly.

"You're a *bartender*?" Abigail asked. "What's that like?"

"You mean Spark?" I asked, confused.

"No, she means bartending," Rosalind interjected, cocking her head to one side and flipping her hair. "It must be so difficult for you—staying up all night, serving all those people."

"It's not that bad," I said. "Actually, it's a lot of fun. I love the people I work with, and I make great money." I managed a confident smile. I wasn't going to let them ruin my afternoon. There was nothing wrong with my job—it was a means to an end, I assured myself.

"I'm sure you do," Rosalind said. "In fact, girls, if I recall correctly, Cassie makes a fabulous sour apple martini."

I smiled uneasily. Even though it seemed she was giving me a compliment, I felt like it was backhanded at best.

"Ooooh, we have sour apple schnapps and vodka in the kitchen," Abigail said, her eyes lighting up.

Rosalind turned and looked at me levelly. "Cassie, would you do me a huge favor and run inside and mix me one of those delicious drinks of yours?"

I stood there wondering how I should deal with the situation, which had gone from uncomfortable to insulting. I wouldn't have minded mixing a drink for a friend, but there was something about the dynamics that made me loath to do anything that might suggest I was part of the working class that had catered to Rosalind and her friends throughout their entire lives. They clearly didn't view me as an equal. I looked around for James for the umpteenth time—I couldn't help hoping that he'd appear at my side, put his arms around me, and pull me in for a kiss, instantly validating my presence at the barbeque.

"I guess I can do it," I said finally. I hated that I was playing into their hands, but if James's and Rosalind's families had really known each other for years, being deferential to these girls—even in the face of their passive-aggressive animosity—seemed like my only strategy. I set down my plate of food and turned to walk toward the kitchen.

"Sorry, ladies," Annie interjected, sidling up beside me and blocking my path. "But today's our day off. If you really want a martini, you can make it yourself. It's not that difficult, really. Didn't they teach you to make the perfect cocktail in charm school?"

The girls erupted into insincere laughter. "Oh, isn't she adorable? What's your name again?" Abigail asked.

"Annie," Annie said with an equally insincere smile, taking a step closer toward them. I put a restraining hand on her forearm, praying she wasn't about to punch one of the Pearls Girls in her Rembrandt-white teeth.

"Hey, guys." James's voice cut through the overwrought air from the kitchen doorway like a shotgun blast. All of our puffed-out peacock feathers slowly settled back into place and the cat fight was averted, at least temporarily. With his slightly rumpled Polo shirt and tousled hair, he looked like he'd just woken up. I felt a happy rush of relief and anticipation—not only did he look as adorable as ever, but I couldn't wait until the moment the Pearls Girls realized that there was something going on between us. If I was good enough to be James's paramour, then I was good enough for them.

"James!" Rosalind trilled, mincing over to him and presenting her cheek, which he dutifully kissed. Buffy, Abigail, and Charlotte flocked behind her. He kissed them all on their cheeks and then made his way toward me and Annie.

"Hey, Annie," he said, also kissing her on the cheek. Then he finally turned to me. "What's up, Cass?" he said, planting a generic kiss on my cheek and then brushing past me and shouting to Tom at the grill, "There better be food left. I'm starving!"

I stared at James's back in disbelief as he walked over to where Tom was manning the grill. He'd barely even looked at me. Only that morning we had been kissing on the beach wrapped up in each other's arms. But now I felt like we were strangers. What had happened? Had he heard my exchange with the Pearls Girls? I looked at Annie, speechless. She gave me a sympathetic look and shrugged her shoulders.

"James, did you get a chance to talk to Elisabeth last night?" I heard Rosalind ask him excitedly as she followed him over to the grill.

"Yeah, I hung out with her for a while," James said. "It was so good to catch up. I haven't seen her since Marbella last summer. She told me her dad's finally closing on that Aspen house for her."

"I know! Isn't it exciting? It's literally down the road from my family's house. This winter's going to be the best one yet!"

Marbella? Aspen? James and Rosalind were casually mentioning places I'd read about in *People* magazine as the most exclusive celebrity retreats as though they were the Red Roof Inn in Albany. I stood around awkwardly, feeling stupid. I certainly had nothing to add to their conversation. How did I ever think I'd be able to ever fit into his world?

Suddenly Charlotte put down her wineglass. "Oh my goodness, what time is it?" she asked, alarmed.

Rosalind consulted the platinum Cartier watch that hung delicately on her slender wrist. "Oh my gosh!" she cried. "It's almost five-thirty. If we don't leave now, we'll miss the Luxury Liner and be stuck taking the Jitney or the train!"

Without another word, they all sprang into action, gathering their belongings, which were neatly piled on lounge chairs beside the pool. In a shahtoosh-filled flash of air-kisses and Chanel quilted bags, they were headed for the door. As I watched them leave, I overheard Rosalind say to Abigail, "I don't understand why they invited those bartender girls in the first place. . . ."

Annie, who thankfully hadn't been privy to Rosalind's final dig, rolled her eyes, laughing incredulously. "Are you fucking kidding me? What the hell is the Luxury Liner?"

I breathed a sigh of relief. I didn't care how Rosalind and her friends had departed, just so long as they were gone.

"Hey, girls," Tom called. "There's lobster left over if you want some."

"Come on," Annie whispered. She grabbed my hand and marched me determinedly toward the grill, where Glen was drinking a Stella, and Tom and James were seated at the table, busily cracking open lobster tails and dipping them in drawn butter.

To my surprise, James pulled me into his lap. "Here," he said, lifting up a forkful of fluffy lobster meat. "Have some of mine." I took a dainty bite. He leaned in and gave me a buttery kiss—on the lips this time. "I'm so glad you came."

"Me too." I smiled back weakly. It felt so good to be snuggled in his lap here in this lushly landscaped yard, being hand-fed lobster as the sun sank lower in the sky. Still, I couldn't shake the awkwardness of the rest of the afternoon and his obvious coldness toward me in front of the Pearls Girls. Was it my imagination, or had he warmed up to me the second they'd disappeared? As I accepted another bite from James's fork, the sumptuous flavor of the rich delicacy mingled with the bitter taste in my mouth.

Seven

SUGAR DADDY

"Nice tan," Billy said as I pranced behind the bar.

"Thanks." It was another slow Wednesday night at Finton's, and I was already counting down the hours (thirty-six to be exact) until I left for the Hamptons.

"Did you make good money this weekend?"

"Yeah, I made *great* money. Everyone out there runs six-hundred-dollar bar tabs on their black AmExes and tip like two hundred percent," I crowed. Now that I'd finally figured out the significance of the black AmEx, I was eager to drop the term casually in conversation. The night before

Alexis and I had been lounging on our couch in the living room, sharing a red chenille blanket, watching *Cocktail*, and I'd seized the opportunity to conduct a little research.

"Lex, I know the difference between the green American Express card and the gold and platinum ones, but what about black? Everyone in the Hamptons has one."

"Well, a black AmEx is the highest one, and the hardest to get," she explained, taking a dainty scoop of Ben & Jerry's Phish Food directly from the pint. "It's called the Centurion. You have to be invited to get one—you can't apply or anything. And there's some ridiculous yearly minimum, like you have to charge at least $250,000 a year on the card. But you get all kinds of benefits, like this amazing concierge service that can get you into any restaurant in the world at a moment's notice. At least that's what my dad told me. Basically, almost anyone can have a gold card or even a platinum one, but you have to be *really* rich to have a black one."

"Wow," I said, marveling as Brian Flanagan and Doug Coughlin executed flawless bottle-tossing choreography to "The Hippy Hippy Shake." "Martin Pritchard has one. And James has one too."

"He does? What does his father do?"

"I don't know."

"You mean you never asked?"

"No. It never came up."

"Well, aren't you dying to know?" she asked incredulously.

"Why? So I can tell him that my dad's a fireman who moonlights as a plumber, and I grew up 'summering' at the town pool? He probably comes from serious old money, and I'm not even new money—I'm no money."

"Don't even worry about that, Cass. He obviously likes you. And if that's what matters to him, then you don't want him anyway. Besides, it's going to come out sooner or later." Her eyes returned to the movie.

Now, as I stood behind the bar at Finton's, I tried to stop obsessing over the striking gap between our social backgrounds. "So, did you do anything besides work all weekend?" Billy asked as he grabbed the bottle of well gin and poured it into a metal shaker along with some pineapple juice, grenadine, and bitters to make that night's $5 special: the sugar daddy martini.

"Yeah, Annie and I went to the beach, and we met these guys at work, and they invited us to their barbeque at this unbelievable house right on the water. It was really fun."

"Yeah, it's a great time out there, but I think I finally just got too old for it. It gets really tiring going back and forth and working all those late nights. By the end of the summer, you'll know what I mean."

The door chimed to punctuate our conversation, and when I looked up, I thought I must be hallucinating. James was strolling toward me. "I didn't expect to see you until Friday," I said, beaming.

"Yeah, well, they let me leave the office for a dinner break, and I heard the bartender here was pretty cute, so I thought I'd stop by." He pulled me in for a kiss.

Brimming with elation, I propped myself on my elbows and leaned in so I was as close to him as I could get with a three-foot-thick piece of wood in between us. Nothing was sexier than James in a suit—he looked so powerful and in charge. "Can I get you a drink?"

"I'll just have an Amstel."

"You got it," I said, grabbing his beer and flipping off the cap with a sassy flair. I handed him a menu.

"And I'll have the burger, medium, with cheddar, please," he said after glancing through it quickly.

"Coming right up," I said, punching the order in on the computer. "So how was your day?"

"Not that exciting," he said, taking a sip of beer. "I'm working on this merger . . ."

"Hi, Cassie," Dan interrupted. I hadn't even noticed him come up to the bar.

"Hey, Dan. James, this is Dan Finton, the owner of Finton's. Dan, this is James Edmonton."

"Hi," Dan said coolly, extending his hand officially, like a politician.

"Nice to meet you," James said. "I think you know a good friend of my father's, Martin Pritchard. This is his favorite place. He talks about it all the time."

"Yes, I've known Martin for years," Dan said. Then he turned and vanished back down the stairs.

I spread out a white napkin on the bar in front of James as a place mat, and placed a folded napkin and silverware neatly on top of it.

"So have you been getting any work done on your screenplay?" he asked.

"As a matter of fact, I worked on it all afternoon," I said proudly. That morning, for the first time since graduation, I'd woken up before ten o'clock and, after hitting the gym for a spin class, opened my computer. I sat typing for hours, buzzing with energy from the weekend, and trying not to check my cell phone every ten or fifteen minutes to see if James had called.

"See, what did I tell you? Starting is always the hardest part," he said.

José delivered James's burger, and I grabbed a handful of his fries, perched on the metal cooler, and started munching as he dug in.

"So, any new developments with your production company?" I asked. But Dan's voice crackled over the intercom before he could answer.

"Cassie, I need you downstairs," he said brusquely.

"I'll be right back," I promised James, hopping off the cooler and descending the stairs two at a time until I arrived at the office. Laurel didn't look up from her paperwork. Dan stood in the doorway.

"Follow me," he said. His terse tone startled me. My stomach tightened as I followed him past the tunnel where we stored the wine and through a storage closet to a door I'd never noticed before. He punched a combination into a keypad and opened the door. I stepped inside and almost fainted at the sight of what seemed like twenty monitors mounted on the wall, showing every single angle of the bar. On one camera I saw an extreme closeup of the small mole on Billy's cheek as he blew his nose in a bev nap. On another screen I saw José polishing silverware, and another showed the guys in the kitchen washing vegetables. Other screens showed images of customers eating in the dining room and drinking in the lounge. There was even some footage of the streets outside of Finton's.

"This is the surveillance room," Dan said evenly. "I've been watching you at the bar, and I must say your behavior so far tonight has been totally unacceptable."

For a moment, I was speechless. I'd gotten used to the idea of cameras at Spark, but I'd never dreamed there were cameras at Finton's. And yet there I was in an elaborate observation chamber where my every move was being examined. "What are you talking about?"

"I don't mind if you have friends come into the bar, and in fact, I encourage that. It promotes business."

"Okay," I said, unsure of where he was going.

"What I *don't* like is when you throw yourself at your boyfriend and flirt with him all night when there are other customers at the bar. That's highly unprofessional, and I expected more from you."

Again, I was too stunned to react immediately. "Dan, I don't know what you're talking about," I finally said. I could feel my face getting red and my sweat glands kicking into overdrive. "First of all, there were no other customers at my side of the bar, and second of all, I didn't throw myself at him, and . . ."

"Cassie. I saw it right here on this screen," he said, indicating the central monitor, which was larger than all the other screens. "I can play it back for you if you'd like."

"That won't be necessary," I said, suddenly feeling very violated—the same creepy feeling I had when I learned that there were cameras in the dressing rooms at Bloomingdale's.

"I don't like my employees dating the customers," he said plainly. "Because then if things don't work out, the customer will never come back."

"But that doesn't make any sense," I protested, trying not to lose my cool. "If it wasn't for me, he wouldn't even be a customer."

"You're missing the point. As a bartender in my bar, it's your job to entertain the customers and make sure everyone is having a good time. You can't do that if all of your attention is being monopolized by your boyfriend."

"He's not even my boyfriend yet," I countered lamely.

"Well, he's certainly been monopolizing your time all night."

"He's only been here for fifteen minutes!" I cried, exasperated. "And there's no one else at the bar!"

"Cassie, I don't want to argue with you. You work in my bar, and you have to respect my rules."

I took a deep breath, held back tears, and forced myself to remember that my job was on the line. "Fine," I said. "It won't happen again." I walked out, mustering every ounce of self-control to keep from slamming the surveillance door behind me.

By the time I arrived back upstairs, James was almost done with his burger. "Is everything okay?" he asked, offering me a French fry.

"It's fine." I sighed. "I just sometimes don't think I have the stomach to work in this business."

"You'll be okay," he said, reaching over the bar and taking my hand. I quickly looked around to make sure Dan, who'd followed me upstairs and taken a seat in the dining room, hadn't witnessed the affectionate gesture. "Just remember, you're not doing this forever, just until you get your screenplay out the door."

I looked into his sympathetic eyes and tried to smile. His confidence in me threatened to spark the tears I'd been successfully holding back.

"So, what time do you think you'll get off tonight?" James asked as I cleared away his plate and put it in the bus pan we kept under the bar.

"Not until at least two," I said.

"I'll probably get out of the office around one. Maybe I can come back for a nightcap and keep you company."

"That's okay, you should probably just go home. I don't want to make you sit here. Besides," I added, busying myself washing dishes, "Dan's been a little grumpy about us entertaining personal friends."

"Okay," he said. "That's probably better anyway. I have

an early meeting tomorrow about the Kmart/Sears merger. But how about dinner tomorrow night?"

"I can't, I have to work," I said.

"Well, what about Friday?" he persisted. "We can do JLX in Sag Harbor. It's Jean-Luc's other restaurant."

"I have to work then too," I said, disappointed.

"Okay, well, don't worry. We'll figure something out. I guess I should get back to the office." He leaned over the bar and kissed me on the cheek. Paranoid, I looked around to make sure Dan hadn't been watching. "I'll call you," he said, and headed for the door.

Around ten o'clock, my cell phone rang. I knew better than to answer it, since talking on cell phones behind the bar was strictly forbidden and I now knew that my behavior was being closely monitored. But I couldn't resist checking the caller ID, hoping that it was James. Instead, it was a 917 number that I didn't recognize. When my phone beeped to signal that I had a new message, I called my voice mail from the landline at Finton's.

"Hey, Cassie, it's Teddy, give me a ring: 917-555-4342."

The bar was entirely empty except for Maya, the new girl Billy was seeing, who'd arrived a few minutes before and was now leaning over the bar playing with Billy's hair. I noted that Billy wasn't getting called out by Dan on *his* demonstrative behavior.

"Billy, I'm going outside for a second to make a phone call," I said, clandestinely slipping my cell into the back pocket of my pants and making my way to the door.

"Hurry back, it's swamped in here," he joked.

I walked outside and turned left onto Grand Street, walking a few blocks until I was sure I was out of the cameras' reach. Then I dialed Teddy's number.

"Hello?" he answered on the first ring.

"Hey, Teddy, it's Cassie."

"Cassie, hey. I need to go over a couple of things with you," he said, quick and businesslike. "First, I need you to come to work a little early on Friday, because there's a private party for Jessica Simpson's makeup line and we need to have everyone in by eight-thirty to set up."

"Okay," I said.

"And another thing," he continued, "We're switching things around a little this weekend. I'm moving you to the back bar and trying a new girl out in the front."

I felt like the wind had been knocked right out of me. "A new girl?" I asked. "Why?"

"Well, to be honest, Cassie, your rings just weren't that high this weekend, and we know we can be making more money up there. We just finished going over all the reports for both Friday and Saturday, and Jake more than doubled your sales."

"But you've seen me up there. I work really hard, and you said yourself I did a great job," I said defensively. "And I sold bottles. I know I sold more bottles than Jake. He said it's a big deal to sell bottles at the bar."

"It is, but it doesn't really matter. Numbers don't lie. Jake still rings circles around you. Don't get me wrong, we still want you to work here, which is a huge compliment—we've already let three bartenders go. It's just that, like I said, I can't argue with the numbers."

My head was spinning. I didn't want to leave Jake, and I didn't want to lose the cash flow of the front bar. "Okay, Teddy," I said, resigned, "I'll give it a try."

"Great," he said. "See you Friday."

Defeated, I walked back into Finton's and grew even more dour when I saw that Dan was comfortably seated right in front of my register. He was drinking Wishing Tree Shiraz out of a globular Riedel wineglass and talking to the attractive young redhead sitting beside him. "When dealing with old-country wines, the grape itself is the primary focus, and winemakers don't concern themselves as much with the casking. With new-country wines . . ." He rambled on to his captive audience of one. "Hey, Cass," he said, interrupting himself to offer me a half-smile when I returned behind the bar. Then he returned to his private tutorial.

While Dan was normally impeccably groomed and even dashing, I was noticing he tended to degenerate as the night wore on. When he indulged in too much red wine (as he often did), his teeth would turn a purplish black and the stain would eventually bleed into the cracks of his chapped lips. The writer in me wondered if that discoloration wasn't a physical symbol of the toll the bar world took on its inhabitants. It was like when I counted out money at the end of a shift at Spark. After handling thousands of dollars in cash, my fingers would literally turn black from the dirt and grime on the bills. When you work in a bar, surrounded by every imaginable vice, it's hard not to have some of it rub off on you.

I walked over to Billy's end where he was reorganizing the CDs.

"Where's Maya?" I asked.

"She just ran out to get some cigarettes," he said, trying to locate the case for Tom Petty & the Heartbreakers' *Greatest Hits*. Then he lowered his voice. "What'd Dan want to talk to you about downstairs?"

"He showed me his secret surveillance room—thanks for the warning."

"I thought everyone knew about that room. What happened—did he catch you giving away free drinks or something?"

"No. He accused me of throwing myself at a customer. He was watching me on the cameras." I handed him the case, which was sitting on one of the beer coolers. "It's such bullshit. He doesn't yell at you when Maya is stretched halfway over the bar making out with you."

Billy laughed. "We weren't making out," he scoffed. "And it's different with me. I'm a guy."

"What's that supposed to mean?"

"Dan can get really weird about some of the girls that work here—really possessive and territorial. He has this fucked-up idea that this is his bar, his domain, and *his* women. He wants to be the only man getting attention when he's here. Sometimes I think the only reason he bought this place was so he could enjoy a little celebrity. Know what I mean?"

"Not really."

"When you own a restaurant or bar, even if it's not some crazy hot spot, you're still a celebrity whenever you're there. Everyone that comes in is always asking 'Is Dan Finton in tonight?' It's in everyone's best interest to be on his good side, so customers and employees kiss his ass. You know how it is whenever he comes in here. Laurel, the waitresses, the regulars, everyone runs over to him. So he doesn't like it when anyone threatens that."

I nodded, mulling over this insight.

"We used to have this manager here a couple of years ago," he went on. "His name was Philipe, and he was pretty much the polar opposite of Laurel. He was from France, and he was really charismatic with both the customers and the staff. And everyone that came in here asked for him. He more than tripled the business of this place, and he would turn tables in the dining room four times a night. He was an absolute genius at bringing in business. Basically, any time pretty girls came in, he would make sure they had a great time, buy their drinks, play great music—everything. Then, of course, they came back with more of their girlfriends to see him. Pretty soon this place got to be known as the spot where pretty girls hung out, so of course all the guys started streaming in and spending all their Wall Street cash. We were mobbed seven days a week. Anyway, one day without warning, Dan fires him."

"Why?"

"He couldn't handle all the attention Philipe got. People thought *Philipe* was the owner, and Dan just lost it."

"But that doesn't make any sense," I said.

"No shit. Now Philipe works for Keith McNally at Balthazar and Pastis. Dan literally gave up a gold mine when he fired Philipe, but he didn't seem to care. He'd rather sacrifice great business and great money than play second fiddle to anyone. That's why he got mad when you were talking to your boyfriend before."

"He's not my boyfriend," I refuted, like a third-grader.

"Well, whoever he was, you two seemed really into each other, and it touched a nerve with Dan."

"CASSSSSSSSSSSSSSSIE!!!" I turned around to see Alexis standing by the front door carrying one of her Manolos, her highlighted hair falling halfway out of the smooth ponytail she usually wore to work. Her chic Balenciaga suit was wrinkled, and I could see even from behind the bar that she had a giant run in her hose. She was hanging on the arm of a middle-aged man with combed-back salt-and-pepper hair who was wearing a dark suit and shiny shoes. I could tell she was absolutely wasted.

"This is my best friend in the entire world," she crowed to the man as she approached and steadied herself by gripping a bar stool. "I don't know what I'd do without her. I love her. I'm *obsessed* with her. She's my best friend."

"Nice to meet you," the man said, offering his hand, his platinum wedding band glinting in the candlelight. "I'm Bob."

"Bob is my managing director who I've been telling you about," Alexis slurred. "He took me out to dinner tonight. We went to Le Cirque, and it was *fabulous*."

"It's nice to meet you," I said to him.

"Shots!" Alexis clapped her hands. "Let's do some shots, Cassie! What do you say? Jameson?" she sputtered.

"Lex, I don't feel like drinking tonight," I said, hoping to thwart her plan for getting even more wasted.

"Cassie, your straight edge is cutting me! Now pour us some shots!"

Reluctantly I grabbed the bottle of Jameson and poured two shots, one for Alexis and one for Bob.

They slammed them, and Bob ordered a Lagavulin neat. Once I'd poured him the expensive single-malt scotch and given Alexis her usual glass of Fumé Blanc, they sat down a few stools from Dan. (His redheaded companion had just jotted her number on a bev nap, slipped it to him, and left the bar.) Bob was smiling at Alexis lecherously. "Alexis," he was saying, "I never get to see this side of you at the office. You're really fun when you have a couple in you."

I wasn't sure how he had seized on the word "fun" to describe her at that moment. To me, she looked like she was about to either throw up or fall over. Bob slid his hand around her shoulders, massaging her neck, while Alexis rambled on to him about something work-related, drunkenly attempting to keep her hair out of her eyes. Suddenly it registered to her that Dan, whom she'd met several times over the past few weeks, was sitting two stools away.

"Dan!" she cried. "I haven't seen you in forever! This is my boss, Bob. Bob, this is Cassie's boss, Dan." She got off her stool and went over to Dan, dragging Bob with her.

For a minute, as I stood there watching them, I was transported to a surreal world where Bob and Dan looked like Alexis's and my fathers. I poured a club soda with a lime and passed it to Alexis, hoping I could trick her into thinking it was a drink. She was now draped up against Bob and drunkenly chattering at Dan, who was looking on with amusement.

I decided that I should try to pull Alexis into the ladies' room for a girls' powwow where hopefully I could convince her to drink some water or, better yet, coffee—and then see if I could sneak her out the delivery entrance to a cab. But when I looked back up, Alexis and her boss were kissing passionately, running their hands over each other.

I sprang out from behind the bar and raced up to them, tapping Alexis on the shoulder as hard as I could without injuring her. When she didn't respond, I tugged on her arm forcibly until she pulled away from Bob and looked dazedly in my direction.

"Lex, wanna run down to the bathroom with me?" I asked, giving her what I hoped was a meaningful look.

"Whatever," she slurred.

I hurried her down the stairs, watching closely to be sure she didn't trip on her one remaining shoe, and not saying a word until the bathroom door was shut safely behind us.

"What are you *doing*?" I hissed.

"Whaddya mean?" she asked, trying to apply her Trish McEvoy lip gloss and smearing it all over her upper lip in the process.

"You're kissing your *married* boss in front of me and Dan and everyone else at the bar!" I admonished.

"What do you care?" she asked.

"Well, first of all, it's a little awkward for me since I work here. And second, are you sure you want to do this? He's your *boss*. What's going to happen when you see him tomorrow at work?"

"I already told him I'm calling in sick." Alexis sniffed.

"But what about the next day? You're going to have to see him again eventually."

"Lighten up," Alexis whined.

"*Lighten up?* He's married. He has a wife. And probably kids."

"Oh, don't be so naïve, Cassie. People do this all the time. I'm just having fun." She stormed out the door and I could hear her tripping up the stairs. I followed her glumly back to the bar, where Dan and Bob were laughing amiably.

"I'm not feeling well, Bob, I gotta go," Alexis said, gathering up her bag and other shoe and doing her best to flounce out the door without looking in my direction.

"Nice to meet you," Bob said to me and Dan as he followed after her.

I watched them leave, hoping Alexis would have enough sense to get in a cab by herself and go home. But given the look in Bob's eyes, I doubted he was going to let that happen. Part of me was in shock—Martin and Lily had been bad enough, but now my best friend was fooling around with her much older, married boss? Was it impossible for some young women to resist the money, power, and prestige that defined many men in Manhattan?

"Hey, Dan, is it okay if I go home with Maya?" Billy

asked. He'd just emerged from the employee bathroom where he and Maya were doing God-knows-what. "It's so dead in here. Cassie, you don't mind closing alone, do you?"

Before I could answer, Dan said, "Not a problem at all. Tell José he can go home too. I can stay with Cassie until she finishes."

I inwardly cringed. The night's events—the surveillance room, Alexis making out with Bob, Bob and Dan fraternizing at the bar, and Bob chasing after Alexis—all swam in my mind, making me wary. I didn't want to think about what Alexis might be doing with her boss right now, and I didn't feel like being left alone with mine.

Once the bar was empty and I had begun to close out, Dan turned to me. "Bob seems like a nice guy."

"Um . . . I guess," I said reluctantly. "But I just can't figure out what he's doing out this late with Alexis when he has a wife at home."

"Having a wife at home doesn't always signify happiness, Cassie," he said.

"No, maybe not. But I'm not sure making out with a twenty-three-year-old does either," I replied. My stomach was suffering an Alexis-induced ulcer of worry and annoyance, and I just wanted to count my money and go home.

"Come on," Dan chided. "Give the guy a break. Here he is with this beautiful young girl who's all over him—"

"She was *drunk*," I said, even more irritated now that Dan was trying to defend the situation.

"All I'm saying is that I can't blame him," he said as he walked around, lowering all the blinds in the bar and restaurant. "Men are simple creatures, Cassie. There are few who could resist an opportunity like that. At the end of the day it's basic human nature. Older men will always be attracted to younger women."

"What are you doing?" I asked as he finished closing the blinds.

"I just thought we should have some privacy as you close up."

Eight

JACK AND COKE

"Up, rocks, or frozen?" the gray-haired bartender asked us. He had a tanned, leathery face and a friendly smile and was wearing a bright red Hawaiian-print shirt.

"Rocks," I said. "Annie, up, rocks, or frozen?"

"Frrrrrrrrrrrrozen!" Annie trilled, popping up beside me at the bar. She looked like a sun goddess in her white sundress and turquoise beads, with her olive skin and glowing blond ringlets.

"Salt?" the bartender confirmed.

"None for me, thanks," I said. "Annie?"

"Nope!"

"Okay, so one margarita on the rocks, no salt, and one margarita frozen, no salt," I recapped, wanting to help out my fellow bartender. He disappeared to make our drinks as Annie wilted onto a bar stool and scooped up some salsa with a dark blue tortilla chip.

"I like this place," she said, looking around at the brightly colored T-shirts and license plates that adorned the walls. The outdoor seating area was packed with families and young couples drinking margaritas and beers, and the inside bar where we sat was just as bustling. "I feel like I'm on vacation. When are the boys getting here?"

Earlier that day, while I was on the train, James had called. His invitation for Annie and me to join him and Tom for happy hour margaritas at the Blue Parrot in East Hampton was the only thing that stopped me from plotting to kill Alexis. In addition to the previous night's sordid display at Finton's, it was on her account that I'd missed the earlier train I usually took, because she was retching all morning in the bathroom. Thankfully, I'd discovered after my first weekend in the Hamptons that there was a train called the Cannonball, which ran only once a week during the summer on Friday afternoons and, as its name would suggest, got you from Penn Station to Amagansett in under two and a half hours, while the local train, comparable to the Slow Boat to China, took well over three.

I'd felt like screaming at Alexis not only because she'd hooked up with her boss, who had gray hair, wrinkles, and a wedding ring, but because it had opened the door for Dan Finton to openly convey what deep down I'd suspected all along—that he believed that May–December relationships between employer and employee were perfectly permissible. I feared Alexis's behavior might inadvertently suggest something to him about me—if my best friend was up for it, why wouldn't I be? The night before, after I'd dropped my money in the safe, I'd hightailed it out of Finton's to escape what promised to be a sticky situation before Dan could make an overt advance. Still, I'd reflected, my predicament with Dan wasn't really all Alexis's fault. Looking back, I wondered if I'd been toeing the line with him since we first met.

"Cassie, I swear I'll never get that drunk or do anything like that *ever* again," Alexis had said, tossing five Advil Liqui-Gels into her mouth and washing them down with a two-liter bottle of Pepsi. "Promise you won't let me drink for at least a week. No drinks after work—nothing."

"Okay," I'd promised, wishing I had the luxury of avoiding alcohol, since it was obviously a catalyst for debauchery and dysfunction. But unfortunately, alcohol was the center of my professional universe, and while it seemed to embolden or empower people like Dan and Bob, their resultant drunken alter egos made *me* ridiculously uncomfortable. If I was going to survive in this world, I decided, I had to start sticking up for myself.

But I'd brushed all my Manhattan drama aside the moment I'd arrived in the Hamptons, and all I could think about was seeing James. "He said they'd be here at eight," I told Annie, glancing at the vintage Coca-Cola clock on the wall, which read 8:04. "But they might have gotten stuck in traffic. Tom specifically requested your presence."

Annie dismissed my comment with a giggle.

"Are you into him?" I asked.

"I don't know. He's cute. I'd fuck him."

"Good to know." I rolled my eyes. "Anything new with Teddy?"

"He booty-called me the other night at three in the

morning," she said cavalierly. "But who cares about that? What's up with you and James?"

"Everything's great. He's incredible. It seems to be going really well. It's just—"

"The Pearls Girls," Annie interjected, reading my mind.

"Yeah," I said. "It drives me crazy that he's friends with those girls. They were so awful to us. It makes me wonder about him. Why would he hang out with them?"

"Maybe they're not really his good friends," Annie suggested. "I mean, they probably just grew up together and their families are friends. I can't imagine how anyone as cool as James and Tom could be friends with those stuck-up bitches."

"Excuse me, ladies," a strange man in a taupe linen suit interrupted. He had a large shiny forehead and a receding hairline of black wiry locks. He wore Coke-bottle glasses, and his breath smelled like Listerine. From all exteriors, he looked pretty harmless, but I detected the subtly slimy look of a private eye from the 1970s—maybe it was the shirt, which was unbuttoned just a little too far. Upon further examination, I decided that he looked like the pimp from the *Facts of Life* episode where the girls go to the city and have a close encounter with a teenage prostitute at a seedy diner.

"Yes?" I asked.

"Gorgeous evening, isn't it?"

"Yes, it is!" Annie smiled. She never had her guard up, especially when it came to men.

"I've see you two around everywhere, and I thought I should introduce myself. My name's Roy, and I wanted to invite you beautiful ladies to a party I'm throwing in the city this week," he said, producing two business cards and handing them to Annie and me. The cards read: ROY FOX: SOCIAL

PARTY THROWER AND MATCHMAKER. "Are you girls going to be in the city Tuesday night?"

"Maybe," Annie said. "Where is it?"

"It's going to be at my apartment on Park and 74th."

"Sorry, we never go north of 14th," I quipped. "We get nosebleeds."

"Well, I beg you to reconsider," the man urged.

"What kind of a party is it?" she asked. "Are you a promoter?"

"Not exactly. I throw parties to help some older gentleman clients of mine meet beautiful women like yourself. They're a lot of fun. Why don't you girls give me your numbers and I'll call you with all the details?"

My antennas went up. "Social Party Thrower" that matches up older gentleman with young women? I wondered if Martin Pritchard was one of his clients. Images of threesomes and other sexually deviant behavior by eighty-year-old men flashed in my mind. "Thanks, but how about *we* call *you*?" I suggested.

"Whatever makes you more comfortable," Roy said. "You have my number, and I already have two great men in mind for you two. I hope you can make it."

James and Tom breezed through the front door, prompting Roy's speedy exit. "Ladies!" Tom called, kissing Annie on the cheek and throwing his arm around her shoulder.

"Hey, beautiful," James said, giving me a lingering kiss on the mouth that made me melt like a frozen margarita in the sun. He was wearing a white button-down shirt paired with Diesel jeans and flip-flops. I couldn't resist tousling his hair, which smelled faintly of Aveda shampoo.

"Sorry we're late. The traffic was horrible!" he said. "It

took us over an hour to get from Bridgehampton to our house. Even the back roads were bumper to bumper."

"Sounds like you need a drink," I said, smiling.

"Exactly," he said. "And a Blue Parrot margarita can cure just about anything."

The bartender returned and furnished us all with margaritas, which the Blue Parrot served in mason jars. "It's good to see you," James whispered, his nose nuzzling my ear ever so slightly.

"You too," I said, smiling up at him. The previous night's trauma with Alexis had completely disappeared from my memory. I felt electrified just being next to James—as though I'd drunk five espressos in quick succession.

We were sipping our drinks and trading war stories about our weeks when a pretty redhead in a ruffly, floral Narciso Rodriguez ensemble suddenly pranced over to us, calling out "James? James *Edmonton*?"

James looked confused but forced a smile.

"James, it's me! *Caroline!*" she sang. "We met in Aspen at Caribou Club last winter. My father's Graydon Mitchell, he works with your father at—"

"Oh, Caroline!" James said, his eyes lighting up. "How are you?"

"I'm great! How are you?" she gushed, tossing her tresses from side to side.

"Doing well, thanks. How's your father?"

"He's wonderful! Busy as usual. It's so crazy that I ran into you, because a friend of mine is putting together the Black Book this year," she began. Alexis had told me that the Black Book was the storied annual issue of *Hamptons* magazine that profiled all the eligible bachelors and bachelorettes in the Hamptons, cataloging them according to profession, party personality, and level of coolness, among other creative distinctions. More often than not, the "occupations" of the chosen were listed as "socialite" or "heiress," as if those were actually all-consuming, important vocations. Needless to say, the "it" people in the Hamptons waited with bated breath to see who made the cut.

"Anyway," Caroline continued, "they asked me to be in it and asked if I could recommend anyone else, and I was thinking you would be perfect for it, and here you are! The photo shoot is next weekend, if you're interested. Rosalind's going to be there . . ."

I scowled inwardly at the mention of Rosalind's name, but I vowed to try to be mature about it. After all, James wasn't even my boyfriend yet, and he was allowed to be friends with whomever he wanted. Still, I waited eagerly for his reply.

"Well, I don't know," he demurred.

"Come on, it'll be fun!"

"I'll think about it," James said. I shifted on my bar stool wondering if he was going to introduce the rest of us to his ruby-haired friend. She hadn't so much as glanced at Annie and me.

"Fabulous!" she sang. "This is fantastic. I was literally *just thinking* how perfect you would be for this!"

James produced a black leather wallet and pulled out one of his business cards. "My work number's on here, or you can e-mail me."

"Perfect! I'll call you next week!"

"Take care, Caroline," James said as she flitted away.

"I had no idea you were among the most eligible bachelors in the Hamptons." Tom smirked. "I can't believe she didn't ask me. Glen's in it again this year too."

"Yeah, but doesn't Glen's dad own *Hamptons* magazine?" James asked.

"Actually, no," Tom said. "I think it's the one magazine in America that he doesn't own."

"So, are you going to do it?" I asked, trying to sound nonchalant.

"Are you kidding? No way," he scoffed.

"I think it could be fun," Annie said, her mouth full of chips.

"I don't know. It's not exactly my idea of a good time," James said, much to my relief. Caroline, like the Pearls Girls, struck me as about as genuine as the Rolexes sold on Canal Street. Perhaps deep down James was made more of my mettle than theirs after all. My amorous feelings intensified a notch.

"Yeah, but Charlotte Freund is kind of hot." Tom guffawed. I'd learned the prior weekend from *Hamptons* magazine that Charlotte Freund was yet another teenage heiress who dated Nicky Hilton's ex-husband Todd Meister. The wealthy playboy and playgirl world of the Hamptons was small indeed.

"Tom, she's jailbait," James remarked.

"Yeah, but we see her out every night," Tom countered. "She's fair game."

When we were on our third round of margaritas—interspersed with Patrón shots for the boys—I happened to catch a glimpse of James's Tag Heuer watch and almost had a heart attack. It was nine-eighteen: The realization that I had to be at work in almost ten minutes hit me like a Mack truck. I grudgingly grabbed my bag and hoodie and tapped Annie on the shoulder, interrupting her repartee with the bartender.

"Hey, we'd better get going, it's after nine," I told her.

"Nooooooo, I don't want to go to work!" she wailed dramatically.

"Me neither. But think of the money we'll make, and maybe you'll get to see Ryan Cabrera tonight at the Jessica Simpson party," I said, trying to look on the bright side, though the last thing in the world I felt like doing was tearing myself away from James, who had his arm around my shoulders and was absentmindedly playing with my hair.

"Where do you girls work?" the bartender asked.

"Spark," I replied proudly.

"It's been busy over there, hasn't it?"

"Yeah, it's pretty nuts," Annie agreed.

"You want one more drink? It's on me. I know what it's like to need some prework cocktails to take the edge off," he said with a wink. Sometimes being a bartender felt like being part of a secret society—admission was difficult and the hazing was grueling, but once you were initiated, all the members looked out for one another. Without waiting for our reply, he placed a pink shot in front of each of us that smelled like Hawaiian Tropic tanning oil.

"Thanks," I said. Then I turned to Annie. "I'll call us a cab."

"You guys can take my car," James offered, taking out his keys. "Tom's got his car here. Then we'll all meet up later."

"Perfect!" Annie exclaimed.

"I don't know if I can drive," I said to James. "I'm a little buzzed."

"I can drive!" Annie volunteered.

"Annie, you've had as many drinks as me, and you don't even have a license in this country!"

"Cass, we'll be fine," Annie pleaded. "We'll just drive *really*, really slowly. You know how Shalina is about getting there on time."

I weighed our options. By the time a cab got here and

took us to Spark, it would be at least ten, and we'd both be fired. Plus, I had to admit I was more than a little enamored with the idea of pulling up to Spark in James's Range Rover. I slurped down some water, popped some Extra Wintergreen gum in my mouth, and took the keys from him.

Thirty minutes later, we were caught in one of the East End's famous traffic jams. The single-lane highway was totally congested with Porsche SUVs, Jaguars, Beamers, and, of course, Range Rovers. When we finally pulled into the Spark parking lot, I cringed as I saw the time, 10:03, lit up on the three-dimensional control panel.

"Holy shit, look at the line to get in," Annie said with a tone that approached reverence. There was a swarm of about three hundred people spilling out of the parking lot and onto the highway, pushing and shoving to join the line to get in the club, which culminated at the ominous-looking clipboard-armed doormen and velvet ropes. Usually Spark didn't fill up until after eleven, but the parking lot was already packed. Then it hit me.

"Annie!" I cried, my heart stopping. "We were supposed to get to work at eight-thirty for that party tonight—not nine-thirty! I totally forgot!"

Annie's face turned white. "Oh my God," she breathed. Instead of being just a half an hour late, we were over an hour and a half late.

I panicked. I'd already been demoted to the back bar and was terrified that Teddy and Shalina would fire me on the spot. With growing horror, I imagined spending the summer back at Finton's—no Hamptons, no $350 tips, and, worst of all, no James.

"Okay, calm down," Annie said. "Pull around to the back."

The employee parking lot was located behind the club by the Dumpsters. James's glistening Range Rover stood out like a sore thumb amid the beat-up Honda Accords circa 1983. Annie and I changed into our uniforms in the car and then sprinted to the entrance. Shalina blazed up to us, blocking our path. "Where the hell have you girls been?" she snarled. "You were both supposed to be here almost two hours ago. If I didn't need you so much right now, I would fire you."

"Shalina, we're really sorry . . ." I could feel my lower lip quiver.

"Do you know how many girls would die for your job?!" she demanded. "This is the most irresponsible, unprofessional—"

"We got into a car accident!" Annie blurted out with a convincingly wounded expression. Startled, I turned around to look at her. There was no choice for me but to play along.

"What?" Shalina asked.

"On Montauk Highway," Annie continued. "Cassie and I got rear-ended by a Hummer. It was really scary, but thank God we're okay. We know we should've called, but we were so shaken up by the whole thing, and we had to wait for the police to show up, and . . ."

"Are you all right?" she asked, her hawklike features almost softening.

"Yeah, we're okay," I said.

"Just *very* shaken up," Annie added.

"Annie, I know you're supposed to work the patio," Shalina said, "but we need you in VIP. We're very short-staffed."

"VIP?" Annie asked, her eyes lighting up as if she'd just won a Daytime Emmy.

"Yes, and I'm sorry, what's your name again?" Shalina asked, turning to me.

"Cassie."

"Cassie, right. You're at the back bar with Kyle. Get there as soon as you can. He's really backed up." She threw my thick bank envelope of cash at me and walked away. Apparently she didn't plan on firing us—at least not while she needed us for that night's shift. As we hurried inside, I was still dizzy with anxiety.

Hundreds of sweaty dancing bodies thrust into me as I pushed through the dance floor to get to the back bar. It must have been about a thousand degrees hotter back there, because my fellow bartender Kyle looked positively feverish. His classically handsome face, framed by Olivier Martinez—type dark hair, was dripping with sweat and his shirt was already soaked through. He was agitatedly making drinks for the hordes of customers already six deep.

"Kyle?" I asked, jumping behind the bar.

"Yeah," he said, looking like a deer caught in headlights. He kept knocking drinks over, and the bar was covered in liquid and ice.

"I'm Cassie," I said. "Sorry I'm late." Immediately I was bombarded with drink orders. I struggled to count out the money in my bank envelope as quickly as possible, but my hands were shaking, which I attributed to the Blue Parrot margaritas, coupled with a liberal dose of Shalina. I was already feeling hungover and the night had barely even begun. "I got in a car accident on the way here," I explained, hoping that in the midst of all the chaos he wouldn't notice my face, which always turned the color of maraschino cherries when I lied. I quickly poured ten "vodka tonics with a splash of cranberry and lemons not limes" for a guy who looked like he was about sixteen. Luckily, at Spark, the bartenders weren't responsible for carding like we were at Finton's.

"A hundred dollars," I said to the customer, already wiping sweat from my brow and looking on in amazement as Kyle stopped making drinks for a full two minutes and chatted with two pretty girls, somehow able to tune out the rest of the screaming customers. I tried to kick my performance up a notch, mixing as fast as I possibly could, all the while groping around for the basics—the bottle of triple sec, the house champagne, the martini glasses. The back bar was like a foreign country, and I cursed as I realized that Kyle had set the well up haphazardly, not in any discernable or logical order.

"So, Cassie, what do you do?" Kyle shouted over Jay-Z ten minutes later, while he poured out twelve shots of Patrón.

"I'm a writer," I yelled back, grabbing six Amstel Lights. "And you?"

"I do a lot of modeling," he said with a self-congratulatory air. "But my agent's trying to help me break into acting." He turned around to grab cash from a customer and knocked over ten of the twelve shots. He took his time getting a rag and cleaning up the Patrón puddle, before starting to re-pour the shots.

"Three Jack and Cokes, Two Ketel sodas, a Stoli-O and tonic, and Four Captain gingers," a customer hollered at me. I grabbed ten plastic cups and started filling them with ice.

"Kyle, where's the Jack Daniel's?" I asked, before noticing that he was crouched down below the sink. "Are you okay?" I bent down to his level.

"You want some?" he asked, offering me a key and a tiny

ziplock bag of white powder. His eyes were bloodshot and he had traces of white around his nostrils, which looked red and inflamed. "We got it as a tip from that guy over there."

"No, thanks," I said. I felt culpable as it was coming to work after a few margaritas. And yet here was Kyle doing coke right behind the bar.

I found the bottle of Jack hidden behind a case of Grey Goose and finished filling the drink order. Kyle had again "taken a break" from serving customers and was helping himself to a Red Bull. No wonder Shalina said he was backed up, I thought bitterly.

"Kyle, can you get those guys down there?" I asked, collecting money from a customer and ringing the order through the register.

"Yeah, in a minute," he said.

"Kyle, where's the Maker's?" I shouted at him.

"Oh. Um, here," he said, tossing me an icy bottle. I had no idea why he was storing bourbon in the ice bin, but I didn't have time to ask.

"You sure you don't want a bump?" he asked a few minutes later, again proffering the tiny bag of cocaine. I looked at him and felt like I was in an after-school special that dealt with peer pressure. I had always aligned coke with the high hair, acid-washed jeans, white pumps, and utter financial gluttony and extravagance of New York in the '80s. I hadn't realized that twenty years later it had trickled all the way down to us, the lowly serving classes.

"No, thanks," I said for the second time. "I was drinking before work, and I'm trying to get rid of my hangover."

"This'll do it. Trust me," he said, trying to hand it to me. I briefly wondered if he was an undercover cop.

"No, really I'm fine," I said. "Thanks anyway."

For the next hour and a half I toiled behind the bar, struggling valiantly to make a dent in the crowd and turning out thousands of drinks until my fingertips turned to prunes and my lower back ached from bending down to get ice. Kyle served customers sporadically when he wasn't snorting coke, chugging Red Bull, imbibing shots of Cuervo, or getting girls' phone numbers. The private party finally ended at midnight (I didn't have time to look up from the bar for so much as a glimpse of Jessica and Nick), and after the guests filed out, there were a few moments of much-needed down-time before the club was reopened to the public.

"Let's do a shot," Kyle said, grabbing two rocks glasses and filling them halfway up with Cuervo.

"That's a really big shot," I said, reluctantly accepting his offer.

"Cheers," he said.

I choked down the shot, and Kyle refilled the glasses.

"One more time," he said.

"I can't," I said, wiping my mouth.

"Yes, you can," he said, handing me the glass. I silently apologized to my stomach as I drank it down, longing for last weekend when I'd drunk five-times-distilled tequila with Jake, a competent bartending partner.

"Is this your first night at Spark?" Kyle asked.

"No, I worked here last weekend. I was at the main bar with Jake."

"How was that?"

"Good," I said. "Jake's great to work with. He's so fast." I hoped he'd get the hint that he needed to pick up the pace for the remainder of the night.

"He's the best bartender in the Hamptons," Kyle said. "He can ring up to ten thousand dollars in a single night.

The man's a machine." He took out the tiny ziplock bag of cocaine once more.

"You're going to have a heart attack before you reach thirty," I said.

He laughed. "I can't believe that guy tipped us in coke. It's like Studio 54."

"I prefer getting tipped in cash."

"I should give Jake some of this," he continued, ignoring my comment. "He hooked me up big time last weekend." Kyle lifted himself over the bar and sprinted toward Jake. I watched the two of them disappear into the bathroom together. Suddenly it all became clear: Jake's hyperefficiency, frequent trips to the bathroom, and crash at the end of the night. I wondered if he'd still be able to ring $10,000 a night without blowing lines and—wryly—if a coke addiction would increase my rings and make me eligible to work at the front bar again.

Kyle returned from the bathroom talking a mile a minute. "So anyway, I'm a model-slash-actor, and I've been getting a lot of gigs in the city but most of it is bullshit catalog work, so I need to work here to make some extra cash, you know? I just read for this stage adaptation of the play *Under Milkwood* by some dude named Dylan Thomas, you ever heard of him? It's pretty cool. Anyway, my agent said I should hear back next week about it, but you never know, sometimes these things take a really long time, but I'm really hoping to get onto the big screen, that's where the money is, you know what I mean? Plus the chicks, I met Cameron Diaz over the winter at Chateau Marmont . . ."

I tuned him out and decided to focus on organizing the bar before the next onslaught. I dipped my head into the cooler to pull out the white wine that Kyle had forgotten to put in our ice bins and looked up just in time to see James sauntering up. He had changed into a yellow, lightweight button-down shirt that accentuated his tanned skin. His presence immediately raised my spirits.

"Hey!" he greeted me. "What are you doing back there?"

"I got demoted," I said.

He laughed. "Demoted? I'll have to put a call into your boss."

I smiled back. "Jack and Coke?"

"No, we're actually sitting at a table tonight."

I looked up and saw Tom, Glen, all four of the Pearls Girls, and some other vaguely familiar people milling around by the front bar, waiting to be seated. I waved at them but felt a twinge of anxiety at the sight of Rosalind and her friends. I hated that they saw me working.

"That's cool," I said. "Are you guys going to be outside on the patio or—"

"VIP," James finished, motioning for his friends to come over. Rosalind was wearing a beautiful white Vince top that showed off her sculpted shoulders and she looked impossibly perfect. Her long blond hair framed her flawless features, and her tiny pearl earrings gave her an aura of classic elegance. She sidled up next to James and slid her arm through his, appraising me coolly.

"So I had so much fun at the Blue Parrot," I said to him, smiling as flirtatiously as possible. "Do you want your keys back now, or should I hold on to them for you?" I knew I was being foolish, but I couldn't help wanting to show Rosalind and the girls that James and I had a relationship. Rosalind turned to James with a not-so-subtle raise of her eyebrows.

"Tom and I ran into Cassie and her friend at the Blue Parrot and had a couple of margaritas before dinner," he explained.

A wave of humiliation and apprehension rushed through me. Why was he making it seem like our date was a mere run-in? Did he not want Rosalind and her friends to know we were dating? I stood there, stung, trying to figure out what—if anything—I should do or say in response.

"So, I'll talk to you later, okay?" James said, leaning over the bar and bypassing my mouth to plant a kiss on my cheek. I tried to smile, but inside I felt the same burning insecurity I had at the barbeque. He'd been kissing me on the lips nonstop at the Blue Parrot.

"Look out for Annie," I said with forced cheer. "I think she's cocktailing upstairs." Rosalind flashed me a menacing smile as they turned to go.

I watched with a heavy heart as James placed his hand solicitously on the small of Rosalind's back as they walked upstairs and settled into the prime table that looked out right over the crowd and offered me the perfect vantage point for viewing every second of their night. I felt categorically rejected. While I was stuck downstairs, behind the back bar, clearly the lowliest of stations at Spark, James and the Pearls Girls would be upstairs mingling with the rest of the Very Important People in the Hamptons. How could I ever expect to compete with Rosalind when I was covered in grime and sweat and wearing a dirty uniform that made me look like a slut? Furious, I grabbed a bar rag and tried to scrub off some of the stains on my skirt, fighting back tears.

"Did you see that guy?" Kyle asked excitedly, his eyes nearly popping out of his head. He was still sweating profusely and kept wiping his brow with bev naps.

"What guy?" I asked bitterly.

"That guy in the gray suit with your friends," he said, gesturing upstairs toward James's group.

"What about him?"

"I just saw him on that HBO documentary about all those rich kids in Manhattan. Do you know what I'm talking about?"

"No," I said.

"Some rich guy made a movie about all his friends—the Trump and Bloomberg kids, and all those dudes that have nothing to do but live it up and party like crazy. And that guy was on it. You should watch it. It's really cool. You get to see how rich people live."

"What do you think we're doing now?" I muttered. But before I could dwell further on images of James drinking expensive champagne upstairs in VIP with the heir to a certain Q-tip fortune, while I was downstairs, knee deep in discarded beer bottles beside a coked-up pseudomodel who didn't know how to bartend, drink orders started flying fast and furiously.

"Hey, Kyle, let's do a shot!" I called out. My hangover was dissolving in Cuervo and a volatile drunkenness had taken its place. I sure as hell wasn't going to spend the night feeling sorry for myself. I turned toward Kyle and poured two enormous rocks glasses full of Cuervo and held one to my lips.

Kyle grabbed his shot and held it up. "Cassie, you gotta look me in the eye when we do a toast before a shot, it's bad luck if you don't—everybody has to look everybody else in the eye, it's like some old bartender legend. And it's probably bullshit but I'm superstitious so I always do it—"

"Just shut up and drink it!" I said as I downed what was clearly ten times a Finton's baby shot in one gulp.

"Hey, gorgeous, what are you doing back there?" I looked up to see Burberry Plaid Man standing in front of me. "I was looking for you in the front."

"I go where they put me," I said.

"I'll take a bottle of Goose," he said. Like a machine, I grabbed the bottle from under the bar and rang it into the register.

"Three-fifty," I said, glancing upstairs to see if James happened to be watching. But he was obscured behind Glen, who was gesticulating wildly while telling a story.

He counted out $600. "Keep the change, gorgeous."

I was annoyed that I had to split my tips with Kyle, who now hadn't made a single drink for over twenty minutes, a lifetime on a busy night. He kept yelling riotously at the customers, "Jack and Coke? You want a Jack and Coke, I like Jack and Cokes, Jack and Cokes are great, I can make a Jack and Coke, did you say you want a Jack and Coke?" His lower jaw seemed to disconnect from the rest of his face, and it swung around like a pendulum. He sucked his spit in loudly while he talked and moved his tongue around maniacally. Sweat poured off him, and he was literally running around in circles behind the bar as he played air guitar along with "Sweet Child o' Mine."

"Kyle, chill out," I yelled at him. "The owners are going to see you on the cameras, and you haven't been making any drinks all night."

His bloodshot eyes widened so much that I feared they would pop right out of their sockets. He abandoned Slash's famous guitar riff. "Shit! Do you think they're watching?"

"I don't know. Jake says they watch the tapes from home every night and that the cameras are connected to the Internet."

"Oh, shit. Oh, no," he said. I watched the color drain from his face as Axl Rose droned in the background, *Where do we go, Where do we go now?*

"Look," I said, "don't worry about it. Just get to work."

For the first time all night, he really tried to buckle down and start mixing drinks, but by this time he had so much cocaine, Cuervo, and Red Bull coursing through his veins that he was pretty much useless. I saw him struggling to make a vodka soda for a girl with fringy bangs and black eyeliner, his hands shaking uncontrollably, spilling liquid everywhere. "I'm really tired," the girl whimpered, looking up at him and batting her eyelashes. "Do you have a bump?"

He disappeared outside with her, and I straightened up and smiled at the relentless crowd of people waving money in my face, even though I felt like screaming. All I could pray was that I looked like I had it together and was having a good time should James be watching. To that end, I flirted relentlessly with all the male customers, hoping that I'd also make enough money to offset the share I'd have to give to useless Kyle. I poured and mixed and shook and changed money, and it took every bone and muscle in my body to avoid looking up at the balcony. But I couldn't resist a peek every now and then. Unfortunately, the one time I actually saw James, Elsie was leaning over him, her breasts practically brushing his face. I could tell even from forty feet away that she was trying desperately to work her skanky charms. I made a mental note to mention exactly what I thought of her and the other cocktail waitresses to James later.

Hey, Cass, can I drive you home?" James materialized out of nowhere around 4:00 A.M., just as the bouncers were herding everyone out the door and I was about to head to the bathroom and give in to beer tears, since he hadn't so much as glanced downstairs all night. Between fretting over James and being furious with Kyle, I'd passed the time doing shots of Cuervo every half hour or so to drown my sorrows.

"I guess," I replied flatly. "But it's the same deal as last time. We have to wait for the waitresses to count out and it's going to take a while."

"No problem. You know I don't mind waiting," he said, smiling and kissing me on the lips.

"Oh, so *now* you want to kiss me on the lips?" I said saucily, then instantly regretted it. My beer tears apparently had been replaced by beer balls.

"What do you mean?" he asked, giving me a funny look.

"You're so weird to me when Rosalind and the girls are around," I glowered. "One minute you're all over me in the Blue Parrot, and the next minute you're kissing me on the cheek like I was your grandmother."

"Come on, Cassie. You were working, and I was just trying to be respectful."

"Well, those girls have been really fucking rude to me and Annie."

"I'm really sorry about that. Try not to take it so personally. It's just that we're a really tight group, and sometimes they can get a little territorial," he conceded, extending a chilled bottle of Cristal, two champagne glasses, and a bucket of ice as a peace offering. "I brought this to share with you."

James looked so cute holding the champagne and its accoutrements that I wondered if I'd been overreacting. I decided again I wasn't going to let a bunch of catty girls ruin what was shaping up to be the best thing that had ever happened to me. "Okay," I said, my expression softening as I rested my elbows on the bar.

"How was your night?" he asked.

"Let's put it this way," I began. "The eighties are officially back."

"What do you mean?"

"I had no idea the coke scene was so huge out here."

He laughed. "Yup, all summer long it snows in the Hamptons." He opened the champagne and the cork flew out with a celebratory *POP!* as if to signify that my night of work was legitimately over. "Champagne?"

"I'd love some," I said. I'd never tried Cristal, but I knew it was listed as $500 a bottle on the Spark menu and was the drink of choice for everyone from Ron Perelman to Ludacris. I took a sip. It was bracingly refreshing, not too sweet, but perfectly flavored with elfin bubbles that dissolved on my parched tongue.

"How about a toast?" James asked, raising his glass. "May all your joy be true joy, and may all your pain be champagne!"

"Cheers!" I exclaimed, thinking how adorable he looked all disheveled from the night's revelry. I gathered up my money and the tip bucket and we slipped into a booth to sip our champagne.

"Cassie, are you closed out?" Chris asked. I hadn't seen much of him in my first two weeks at Spark, but my overall impression was that he was overworked, overmedicated, and overwrought. Even though he was the manager, relatively high up on the totem pole, Shalina treated him like her bitch and ran him ragged all over the club on a nightly basis.

"Yup, all done," I said, handing him my report to look over. "How was your night?" I asked, trying to make conversation.

"It was a fucking nightmare," he said. "I can't wait for Sunday. It's my only day off."

"You should go to the beach," I suggested, thinking he could use some color.

"Nope. On my days off I smoke a blunt, take two Quaaludes, and drink a bottle of red wine. It's great. I don't feel anything." He gathered up my money and report. "Your ring was good tonight. How was it working with Kyle?"

"A little erratic," I said.

"Yeah, that kid's a trip. I swear, he sprinkles coke on his cornflakes in the morning. See you tomorrow."

After an hour or so, James and I had polished off the rest of the Cristal, but the waitresses still weren't finished closing out. I ran back behind the bar to grab us two Bud Lights and, on my way, noticed Jake and Elsie huddled in a corner. He was snorting coke off the web of her hand. When he saw me coming he wiped his nose and straightened up. "Hey, Cass, how was your night?" he called. "Miss me?"

"Um . . . yeah," I muttered.

The sun was just starting to peek through the skylights, and I almost laughed out loud when it occurred to me that most of the staff looked vaguely like characters from *The Dawn of the Dead*: coked-out zombies with dark circles and mascara stains under their eyes. They seemed surreal and slightly terrifying.

"This place is crazy," I said, sliding back into the booth and burrowing into James. "No wonder it takes everyone three hours to close out. Everyone's wasted—including me."

"You seem to be in pretty good shape," James said.

"I don't know. First I had those margaritas, and then I drank about a liter of Cuervo with Kyle, and then I drank half a bottle of champagne with you, and now we're drinking beers, and I'm technically still *at work*."

James smiled as he twisted the cap off his beer. "Hey, what are you complaining about? I wish I could drink Cristal at work. Think how much better life would be."

"I know, it's just so weird, you know?" I said, taking my

first sip of beer. "Still, I can't imagine working here sober. It's hard enough to relate to these people when I'm drunk."

"Cassie, wake up," Travis urged, his hand shaking my shoulder. It was eight-thirty in the morning, and after another late-night/early-morning beach rendezvous with James, I had been asleep for only fifteen minutes.

"Why?" I moaned, twisting around under the sheet and pulling the pillow over my head.

"The owners are coming, and we all have to leave."

"What?" I asked, struggling to open my eyes.

"The owners of the house just called. They're coming over right now, and we need to leave."

"I don't get it," I mumbled. "Why do we need to leave?"

"Because according to the lease, there are only supposed to be four of us renting the house, and at least thirty people slept here last night. If they see all of us here, they're gonna freak out."

"What?" I cried, alarmed. We usually had a minimum of about four people per *bed*. Wearily I sat up. "Where should I go?"

"Just hang out at the beach for a little bit. I don't think they're gonna stay here that long, they just want to check in on the house."

"Okay," I said, stumbling out of bed. I wondered if I would have the opportunity to sleep at all over the summer, or if like everyone else at Spark I was going to be a chemically fueled Frankenstein for the next twelve weeks.

"Thanks a lot. Sorry about this," he said before disappearing out of the room to try to scatter the other twenty-nine people. I pulled my favorite key lime Banana Republic bikini out of my bag and slipped it on, threw my hair in a ponytail, slathered on some sunscreen, stepped into the same cotton dress I'd worn on the train, and headed out the door. Annie was already standing in the hallway, holding a beach bag and a pro Kadima paddle ball set.

"Come on, lady, let's hit the beach," she cheered.

"How can you be so perky?" I grumbled. "It's not even nine o' clock."

"No whining," she said. "Grab your sunglasses and a towel, and let's get out of here."

I wordlessly did as she'd instructed, pausing only to toss my notebook and a pen into my beach bag in case inspiration struck later on.

"I'm bringing the Kadima set," she said cheerfully. "We can have an active beach day. Wanna go for a run later?"

"I want to go back to sleep for another eight hours," I groaned as she swung open the rickety screen door and we started walking south toward Indian Wells Beach.

It was a perfect beach day—already about 85 degrees, with a warm breeze blowing off the ocean and bright blue skies stretched overhead. As exhausted as I was, I was happy I wasn't wasting such a flawless day cooped up inside the share house, breathing in the stench of sweaty socks and mothballs. Annie practically skipped the whole way.

"It's so amazing to be alive on a day like today," she said. "Don't you *love* the Hamptons?"

"What's gotten into you?" I asked.

"Oh, nothing. It's just that I had the most *incredible* sex last night." She beamed.

"With Tom?" I asked, incredulously.

"No, with Teddy. In the office. It was so hot, Cass, he lifted me up onto the desk, and he did this thing with my legs, where he lifted them up over my head, and—"

"That's enough!" I said, shielding my ears with my beach towel.

"—and *then*," Annie continued, giggling (she loved to make me squirm), "he turned me over on my stomach and started doing me from behind—"

"Annie, stop!" I screeched.

"It was incredible. By far the best sex I've had since I slept with that Christmas tree guy. Remember him?"

"Yes, you told me *all* about him." During the Christmas season in Manhattan, rugged men from Canada and New England came to the city to sell Christmas trees on the streets. They were all strong, handsome, outdoorsy types who smelled of pine, and New York women went crazy for them.

"Well, Teddy was just as good, if not better. The only problem is, I think he threw my lower back out. It was worth it, though. So, have you slept with James yet?"

"No, not yet."

"Well, what are you waiting for?"

"I don't know, I just really like him, and don't see any reason to rush it."

"Okay," she said. "But if it doesn't happen by the Fourth of July, I'm going to be seriously disappointed in you."

Just as James's name was uttered, I looked up and saw that we were approaching Further Lane. The walk to the beach from Animal House took us past eclectic scenery like the Amagansett School for Applied Arts, the Mobil gas station, and of course mammoth houses framed by neatly clipped hedges. I looked longingly down the road in the direction of his house, where I was sure he was sleeping peacefully, free of the rude awakenings and forced diaspora that were inevitably part of an overcrowded share house. A few minutes later we arrived at Indian Wells and looked around the stretch of sand for a good spot where we could stake our claim.

"What do you think, to the right or to the left?" I asked, squinting underneath my counterfeit Gucci sunglasses.

"Well, Travis and the guys usually go to the left," Annie said.

"Then we should go to the right," I said.

"Why?" Annie asked.

"Don't get me wrong. I love those guys. But James told me last night that he and Tom might come meet us later on, and I don't feel like explaining all the empty forties of Colt 45."

Annie giggled. "Good idea." We walked to the right for a few minutes until we found a perfect plot of pristine white sand not too close and not too far from the water. Annie spread out our beach blanket and placed flip-flops and water bottles on each corner to keep it from flapping in the wind. Then she rolled up our towels into makeshift pillows, determined the exact location of the sun, and positioned our bodies so they would achieve maximum sun exposure. She checked her watch. "Okay," she said. "At exactly nine twenty-three we'll flip onto our backs." She prided herself on being an expert on how to achieve the perfect tan.

The sun beating down on my back, I opened my notebook to a fresh page and started jotting down the ideas that were festering in my head from the previous night, even though I didn't know exactly how or if they'd fit into my screenplay. I thought about what Alexis had once told me about working on Wall Street and needing something to fuel you through the long hours. It seemed completely unnatural for a person to work hundred-hour weeks—just as it was unnatural for a person to stay up until seven in the morning making drinks. There was a reason that the financial and club worlds were so closely tied—in fact, they were bound together by a tightly knit symbiotic relationship. There was no way that a city like New York, where the wheels of the world are set in motion, could function so frenetically and efficiently without some chemical help. I just hadn't expected to come face to face with it in quite such a dramatic way. For a moment I wondered if I really belonged in this chaotic world. But I looked out at the ocean and conjured up James's face and realized it was a trade-off I was more than willing to accept.

"Cassie, go long!" Glen called out. I ran out toward the surf to catch the Frisbee, but before the pass was completed, a wave clobbered me.

"Are you all right?" James asked. He was standing at the water's edge and trying hard not to laugh.

I righted myself and, after checking to make sure my bikini top was still on and pulling some seaweed out of my hair, stood up and whipped the Frisbee in James's direction. "I'm fine!"

James, Tom, and Glen had shown up around one, and we had been running around ever since, swimming, playing Frisbee and Kadima, and drinking beers. The sun was hot, and as I wrung out my hair, I decided it was time for another break.

"Want an Amstel?" Tom asked as I approached the coolers.

"No Amstel for her," James said, collapsing into a beach chair and handing me a Budweiser. "I bought these especially for you."

I jumped into his lap and threw my arms around his

neck. He looked irresistible with his shirt off, and as my hands rested against his smooth, firm abs, I felt like I could spend all day just looking at him. The touch of his hand on my bare skin was enough to send me flying like one of the ad banners that sailed behind the planes riding over the shoreline. Even though I could feel the puffiness beneath my eyes, I felt like I didn't need to sleep for days. "Thanks," I said, kissing his neck.

"So," Glen said, eyeing the label on my bottle of Bud, "I'll buy drinks for everyone at Cyril's later if one of you can tell me what 'Budweiser' stands for."

"What do you mean?" Tom asked. "It doesn't stand for anything."

"Yes, it does," Glen said. "Each letter stands for something. Come on, I'll buy all you guys drinks if you can figure it out."

I looked around expectantly at all of their blank faces. I couldn't believe they didn't know something so simple and American. "Because U Deserve What Every Individual Should Enjoy Regularly," I sang triumphantly.

"How'd you know that?" Glen asked, trounced.

"I'm a bartender," I said. "Besides, that's not really what Budweiser stands for. It's probably just something some frat guy made up at five in the morning, after drinking Buds all night. I think it's really just a combination of the two names: Anheiser and Busch, but I don't know."

"Congratulations, Cassie! You get free drinks all night, but it doesn't matter since you have to work and will drink for free anyway!" Annie laughed, raising her bottle in a toast. She had climbed into Tom's lap, and I couldn't help but think about how less than ten hours ago she'd been having passionate sex with an entirely different person.

James leaned over and kissed me on the top of my head. "You're so refreshing," he said. I beamed.

"Well, I can at least buy you a BBC at Cyril's before you go to work," Tom suggested. Cyril's was a divey outdoor bar and restaurant located on Napeague Stretch between Montauk and Amagansett, where they served fried seafood in red plastic baskets. It always looked like a scene out of *Beach Blanket Bingo*—people pulled up in cars and trucks with surfboards hanging out of the back, or mounted on the roofs, and most of the customers didn't wear shoes; in fact, a majority of them were still in their bathing suits, with towels or sarongs wrapped around their waists.

I knew I probably shouldn't have another drink before work, but I had trouble turning down offers for alcohol in the Hamptons. When it came right down to it, I'd been drinking all day. But at least, I reminded myself, I could make it through a night of work without snorting coke. As the sun slowly started to sink in the sky, James leaned in to gently kiss me on the mouth. At the end of the day, some addictions were better than others.

Nine

THREE WISE MEN

Sweating, I adjusted my grasp on the sides of the plastic checkered crate and, for the fifth time, attempted to heave it out of the stifling liquor storage room. Piled high with five Ketel Ones, four Citrons, four Jack Daniel's, three house vodkas, and three triple secs, it didn't budge. I began to drag it, scratching the hardwood floor until Miguel, the new bar back, who was a good five inches shorter and probably thirty pounds lighter than I, came through the door, took one look at what I was doing, and effortlessly picked it up, sailing back out into the bar. I was sure Kyle would be late, as usual, so I decided to set up both sides of the back bar. He took so many "breaks" when we worked together that I ended up making better use of his side of the bar than he ever did anyway.

"We need more Cuervo!" I shouted, almost inhaling a fruit fly. The back bar was a disaster. Every conceivable surface was sticky, covered in hardened Rose's Lime Juice and fluorescent pink Pucker Watermelon Liqueur. Hordes of fruit flies circled my head, and the smell of stale beer and mildewed garbage permeated the humid air.

"How many?" Miguel asked.

"I don't know . . . I guess just bring out a case. I'm sure we'll go through it all."

I felt like I was in one of the Y's "Sculpt and Stretch" classes. Lunge to the crate on the floor, grab bottle, lift and place up on shelf . . . repeat thirty times. I was in a zone and barely noticed as Teddy, holding his ever-present clipboard, walked down the stairs, a flushed Annie in tow.

"Here early, huh?" he asked.

"Yeah," I replied. Over the past few weeks I'd made an effort to be always at least a little early, demonstrating that I was as responsible as possible, especially since the fiasco after the Blue Parrot. I'd somehow gotten away with that little incident, and even though we'd never mentioned it, I was pretty sure that Annie's special relationship with Teddy had had something to do with it. I was determined to keep this job and the average of $800 I was making per weekend. Plus, it was Fourth of July weekend, and I wanted to equip the bar for the impending frenetic rush.

"Go set up the front bar," Teddy directed.

"Can I just finish this one first?" I said. I made a mental note not to show up quite so early the next time. I didn't want to get stuck single-handedly setting up the entire club just because I lived in fear of getting fired.

"Kyle can set this one up when he gets here. You're gonna work with Jake at the front bar," he said distractedly, muttering "shit" as he paged through the list he held. Before I could ask why, he walked away, holding his Nextel cell phone in front of his mouth in walkie-talkie mode demanding, "Why the fuck is Lulu Johnson getting the table by the door?"

"Thanks, Teddy," I said, still a little surprised. I jumped over the gluey bar, careful not to saturate my new Seven jeans in week-old Southern Comfort, and headed north to my new station. I was setting up my speed rack when Annie pranced over to me.

"I'm back at the front bar!" I cried.

"I know," she said with a self-satisfied smile.

"How do you know?" I asked suspiciously.

"Let's just say I worked some of my magic with Teddy."

"You're kidding!"

"I just helped him take care of some things in the office, if you know what I mean," she said impishly. Her cheeks were glowing and her lipstick was smeared. She hadn't even bothered to rearrange her tousled curls or straighten her skirt.

"I'm afraid to ask."

"Anyway, as things were really heating up, I was like 'Teddy, why'd you stick Cassie at the back bar?' and he was like, 'Let's talk about this later,' and I was like, 'No, let's talk about this now, she hates it back there. Can you switch her back?' And he was like, 'Anything you want, baby,' and then he came *so hard*, I thought he was having an epileptic seizure!"

"Okay!" I said, clapping my hands over my ears. "I get it."

"So am I the best friend ever, or what?"

"You're pretty amazing," I said. "Thanks."

"I was thinking the whole train ride that it wouldn't be

worth it for you to come out here on a Thursday just to work the back bar and make no money, you know? Especially after you had to go through all the crap of getting the extra night off from Finton's and pissing off Dan and Laurel. So I took matters into my own hands, so to speak, and now you're back at the front bar permanently."

I looked at her incredulously. Teddy had made such a big deal about how "numbers don't lie." I guess when he talked about numbers, he was referring to how many times he and Annie had gotten it on in the office.

As I continued shelving bottles of Mount Gay rum in the racks beneath the register, I pondered the surreal landscape of my postcollege environment. Two of my best friends were happily advancing in their respective fields—but more through their feminine wiles than their actual talents and intelligence. While I was grateful to Annie for getting me back at the front bar with Jake, I had to question where to draw the line. It was clear that being an attractive woman could get you far in this world, whether on Wall Street or on Montauk Highway.

The day before I'd been on my way to my regular Wednesday shift at Finton's when my cell phone rang. I'd hoped it was James; he'd been buried in work all week so we hadn't spoken much. To my disappointment, it was Teddy.

"Hi," I said timorously. I figured he was calling because my ring at the back bar had slipped since I'd started working there earlier in June. At this point, I could only go lower at Spark if they set up a station for me out back by the Dumpsters.

"I need you to work tomorrow night," he'd informed me. "We have an open bar party booked from nine to twelve, and I need all my bartenders there. A buddy of mine over at Jive Records is throwing a release party for Britney Spears. You should be there at eight."

"Let me see what I can do," I said. "I usually work at my job in the city on Thursdays, but I can try to get someone to cover for me." I crossed my fingers that Sean was available.

"I can't take no for an answer. The owners said they might come by so I need all the bartenders on." He hung up without another word.

I'd still never met the ominous owners of Spark and wanted to be there should they show up. Plus, Spark money was always better than Finton's money by leaps and bounds. My tail between my legs, I arrived at Finton's and decided not to waste any time approaching Laurel, who was sitting at the bar devouring a hangar steak entrée, hunched over a dated edition of *Wine Spectator* magazine.

"Laurel, I have to ask you for a favor," I began, just as Dan Finton emerged, presumably from his observation chamber downstairs. Ever since I'd bolted that night we were closing alone together, Dan had been acting decidedly cooler toward me. For the most part, I was relieved.

"Hi, Dan," I said cheerily. He gave me a half-smile and a sharp nod of his head.

"You were saying?" Laurel asked.

I didn't want to ask for Thursday night off in front of Dan, but decided I had to bite the bullet. "Um . . . well, I just got a phone call from my boss in the Hamptons—" I fidgeted with my necklace "—and he said that there's a really big Fourth of July party at Spark tomorrow night, and he needs me there to work, because—"

"If someone can cover your shift, then I don't care," she said flatly. "I can't be bothered with this anymore."

I was stunned.

"Okay, great," I said, not believing my luck. "Thank you so much, Laurel. I'll call Sean right now."

Just as I turned to skip over to the phone, Dan commented coldly, "It's amazing how quickly your loyalties have shifted."

"Excuse me?" I said, feeling both insulted and surprised, but he'd already vanished out the door of Finton's. I'd expected attitude about the schedule change from Laurel, but from Dan? On one hand, I was glad to have a little more distance from him, especially after our loaded exchange about Bob and Alexis. On the other hand, things had been undeniably easier when Dan had taken special care to look out for me. Thinking back, it was clearly the reason I'd gotten my job at Finton's in the first place and how I'd been able to get away with spending my weekends at Spark. I finally had to admit to myself that I'd been taking advantage of the perks that came along with being a woman in the bar industry all along.

Now, however, I was experiencing the flip side of the coin with Dan. I'd seen this all too often in my short tenure behind the bar. In the beginning of the night, men would be polite and tip well. As the night wore on, they would get drunk and make advances. When I didn't oblige them, they got belligerent, rude, and stopped tipping. In the case of Dan, it seemed, I was no longer his shining star.

I'd called Sean, who agreed to cover my shift, and then headed back out to the bar.

"Hey, kid!" Billy called out. "How's it going at Spark?"

"Great. I'm going out there tomorrow morning."

"Yeah, you've got a big weekend ahead of you. We used to bank over two grand on the Fourth of July. It was a beautiful thing."

"If I could make two grand this weekend, I'd be the happiest girl in the world."

"How are the other bartenders you work with?"

"They're all right. But most of the tips they make end up going up their nose."

"Welcome to the Hamptons," Billy laughed.

"Was it like that when you were out there? I mean, everyone's so fucked up all the time—it's insane!"

"What do you think? I was there in the *eighties* working at a *gay club*," Billy commented drolly. "It was a lot of fun, but I don't think I could handle it now. You have to be careful, you know? If you do it every now and then it's okay, but when you need to drink five martinis at six o'clock in the morning so you can go to sleep—" He shook his head. "It's not good."

Slow down, Cassie," Jake said. "Don't bust your ass. It's open bar."

"So what?" I panted as I peeled the foil off the top of a bottle of Grey Goose, pulled the cork out, and stuck a speed pourer in. I'd thought it would be an easy night, considering I didn't have to deal with cash, credit cards, or payment of any sort, but everyone that came up to the bar ordered fifteen drinks at a time.

"I fucking hate this open bar shit," Jake groused. "But at least we'll be outta here by twelve." He grabbed four bottles of Bombay Sapphire and stocked them ferociously on the shelves behind him. "We're getting paid nothing for this party, so if they don't tip, don't serve them," he added. "We don't work for free. And pour light. Whenever it's open bar, you always pour light."

I took his advice and slowed down. He was right, 90 percent of the people weren't tipping. But it was hard to ignore the patrons staring me down for drinks. Eventually the mob got the point and started waving cash to get our attention. We served them immediately, and the crowd died down. For the first time all summer, I wasn't stressed out while working at Spark.

The doors had opened promptly at nine, and I'd waited expectantly, thrilled to be back next to Jake at the front bar working a celebrity's party. A little overzealous, I'd already arranged ten plastic cups filled with ice on the bar mat near my gun.

By nine-fifteen, exactly three people had trickled through the door.

An hour later, the bar had filled, but Britney hadn't even shown up, even though she was supposed to be "hosting" the party. In between Jake's manic fits of productivity, he managed to explain that most New York City or Hamptons parties "hosted" by celebrities were really just elaborate smoke-and-mirrors schemes by event planners and publicists designed to get the maximum number of (preferably well-to-do) people coming to an event. But the actual celebrity rarely ever made an appearance.

As I surveyed the crowd, I noticed most of the people were a far cry from our regular Spark clientele and would've never made it past the velvet ropes on a normal night. I'd heard of the phenomenon of arrivistes keeping publicists on retainer to help them climb the social ladder of the rich and established, which meant getting them into hot parties where they hoped to be exposed to *real* socialites and celebrities. And from the awkward social interaction of these less-than-Beautiful People, I guessed that the publicists really had exhausted their Rolodexes of wannabes to fill the party.

Snoop Dogg came blaring out over the speakers. "I love this song!" Jake screamed. *Laid back, with my mind on my money and my money on my mind . . .*

When Jake wasn't rapping, he paced back and forth around the bar, adjusting pourers, putting the shakers in height order, picking up a stray bottle cap from the floor, and thrashing around wildly to that night's DJ's mix of rap and rock. I giggled to myself—we had never worked at Spark when it wasn't absolutely slammed, and it was clear that Jake didn't know what to do with his energy when he wasn't busy with seven hundred customers.

"Shots?" Jake asked, a bottle of Patrón in his hand.

"We'd be crazy not to at this point," I said.

"Good to have you back up here, Cassie!" he roared, swinging the bottle of Patrón in his hand.

"Good to be back!" I said, slamming the tequila.

Finally, at around eleven forty-five it was patently clear that the party had dwindled to nothing. With the exception of one short-lived rush, the party was a bust. My enthusiasm was dampened slightly by the thought of my ever-empty bank account. I wondered if I could have made more money at Finton's. I sighed and sucked on a lime.

"You can close out, guys," Chris told us.

"What should we do to close out?" I asked, pressing a cold Bud Light against my overheated forehead. At some point during the party, the air-conditioners had short-circuited. As if Long Island air weren't humid enough, the atmosphere was further saturated by the sweat of people straining to climb the social ladder.

"Nothing," Jake said, "That's the beauty of open bar. We

have nothing to cash out. We just have to wait for our shift pay and count the tips."

Moments later Shalina sashayed over to us, a green silk scarf trailing behind her. Her breasts were spilling out of her corseted top, and her white pants looked like they'd been painted on. I marveled at her tiny waist, thinking she must spend at least four hours a day at the gym. "Here's your shift pay," she said, handing Jake and me each a sealed envelope.

I opened it up. Fifty dollars.

"Fifty dollars?" I whined to Jake. "That's ridiculous!"

"That's why I told you not to bust your ass. Hand me the tip bucket."

Jake and I were organizing the tips into neat piles of singles and fives (to our dismay, no tens or twenties had made an appearance that night—another downside to serving the wannabes rather than the genuine high rollers), when I overheard Teddy say to Shalina, "I just ran the guy's credit card. He said everyone had a great time."

"Perfect," she said. "We need to make sure he's happy. This party cost him over fifty thousand dollars."

At first I was shocked. Then I was furious. Fifty thousand dollars and I was paid out *fifty*? That was one-tenth of 1 percent.

"Here you go, Cass," Jake said, handing me my share of the tips. "Forty-eight." Combined with the shift pay, we hadn't even broken $100. After Billy's promise of two grand over Fourth of July weekend, I sulked, realizing I was about $600 off schedule.

"Thanks," I said grouchily, shoving the cash into the back pocket of my skirt. "I can't believe they're only giving us fifty dollars. At Finton's if we work an open bar, we always get a couple of hundred."

"That's how it is at these big clubs. They screw you over, because they know if you quit, there are thousands of other sorry-ass bartenders salivating to work here."

"Sounds like Marxism," I said dramatically.

"Huh?"

"You know, Karl Marx. 'Bartenders of the world unite, you have nothing to lose but your derisory shift pay.' "

"What the fuck are you talking about?"

"Forget it." I said.

"Anyway," Jake continued, "the good news is that on most nights you can make a lot of money here. But you're right, Shalina and the owners are such fucking money-grubbing scumbags." I looked over at Shalina and Teddy and imagined I saw dollar signs where their pupils should have been. At least the holiday weekend had started out with a bang for somebody.

"We're going out!" Jake yelled. "Cassie, you're coming!"

"I should probably just go home," I said. I was already more than a little drunk, and I knew I had two intense nights of work ahead of me. I was also feeling too poor to spend money on beer. Not to mention that the prospect of a decent night of sleep in my empty share house was tremendously appealing.

"No way!" Annie appeared at my side. She'd already changed out of her uniform into a short jeans skirt, wifebeater, and strappy heels. "I need a drink after dealing with all those losers asking my for my phone number!"

"Why don't we go to the Talkhouse?" Jake suggested. "It's right near your house. You can walk home whenever you want."

It was true—the Talkhouse was practically next door to Animal House. Plus, as usual, I was still wired from work, and it would be helpful to have that wind-down drink.

Annie and I piled into Jake's car. He revved the engine like a race car driver and peeled out of the lot, flicking his middle finger toward Spark and screaming "Fuckers" out the window with a demonic laugh. He made a left out of the Spark parking lot, heading east toward Amagansett.

"Are you sure you're okay to drive?" I asked, hastily buckling my seat belt and gripping the door handle until my knuckles were white.

"I'm fine," Jake said, defensively.

"I'm just asking, because we had a lot of shots and—"

"Cassie, he's fine," Annie said, manually rolling down her window.

"Okay," I said meekly.

Jake kept his eyes on the road as he flicked on the radio and jiggled the dials.

"The only thing I can get on this thing is Big Band music on AM," he said, laughing maniacally again.

"Really?" I asked.

"Fuck, no!" Jake cackled, blasting Biggie's "True Player." I thought his crackling speakers were going to explode; the bass caused the seats to vibrate, tickling my back.

We pulled up in front of the Talkhouse around twelve-thirty and parked across the street. It looked exactly like a medium-size summer share house, complete with brown, weathered shingles that were half falling off and a sprawling concrete "yard" on the side, complete with a tiki bar. Unlike Spark, there was no line to get in and no velvet ropes in sight, but a doorman sat on a battered bar stool by the front door collecting money under a chalkboard sign that read "Thursday, July 2nd, Nancy Atlas, The Niagaras, $25." Jake had told us that the Talkhouse had appeared in *Maxim* under the heading "100 Best Dive Bars in America."

On the ride over, I'd exchanged my closed-toed work

shoes for a pair of pale yellow flip-flops, shimmied out of my white Catherine Malandrino skirt, and slipped on a ripped jeans skirt I'd had since high school and a red tank top. Feeling only moderately disheveled from an abbreviated night of work, I applied a coat of lip gloss and walked confidently to the door. I was opening my wallet to find $25 for the cover when I heard the doorman call, "Jake, you bastard, how the fuck are you?!"

Jake ran up to him and the two men embraced each other in the typical guy half hug, thunderously pounding one another on the back. "How are you, bro?"

"Can't complain. You?"

"Pretty good. These are some friends of mine from Spark. This is Rex."

"Hi." Annie and I smiled.

"Hey, ladies," Rex replied. He was a well-built man with a thick neck and curly black hair. He was wearing a white T-shirt with a picture of a man's face on it and below it the caption, FREE KENNY. I stepped forward and tried to hand him the money.

"Don't worry about it," he said, stamping my hand with a red circle. "Your money's no good here."

"Thanks," I said.

We stepped inside and I was immediately floored by the masses of people and the loud live music. It was a dark, dank space with a small stage and a long bar where two heavyset older men and a younger, good-looking guy with a bandanna tying back his longish blond hair were mixing drinks. The wood-planked floors were uneven and the ceiling sagged, looking like it was about to buckle and cave in. It smelled like a not entirely unpleasant combination of beer, dusty old wood, and sweat.

Jake pushed his way through the crowd, shaking hands

and pounding fists with nearly every patron and employee. "Andy!" He let out a whoop in my right ear that almost stopped my heart, though nobody else batted an eye.

"Yo, Jake!" Andy was the young bartender slinging drinks at a Jake-like speed behind the bar. He wore a drenched, T-shirt with the sleeves ripped off, surfer shorts, and a rasta sweatband around one wrist, and a Puma band around the other.

He came over to Jake, leaving behind a line of customers waiting for drinks. When one customer loudly voiced his disapproval, Andy glanced over his shoulder and yelled, "Shut the fuck up, asshole!" I cringed, but nothing seemed to come of it, even though I knew that if I ever spoke like that to a customer at Spark or Finton's, I'd have to start collecting unemployment. Andy turned back to us, smiling angelically, and said, "Come on, you guys, let's go out and smoke a blunt."

"Sounds good," Jake said. "This is Cassie and Annie—I work with them at Spark."

"Hey, girls!" Andy barreled through the crowd toward the back of the bar. We followed him past the bathrooms and then out a swinging door into a small, quiet lot littered with junky old Jeeps, enormous potholes, and the shell of an abandoned school bus. When the breezy night air hit my skin, it felt like a cool shower.

"So you work at Spark with this guy?" Andy asked, pulling a joint roughly the size of cigar from his pocket.

Annie and I nodded.

"I'm there Monday, for industry night—all the bartenders and waitresses who work out here go. I make sick money and do half the work."

He wasted no time in lighting up and inhaling with all

his strength. He exhaled the smoke with a long "Aaaah," then passed the blunt to Jake, who took a similarly deep hit. He passed it to Annie, she puffed, and then passed it to me. I took a small hit.

"You *smoke*?" Jake asked mockingly.

"Shut up," I said. I'd really only smoked a few times in college. Pot just didn't do it for me—it always made me paranoid, eat an entire box of Oreos, and then promptly fall asleep.

"A little weed is good for the soul. It opens your mind," Andy said.

Annie laughed. "Spoken like a true pot head."

Andy appeared not to have heard her. His pupils had dilated to the size of quarters. He glanced casually at his watch. "I guess I better get back in there."

"We'll see you later, bro," Jake said.

"Good to meet you girls," Andy said, and strolled inside.

We followed Jake back inside and into another room with a smaller bar, several TVs, and two pool tables. The bartender's face lit up when he saw Jake, and before even saying hello, he'd grabbed the bottle of Patrón and poured two mammoth shots.

"Hey, Pat!" Jake said.

"What's going on, Jake? Ladies," he said, smiling in our direction.

"Pat, this is Annie and Cassie. They only drink beer and whiskey," Jake said, slamming the tequila.

"I think I'm in love," Pat stated, grabbing the Jack Daniel's and pouring it into a rocks glass along with Jim Beam and Cuervo. "Try this: Three wise men."

As I choked down the toxic mix, Pat poured another round of shots and gave us each a Budweiser.

"These are on me," he said. "And so's whatever else you guys want. You're on scholarship tonight."

Jake threw a twenty on the bar and held up his shot.

"Cheers," said Pat.

"Cheers," I said, bringing the second shot glass to my lips. As the three wise men traveled through my system, I felt a tiny bit better about not making any money at the party.

Pat seemed friendly enough, but as I studied him, I was amazed. At Spark, all the bartenders were perfectly groomed and attractive. Even Jake managed to pull it together. Pat looked like he hadn't showered in days. His greasy reddish hair was plastered behind his ears, and he was long overdue for a shave. His large beer belly hung over the waistband of his stained jeans, and I noticed he was wearing the same T-shirt as the doorman, Rex. I scrutinized the picture of the man's face and the caption, FREE KENNY, but couldn't for the life of me figure out who the man was. I was embarrassed to ask, worried it might be someone as important as Nelson Mandela. Eventually curiosity got the best of me. "Who's Kenny?" I asked.

"Huh?" Pat said.

"The guy on your shirt."

Pat and Jake exploded in laughter. "What?" I demanded.

"Kenny was the resident 'supplier' of the Talkhouse," Jake said, "but he got caught, and now he's serving time in Riverhead."

"Oh," I said. I felt such an idiot, but how was I supposed to know they paid homage to their drug dealer on the front of their T-shirts?

I looked around and noticed several black-and-white photocopies of a woman's breasts and butt hanging over the bar, behind the bar, and on the walls over by the pool table.

I nudged Annie and pointed them out. "Whose boobs are those?" she asked, amused.

Pat chuckled. "Jasmine's. She's the owner's girlfriend. She was pretty shit-faced last night. She disappeared to the office for a couple of hours, and when she came back she was hanging these up everywhere and handing them out to customers."

I shot Annie an incredulous look.

"Jasmine kills me," Jake said, admiring the photocopies. "That girl can booze."

"So, how do you two know each other?" I asked.

"I used to bar back at the Talkhouse. These guys taught me everything I know. I'm still on the T-house softball team," Jake said.

In the Hamptons bar world, it seemed everyone knew each other from past summers and other bartending stints. Even if they worked in Miami or Palm Beach during the winter season, or just found other gigs back in the city, all the bartenders, promoters, owners, and managers came back in the summer to their drug of choice: the Hamptons. I thought it might be fun to return the following summer to work now that I'd made so many connections, but God knows I didn't want to morph into a Jake or a Pat—I'd much rather start getting paid for writing rather than slinging drinks.

"So how's Spark treating you guys?" Pat asked, leaning back on one of the coolers, his belly spreading out over his thick thighs.

"Good," I said. "The money's great."

"I could never work at a place like that," Pat said, using the bottle opener he wore on a tattered rope around his neck to fling the top off a Heineken. He drank half the bottle in one sip. "Too much bullshit," he said, letting out a belch.

"It is a lot of bullshit," Annie agreed.

"Do you guys do okay here?" I couldn't help but ask him.

"Yeah," he laughed. "We pull in probably around eight bills on Saturday, we play our own music, there's no manager walking around—Larry the owner is really great. I hear the guys over there at Spark are real dirtbags."

"How many promoters work here?" I asked.

Again, Pat shot a look to Jake and they laughed. "We don't have promoters here," he explained. "We don't let that kind of riffraff in. All they do is rob the place blind."

"Oh," I said, thinking that if tonight's experience was any indication, he was probably right. Jake had mentioned that the promoters and their subpromoters got a huge cut of Spark's cover charges, as well as a percentage of the register rings. He also said that they stole money left and right. The easiest way was for them to pocket a lot of the cover charges they collected at the door. On top of that, the waitresses had to tip the promoters out at the end of the night too, in the form of a "host" tip. Jake had informed me that promoters and their favorite waitresses were usually in cahoots, in elaborately organized schemes to steal money.

I looked around at the hordes of Talkhouse customers spilling out onto the outside deck and couldn't believe the place was packed to capacity without promoters. "Is it this busy every night?" I asked.

"This is nothing," Pat said, finishing the second half of his beer. "On the weekends it's twice as busy."

I was green with envy—the bartenders at the Talkhouse clearly made a lot more money than I did and had to put up with zero club politics. "What time do you guys get out of here?" I asked.

"Three forty-five or four at the latest. We just leave the money in the register, take our tips, and go."

"Are you *kidding* me?" I asked. "We don't get out till at least seven."

"Yep. Sucks." He wiped his mouth with the back of his hand.

"So how long have you been working here?" Annie asked him.

"A little over twenty years," Pat replied, letting out another, longer belch.

"Twenty years?" I marveled. "That's a long time."

"I love it here," he said. "I'll never leave."

"I can't blame you," Jake said. "Your setup here's amazing. It's always packed with serious drinkers—unlike Spark, where you get all those people who just come in for the 'scene,' stay all night, and only order one drink."

"And it's steady," Pat added. "We can always count on making a certain amount."

I felt my back pocket buzzing and realized my cell phone was ringing. I felt a jolt of excitement when I saw the Caller ID: "James cell."

"Excuse me," I said, dashing out the door and onto the patio, where I did my best to step away from the crowd.

"Hey!" I said happily.

"Hey, how are you?" James's voice answered.

"Great! How are you?"

"Good. It sounds noisy. Are you still at work?"

"No, I'm at the Talkhouse with Jake and Annie. Are you in the Hamptons yet?"

"No. I'm coming out tomorrow night. My dad and I just finished dinner at Perse. Now we're at the Oak Room having a drink with a couple of his business partners who're in town."

"Cool," I said, looking over my shoulder at Annie and Jake who had left Pat and were now dancing wildly to "Pour Some Sugar on Me." "Oh, I love this song!"

"I'll let you go, Cass, it sounds like you're having a good time. But hey, I wanted to ask you, are you doing anything on Saturday during the day?"

"Nope. I don't have to be at work until nine-thirty. Why?"

"Do you like polo?"

"Uh . . . sure."

"Would you like to be my date at the Bridgehampton polo match?"

I'd never heard of the Bridgehampton polo match, but it sounded impossibly elegant. Images of wide-brimmed hats, slim trophy wives, poised horses, and mimosas in crystal goblets swirled in my head. I pictured myself arm in arm with James wearing a polka-dotted dress evocative of the one Julia Roberts had worn in *Pretty Woman* during the famous polo scene. "I would love to."

"Great. It starts at noon. Will I get to see you tomorrow?"

"That could be arranged," I said, smiling.

"I'll call you on my way out there."

"Okay. Bye."

I closed my phone with a sigh and spent a gleeful moment thinking about James. I did a little bounce as I returned back inside to where Annie, Jake, and Pat were toasting with yet another round of shots.

"Hey!" Annie said, smiling. "Who was that on the phone?"

"James," I said amorously.

"Your boyfriend?" Jake taunted.

"Yes," I responded proudly. "My boyfriend."

I loved saying that. I couldn't say it enough. The previous weekend James had taken me to Main Beach in East Hampton before work for a picnic of '97 King Estate Pinot Noir, Cabot's Vermont sharp cheddar cheese, and grapes from the Farmer's Market in Amagansett. Who'd have thought little Cassie Ellis from 217 Poplar Street in Albany, New York, would be sitting on a pristine beach in the Hamptons enjoying expensive wine with the man of her dreams? No longer were the Hamptons merely a backdrop for Martin and Lily's pill-popping and swinging—they had finally started to become my haven as well.

As we reclined on the blue blanket, sipping the wine, James had turned to me and said, "I don't want to see anyone else, Cassie. Just you."

Five minutes earlier I hadn't thought I could feel any happier, but his proclamation made me elated. I couldn't have scripted a more perfect fairy-tale scenario. "Me neither," I replied blissfully, and we'd consummated the agreement with a lingering kiss. As I sat there in James's arms looking up at his contented expression, I felt like I was right where I belonged.

James's phone interrupted our moment. He retrieved it from his pocket and snapped it open. "Hey, Rosalind," he'd said. And just like that my security and happiness vanished in the sea air. Rosalind represented everything I could never be—a wealthy, impossibly well-bred woman who navigated James's elite world with ease because it was her world as well. She was a symbol of the side of him I still wasn't sure I could ever relate to—even if I was his girlfriend. "No, I'm not going to be able to make it," he went on. "I'm spending the day with Cassie."

My spirits lifted immediately and I wrapped my arms around his neck in a rapturous embrace. It was official. He'd chosen me over Rosalind.

Annie, Jake, and I trailed around the Talkhouse, drinking beers and dancing in all of the rooms, first to live rock then to reggae, then to 1980s' hits. We didn't have to pay for a thing, though as the night and the drinks wore on, I was more inclined to leave twenties for every bartender who served me even a simple beer. I was probably spending more than I would have if I was paying for everything.

"I'm starving," Annie howled, grabbing her flat stomach.

"They have hot dogs and oysters out back," Jake said.

"Really?" Annie asked. "Live music, pool, cheap beer, and hot dogs? This really *is* the best bar in America."

I followed Annie outside in search of late-night snacks. A bright white banner proclaiming "Shuckergirl" hung above a homespun wooden stand. Two girls wearing shirts that read MOTHERSHUCKER were standing over oysters nestled in crushed ice. Hot dogs were roasting on the grill behind them, next to bags of potato chips and vats of cocktail sauce.

"I'll have a hot dog please," Annie said.

"Make that two. And six oysters," I added.

One of the girls tucked two hot dogs into yellow Martin's Potato Rolls, while the other dug through the ice and started shucking oysters at a remarkable speed. I left a twenty for the girls. I didn't have a care in the world, and better yet, on Saturday, I was going to one of the biggest events of the Hamptons summer season with my boyfriend James.

Annie squirted fluorescent yellow mustard on her hot dog, and I pulled out my cell phone to check the time. "Oh my God, it's already almost three. I should go."

"Why? We're having fun," she said, slowly biting into her hot dog, the mustard oozing out the sides. Only Annie could make eating processed pork look sexy.

"Because we have to work tomorrow night, and I've been getting no writing done. I was going to try to squeeze some in tomorrow before Travis and the crew get here. I feel like all I do is work and drink."

"I know, but it's the summer. It's so hard to resist going out."

"Tell Jake, Pat, and Andy I said good-bye," I said, standing up. "I'm afraid to go in and tell them myself, because they'll end up convincing me to stay and have one more shot."

"Okay. I'll see you back at the house."

As I was heading out toward the street, a stark-naked woman suddenly bolted past me, screaming her head off.

"Are you okay?" I called after her, alarmed, fearing she had been the victim of some thug's drunken sexual rampage.

"She's fine," Andy called from the Talkhouse doorway. "I told her I'd give her twenty bucks if she ran down Main Street naked. I can't believe she did it."

Ten

PEARL DIVER

"This is adorable!" Annie gushed, holding up a short, ruffly, sunshine-yellow Miss Sixty skirt. We were in the middle of an East Hampton shopping spree, stalking Main Street and Newtown Lane for the perfect polo outfit.

"It's a little short for the event, don't you think?" I mused. "I think I'm better off sticking with something a little more classic."

"I don't think it's too short," Annie said. "It's so cute, and you have hot legs. With a pair of strappy heels and your tan, this would be so sexy."

"I'm just not feeling it," I said. "Let's

go check out Henry Lehr." We left Scoop Beach, which catered to women who were young, hip, and a little flashy, and crossed the street to Henry Lehr. Contrary to Scoop, where bright terry-cloth beach dresses were splashed across the window display like paint in a Jackson Pollock piece, Henry Lehr's window displayed an elegantly tailored summer suit the color of crème fraiche.

"This looks like stuff my mom would wear," Annie said disdainfully, eyeing a sea-foam green blazer.

"You're right," I agreed. "Let's go to Calypso. I love that pink dress they have in the window."

"Cassie, that dress has got to be at least a thousand dollars," Annie warned.

"I'm not saying I'm going to buy it," I said testily. "I just want to try it on."

We crossed the street again and walked into the stately brick building that housed Calypso, one of the high-end favorites of East Hampton. Dozens of feminine floral prints and gauzy, flowing materials graced the mannequins. The boutique's signature gold and silver thong sandals, which I'd seen on nearly every woman since I'd arrived in the Hamptons, were displayed throughout the store. I went straight for the sunset-pink dress and held it up against my body. It was made of silk and cut on the bias. "I think this is perfect," I breathed.

"How much?" Annie asked.

"When did you become the practical one?" I teased. I checked the price tag and winced: $900.

"I just don't want you to blow a month's rent on a dress you're only going to wear once. I know James is great, but I bet he'll think you look just as beautiful in Banana Republic as you do in Calypso."

I wasn't sure how to admit to Annie that deep down I was

pretty sure James was more of a Calypso kind of guy—and that the thought of showing up improperly attired to the Bridgehampton polo match terrified me. I thought back to how I'd felt at the barbeque standing next to Rosalind and her friends—and no matter how unglamorous and juvenile I'd felt that day, I knew that this would be much worse. I didn't want him to regret taking me. While in most situations it seemed like standing out and leaving your mark was optimal, I knew that with James's crew, blending in was much more important. Now that I was James's girlfriend, I had to look like I belonged with him. Plus it was a gorgeous dress, and after all the times in my life when I'd made the practical, less-expensive choice, I felt like I deserved it.

"Well, the good news is it's slightly cheaper than a month's rent," I said.

"Cassie . . ." she started to protest, but I was already halfway to the dressing room. Just as I got there, an aggressive saleswoman, who no doubt worked on commission, snatched the dress from my hands and said with a forced smile, "Would you like to try this on?"

"Um . . . yes, please," I stammered.

Her eyes quickly scanned my less-than-stylish outfit, lingering on my Old Navy flip-flops. "Would you like to borrow a pair of heels so you have a better idea of how the dress should look?"

"Yes, thank you," I said. "That would be great."

She vanished, and after I'd pulled the door closed, I tugged my J. Crew wife-beater over my head, slinked out of my cargo skirt, and stepped into the pink dress. As I was in the midst of yanking it up over my torso, the saleswoman returned and without warning threw open the dressing room door.

"Never step into a dress," she instructed. "Women should always dress by putting the garment over their head."

I stepped out of the dress, painfully aware of my SpongeBob Squarepants thong, and lifted the dress over my head and let it cascade down over my body.

"Turn around," she said authoritatively. She zipped me up. "Now slip on the heels."

I took the delicate strappy silver heels and pulled them onto my unpedicured feet, hoping I wasn't desecrating some cardinal rule about how a woman is supposed to don sandals. I stood up and bravely faced the mirror. What I saw almost took my breath away.

The dress was beautiful. *I* was beautiful. The pale pink contrasted dramatically against my tan skin and dark hair. It fit me perfectly, smoothing out all my imperfections. It embraced each curve of my body without clinging or puckering, hugging my hips and flowing down over my legs.

"The dress fits you well," the saleswoman remarked, more gently this time. I couldn't wait to show Annie.

"Wow," she gasped. "You look like a princess."

"I have to get it, Annie. And the shoes."

"Are you sure?" she asked, "It's really beautiful, but it's a lot of money. Are those Pearls Girls really worth it?"

I looked away, knowing she'd read me like a book. "I really want to look good. It's the first big Hamptons event I'm actually going to be a part of."

"That's not true," Annie said playfully. "We're at all the big Hamptons parties!"

"Yeah, behind the bar! This is the first one I'm actually invited to."

"Well, we did make really good money last weekend," she conceded. "And I'm sure tonight will be huge, especially since you're back at the front bar with Jake."

"Yeah," I said, "I'll make it all back this weekend. This will be my one big summer splurge, and after this, no more."

I slipped back into the dressing room and quickly changed out of the dress, then brought it along with the shoes to the register.

"Charge it," I said, handing over my plain old AmEx Blue card. I felt a small sense of satisfaction recalling how the saleswoman had looked at me when I'd walked into the store; it felt good to show her that appearances could be deceiving, and that I could actually afford the dress. At the same time, I hoped my card wouldn't get denied.

"So did you get any work done while I was at the beach this morning?" Annie asked as we left Calypso and sauntered down Main Street.

"Yeah, I actually got a lot done," I said. Even though I had woken up with cotton mouth and a headache, I hadn't been able to pry myself away from the computer. I'd sprung out of bed, inspired to work on my screenplay, and found myself overflowing with ideas. Suddenly, faced with the prospect of going to the Bridgehampton polo match with James, my Cinderella character's perspective was perfectly clear to me. I'd been in the middle of feverishly tapping out a description of the Pearls Girls as a sort of slew of wicked stepsister types when Annie had burst through the door, wearing a bright pink bikini and smelling like a beachy combination of fresh air and tanning oil, to accompany me on our shopping excursion.

"I like shopping in the Hamptons so much better than the city," I confessed to Annie, as we stopped into Scoop du Jour and emerged with two enormous neopolitan cones.

"Why? There's such a better selection in the city," she said.

"Yeah, but *everyone* out here goes shopping with beach hair and flip-flops," I said.

"Not just any flip-flops—haute couture flip-flops,"

Annie corrected me with a scoff. "And their beach hair is probably styled by Garren himself for a mere five thousand dollars a tousle." Garren was *the* celebrity stylist who was on call all summer long in the Hamptons for the emergency hair fixes of heiresses and socialites.

"Oh, come on," I said, pausing to look in the Tiffanys window.

"I'm serious. Remember when we saw Gwyneth Paltrow at Spark that night and we loved her because she was all casual and beached out?" Annie asked.

"Yeah."

"Well, later on I saw her picture in *Us Weekly* and it gave all the details of her outfit and that tank top was like eight hundred dollars and her flip-flops were actually Manolos!"

"You're kidding!" I laughed. "And here I thought she shopped at Target like the rest of us."

We decided to stop in Tiffanys just for the fun of it, and Annie asked to try on a $500,000 engagement ring. "I can dream, can't I?" she said with a wink as a man in a three-piece suit removed it from the case. While she was admiring her sparkling hand, I noticed a delicate choker of freshwater pearls in a glass case at the far end of the store. I walked over for a closer look.

"Can I help you with anything, miss?" a salesman asked.

"No thanks, I was just looking," I said.

"Would you like to try them on?" he asked, following my gaze.

"Um . . . okay."

He took a tiny key out of a pocket on the inside of his suit jacket, opened the case, and carefully pulled the pearls from the display. He helped me fasten the clasp around my neck and then handed me a mirror.

"What are you doing?" Annie asked, suddenly appearing beside me.

"Nothing. I was just trying them on."

"Pearls?" she said, with a dramatic roll of her eyes. "You've been in the Hamptons too long."

I felt a tingle of excitement when I woke up on Saturday morning, even though my head pounded with my second hangover in two days (this one brought on by a late-night champagne celebration with Jake, Kyle, and the other Spark bartenders after we'd each made $705—almost the cost of my clothing splurge earlier that day). I forced myself to guzzle a big glass of water as I waded through the cigarette butts and slumbering bodies on my way to the shower. I toted a plastic shower caddy equipped with Dove Body Wash, Pantene Pro-V shampoo and conditioner, a pumice stone, a loofah, and a fresh razor, determined to beautify myself as much as humanly possible. My hair still smelled of beer and cigarettes.

"You look soooooo gorgeous," Annie said breathlessly from her perch on the edge of her bed an hour and a half later, after I'd strapped my second sandal, spritzed on her Michael Kors perfume, and stood in front of her for inspection. I had a nice bronze glow from the beach, which I accented with Benetint cheek glow makeup, a soft pink Becca lip gloss, and chandelier earrings. All purchased on yesterday's shopping outing for the low price of $178.

"Are you sure I look okay?"

"You look amazing," she said. "Knock 'em dead."

On my way out the door, I found Travis collecting empty beer cans on the porch and putting them in the recycling bin. "Wow," he said when he saw me. "You look beautiful."

"Really?" I asked. His unexpected compliment had a calming effect, and I was able to stop obsessively fidgeting with my dress.

"Really," he confirmed. And then again: "Wow." I heard the wheels of James's Range Rover crunching over the gravel driveway.

"I gotta go." I smiled. "Wish me luck!" Then I dashed out into the sunlight.

James was already halfway to the door when I stepped out onto the porch. He looked me up and down admiringly. "You look beautiful," he said softly, in a single moment making every penny of my splurge well worth it.

We drove in comfortable silence through East Hampton and Wainscott. Just before James turned off the highway to follow the sign for the Mercedes-Benz Polo Challenge, I looked to my left and happened to spot something that made the little kid in me jump for joy.

"I didn't know they had Carvel ice cream out here!" I said jubilantly. "I love Carvel! Every year on my birthday, my parents used to get me a Carvel ice cream cake. Did you ever have one?"

"Yeah, of course I've had one," James laughed. "But that one's really sketchy. Look at all the grafitti all over it. And this whole plaza doesn't exactly fit in with the rest of the Hamptons. This is the not-so-nice area of Bridgehampton. There's actually a lot of crime around here."

"What? There's crime in *Bridgehampton*?" I asked incredulously. The Carvel was situated across the street from a Kmart, a Payless Shoe store, and a TJ Maxx, all laid out in typical suburban shopping plaza fashion. There was a little graffiti on the side, but it all looked harmless enough to me.

I sat vigilantly looking out the window for thugs and criminals, but all I could see was the sun reflecting off the luxury cars as we wove closer to the polo match. We finally followed a white Rolls-Royce and silver Lexus onto a dirt path, which led us to a huge parking area stretched across a grassy lawn. When we climbed out of the car, I had the urge to take my shoes off and run through the soft greenery. The fragrant air was warm and breezy, and in the distance, I could see the far end of the polo field, where gorgeous men wearing their navy blue and white polo uniforms sat atop sinewy horses like knights.

I felt a thrill as James took my hand and we strolled over to the entrance, where a red carpet was cordoned off by—surprise—a velvet rope. Photographers and reporters obstructed my view as they swarmed like vultures around the people preening and posing on their way inside.

"Lydia! Down to the left!"

"Amanda! Over here!"

"Olivia! Smile up to your right!"

"Kimberly, can we get a back shot?"

The roar of the photographers' pleas and the incessant *click-click-click* of their cameras filled the air with a palpable fervor. Immediately I could see that there were ten times more spectators gathered around the red carpet than there were watching polo. I trailed slowly behind James as he avoided the cacophony by veering behind the army of paparazzi and reporters. He bypassed "General Admission" and headed for "VIP Admission" instead.

I craned my neck to steal a glimpse of the action on the red carpet as we passed. I expected to see classic New York pairings of über-celebrities like Sarah Jessica and Matthew, Donald and Melania, Harrison and Calista. To my shock, I didn't recognize a single one of the rail-thin, platinum-blond teenagers with hair extensions who were basking in the incessant flashes.

"Who are those girls?" I asked James in wonder.

"Camera whores," he laughed. "Socialites. They're only famous for being rich, and the only thing they'd love more than getting their picture taken would be having their own reality TV show."

Social climbing, I was learning, was an extreme sport in the Hamptons—and way more challenging than polo. It never seemed to end. No matter how rich or well connected a person was, he or she always aspired to ascend to the next rung on the social ladder. In my opinion, their clamor to get invited to the right parties, have the right friends, belong to the right country clubs, and get their pictures into the right publications made for an extremely stressful lifestyle. These adolescent girls—clawing for camera time on the red carpet—acted as though their survival depended on getting their face into *Hamptons* magazine. I'd already encountered a lot of status hysteria at Spark, but here at the Bridgehampton polo match, it was all the more acute. By all appearances, the only role model these "camera whores" had ever known was Paris Hilton.

"Good afternoon, Mr. Edmonton," the man who handed us our VIP admission bracelets greeted us solicitously. As he fastened the red bracelet around my wrist (general admission was yellow), I marveled at the endless strata of status in the Hamptons. Exclusivity bred exclusivity, like bad behavior begot bad behavior. At first I'd thought it was considered elite just to physically be in the Hamptons for the summer. Then it was a mark of distinction to be invited to the Bridgehampton polo match—and now here I was entering the VIP tent. What was next?

We meandered through the gates past the brigade of beefy security guards. The sun shimmered across the freshly cut grass, which filled the air with a distinctly summer smell. Along the way we passed clusters of people dressed in their summer best, talking to each other while looking around for someone better to talk to. Most of the women were svelte and beautiful. A few, however, sprinkling the crowd had the distinctive lioness look of a plastic surgery mishap. Their multiple nose jobs, skin pullings, cheekbone work, collagen-implanted lips, and Botox-injected foreheads made even Joan Rivers look natural.

James and I circled around the tent, grabbing the featured pearl diver martinis from a passing waiter's tray. In the center of the VIP tent was a roped-off VVIP section, where Star Jones sat like Jaba the Hut—the only nonwhite face in the crowd. I watched as a young female reporter carrying a notebook and tape recorder respectfully approached her. Star shook her head slowly from side to side like Marie Antoinette rejecting a prisoner's plea for clemency. Who knew a mere talk-show host was in a position to turn down media attention?

Kim Cattrall stood a few feet away examining her nails, looking bored. A young woman, presumably a fan, clamored on the outskirts of the VVIP section for her autograph, but Kim never even looked up from her manicure.

"Oh my God, that's Kim Cattrall!" I whispered excitedly to James. "That's *Samantha*! Did you see her?"

"Yeah, she's here every year. Look at you, you're star-struck," he teased.

"No, I'm not," I protested, taking a long, satisfying sip of my ice-cold martini. The coconut flavor from the Malibu rum was the perfect summer tonic. It hit me that I hadn't eaten anything since my pit stop at Twice Upon A Bagel on the way home from Spark at 7:00 A.M. "I'm going to get something to eat. Do you want anything?"

"No, thanks," James said. "But make sure you try one of the chocolate peanut butter cookies from Levain Bakery. They're awesome."

"Twist my arm," I joked.

As I walked around the tent visiting all the buffet tables and selecting delectable hors d'oeuvres from each one, I couldn't believe how many people I recognized. Ironically, I realized, I already knew all the "right" people in the Hamptons, but in a different way: I could look at almost any given face and know exactly what they drank, how they paid, and what kind of tipper they were.

My mouth already full of prosciutto-wrapped melon, I accepted a grilled shrimp flatbread from a smiling chef, along with a wild mushroom tart and a piece of havarti dill cheese and some strawberries. I made my way over to the cookie station and filled a second plate with a chocolate chip cookie with walnuts and an oatmeal raisin cookie in addition to the highly recommended chocolate peanut butter cookie. Realizing that my martini was dangerously low, I then headed over to the bar, all the while scanning the crowd for Rosalind and her clique. Part of me hoped that I'd run into them now that I was armed with an expensive dress and gorgeous shoes. I hoped I hadn't spent close to a month's rent on an outfit they'd never see. I looked down and saw that I'd already gotten a dab of chocolate on my dress (so I couldn't even return it after the match, as Annie had impishly hinted the night before). As I crossed the tent balancing my plates of delicacies, I realized I was the only one in the entire VIP section who was actually eating.

"What can I get for you?" the bartender, dressed in the

usual catering uniform of a cheap tuxedo, asked me as I approached.

"Hi. How are you?" I asked him, juggling my plates and setting down my empty glass.

"I'm fine. Thank you for asking. How are you?"

"I'm wonderful, thank you. Can I have another pearl diver, please?"

"Of course." He turned and reached for the pineapple juice.

"There you are," James said, coming up beside me. "Cassie, I'd like you to meet some friends of mine."

Flustered, I looked around for a place to set down my heaping plates. I was suddenly embarrassed to be the only one in VIP not only eating but eating a lot. But the bar was too cluttered with cocktail glasses and there was no available space for me to put my food, so I finally just dropped the plates into a trash bin next to the bar.

"This is Mr. and Mrs. Hildreth," he said, introducing an impossibly well-kept older couple. "They're very good friends of my family. This is Cassie Ellis."

"It's nice to meet you," I said, shaking their hands and stretching my mouth into the widest smile I could manage. I felt a little like Miss America.

"Likewise," Mr. Hildreth said. "So, Cassie, how do you know our James? Did you go to Yale?"

"No, actually Cassie went to Columbia," James answered for me. "Martin Pritchard introduced us."

"How wonderful. How is Martin?" Mrs. Hildreth inquired.

"He's doing very well," I guessed. I hadn't seen Martin in Finton's much as of late and assumed he'd been spending most of his summer out here.

"Lovely," Mrs. Hildreth said. "I just adore Martin. He has exquisite taste."

"Did you grow up in Manhattan?" Mr. Hildreth asked.

"No, actually, I grew up in a suburb outside of Albany," I said.

The Hildreths stared blankly. "How nice," they said.

"And what is it that you do?" Mrs. Hildreth went on.

"I'm a—"

"Cassie's a writer," James interjected. "Screenplays."

"Hey, gorgeous!" an all-too-familiar voice heralded in my direction. I looked up and saw Burberry Plaid Man, my high-tipping regular from Spark, sauntering over. "You clean up pretty good," he said, standing too close to me.

"Hi," I said weakly, turning back to the Hildreths and trying to keep the awkwardness of the encounter in check.

"Why aren't you behind the bar?" Burberry Plaid Man boomed.

I fidgeted uncomfortably. Here I was, dressed to the nines, chatting with the VIPs of the Hamptons, and actually starting to feel like I belonged at the polo match. And now Burberry Plaid Man had changed all that with one sentence; it was as if I had been unmasked. I forced a smile and tried to ignore the comment, hoping the Hildreths weren't paying attention.

"Here's your martini, miss," the bartender said. I was grateful for the shift in attention. Fortunately, Burberry Plaid Man was soon distracted by a socialite in a particularly revealing dress.

"So where are all your friends, James? Glen, and Tom, and that lovely Rosalind we met at your father's party in May?" Mrs. Hildreth asked.

"Glen and Tom are meeting us later, but I'm afraid

Rosalind isn't going to be able to make it," James replied. "She's in Paris for the weekend with her father."

"Oh, that's too bad." Mrs. Hildreth sighed. "She's such a charming girl. It will be a lucky fellow who manages to put a ring on her finger." She gave him a pointed look. I stared at my shoes, feeling small and overlooked. I wasn't sure what was worse: that this woman obviously assumed that James and I weren't a couple, or that she clearly felt that he and Rosalind should be. Leave it to Rosalind to ruin my day without even being there.

"Well, we have to be going," Mr. Hildreth said suddenly, shaking James's hand. "Please give our best to your father." Mrs. Hildreth kissed James on two cheeks, European style, and then the two of them swooped away into the crowd without saying good-bye to me.

"It was nice to meet you," I called after them, but they were already too busy making their rounds, ensuring they said their "hellos" to everyone in VIP. For people so allegedly well-pedigreed, they didn't seem to have an ounce of manners or decency. The snobs here breed more selectively than the polo horses, I thought.

The Hildreths' slight of me seemed to have escaped James's attention entirely. As he looked around cheerfully for the bartender and signaled for another round of martinis, I contemplated how exactly I'd wanted him to react. After all, it wasn't James's fault that his father's friends had been rude to me. But I did wish he'd been a little bit more conscious of my feelings—not to mention more forward about introducing me as his girlfriend.

I was thankful when my crisp, refreshing (third) martini was ready. I drew a long swallow from the glass and almost choked when I realized that in the two seconds I'd turned around to collect my cocktail, Amanda Hearst herself and her coterie of ladies-in-waiting had captured my boyfriend's attention.

"Mandy!" James enthused. His usual calm and confident demeanor had evaporated like spilled vodka and been replaced by a giddy, schoolboy animation. "How are you, sweetie?"

Sweetie? I'd never heard him use that term, even with the Pearls Girls. My heart sank as I recalled Martin mentioning he'd heard through the Hamptons rumor mill that James had once dated Amanda Hearst.

"Hi, James." She yawned, barely pausing to send him an air kiss. He watched her admiringly as she and her fawning contingent continued making their rounds.

"That was Amanda Hearst," James said, turning to me as though he'd just remembered that I was there. "Sorry I didn't introduce you. She's so interesting, you'd love her. She's really smart—she finished college in two years—she's only nineteen, and she's already set to star in the next Steven Soderbergh film . . ."

As James continued to gush over the simpering teenage beauty, I couldn't believe my ears. Was this starstruck Amanda Hearst sycophant the same guy who only moments ago was calling her contemporaries camera whores?

"Did you used to date her?" I blurted out before my jealousy filter kicked in.

"What?" James asked, pausing in his reverie.

"Martin mentioned he thought you used to date her," I said lamely.

"No. I met her in Gstaad a few years ago. And I always bump into her out here, but we're just friends."

"Oh." Even though he claimed their relationship was innocent, it still bothered me that he was so dazzled by her presence. But then it occurred to me: even a Hamptonite like James could be affected by a "celebrity" like Amanda Hearst, who, for him, represented the next realm of high society. There were wealthy people. And then there were wealthy, established people. And then there were wealthy, established people like Amanda Hearst who came from an actual dynasty. There were lots of people in the Hamptons who had more money than the Hearsts, but nobody could touch their family name, which eclipsed all else in this world.

I finished my still-cold martini in one gulp.

They weren't even bartending nightmares anymore, just dreams where my body—now so used to mechanically making hundreds of thousands of drinks into the wee hours of the morning—couldn't stop, even when I slept. Especially after I'd worked the longest, busiest shift of my life as I had at Spark the night before. I'd left the bar close to 8:00 A.M. on Sunday morning, dripping in sweat and dollars. In my sleep, I'd found myself straining for a nonexistent bottle of vodka perched on the highest shelf.

Agonizing lower back pain woke me up, and the sunlight pouring through the window made my dry eyes burn. Even though it was a perfect beach day, I had no plans to get out of bed. I'd worked roughly twenty-four hours in the last two days, and even though I was $1,350 richer, I was mentally and physically drained. I reached around the floor for the FIJI water bottle I'd embezzled from Spark only hours before. As I sat up, my head began to throb, and even raising the bottle to my lips caused my arm to ache with exhaustion.

I rolled over and did some calculations in my head. Even

after accounting for the monstrous expense of my new out-fit, I'd still netted more than $300 for the weekend, which meant my July rent check wouldn't bounce. I squinted over at Annie's reclining form and saw that her eyes were open.

"What time is it?" she asked in a hoarse whisper.

"About eleven," I said.

"God, we've only been sleeping for three hours. I feel like shit."

"So do I."

"I can't do that ever again," she groaned.

"Me neither."

She sat up in bed, grabbing her own bottle of water. "My head hurts."

"So does mine, and my back aches, and my arms are sore."

"I feel like I've been beat up."

"Me too." I took another sip of water. "You know, it's not just the working," I said thoughtfully. "It's the drinking. If you think about it, we're doing all this strenuous work, lifting cases of liquor, bending down a million times, running around like maniacs, and on top of that I feel like I'm constantly doing math problems in my head all night long, you know—adding up all the drink prices? And keeping track of all those tabs—sometimes I have fifty credit cards at once. And then on top of all that, we get wasted. As if our bodies aren't getting enough abuse. No wonder my muscles hurt."

"I know," Annie agreed. "It's awful." She reached into her backpack and pulled out the train schedule. "I think I'm just going to go back to the city now. I have to clean my apartment and do some laundry, and I have some serious catching up to do on my sleep. If I stay here, I'll end up at the beach with a beer in my hand."

"Okay. I think I'm going to stick around tonight and try to get some writing done after all the boys leave. I told James

I'd show him my screenplay when he stops by Finton's on Wednesday."

"Good idea. The house should be pretty quiet," Annie said, sitting up and pulling her curls into a chaotic ponytail. She rolled out of bed and started shoving her things into her backpack. "Is James staying out here today?"

"No, he's going back early for work, so I won't have any distractions," I said. But secretly I was still mulling over everything that had gone down at the polo match. I was 90 percent certain that James really did have to make it into the office that afternoon, as he'd said. But after yesterday, my doubts had resurfaced. I worried that he was thinking I wasn't right for him. I hoped he wasn't thinking about Amanda Hearst.

I'd set up my laptop, spread out my notebook, along with a bunch of crumpled bev naps that contained scribblings of my late-night wisdom, and had written about six words when I heard a knock at my door.

"Come in," I said.

"Hey," Travis said, standing in the doorway.

"Oh, hey, Travis, I thought you went back to the city."

"No, I decided to take tomorrow off. How was your weekend?"

"I made good money, but I worked my ass off."

"I was thinking about going to Montauk tonight for some dinner. Do you want to come?"

"I really shouldn't," I said, staring at the blinking cursor on my computer screen. "There's no way I can go out and drink again."

He laughed. "Come on, it's gorgeous outside, and I want to go to Duryea's. Have you ever been there?"

"No."

"Then you have to come. It's amazing, it's right on the water in Montauk Bay, and it's bring your own, so we can pick up some beers on the way. Do you like lobster?"

"I love lobster," I said, tempted, biting my lower lip.

"Then you'll love this place."

"Travis, I can't. I haven't been able to get much writing done because of work, and . . ."

"That's okay, I understand," he said, and started to go.

"Wait!" I said. "I've always wanted to go to Montauk." Montauk was the farthest point east on Long Island and was a famous old-world fishing town that retained a lot of its original rustic flavor, unlike the rest of the East End.

"Then get in the car."

"Okay, just give me a minute to change."

"You can go in what you're wearing."

I looked down at my faded tank top and khaki skirt. My hair was unwashed and piled on top of my head. "I can't wear this."

"Trust me, it's really casual. Just bring a sweatshirt, 'cause it gets really cold down by the water when the sun goes down."

I shut down my laptop, grabbed my bag, and twenty minutes later, after picking up some Budweiser at the Amagansett IGA, we hit the road. Cyril's whizzed by on my left as we traversed Napeague Stretch on our way to the tip of the South Fork.

I flipped through the radio stations and started singing—admittedly a little off-key—along with the Rolling Stones. *You're just a memory* . . .

"Did you know that Mick Jagger actually wrote that song at the Memory Motel in Montauk?" Travis asked me.

"Really?"

"Yup. The Stones used to come out to visit Andy Warhol's place in Montauk all the time."

"Look," I said, pointing to the bumper sticker on the car in front of us. "It says 'Montauk: a drinking town with a fishing problem!' "

Travis laughed.

Montauk was by far the least pretentious of the Hamptons towns. There were no swanky stores or women walking around carrying Malteses in $3,000 handbags. There were lots of families wandering around eating ice cream and fudge, and the atmosphere was like a big carnival.

"That's Mr. John's Pancake House," Travis said, pointing to the left. "Best breakfast. You have to go before the summer ends and order a number two."

"What's that?" I asked.

"Two eggs, two pancakes, two pieces of bacon, two pieces of toast, and homefries."

"Yum," I said.

We pulled off the main road and onto a rocky, hilly path that ran parallel to the shore of Montauk Bay. Seagulls circled over the rocky beaches of the bay and quaint summer cottages dotted the bucolic landscape.

"That's the Montauket," Travis said, pointing to a divey-looking hotel and bar off to the left. "It's a great bar. Local spot."

Finally we pulled into Duryea's parking lot. There was an expansive wooden deck facing the bay framed by rock jetties and covered with no-frills white plastic lawn furniture and picnic tables. The sun, a fireball in the distance, had just started its final plunge below the horizon, and there was a slight breeze wafting off the water. We approached the tiny ordering window, and I happily placed my order for a two-pound lobster, which Travis assured me was the best in the world. We sat down at a table and cracked open some beers. Travis went to get us some napkins and plasticware.

"It's beautiful here," I said, taking a long sip of Budweiser and looking out at the choppy water breaking on the rocks and lapping up against the deck.

"Montauk's my favorite place out east," Travis said. "Most of the locals out here are fishermen. It's not as Hamptony as the rest of the East End."

"Yeah, James was telling me that because it's the farthest away from the city, it's the least developed."

Travis took a swig of his beer. "So, when am I going to meet this James I hear so much about?"

"I don't know," I said, trying to imagine the two of them meeting. Somehow I wasn't sure if they would get along. I didn't know what Travis would make of James's rarefied world. "Soon."

They called our number, signaling our food was ready, and after a full hour of claw-cracking, tail-dipping, and beer-sipping, we were messy, happy, and delightfully stuffed.

"That was the best lobster I've ever tasted," I said, ripping off my plastic lobster bib.

"I told you you'd love it here," Travis said as we bused our butter-soaked paper plates. "You want to stop by the Montauket for a beer?"

I only thought for a split second. "Sure," I answered.

The Montauket was dark inside, and the girl who was tending bar looked like a real seafaring "broad"—she had a leathery face and chapped lips, smeared with coral lipstick that bled into the tiny cracks around her mouth. She was wearing a T-shirt tucked into high-waisted denim shorts, and her dried-out, bleached blond mullet was pulled halfway back into a ponytail.

"What can I get for you, honey?" she asked in a raspy voice.

"Two Buds, please."

Travis and I took a seat, and I looked around at the all-male faces of the motley crew that had settled on the other stools. They looked like they belonged in Richard Avedon's vagabond portraits. Their wrinkled faces, dirty fingernails, and worn flannel shirts told the tale of the toll life had taken on them. Their skin was deeply tanned, and when they moved their faces, I could see white skin inside the creases of their wrinkles. One of them, a particularly dog-eared fellow, kept looking in my direction. It was a few minutes before it registered who he was.

"Pat?" I asked uncertainly.

"Jake's friend, right?" he said, swigging a Heineken.

"Yeah. Cassie," I said. "And this is my friend Travis."

"Nice to meet you," Travis said, offering his hand, which Pat accepted with a hearty shake. "You work over at the Talkhouse, right?"

Pat nodded.

"I go there a lot. Great bar," Travis said.

"Do you live out here?" I asked.

"Yup. Born and raised."

"It's my first time in Montauk," I said. "We just had dinner at Duryea's. I really like it out here. It's different from the rest of the Hamptons."

"Not anymore," Pat said in his gravelly voice. "It used to be. Every time I drive to work I see more construction. They're selling these tiny little houses on no land for millions of dollars. It's gotten so none of us can afford to live here anymore."

I thought back to our drive out to Montauk. Almost the entire stretch of highway between Amagansett and Montauk had been an eyesore of construction sites or brand-new mammoth homes made of not-yet-weathered blond wood. Unless the land was earmarked as federal or state property through the park systems, it was up for grabs.

"I grew up in Smithtown, and every summer we'd rent a house out here for a week. It's definitely a lot more built up than it used to be," Travis agreed. "But the good news is, you can now sell your house for a minimum of two million dollars."

"I don't give a shit. I like my little house, and it's been in my family for three generations. It's still a great place to live," Pat said. "But the traffic gets worse and worse, and it feels like the Hamptons eats into Montauk a little more each year."

"Can I buy you a beer?" Travis offered noticing Pat's empty Heineken.

"No, thanks. I'm meeting some friends over at The Point. You guys should swing by."

"Okay," we said.

Pat negotiated his large body off the bar stool. "Nice seeing you again." He tipped his hat to the bartender and walked out the door.

"So you want to check out The Point?" Travis asked.

"Why not?"

We climbed back into Travis's '97 Mitsubishi Galant and drove the quarter mile to The Point. Inside it was slammed. "Paint It Black" was blaring from the speakers, the bass so strong you could feel it in your chest. We tried to claim some real estate at the bar, but no stools were available and I couldn't get the bartender's attention. Finally I felt a tap on my shoulder, and I turned around to see Pat struggling to hold three shots, two Buds, and a Heineken.

"Thanks!" I shouted, grabbing two of the shots in one hand and the two Buds in the other. The three of us hollered, "Cheers!" and downed the shots with little hesitation. As I smiled at Travis, I realized I was well on my way to yet another night of inebriation. The lights were streaking when I turned my head, and my teeth felt numb. I was about to ask Pat to get me a glass of water when AC/DC's "You Shook Me" started playing.

"I love this song!" I shouted happily, throwing my body into an energetic dance.

"Then get on the bar," Pat said.

"No way," I said, shaking my head dramatically.

"Come on, Cassie," Travis encouraged. "I'll help you up."

Before I knew what I was doing, Travis was lifting me up onto the bar. The crowd started cheering like crazy, and something came over me—all of a sudden I felt like I was Beyonce. I thrashed my head and hips in rhythm to the strains of *Knockin' me out with those American thighs* . . . I felt a complete sense of reckless abandon. For the first time in the Hamptons, I wasn't worried about anything. As long as I could swing my hips, bash my head, and sing along, everything would be just fine.

Like almost every other morning that summer, I woke up on Monday with a massive hangover. I checked the clock on my phone and couldn't believe it. I had slept until two in the afternoon. I forced myself to get out of bed, brushed my teeth, and went to the kitchen for some water. On the refrigerator was a note from Travis. "Went back to the city.

Had a great time last night. There's some orange juice and a bagel in the fridge. See you next weekend."

I smiled as I poured myself some juice, thinking about the lobster dinner and the dancing on the bar. Then I grabbed my bagel, went back upstairs, and climbed back into bed with my notebook.

After last night, I've decided I'm blue collar, I wrote. *A perfect match for James's blue blood? I had more fun at a dive bar in Montauk than I did at the Bridgehampton polo match. . . .*

My rambling thoughts were interrupted by my cell phone ringing and a 631 number I didn't recognize flashing on the screen.

"Hello?" I said.

"Cassie? It's Chris from Spark."

"Hey, what's up?" I said, wondering if I was in trouble for something.

"Not much. Listen, tonight's industry night, and I'm short a bartender. I was wondering if you were still in town and if you could work."

"How are industry nights there?" I asked. I wasn't about to give up my free night for nothing. Especially since I had to be back in the city in time to work the Tuesday day shift at Finton's.

"Pretty good. It's a party just for people in the restaurant industry, bartenders, waiters . . . It's a great night to make money, because everyone tips really good."

I mentally considered the offer. If I stayed, I'd have to take a really early train out of Amagansett in the morning. I hadn't been getting enough sleep, my apartment back in the city was a mess, and I definitely hadn't been doing enough writing. On the other hand, the offer was seductive. The weekend had already been incredibly lucrative, even with my little shopping spree, but I certainly wasn't in a position to turn down more money.

"I can do it," I said.

"Great. Show up at nine-thirty. Oh, and you can wear whatever you want. I'm the only one there tonight."

"Okay. See you then."

As I hung up the phone I wondered if I was a glutton for punishment—or if I was becoming addicted to making money or to alcohol, or to both.

A night at Spark without Shalina and Teddy and the zillion other promoters and managers reminded me of the one glorious occasion when Laurel had been out sick and there was no manager on duty at Finton's. I could actually relax at work.

Only one bar was open on Monday nights, the front bar. I was working with Andy, my new friend from the Talkhouse, and the entire energy of the place seemed different. It was really laid-back, and as Chris had promised, all the customers were patient and friendly and huge tippers. I couldn't help thinking that everyone should work in the service industry at least once in their lives in order to appreciate how hard it could be.

I was wearing my navy blue Pumas, jeans, and a wife-beater, and for once I felt like myself at Spark. It made all the difference in the world not to be wearing Shalina's offensive uniform.

"Hey, wanna see a trick?" Andy asked me. His eyes were bloodshot and the distinct smell of weed wafted off his clothes.

"Sure," I said.

He opened up a fresh bottle of Grand Marnier and stuffed a bev nap in the neck. Then he took out a book of Talkhouse matches and lit the napkin. "This is sick!" he exclaimed. "Watch—in a minute, the bottle'll be like a torch."

I watched for a moment, before getting distracted by a customer in need of six kamikaze shots. I was reaching for the bottle of triple sec when I heard a loud explosion and felt a rush of heat behind me. Instinctively I hit the deck, saturating my jeans and shirt with bar sludge. Shards of glass rained down on my back as Andy screamed, "Oh, shit!" His little trick had backfired. Literally.

"Are you okay?" he asked, laughing, extending a hand.

"What the hell just happened?" I cried.

"The bottle exploded. Sometimes that happens if the bottle's too full," he explained casually.

After helping him sweep up the mess, I finally got back to work. Mondays certainly were different. Andy's experiment could have killed someone, and no one had said a word about it. In fact, Chris looked amused.

"Hey, Chris!" Andy shouted suddenly. "You feeling dirty?"

Chris smiled widely and grabbed two unopened bottles of Jägermeister from a shelf behind the bar and handed one to Andy. "I think we need a Jäger bath," Chris concluded solemnly. At that, the two of them simultaneously unscrewed the tops, clinked the bottles, took a long swig, and then proceeded to pour the rest of the black syrupy liquor over their heads until the bottles were empty. I watched on in disbelief as they guffawed, then turned back to the customers, shaking my head.

"Cassie!" Andy called. "You can keep all our tips tonight if you do a bar mat shot."

"What's that?" I asked suspiciously.

Andy grabbed a soaking bar mat off the bar and filled a plastic cup to the brim with the brownish sludge that had collected on it over the course of the night. He held it out to me.

"No, thanks." Even though I needed money, I had to draw the line somewhere.

"Hey, you look familiar," a greasy black-haired man said after I fixed him a Patrón on the rocks. "You're Martin's friend, you came into my restaurant looking for a job."

"Hi." I smiled. "Tony, right? You work at Saracen?"

"That's right, beautiful. Thanks for the drink," he said, slipping me a $100 bill. "That's for you. But next summer, I want you behind my bar."

I smiled again and then turned to Andy. "I think we're going to make some cash tonight. That guy just gave me a hundred dollars for one drink."

He chuckled. "Well, everyone that's come in tonight's asked for you. You should run for mayor of this town."

Eleven

THUG PASSION

My swollen bladder straining against my abdominal wall, I barrelled through the hordes of oblivious dancing bodies in VIP to reach the employee bathroom. Cursing myself for drinking a hundred ounces of water on such a busy night, I pushed the unlocked bathroom door open without knocking. Teddy was inside standing with his back facing the toilet and his pants down. A slender bleached blond, wearing a skintight white Moschino crop top and low-cut Chloe jeans, was on her knees before him.

"Oh my God, I-I'm so sorry," I stuttered, backing out of the tiny bathroom.

"That's okay," the girl answered, wiping her mouth with the back of her hand. "We're finished." She rose to her feet as a flushed Teddy pulled up his pants. On her tiptoes she planted a brusque kiss on his lips. "After this little favor, I don't think I should have to wait on line to get into the club anymore," she said with a sexy laugh before brushing past me to join her cluster of dancing friends in VIP.

"Teddy, I'm really sorry. I should've knocked," I said, flustered. The air in the bathroom was thick with marijuana smoke, and Teddy slugged the rest of an Amstel Light before straightening his metallic-green tie and squeezing by me. Still overwhelmed by embarrassment, I closed the door and made sure to lock it.

As I made my way back through VIP, I promised myself I would never again barge through a closed door at Spark—you just never knew what lurked behind. I thought of Annie and wondered just how many women Teddy managed to score on any given night. Annie seemed to have tired of him (and Tom, too, come to think of it)—lately she only mentioned the wealthy Mr. Big types who seemed to populate VIP and were always responsive to her charms—but I wondered if she knew what he was up to all the same. Then again, knowing Annie, she probably wouldn't care. I had a hard time just keeping track of her suitors.

Earlier that night, when Annie and I had arrived for work, a burly bouncer had blocked our entrance. "Sorry, girls, the back of the line is that way," he'd barked.

"We work here," I'd said, mildly proud that I wielded a little velvet-rope power, a true mark of distinction in the Hamptons.

I'd noticed that two separate lines had formed in front of the door, and I remembered Teddy mentioning he was bringing in a different promoter to host a Latin night on Fridays. The line on the right side consisted mostly of people of Hispanic origin who were being shepherded through a metal detector administered by unfamiliar security guards and getting frisked before being admitted. The other line looked like the typical Spark clientele: girls in Jimmy Choo stilettos, short Chip and Pepper skirts, and brightly colored Dior tanks; guys in the standard male uniform of Hickey Freeman or Ascot Chang button-downs rolled "casually" to the sleeves, and Cole Haan or Gucci loafers. While one line ended in a cursory guest list check, the other ended in a full body search.

Cassie! Can I get two Ketel cranberries?" Elsie asked. "I would've gotten them from the back bar, but they hired some idiot girl when they fired Kyle and she can't bartend for shit."

"They fired Kyle?" I asked, dressing her cocktails with limes.

"Yeah. He came in tonight all the way from Hampton Bays and when he got here they told him to go home. Teddy's fucking some chick and he hired her friend back there. She's a total bitch." She put the drinks on a tray and teetered back into the crowd.

Whenever a bartender or waitress was fired, an epidemic of fear infected all Spark employees. Those of us who remained tried to determine the exact reason the employee had been dismissed, in order to avoid getting sacked ourselves. I imagined that the portentous owners had witnessed Kyle blowing lines behind the bar from their cameras at home. Still, with new faces appearing right and left, it was getting so I actually felt comforted when I saw Elsie and the girls—at least they were familiar.

I buckled down and got back to work, my arms and mind moving as fast as they could. I started making watermelon martinis for two "Lawn Guyland" girls—with thick local accents, long pink fingernails, and teased hair. Before I'd even had a chance to get the Pucker Watermelon Liqueur, I looked up to see James and Tom standing right in front of me.

"Hey, guys!" I said, lighting up and abandoning drink-making for a second while I leaned over the bar to kiss James hello. "I didn't know you were coming!"

"We decided to stop by for a quick drink," he said. "I don't think we're going to stay long. I have to wake up early tomorrow to go golfing with some guys from work."

I shot him an exaggerated pout as I added vodka to the watermelon mix, and he laughed. "You want a Jack and Coke?" I asked, smiling.

"Sure, thanks. How's your night going?" he asked.

"Good. It's busy," I said, looking around at the masses.

"Yeah, it's crazy in here tonight," Tom agreed.

"How was dinner?" I asked, shoveling ice into the watermelon concoction and shaking energetically.

"Good," James said.

"Where'd you go?" I asked, handing the girls their martinis and accepting their cash.

"Nick and Toni's," Tom said. "It was delicious."

"So . . ." James said, leaning in over the bar.

"Yeah . . ." I said, leaning in even closer so our noses were almost touching.

"I know you're really busy, but I just wanted to tell you I finished reading your screenplay this afternoon, and I loved it. It was brilliant."

"Really?" I asked. Time seemed to stop, and for a moment I was utterly unaware of the fact that I was behind a bar in front of hundreds of impatient customers. Ever since I'd given him a copy of my screenplay at Finton's this past Wednesday, I'd been waiting with bated breath for his reaction.

"Really. I loved it."

"Really?" I asked again, feeling the blood rush to my cheeks.

"Yes. It was amazing. I'll talk to you more about it later, but I'm going to make some calls and see what we can do to shop it around."

"What do you mean?" I asked. I got chills thinking about the possibilities. I wondered how far his connections actually extended in the film world, since in all of our conversations we'd never really talked about specifics. I wondered excitedly if he could actually get my screenplay produced.

"Can I get a drink over here?" a man called from a few feet away.

"Go back to work. We can talk about it later. I just wanted to let you know I loved it." James turned and disappeared into the crowd with Tom.

I faced the angry rabble with a proud smile. In a matter of weeks I probably wouldn't even need to bartend anymore.

"Three Ketels and sodas, two Jack and Cokes, a sour apple martini, a glass of champagne, four Amstel Lights . . ." Customers were barking, but all I could hear was "and the Academy Award for best screenplay goes to . . . Cassie Ellis."

"Excuse me," a man's voice beseeched, forcing me back down to earth.

"Hi! How are you?" I asked, turning and smiling brightly at the man, still intoxicated by James's praise.

"I'm good, thanks. How are you?" He was a grizzly-looking guy, and his red and white checkered button-down shirt was wrinkled and sloppily tucked into furrowed khakis. Not exactly the typical polished Spark fare.

"Great!"

"Can I buy a bottle at the bar?" he asked.

"You sure can," I said. "What can I get for you?"

"Do you have Ketel One?"

"We sure do!" I bent down to the shelves stacked with vodka reserves and grabbed a bottle of Ketel, all the while dancing along to Donna Summer's "She Works Hard for Her Money." Spark constantly rotated in new DJs, and this one was spinning lots of my favorite 1970s and '80s classics. "Here you go," I said. "That'll be two hundred fifty dollars."

"And a Bud for me."

"Two-sixty."

"Ten dollars for a Bud?" he asked.

"I know. It's crazy," I sympathized. "But it's the Hamptons."

The man pulled a slapdash wad of bills out of his pocket and counted out $260 and handed it to me. Then he grabbed my hand and slipped me a hundred-dollar bill. "That's for you," he said. "You're the first person I've ever met at these clubs who was nice to me before I dropped five Gs."

"Thanks," I said.

"Let me tell you something. I was at Jet East last weekend, and they wouldn't let me in to the club until I told the doorman I was willing to buy some bottles. He finally sat me at a table, and the cocktail waitress was such a bitch until I ordered three bottles of Cristal and four bottles of Ketel. Then all of a sudden I'm the most popular guy in the club. The waitresses were all over me."

"Money talks," I said, tossing the hundred into the tip jar.

"You got that right," he concurred.

I watched as he walked away, wondering why so few people in the business had learned what seemed to me an obvious secret: that one smile and a little conversation could get you an enormous tip.

James walked back toward the bar and set his empty Jack and Coke cup down. "I'm heading out, Cass. Do you want me to come back later and pick you up?"

"Oh, no, don't worry about it. Get some sleep. I'm sure Jake'll drive me home," I said, suppressing a little bit of surprise and annoyance. True, he'd said he wasn't staying long, but I didn't realize that he'd be leaving quite so soon. I attributed my feelings to PMS and put a big smile on my face, playing the role of the ultra-cool girlfriend. "I'll see you tomorrow."

"Definitely. I'll give you a call in the morning," he said. And with another quick kiss, he was gone.

"Jake! Shots!" I called.

"You got it, babe." And without missing a beat, Jake pulled the Patrón off the shelf, filled two shot glasses, and we knocked them back in a matter of seconds.

The rest of the night passed by quickly. At around a quarter to four, right before we were about to close, a woman struggling to walk in her six-inch heels hobbled over to the bar requesting seven shots of Jägermeister.

"That'll be eighty-four dollars," I stated wearily.

She tossed five twenties in my direction, slurring "Keep it."

I picked up the money and was on my way to the register when Jake muttered under his breath, "Just throw it in the tip jar."

"What?" I asked, confused.

"Just throw it in the tip jar," Jake said, already starting the nightly ritual of gathering the bar mats, and clearing the bar of the cups, bottles, glasses, straws, and napkins.

Never questioning Jake's authority, I flung the money in the tip jar. A bout of severe paranoia followed. I assiduously avoided looking at the ominous, omnipresent cameras, fearing they had recorded my theft and were at that very moment transmitting my crime to the owners. I wanted to dig $84 out of the tip jar and ring it into the register, but thought it might look even more suspicious if the cameras captured me rooting through the tips and then putting money in the drawer. But then I started rationalizing. Shalina, Teddy, and, by extension, the owners didn't bother in the least to take care of their employees, firing and demoting us at will. I thought of the $50 shift pay I had gotten at the Fourth of July party, and that put the nail in the coffin of my guilt.

I grabbed the tip jar righteously and sequestered myself, along with James's hooded Yale sweatshirt and a Bud Light, in the dining room to start counting.

"Your boyfriend left early tonight," Jake commented as we sat waiting for the waitresses to tip us out.

"Yeah, he has to wake up really early tomorrow to go golf with some guys from his work," I said, finishing my beer with a gulp.

"What a yuppie."

I ignored his comment. "Can you drive me and Annie home?"

"Sure," he said. "I might swing by the Talkhouse anyway."

After the waitresses finished closing out, Annie and I bundled up our things, grabbed two more Bud Lights, and followed Jake out to the car.

"I think this is the earliest we ever got out." Annie yawned. "I'm actually going to get a good night's sleep." Jake grunted his assent.

"I know, I can't believe it's only six," I agreed, realizing how absurd it was that a good night's sleep for us meant we'd gotten out of work before 7:00 A.M.

On the way home, I was tempted to ask Jake how often he took money from customers and bypassed the register in favor of the tip jar. But I fought the urge, deciding it had to be something that bartenders never spoke of out loud. See no evil. Hear no evil. Speak no evil.

The sun was rising as we drove down Main Street in East Hampton, and people were already out and about walking their dogs and getting coffee at the Golden Pear. "I can't believe these people are already starting their days, and we haven't even gone to sleep yet," Annie marveled. I looked down at the beer I was holding and felt sick. What was I doing drinking at six in the morning?

We pulled into the Animal House driveway, and Annie and I jumped out. "Crazy night, huh?" I commented to her as we walked across the dewy lawn to the porch arm in arm.

"As usual," she sighed.

"Oh my God! I forgot to tell you about Teddy!"

"What about him?" she asked, her eyes widening.

"I walked in on some girl giving him a blow job in the employee bathroom," I said evenly, looking to see her reaction.

She laughed. "Someone's stealing my bag of tricks!"

"So you're not upset?" I asked.

"*Please*, Cassie. He's like the biggest loser on earth. We were just having fun."

We approached the porch and stumbled on Travis, who was reclined in a lawn chair, making out passionately with a teeny blond wearing a pink and blue Lily Pulitzer dress that was inched up to the tops of her thighs. Her shoes, bag, and cardigan were strewn on the porch beside the chair, and the first few buttons on Travis's shirt were undone.

"Good morning!" Annie sang out, chuckling.

"Oh . . . hey." Travis sat up and shifted around uncomfortably.

"Don't mind us," I said, opening the screen door and stepping into the house. Annie and I erupted into giggles once we were inside.

"Did you see his face? He was so embarrassed!" she squealed. "Who was that girl?"

"I don't know. I don't think I know her. I couldn't get a good look at her face."

Inside, couples were strewn all over the living room floor, most of them curled up, disheveled and passed out.

"What did they have some kind of orgy in here while we were gone?" Annie wondered, noting a condom wrapper on the floor.

From where we were standing, we could hear the unmistakable sounds of a couple in the throes of sexual dealings coming from the direction of the stairs.

"Excuse me," Annie said, stepping over the tawny-haired meathead and the girl with him. I took a deep breath and followed suit. The couple never stopped gyrating and acted as if we didn't exist. Armed with her usual kitchen utensil, Annie jimmied the lock open.

"We're living in a brothel," I announced, once we were safely inside and turning down our beds.

Annie giggled through a gaping yawn.

"Next summer, when I'm an Academy Award–winning screenwriter, I'm gonna buy us a ten-bedroom house right on the ocean just like James's," I said, pulling the covers over my head. "And we'll laugh about the times we lived at Animal House and had to crawl over couples having sex on the stairs."

It seemed like the cycle of going to sleep when the sun came up, getting up midday, going to the beach, going for a few preshift cocktails, and then coming to work would never end. Before I knew it, Annie and I were back at Spark, ready for Saturday night's mayhem. "Hey," I said, waving at one of the doormen as I walked through the entrance.

"Hey, how are you?" he said, dragging the plush red velvet rope to its rightful position and foiling any fool's plans for easy entry.

"I'm good. I was wondering if you could do me a favor," I said, producing a piece of paper from my backpack. Travis and our other housemates had been trying to get into Spark all summer, but were having trouble getting past the ropes. Earlier that morning Travis had told us he needed to get in to impress the new girl he was dating, and Annie and I had promised we'd pull some strings and get him and the rest of the guys on the guest list. "Do *not* all come together," I'd warned. "Come two guys at a time—max. And try to bring as many hot girls with you as you can. If you all show up as a big group of guys like you do at the Talkhouse, you'll never get in."

"This is a list of some of my friends," I said, handing over a piece of loose-leaf to the doorman. "Can you make sure they get in?"

He glanced down at the list. "Travis, Brian, Scott, Mike . . . these are all guys' names. You're killin' me."

"No, there's a girl on the list."

He shugged. "You know how it is," he said, handing it

back. "We can't let a group of all guys in unless they're gonna get a table and spend a lot of money."

"I know, but these are my roommates, and they've never been here before. Just put them on the list. Just once, pleeease?"

"I'll do my best," he said, reluctantly accepting the sheet of paper once more. "But no promises."

"Thanks."

I set up the front bar in record time. The doors opened at ten, and Jake hadn't even arrived yet. Just as I was doing a final beer check, I couldn't have been more shocked to see Martin Pritchard and Lily promenade into the bar. With the exception of Martin's rare summer cameos at Finton's, I hadn't spent time with either of them since that first weekend in the Hamptons, ages ago.

"Hi, guys," I said, knowing all too well how they'd gotten in. Lily was definitely attractive, in a conservative Pearls Girls sort of way, and while Martin was old and crusty, I was sure he'd liberally greased the doorman's palm.

"Hello, dear," Martin bellowed, beckoning me with his stubby right hand to lean over the bar and give him a kiss. Feeling I had no choice but to comply, I stretched across the bar and pecked him on his shriveled cheek, holding my breath to avoid his acrid, musty odor. "It's lovely to see you."

"Lovely," Lily echoed, perched on a bar stool, her posture so straight and perfect she looked like she could balance twelve books on her head.

"It's great to see you too," I said. "How've you been?"

"Fine, fine, dear," Martin answered, rubbing his protruding belly. "Just had dinner at Della Femina."

"How was it?" I asked. "I hear that's the best restaurant in the Hamptons."

"Don't believe everything you hear," he grumbled. "It's mediocre at best."

I busied myself wiping down the bottles in my speed rack, while Martin went on about how his New York strip steak had been tough and chewy, and Lily's pasta had been terribly overcooked. I looked over at Lily's infinitesimal waist, imagining that after eating one lonely strand of linguini, she announced that she was "uncomfortably full, and couldn't stand to eat another bite."

"What can I get you to drink?" I asked them.

"I'll have a Ketel tonic, and Lily would like a Ketel soda," Martin said, placing a fifty-dollar bill on the bar. "And I believe some congratulations are in order."

"Congratulations? For what?" I asked. I couldn't think of any recent accomplishments, other than perhaps my hard-earned gold medal in burning the candle at both ends.

"The word around town is that you've been having a very successful summer," Martin said, savoring his drink.

"Yeah," I answered. "Spark's been great. I'm having a lot of fun, and making a lot more money than I do at Finton's."

"I'm not talking about Spark, darling," he said, raising his grizzly eyebrows suggestively.

I looked at him uncertainly. "What *are* you talking about?"

"My sources tell me that you've landed the most eligible bachelor in the tristate area," he remarked coyly. Lily smiled down into her drink, gently stirring her straw.

I had no idea how to respond, so I nodded my head awkwardly, feeling more than a little vulnerable. While part of me was happy to know that someone in the Edmonton clan had been talking about me, rendering our relationship official, images of Martin and James Edmonton II playing golf and talking about how James Edmonton III, heir to the throne and family fortune, had taken up with a mangy barmaid instead of the prescribed socialite/heiress tortured me.

"You must be very proud," Martin continued, placidly sipping his drink. "His father says that James usually dates quite the bevy of models and actresses but seems to have eschewed them all lately in favor of you. You must have done a real number on him. Good for you."

"Yeah, well . . ." I stammered, feeling my face flush a dangerous shade of crimson. I only hoped he didn't notice my eyes sparking with resentment.

"Please excuse me while I go to the little boy's room," Martin said suddenly, sliding his stumpy body off the stool and ambling over to the restrooms.

Lily was staring into space, her eyes vacant, and I could tell she'd had a little too much to drink. I hoped I wouldn't have to make conversation with her. She sucked delicately on the little red stirrer straw until her glass was empty, then stood up unsteadily and leaned her porcelain arms on the bar. "I'd love another drink," she said.

"Sure," I said, grabbing another plastic cup.

"No plastic, please," she interjected. "Can I have a real glass?"

"Okay," I tossed the cup in the trash and bent down to where the glasses were stored.

"Thank you," she said, pulling a Chanel lip palette from her Louis Vuitton clutch and painting her lips a bold shade of red. The combination of her pallid complexion, blank eyes, auburn hair, and red lips made her look like a haunted Snow White.

I handed her another Ketel soda. "Fabulous," she said, taking a long sip.

I tried my best to occupy myself over by my register, but

soon she summoned me back over. "Cassie!" she called, interrupting my stewing over exactly how, and under what circumstances, Martin had learned about me and James.

"Yes?"

"Come here," she motioned, draping her upper body along the bar. "I need to talk to you."

I leaned in. "What is it?"

"Don't worry about what Martin said," she began, elucidating a thought for the first time since she'd arrived. "He's always saying that a young girl needs a benefactor. He's just happy for you that you've found somebody who can take care of you."

"James isn't my benefactor, Lily. He's my *boyfriend*."

She took the straw out of her glass, then put her mouth to the rim and downed half the drink. "I know what you're thinking," she slurred.

"I don't know what you're talking about," I said.

"Of *me and Martin*," she went on. "But I want you to know, we've been together for almost two years now. Did you know that?"

"No, I didn't."

"We broke up for a couple of months last summer, and I dated this man in Pacific Palisades, where my parents live. He was sweet, but he was in his mid-sixties and he still didn't have his life together . . ." Her voice trailed off.

I didn't know how to respond, so I said nothing. Apparently Martin wasn't her only lover three times her age. I started to walk away, but she called me back. "Cassie," she pressed, "don't you understand? That's what I like about Martin. He has his act together, you know?" Her eyes were glassy and expressionless. "I'm just accustomed to a certain lifestyle. I'm not going to give that up."

Just then Martin hobbled back to the bar. "What are you

little girls buzzing about?" he asked, taking a seat and placing his hand on Lily's thigh.

As the two of them sat stroking each other, I thought about all the young women in New York City who would rather have someone provide for them than go out and try to make it on their own. And the hordes of older men who were more than willing to raise their liver-spotted hands for the assignment. I couldn't really blame these women for preferring Lily's Manolo Blahniks over my ragged, flat bartending shoes that were permanently sticky on the bottoms. Still, it didn't seem like an equitable trade-off.

My mind wandered to the previous week at Finton's, when I'd been serving Sal and Vinny, two goomba "associates" of Baby Carmine. Sal was a nice, quiet guy who came into the bar maybe once a month and drank Amaretto di Saronno with one ice cube. Vinny was a chauvinistic pig who looked on lasciviously whenever I bent down to get his Beck's out of the cooler.

"Sweetheart, I'll order Beck's all night long if you keep bending over like that for me," he slobbered, pulling a fifty-dollar bill out of his gold, diamond-studded money clip and placing it on the bar. "That's for you. God bless you, honey, you got gorgeous legs."

I'd looked down at the fifty-dollar bill, wondering just how much that money was worth. He'd been slipping me big bills all night long, and while I wanted to reprove him for his lecherous comments, I found myself biting my tongue in favor of taking his money. But once the money was in my tip jar, there was a tangible shift in power. I felt like I owed him something, and he knew it.

"You give great head," he'd said with a wide grin, after I'd poured a customer a pint of beer with a lot of foam on top. Then, "Six dollars for draft beer? Does he get a blow job with that, honey?" He knew just by the mere fact that I was behind a bar that I needed money, and he was testing me to see just how much I'd put up with as long as the tips kept rolling in. In the end, I'd swallowed his comments all night. But there had been a bar between us the entire time—very different from crawling into bed with the man who furnished your lavish lifestyle.

"Darling, I'll have another Ketel tonic," Martin ordered, forcing me back to Spark and the present. I grabbed the bottle of Ketel and hastily poured his drink. The crowds were starting to trickle in, and I hoped a new wave of customers would give me an excuse to abandon Martin and Lily.

"Cassie and Jake, I need to speak to you for a moment," Shalina snapped. Jake had finally just shown up, and we hurried over to her, as she went on. "I just received a call from P. Diddy's personal assistant. She said he's on his way over and will be here any minute. Now, while he'll clearly be seated at a table in VIP, a couple of his friends may choose to order some drinks at the bar. Obviously, I need you to be extremely gracious with them. P. Diddy expects to be treated like a king, and with the amount of money he spends, he very well should be."

"No problem," Jake said, nonplussed, while I felt a surge of excitement. There were celebrities and then there were *celebrities*. I'd seen Carson Daly and Nick Carter skulking around a handful of times and hadn't been that impressed, but P. Diddy was the king of the A-listers. "We'll have the bar back stock up on Hennessy." Jake turned to me. "All they ever order is Cristal, thug passions, and incredible hulks."

"Cassie, darling." Martin was beckoning me back over.

"Excuse me," I said to Shalina, and walked back to Martin. "Yes?"

"Lily needs another drink, dear."

I glanced over at Lily, who looked like she needed a lot of things, but a drink was not one of them. I grabbed the bottle of Ketel One and poured her a very weak cocktail.

"So tell me," Martin said, "has James taken you out to his mother's home on Nantucket yet?"

James had never even mentioned that he had a mother. I'd always been too afraid to ask about her, since he never brought her up. I figured we'd get there in due time.

"Nope," I said, forcing a smile. "Not yet."

"Well, you must have him take you there. It's stunning. In the divorce settlement, James's father kept the Hamptons residence, but his mother got Nantucket. If you ask me, though, Jim got the better end of the deal. Then again, he did have Raoul Felder, the best divorce lawyer in Manhattan . . ."

Martin's ramblings were suddenly interrupted by a screech of microphone feedback and then a booming voice that yelled: "Yo! Yo! Yo! Party people at Spark!"

I looked up from my ice bin just in time to see a ghetto fabulous entourage of about fifty parade in, led by a man holding a microphone.

"I'm Doug E. Fresh and I'm gon' be your emcee tonight. Let's get this party started. Unh! Unh! Unh!" he shouted, as Run DMC came blasting out of the DJ booth.

True to all stereotypes, I was immediately blinded by all the bling. It looked like Jakob the Jeweler, the L.A.-based diamond mogul who catered to the hip-hop crowd, had personally overseen the assemblage of each and every outrageous accessory now swarming around the bar.

Gaudy diamond nameplates spelling names like Deebow, Kid Funk, and T-Money were everywhere. I caught a glimpse of a colossal gold dollar sign titivated with glinting diamonds and a similarly jewel-encrusted emblem in the shape of the Cadillac seal. Every last one of the guys had at least four huge diamond studs in his ears—stones that easily rivaled those set in the engagement rings of some of the Hamptons' richest socialites. High-end monograms—Gucci, Fendi, Chanel, Prada, Hermès, and Louis Vuitton—were emblazoned on every available surface on their clothing, and they all wore bright white sneakers. One guy was even wearing a floor-length mink, despite the 90-degree heat of the Hamptons summer.

Doug E. Fresh's voice beat-boxed over the din of the music, while the rest of the Spark crowd parted like the Red Sea to let them pass. They were a royal procession, beating a path for their king: P. Diddy. He appeared wearing the signature diamond-encrusted Sean John shades that he'd personally designed and listening to his diamond-encrusted iPod, which, according to some show I'd seen on VH1, was worth $100,000. The way Shalina, Teddy, and even Chris were watching in nervous awe, I expected one of them to genuflect and kiss the enormous canary diamond ring glimmering on his right hand like a disco ball.

"Let's all say a big wazzzzzzup to the man of the hour, P. Diddy! Unh! Unh! Oh, yeah!" bellowed Doug E. Fresh, chanting along to G. Unit's "Stunt 101," *The ice in my teeth keeps the Cristal cold.* . . .

P. Diddy waved at the crowd grandly, basking in the warmth of their admiration. Martin, however, was looking on scornfully. "These thugs are taking over the Hamptons," he muttered.

"It's horrible," Lily slurred in agreement.

"We've been trying to do something about it, but we can't

seem to get rid of them, which is exactly why we're working toward establishing Dunehampton. We need to preserve the unique feel of what the Hamptons were like before people like this could ever afford to come out here. Cassie, have you heard about Dunehampton?"

"No," I answered, thinking that if Martin had his way, the old-money residents of the Hamptons would be allowed to shoot the "other" people trying to get in, just as they might take out a pesky deer in their oceanfront backyards.

"One town councilman had the nerve to call it 'Richampton' when they rejected our petition," he went on, "but we're not giving up. We're going to keep fighting the town until they let us incorporate. Then we'd have voting rights. The bottom line is that most people would prefer *not* to be accosted by a booming microphone and out-of-control behavior. Let's face facts, these people would rather buy their 'bling-bling' than feed their children. Is that the kind of people we want running around the Hamptons?"

I took a deep breath and held my tongue, but inside I wanted to throttle him. Here he was, running around, hosting orgies at his house, and yet he considered himself superior and his own morally dubious behavior acceptable simply because he came from old money. In fact, he was just as fucked up as anyone I'd ever met. The hypocrisy was so thick I felt like I could tie it around his neck and choke him with it.

"Excuse me, miss," a member of P. Diddy's entourage said, disrupting Martin's sermon. He was wearing a Kareem Abdul-Jabbar throwback jersey and a thick gold chain bearing a diamond Mercedes-Benz symbol. He wore his Gucci monogram baseball hat with a gangsta' tilt, so that only one of his big brown eyes was visible.

"Yes?" I said.

"Can I buy bottles of champagne at the bar?"

"Of course."

"Can I get four magnums of Cristal?"

I fought the urge to gape at his request. Magnums of Cristal sold for a grand each. "That'll be four thousand dollars," I told him.

He reached into his pocket and took out the thickest wad of hundreds I'd ever seen, held together by a rubber band. He counted out fifty of them. "There you go," he said, with a wink.

I did the quick math. A $1,000 tip! By far the biggest tip I'd ever gotten. Not to mention that my ring would definitely exceed Jake's with a single sale of $4,000. I looked forward to Teddy's reaction when we closed out.

"Thank you so much!" I exclaimed, glancing over at Martin, certain he'd be grousing to Lily about his distaste for the flagrant displays of wealth perpetuated by the nouveaux riches. But it seemed my new clientele's presence had been too much for him—he and Lily were nowhere to be seen, though I noticed they'd left a $5 tip for me tucked under Martin's empty glass.

I pulled four oversized champagne buckets from beneath the bar and filled them with ice, lining them up in front of me next to a multitude of polished champagne flutes. I gathered some cloth napkins together and wrapped them around the neck of each bottle, then reached for the first one to open it. But the customer grabbed it out of my hand with a flourish.

"I'll get that," he said. "I like to open them myself." He expertly popped open the top and slowly poured the first glass at a side angle. He poured another, then handed one to me. "This is for you."

He rammed his glass into mine. "Cheers." The champagne fizzed as our glasses collided and spilled out of the flutes and onto the bar. I brought my lips to the glass and savored the delicate bubbles. I would never get over the thrill of drinking champagne that cost more than my rent.

I contemplated that the hip-hop personalities in the Hamptons really did epitomize what it meant to be nouveau riche. A lot of them had grown up impoverished in the ghetto and were now dripping with cash and Cristal. I looked around at all the diamonds and name brands they were wearing, thinking they must swathe themselves in status symbols to make up for their humble beginnings. Then, thinking back to when I'd tried on the string of pearls in Tiffany, I realized that I wasn't much different. The second I had a little disposable income, I ran to the extravagant stores on Main Street to drape myself in expensive clothes and accessories, trying to impress James and the Pearls Girls. The main difference was that I couldn't really afford it. In the Hamptons and New York, it was nearly impossible not to fall into the consumption trap.

Drink orders were flying left and right, so I multitasked, sipping my champagne while shaking cosmos for two hootchie mamas wearing golden glittering pasties and Daisy Duke jeans shorts—hangers-on of P. Diddy and his entourage. Before long James and *his* entourage of Tom, Glen, and the Pearls Girls made their way up to the bar, a surreal parody of P. Diddy's group. When it came right down to it, the Botkier bags and Carolina Herrera ensembles sported by the old-money socialite set were interchangeable with the more overtly labeled attire of P. Diddy and his crew. A diamond and platinum watch from Cartier or a $300,000 ice-encrusted watch from Jakob the Jeweler's—what was really separating them, except for taste? Except that, unlike the rappers, the old-money set didn't generally feel the need to broadcast flashy monograms. Doug E. Fresh was still thumping "Unh! Unh! Unh!" and I smiled, thinking there was something highly amusing about seeing Rosalind and her friends climbing the stairs to a soundtrack of Biggie, who appropriately proclaimed, *Damn right I like the life I live 'cause I went from negative to positive . . .*

"Hey!" James said as he walked up to the bar. He was wearing yet another moniker of status—a perfect golden tan from a long day on the golf course.

"Hey, baby!" I said, leaning over the bar to kiss him. "Are you guys gonna hang out down here tonight?"

"No." James sighed. "It's Rosalind's little sister's twenty-first birthday, and they have a table reserved upstairs."

"Okay. Have fun!" I called after him, trying to sound positive, but feeling a tinge of jealousy as they were seated at a table right next to P. Diddy's contingent. A few minutes later I saw Elsie bring them identical magnums of Cristal.

My own champagne glass was empty, and I needed another drink. "Jake, are we allowed to drink champagne?"

"Of course not," he answered, laughing. "But we're not allowed to drink Patrón either, so who cares. As long as you don't get caught, you're fine."

"I know, but they must keep track of the good champagne, and I don't feel like drinking the cheap stuff."

"So the Virgin Mary wants to steal a bottle of Veuve, is that what I'm hearing?"

"No!" I protested, looking around to make sure Shalina and Teddy hadn't overheard Jake's accusation.

"Relax, I don't care. I'll split a bottle with you. We work hard. We deserve it."

"Okay, but won't they realize a bottle is missing when they do inventory?"

"You'd be surprised, babe. This place is run so bad. They don't keep track of anything."

Minutes later Jake and I were raising our Veuve Clicquot, which we'd disguised as ginger ale by drinking it out of plastic cups, in a toast.

After another hour or so had passed, there was a brief lull in the crowd packed around the bar, so I took the opportunity to check my cell phone. I had ten missed calls from Travis. Without even listening to the messages, I knew he was calling because he was standing outside and the doorman wasn't letting him in.

"I'll be right back," I said to Jake.

I ducked under the bar and pushed my way through the crowd until I arrived outside at the velvet ropes. I scanned the masses of people waiting to get in, all screaming about how they knew "so and so" and should be granted access. Travis and the guys were nowhere in sight.

"Hey, what happened with my friends?" I asked the doorman, fighting through the bottleneck of relieved recipients of the vaunted Spark plastic admission bracelet who were clustered around the doorway.

"I did everything I could, but Shalina was at the front, and she wouldn't let them in. Sorry."

"That's okay. It's not your fault," I sighed.

I scanned the crowd one final time, and as I did so, my eyes landed on the man in the Gucci baseball hat who'd bought the four magnums of Cristal. He was standing next to a white limo Humvee idling in front of the ropes.

"Are you ready?" I heard him say to two of his friends as they all shook up their bottles of champagne.

"What are they doing?" I asked the doorman.

Before he could answer, they all burst their champagne

open with a loud *POP!* and, pressing their thumbs up against the mouths of the bottles, sprayed each other with the $1,000 foam, laughing uproariously the whole time and attracting a huge crowd of spectators. Champagne splashed across the entrance and the onlookers, who cheered as the sweet fizz landed on their faces and their clothes.

"Holy shit!" I cried. "They just paid thousands of dollars for that champagne, and now they're spraying each other with it!" Covered in the bubbles, I laughed to myself that it was the most expensive thing I ever wore.

"That's the Hamptons for you," the doorman chuckled.

Back inside, I poured myself a third glass of champagne and set about fielding drink orders. Soon the Veuve was gone, and I was drunk. I felt sexy and sparkling and full of life. I decided that I needed to see James immediately.

"Jake, I'll be right back," I promised. Normally, I would've been worried about taking a break at all, but that night, after selling $4,000 worth of champagne, I felt confident that I was keeping up with Jake and the pressure to "sell, sell, sell" was dramatically reduced.

I fought my way through the dancing bodies, past the VIP ropes, up the stairs, and into what many might have considered the most privileged social scene in the western world. The anthropological significance of P. Diddy and his entourage beside James and his posse was just too delicious to overlook.

"Hey, what are you doing up here?" James said when I grabbed his arm and pulled him to his feet.

"Come with me," I said, smiling and giving him my best bedroom eyes. I could almost feel champagne bubbles bouncing against the libidinal zone of my brain, and I already knew I'd definitely feel them the next morning—that's the funny thing about champagne—you get a hangover while you drink it. Plus, I couldn't resist flaunting my prize a little—here was this gorgeous man sipping Cristal in VIP, and he was all mine. He thought I was refreshing and beautiful and a brilliant screenwriter. And Rosalind and the rest of the girls could eat their hearts out.

"Where are we going?" he asked.

"There's a secret bathroom," I whispered, looking around like a spy. I dragged him through the VIP area and into the vestibule that housed the office, which was empty, and the employee bathroom. Shutting the bathroom door behind me, I pushed him up against the wall and, taking his face in my hands, kissed him. I started unbuttoning his shirt, my lips moving down his chest.

"Wow!" he breathed. "What's gotten into you?"

I was unbuckling his belt when Teddy burst through the door.

"Oh my God!" I shrieked.

"Oh, ah . . . sorry, guys." Teddy backed away and closed the door behind him.

I turned to James, who was standing there with his shirt open, flushed. "Who was that guy?"

"He's sort of my boss," I said sheepishly, suddenly sober. "I guess I should get back to work." I straightened my halter top and gave James a final kiss.

"We'll have to pick up where we left off later," he said, grinning suggestively and tucking my hair behind my ear. I followed him back outside into VIP, where I walked right into Teddy.

"Well, I guess we're even," he said, smirking.

"Guess so," I said, briefly musing that in the bizzare world of bartending, getting busted hooking up in the bathroom during a shift was perfectly permissible.

I cast one last look at the scene in VIP, then I almost did

a double-take when I saw Elsie, shirtless, straddling P. Diddy while his entourage looked on appreciatively. Wearing only a transparent pink lace bra, she had one arm around his neck and was pulsing up and down on his lap. P. Diddy couldn't have appeared less interested as he gazed over her shoulder out onto the crowd.

"What is this, Scores?" I remarked to Teddy, referencing the famed strip club in Manhattan known for its "high-end" clientele like Howard Stern.

"What can I say?" he shrugged. "These girls know how to work it. That's how they make their money."

Back downstairs, I quickly slid behind the bar. Jake was rummaging through the tip jar.

"Jesus, there's a lot of money in here," he said, his eyes fixated on the folded stack of hundred-dollar bills.

"Well, that guy who bought the Cristal tipped me a thousand dollars," I said.

"Cassie, this is insane," he said, almost shaking with pleasure. "We're gonna make sick money tonight. You know, you're the only one I pool with."

"What do you mean?" I asked.

"You're the only one I share my money with, because you're the only one here who knows how to hustle."

"But I thought we *had* to pool."

"We're supposed to, but if somebody gives me a hundred-dollar tip, I'm not gonna throw it in the tip jar and share it. Everything bigger than a twenty, I keep."

"Well, that sucks, Jake. I share all my tips," I said, growing angry thinking of all the money I could have made if I'd kept my bigger tips to myself.

"You didn't pool all your money with Kyle when you worked the back bar, did you?"

I could feel my face go red. I felt like an idiot. "Yes, I did."

Jake laughed incredulously. "How could you share your money with that dipshit?"

"Because that's what I was told to do," I snapped.

"Sometimes you gotta bend the rules," he said plainly, "and look out for yourself."

For the rest of the night, I watched Jake like a hawk, making sure he deposited all of his tips into the tip jar. But my closer scrutiny revealed more than I bargained for.

"That'll be sixty-five dollars," he said to a customer.

The man handed him four twenties and said, "Keep the change."

Jake threw the entire $80 in the tip jar. No wonder I always made more money with Jake. Not only was he the fastest bartender in the Hamptons, he was also a rabid thief. Later on I saw him take $100 from a customer and then bend down pretending to tie his shoes, while he slipped the money into his sock.

"Hey, beautiful," James said a little after four, just as the bouncers were starting to usher everyone out of the club. "I'm gonna go get something to eat with these guys at the Princess Diner in Southampton. I'll come back around five-thirty and pick you up."

"Okay," I said, coming out from behind the bar to wrap my arms around him. He pulled me into his chest and nuzzled my neck.

"Will you stay at my place tonight?" he asked.

"Absolutely," I said, kissing him again. Teddy apparently knew what he was doing—secret trysts in the employee bathroom really got a person in the mood. Though we had hooked up plenty of times on the beach at sunrise, we still hadn't had sex, and I had yet to spend the night at his house. It wasn't like I didn't want to sleep with him. But my crazy hours had made it tough to find long stretches of time alone together, and truth be told, the old-fashioned romantic in me was enjoying taking it slow. I liked the fact that he respected me. Especially given all the casual sex and debauchery that I saw firsthand all around me.

"I'll see you in a little bit," he whispered, kissing me again.

I bundled up my money, grabbed a beer, and settled in a booth to start counting out the tips. Elsie, who had finally put her shirt back on, was following a man in a bright turquoise, short-sleeved, silk button-down who looked like a shorter version of Antonio Banderas, through the club toward the exit.

"So I'll call you this week," she said. Then she jumped up on him, wrapping her arms and her legs around his body and kissing him long and hard on the mouth. "Do you promise to come back next weekend?" she asked in a whiny baby voice, jutting her full lower lip out into a pout. "I'm gonna miss you."

"Yeah, I'll be back next Saturday," the guy said before patting her on the ass and exiting the club. Elsie walked over to a table, where she immediately threw a sweatshirt on over her tank top and pulled sweatpants on under her miniskirt.

"Who was that?" I asked curiously.

"He's just some customer," she said, lighting a cigarette.

"Oh. I thought maybe he was your boyfriend," I teased.

Elsie snorted with laughter. "Are you fucking kidding me? I'd never date that loser."

"Then why did you say you'd miss him?"

"Because I want him to come back next weekend and sit in my section. He had a five-thousand-dollar tab, and he left me a huge tip. Most of these guys with money are such douche bags. If you give them a little attention, they'll give you all their cash."

I couldn't see how making out with a customer and giving him her phone number constituted "a little attention," but then again, I wasn't really one to talk. While I never gave out lap dances, I knew by this time that I was a lot more successful behind the bar when I flirted with men and women alike. As usual when I hopped on board this train of thought, I couldn't help thinking back to Dan Finton. I wondered what the perks might include if I actually gave him everything he wanted. Not that that was a viable option.

"So you must have done really well tonight," I said. I couldn't even begin to imagine how much P. Diddy and his entourage left her.

"Yeah, I did amazing. Cocktailing in the Hamptons is by far the most money you can make with your clothes on."

You didn't keep your clothes on, I thought. But I didn't say it.

Twelve

SEX ON
THE BEACH

I peeled my sweaty lower back off the black leather seat of James's Range Rover and settled in for what could easily be a forty-five-minute drive from his house to Animal House, even though the journey was little over a mile. On summer weekends, Montauk Highway was a never-ending snake of luxury SUVs with mountain bikes and kayaks bungee-corded on top. We drove down Hands Path where parents were loading kids, beach toys, umbrellas, towels, blankets, coolers, boogie boards, and Frisbees into Land Rovers bearing the coveted town beach pass stickers that allowed you to park a mere few feet away from the dunes and avoid the long schlep that we always had to make from our house. Looking out the window in my sleepy haze, I felt like I was viewing a silent movie.

"I swear this intersection is busier than any intersection in Manhattan," James said, bringing me back to earth and the heavily air-conditioned interior of the car, as he slowly crept up behind a yellow Lamborghini Spider. "I've been trying to make a left for twenty minutes. They should put a traffic light here."

I tried to imagine what a traffic light would look like in the heart of charming Amagansett. The quaint country town looked like the backdrop to *Little House on the Prairie,* and I was sure the summer residents would shun a run-of-the-mill traffic light that would mar the village's old-fashioned ambiance.

"Hey, are you okay?" James asked as he reached over and smoothed my hair with his hand. "You're quiet."

"I'm fine," I said. "Just a little tired." This wasn't a lie exactly. I hadn't gotten a good night's sleep since before Memorial Day.

"You sure?"

"I'm okay, I just want to get home. I still have my clothes on from last night and I need to shower." I looked down at my stained and smelly Spark uniform. My hair, which the night before had been a perfectly tousled mix of ocean air and KMS Beach Head hairspray (made with genuine salt water), now looked more like a nest of seaweed. I felt disgusting.

And there was another reason for my reticence. The night before, after James had picked me up from work, we went back to his house. Our steamy bathroom hook-up had provided the perfect overture, and we'd finally consummated our relationship.

I know I'm pregnant, I thought, as James crept up another inch behind the Lamborghini. We'd used a condom, but the nuns at my high school had ingrained in me that some sort of punishment would immediately follow an act of premarital sex.

"Finally!" James huffed, as the Spider peeled out and took a sharp turn off to the left. Impatiently James snuck out behind him, cutting off a Lexus SUV and causing its driver to flip us off.

I looked over at James's handsome profile and wondered why I felt so conflicted and weird. The sex with James had been amazing, by far the best I'd ever had in my relatively short sex life. I'd made a mental note of all the little details I had to tell Annie—finally *I* had something to share. He didn't balk when I asked him to use a condom, and he certainly seemed to care more about my pleasure than his own. He was textbook perfect afterward too, snuggling naked with me and whispering in my ear about how beautiful I was and how much he cared about me. I was in heaven.

But then I'd woken up with my usual early-morning anxiety—I haven't written for days, I have to work tonight, I ate two cheeseburgers yesterday, I just had sex with the boy I hope to marry—and immediately felt like something was wrong between us. I was pretty sure it was all in my head, but I couldn't help feeling like a lost puppy as we drove along the back roads of East Hampton. He was obliviously singing along as Tom Petty played on 104.7 The Wolf. I looked in the mirror and swiped at last night's makeup still crusted under my eyes.

"Hey, do you want to stop at the Farmer's Market for coffee?" he asked.

"Actually I don't drink coffee, only tea," I said, my mind spinning a neurotic diatribe: If you knew me at all, you would know that. How could we have just slept together and you don't even know that coffee makes me ill?

I sat in stony silence for the rest of the ride. I knew I was overreacting, but I couldn't help it. Having sex was a fairly big deal and I was hungry for reassurance. Was he taking me for granted? I'd been hoping to spend the day with him, but he'd rushed out of bed, saying he had to get ready for some benefit that evening that "everyone" was going to, and he hadn't even invited me along. True, he knew I had to work that night, but he could've at least *invited* me. I wondered how many girls he'd had sex with. Given his bedroom skills, there must have been thousands. Was he on the verge of breaking up with me? I hated him.

It was a little after twelve when we finally pulled into the driveway of Animal House. As usual, a couple of meatheads who'd been too lazy to walk to the ocean had set up a cooler of beers and some beach chairs on our lawn. In between them was a growing pile of empty Miller Genuine Draft bottles, indicating that Miller had been on sale at the IGA.

"Are you sure you're okay?" James asked, putting the car in park.

"I'm fine. I promise," I said, forcing a smile.

"You seem pensive."

"I'm just tired. I think I'm gonna try to take a nap before work."

"Okay." He leaned over and kissed me on my forehead.

"Are you going to stop by Spark tonight?" I asked.

"I can't. I have that benefit for Sloan Kettering at Shinnecock Hills, remember?"

"Well, maybe you could swing by after?"

"Maybe, but it's all the way in Southampton, and I have a feeling there's going to be a lot of boozing going on. I'll probably end up staying overnight."

"Where would you stay?"

"Some friends of mine from Yale have a house right on the golf course, and I haven't seen them in a while. I might play golf with them tomorrow morning. And if that doesn't work out I can always crash at Rosalind's uncle's house."

"Okay," I said, trying to sound laid-back. But in reality I felt like reaching over and ripping his face off. So you'd rather spend the night with Rosalind and the Pearls Girls than with me? Fine. I'll show you. You know how many men would die to have a girl like me?

I had started sliding down the slippery slope of neediness, and I wanted him to leave before I said something I'd regret. It was remarkable how the aftermath of sex with someone you really cared about could be so psychologically turbulent. When we'd gone to sleep, I'd felt so comfortable and close to him. But now that we were parting ways and resuming our everyday lives, I felt as though I were being abandoned. I chastised myself—he was going to a charity event to benefit kids with leukemia, for Christ's sake. It wasn't like he was forsaking me to spend the evening at some strip club.

I slammed the passenger door shut, and his tires crunched on the gravel as he slowly backed out of the driveway. "Cassie!" he called out his window.

"Yeah?"

"Don't forget, we're having brunch with my father tomorrow at the club."

"I know," I said. In reality, I'd been purposefully blocking it out of my mind all week, trying not to let my imagination run wild. In a nutshell, I was terrified of his father, and had been ever since he'd been so rude to me at Finton's. "What time are you picking me up?"

"Ten forty-five. Brunch is at eleven sharp, because my dad has to get back into the city early."

"Okay, I'll see you then."

James slowly pulled away from the house and inched back into the traffic.

"What's up, Cassie?" the meatheads called as they shoveled Cheetos into their orange-dust—encrusted mouths. I was pretty sure there names were Todd and Brad and that they'd been at the house a couple of times before. Each had his own family-size bag, and they reminded me of two donkeys feasting on giant feed bags.

"Hey, guys," I said, traversing the lawn. The grass was warm in the noonday sun.

"Want a beer?" one of them asked, dipping his chubby forearm into the cooler.

"No, thanks," I said, climbing up onto the porch. The rickety wooden stairs creaked under my flip-flops.

"Hey, Cass," I heard someone else call.

I shielded my eyes from the sun with my hand and saw Travis nestled in the chaise I'd used as a bed on Memorial Day, with the same petite blond girl Annie and I'd caught him making out with. She was wearing a short pleated tennis skirt and a pale yellow cable-knit cashmere sweater with a pink Polo icon on it.

"Hey," I said, walking up to them.

"Hi!" Travis's warm smile took the edge off my anxiety. "Cassie, this is . . ."

"Camilla Claremont," the girl said with all the airs of Camilla Parker Bowles. She stretched out her toned arm, offering me a dainty hand complete with a perfect French manicure and a slender wrist decorated by a diamond Tiffany cocktail watch. Travis was still in his boxers and a T-shirt. Evidence of another sleepover.

"It's nice to meet you," I said. "I'm Cassie."

"I know, Travis told me all about you," she said. "You work at Spark and you're a writer, right?"

"Well, more like an aspiring writer," I said ruefully. "And yes, I do work at Spark."

"Well, that's certainly the place to be this summer," she said authoritatively.

"Yeah, it's been really fun," I said. I had to admit that I enjoyed the little boost of coolness Spark gave me.

"I'm surprised I haven't met you before. You have a share here too, right?" I detected a faint whiff of a southern accent—a kind of WASPy drawl.

"Cassie doesn't stay here any more now that she can sleep at her boyfriend's mansion," Travis joked.

"That's not true," I said. And then turning to Camilla: "As you can imagine, there aren't exactly enough beds here for all of us . . ."

"Ew! I know. This place is so overcrowded and disgusting," she said, making a sour face.

While I would normally have been the first to call the place revolting, I found myself feeling insulted. What right did she have to speak that way about my house?

"It's not that bad," I said.

"Come on, Cammie, you love it here," Travis teased, grabbing her tiny waist and pressing her against him. She extended her neck to kiss him on the cheek, and a string of pearls peeked out from beneath her yellow cashmere to catch the light of the afternoon sun. I fought the urge to roll my eyes. I was beginning to think that Pearls Girls could be added to the list of local exports along with wheat, peaches, corn, and strawberries. They sure seemed to thrive in the Hamptons climate.

"So how is the mysterious James?" Travis asked.

"He's fine."

"Not James *Edmonton*?" Camilla perked up.

Oh, no, I thought. Camilla had slept with him too. I was just another notch on his Gucci belt. "Yeah."

"Oh my God! James and my cousin Rosalind are like *so* close! I'm sure you've met her before, she's tall, blond, completely gorgeous . . ."

"Yes, I've met her," I said, cutting her off.

"My uncle Stuart, Rosalind's father, and James's father have been trying to get those two together forever! The family joke is that they've been engaged since birth!"

I'd heard enough. If I wasn't already annoyed enough with James, I really hated him now. "I'm gonna go upstairs to take a nap." I scowled.

"It was a pleasure meeting you," she cooed.

Even though she'd inadvertently offended me, I had to admit that Camilla looked perfectly at home in Travis's arms, snuggling in the chaise, and as I opened the screen door, a small green-eyed monster crept up behind me. I couldn't believe it was "the morning after," and James was off to a glamorous event with "everyone" but me, while these two were probably going to spend the whole day together. I walked through the house, stepping over piles of sand that looked like little ant hills, empty beer bottles, beef jerky wrappers, cigarette butts, and a tiny bag of weed, all the while questioning how salt-of-the-earth Travis had ever gotten involved with a Pearls Girl.

So you finally gave it up. Thank God!" Annie said later that afternoon. She was reclining on one of the mildewed lounge chairs on the porch of Animal House and sipping a cappuccino from the Farmer's Market. "How was it?" she asked gleefully. "I want to hear every detail."

"It was good," I said with a sheepish smile.

"Good? You're going to have to do better than that. And don't tell me you were in the missionary position, or I'll kill you."

"Actually, I was in several positions."

"You slut!" Annie yelled, and we both collapsed laughing.

"Heads up, girls!" Travis called out just before a football came spiraling toward my head. I ducked just in time, and the football sailed past me and knocked over Annie's cappuccino. "Whoops, sorry!"

Annie picked up the overturned cup and threw it at Travis. "You owe me five ninety-five!" she joked. "Coffee's not cheap in this town."

"Nothing's cheap in this town," Travis agreed. "I took Camilla to Jean-Luc last night and spent three bills on dinner. Now I can't eat for the rest of the week." He grabbed the football and sprinted back out to the lawn to join the rest of his shirtless posse.

Travis's comment made me realize with a start how far my life had deviated since the beginning of the summer. I used to scrimp and save just to eat Kraft mac and cheese in my tiny apartment—and now was set to have brunch at the Maidstone Country Club with my wealthy boyfriend. Maybe Lily and I had more in common than I thought.

Cassie, shut off your alarm," an irritated Annie grumbled from under her covers the following morning.

Sleepily I kicked the sheet off my tanned legs and sat up.

My head was pounding, my ears were ringing, my lower back burned, my lungs ached, and I had a severe case of cotton mouth—all the symptoms I'd come to associate with a morning after working at Spark. This morning, however, I had an added cause for anxiety: the dreaded brunch with James's father.

The previous night had been a blur. "I was in Vegas all week and I haven't slept in five days," Jake had boasted as soon as he walked in the door. His face was as gray as the ash at the bottom of the ancient hibachi at Animal House, and his eyes were rimmed with huge dark rings. Even his lips seemed to have been drained of all color. He looked like a crack addict with sickle cell anemia.

"Doesn't your body go to sleep on its own? I read a study that said the brain just shuts down or something. I mean, don't you *need* sleep?" I'd asked, fascinated.

"Yeah, idiot, most people do need sleep," he said. "But not when you're the Jake Man."

I decided to ignore him for the rest of the night, save for the twenty or so Patrón shots we did together, starting at about ten. Jake had warned me at the onset that he needed to get really drunk—probably because it was the only way he could come down from all the chemicals I imagined were careening through his veins.

I kept checking my cell phone, but James never called me and didn't make a Spark appearance. He'd told me that would probably be the case, but I was still disappointed. As I turned out what felt like millions of drinks, I pondered everything I was feeling about him. It was the mark of an experienced bartender: after all these weeks, I could finally hustle and "bang it out" while actually thinking about other things besides the ingredients in a margarita.

Around four he'd sent me a text message: "I miss you."

My heart warmed, and I'd decided right then and there to relax about the whole thing. James was crazy about me, and I was just plain crazy. Annie and I had arrived back at Animal House a little after six and, after removing a jock strap from our locked bedroom doorknob, had promptly passed out.

The alarm sounded again, and I turned it off. I crunched over stale tortilla chips in the hallway on my way to the bathroom. The one good thing about being up at the ungodly hour of 10:00 A.M. on a Sunday was that you could rest assured the bathroom would be free. Unless, of course, someone was passed out in the tub.

I turned on the water, stripped down, and looked at myself in the mirror. Truth be told, I didn't look much better than Jake. My face was pasty, and my cheeks were sunken in. Dark circles swathed my eyes, and my body looked bloated from another night of excessive drinking. My stomach roiled. I couldn't tell if the turmoil was from the shots or the anticipation of sitting with Mr. Edmonton for two hours and trying to find some common ground. James was picking me up in less than an hour to take me to the Maidstone, the most exclusive country club in the Hamptons, and I looked like I hadn't slept or eaten a vegetable since before the war.

As the warm water trickled down my face, I reflected on the conversation I'd had with Alexis only the day before, when she'd called me on my way to work.

"Cass, I'm a little worried about you," she'd said. "You seem so frazzled and burned out lately. What's going on?"

"I don't know. I think this whole lifestyle's just wearing me down. I'm exhausted. It's really hard to keep up, and then on top of all of it, I slept with James . . ."

"Well, that's great! You really like him, right?"

"I know. But now I have to go to Planned Parenthood,

because I want to go on the pill, and I don't have health insurance. I just sometimes wish that I had a normal job, so I could go to a normal doctor like a normal person instead of the ghetto gyno all the way in Brooklyn."

"But you have the best job in the world! You go to the beach during the day, you get to meet celebrities at night, and you have this amazing boyfriend who's practically New York royalty . . ."

"I know," I'd said. "I think I just want to know that I'm on some other path. I don't want to be a bartender for the rest of my life."

"Cassie. You're *not* going to be a bartender for the rest of your life. I think you're being a little dramatic. You've only been bartending for a few months."

"But there's no end in sight. And a lot of the people I work with are way older than me and they're still bartending. The money is kind of addictive, Lex, and then you start spending and it goes so quickly that you feel like you need more and more. I'm so afraid I'm always going to be a bartender."

"That won't happen," she'd said confidently. "You're a writer, Cass, *not* a bartender. At the moment you have to bartend to pay the bills, but so what? And you're having so much fun, right?"

I'd almost burst into tears. "I guess, but it's all so overwhelming." The floodgates opened: "Rosalind and those stupid girls are such bitches to me, so I bought a thousand-dollar dress to impress then, and they didn't even see it, and my credit cards are maxed out, and I have brunch with James's dad tomorrow, and he hates me."

"Okay, slow down," Alexis soothed. "Nobody hates you. His dad is probably like mine, just really busy so he comes off kind of gruff."

"I don't know, Lex," I'd replied. "When he came into Finton's he barely said two words to me."

"So what? You're not dating his dad. You're dating him, and he seems to really care about you. And those girls are just jealous."

During our conversation, I'd felt the first twinge of excitement over moving back to New York in September. I missed spending time with my best friend. She could always put things in perspective.

After a quick shower, I wrapped a towel around my torso and trudged back to our room to tackle a new predicament: what to wear. My mom had always told me that when in doubt, go dressy and classic. Unfortunately, between Annie's and my paltry selections, there wasn't anything dressy *or* classic. The day before Annie had agreed to lend me her white eyelet dress, but I worried it was too short. I put on her small CZ earrings, squelching all thoughts of running out to Tiffany and blowing last night's $594 on the pearl choker I'd tried on earlier in the summer, slipped on tasteful Ann Taylor kitten heels—my sole pair of "grown-up" shoes—and went to work applying some color to my face.

When I'd finished my makeup, I looked down woefully at my ragged nails and wished I had thought earlier to get a manicure. It was impossible to keep your nails looking decent when you worked as a bartender. I'd have to remember to keep my hands in my lap. I picked up my beige clutch and walked down the rickety stairs.

"You look beautiful," James said brightly when I opened the screen door and stepped out onto the porch. He pulled me close to him and kissed me. "I missed you last night."

"I missed you too," I said, all of yesterday's neuroses evaporating in the warm sun.

"Are you ready?" he asked.

"Yes, I'm starving," I said, thinking that a hearty brunch would help combat my hangover and set me straight. I'd heard that the Maidstone was leagues more sophisticated than the Southampton Country Club and couldn't wait to see the spread that was awaiting me.

It would my first time at the Maidstone, which *Hamptons* magazine rated #1 on the list of the hardest places to get in to on the East End (Spark was #5 on the list, directly between Nick and Toni's and Della Femina), and Page Six had cited the club as one of the most exclusive in the world. Allegedly there was a twenty-year waiting list to become a member; membership status was a privilege you had to either be born into or wait half your life for. While other Hamptons country clubs, like the Atlantic, had insanely high initiation fees (seven figures), the Maidstone's membership fee was relatively low ($200,000)—obviously it was the admissions process itself, not the dues, that kept people out.

James avoided Montauk Highway, taking the back roads whenever possible. We finally pulled onto Further Lane and continued on past his driveway until the large clubhouse loomed in the distance, enveloped by the lush emerald green of the golf course. At the beginning of the driveway, a giant white wooden sign marked PRIVATE warned nonmembers not to go any further. When we arrived in the parking lot, I noticed that each spot had a member's named stenciled on it. James maneuvered his Range Rover into the spot marked "J. Edmonton III."

As we walked from the parking lot to the clubhouse, James waved and smiled at the people we passed, all of whom seemed to know each other: little girls in damp bathing suits, men in golf carts, women in perfectly pressed pants and Polo shirts on their way out to the first hole. A small tree-lined passageway led us into the outdoor part of the club—which housed its vast pool and 150 or so cabanas (also with names stenciled on the doors).

"Over there on the lawn is where they used to have high tea during the summer," James said, pointing south toward the ocean.

"Where are the tennis courts?" I asked, rather impressed with myself for knowing that it was also a tennis club.

"They're at another location. I'll take you there later if you want. It's mostly lawn tennis, but we have two clay courts."

"I don't think I've ever seen a lawn court," I said.

"It's very British," he replied.

"Oh."

James smiled and squeezed my hand. "The Maidstone has a lot of British heritage. It's named after a small city on the coast outside of London. Apparently a lot of the early settlers in the Hamptons were from there."

We walked in the front door of the clubhouse and passed a small sitting room where two older women in wide-brimmed hats were sipping tea. Borrowed British culture was ubiquitous in the Hamptons, I reflected: polo matches, high tea, lawn tennis. If the Hamptons were a replica of England, I decided, then the Maidstone was Buckingham Palace.

We walked up the polished mahogany grand staircase to the dining room. Nervously I scanned the room for James's father.

"Good day, Mr. Edmonton," said a rotund, mustached man in a green suit jacket that made him look like he'd just won the Masters Golf Tournament.

"How are you, Roger?" James said. "This is my girl-friend, Cassie."

"It's a pleasure to meet you, miss," Roger said, bowing his head.

"Roger is the general manager of the Maidstone," James explained. Then he turned back to Roger. "Is my father here yet?"

"No, sir, he's not. Why don't you and Cassie have a seat at the bar, and I'll seat you at your table when your father arrives."

We left the dining room and walked to the bar, where I settled on a stool. (Funny how I already felt less anxious now that I was in familiar surroundings.) I took a deep breath and looked around. Everywhere I turned I saw spectacular views of the ocean.

"Cass, I'm going to run to the bathroom. Will you be okay here for a minute?" James asked, brushing a stray hair out of my eyes and momentarily warming my icy hands when he held them briefly in his.

"Sure." I smiled.

"Can I get you a drink, miss?" the bartender asked. He was at least sixty years old and, like Roger, wore a green suit jacket.

"Hi," I said cheerfully. "How are you?"

"Fine," he replied tersely. "Would you like something to drink?"

"Uh . . . yes, please. Do you have Pinot Noir by the glass?"

"Certainly," he said curtly, furnishing a glass. I decided that he probably wasn't allowed to delve into personal conversations with the patrons. As I'd once overheard Martin Pritchard say, the best servants are invisible—you shouldn't even know they're there.

Billy had once told me about the time he'd trained for a job at the Soho House, a highly exclusive, invitation-only, private club in Manhattan based on the London club of the same name. "I trained there for one shift," he'd said. "It was fucking hell. You're not allowed to use the front entrance. You have to walk up seven flights of stairs—because you're not allowed to use the same elevator as the guests—and you can't use the bathrooms. If you have an emergency, you have to walk up another three flights and use this disgusting toilet in the stockroom. You're barely allowed to look at the customers, and are allowed to talk to them only if you're taking drink orders. You're not even allowed to go near the place on your nights off, because you're 'the help.' "

I looked up from my glass of wine to see Mr. Edmonton in all his fit, silver-haired glory, striding up the stairs and heading in my direction. My first panicked thought was, Where the hell is James? but I quickly got control of myself and slid off my stool, doing my best to paste a warm, welcoming smile on my face.

"Hi, Mr. Edmonton, it's nice to see—"

"Ed Hollinger, how the hell are you?" he asked, completely bypassing me and clapping a middle-aged man seated behind me on the back.

"Great, Jim, good to see you . . ." The small talk continued and my face burned in mortification. I was sure everyone had seen him ignore me. I wondered if he had done it on purpose but decided that was just too cruel. Was it possible that he didn't remember meeting me at Finton's? He was one of the richest lawyers in New York City, and I was willing to bet he had a pretty sharp mind. I sat there stewing until I saw James walking back toward the bar. I wanted him to hurry up and rescue me.

"Cass, did you say hi to my dad?" he asked, looking at the back of his father's pressed golf sweater, confused. At the sound of his son's voice, Mr. Edmonton turned around.

"Hello, Dad," James said formally, offering his hand to his father. "Didn't you see Cassie? She was standing right here next to you."

"I must not have noticed," he said coolly. "Why didn't she say something?"

"Oh, I'm sorry, Mr. Edmonton, you were in the middle of a conversation, and I didn't want to interrupt—"

"Roger!" Mr. Edmonton cut me off, snapping his fingers in the air. "Is our table ready?"

James signed for my glass of wine. Seconds later James Edmonton III, James Edmonton II, and I were seated at a window-side table overlooking the ocean. Waves crested and broke into a rolling thunder in the distance, and you could just barely make out the bobbing heads of surfers waiting for a decent swell. Mr. Edmonton pulled out Friday's edition of the *Wall Street Journal* and started poring over it. Apparently he didn't like what he was reading. "Goddamn it! If the blue chips continue to drop like this I'm going to have Ray Sullivan killed."

James said nothing, and I surreptitiously popped two Advils in my mouth and washed them down with a gulp of wine. My head had started throbbing the moment we entered the dining room.

A waiter approached our table. "Hello, how's everybody doing this morning?"

"Ketel Bloody Mary and eggs Benedict," Mr. Edmonton cut in, still immersed in his paper.

"Okay," the waiter said. "And what can I get for you?" he asked me.

I hadn't even opened the menu. "I'm not sure . . . Let me just look . . ."

"I'll have the wild mushroom frittata," James said. "And a coffee, black."

The waiter scribbled some notes on his little white pad, while I frantically searched the menu. My eyes were moving so quickly I couldn't focus on anything. "And for you, miss?"

In a panic, I blurted out the first thing I saw. "I'll have the eggs Sardeaux, please." I had no idea what I'd just ordered. The waiter removed my menu, and I sat on my hands to keep from biting my already unimpressive nails.

"So," Mr. Edmonton said as he brusquely folded up the paper. "Did you and James meet at Yale?"

"No, I went to Columbia," I said, hoping my teeth weren't stained magenta from the wine and berating myself for not ordering a mimosa. What was I doing drinking wine at eleven in the morning?

"Did you grow up in New York?"

"Yes," I said.

"Where?"

"Upstate in a suburb of Albany."

"How long have you been coming out to the Hamptons?"

"This is my first summer."

"What brings you out here?"

His rapid line of questioning was making our brunch feel like an FBI interrogation. "I actually came out here to bar—"

"Cassie's a writer," James interjected. "She came out here for inspiration, hoping to join the ranks of Hamptons bohemians." I tried to ignore the fact that this was the second time he'd stopped me before I made the mistake of admitting I was a bartender.

"Interesting," Mr. Edmonton said. His Bloody Mary had arrived and he was slowly stirring it with a celery stalk. "What is it that you write? Novels?"

"Uh . . . well . . ." Stammering had somehow become my most frequently used mode of communication in the Hamptons. "Right now I'm working on a—"

"Have you ever been published?" he interrupted.

"Oh. Well, no," I said, "but I'm hoping to—" My voice was silenced by the loud ring of Mr. Edmonton's cell phone.

"Yes?" he barked, picking it up on the first ring. As he carried on a tense conversation with one of his secretaries, James put his hand on my knee under the table and offered me an encouraging smile. I tried to smile back, but I felt like the wine and nervous adrenaline had teamed up in my stomach to burn through my abdominal wall, resulting in the worst nausea and heartburn of my life. I needed to eat something. A fair-haired child to my left was munching on French toast with fresh berries, and my stomach rumbled with hunger.

"So did you go to high school up in Albany, or did you go to boarding school?" Mr. Edmonton asked as soon as he snapped his phone shut.

"In Albany," I answered. "I went to Colonie High School."

"Is that a *public* school?" he asked disapprovingly.

"Uh . . . yes. Yes, it is." I said, trying to smother my shame. "So, how often do you get out to the Hamptons?" I asked him, hoping to reverse the line of questioning.

"I try to get out as often as possible. I like to play golf at least three times a week when the weather's nice. Do you play?"

"No," I said. "But I'd love to learn."

Silence. I looked out the window and wished fervently that I was one of those surfers out in the ocean, swimming freely in the clean blue water. I glanced at James for some support. He put his hand on top of mine and squeezed it.

After what felt like an eternity, the food arrived. To my dismay, my plate was a gooey mélange of runny eggs and hollandaise sauce spread over some unrecognizable green mush. Mr. Edmonton ripped into his eggs Benedict, tearing the thin white membrane and causing the bright yellow yolk to bleed all over his plate. Both father and son dug in as I buttered a piece of whole-wheat toast, avoiding my pulpy egg pottage.

"So, Cassie," Mr. Edmonton said after finishing his meal in under two seconds and resting his silverware on the edge of his plate. "What do your parents do up in Albany?"

I cleared my throat and swallowed hard. "My father's a fireman and my mom's a secretary at a law firm."

More silence. I smiled like one of the mannequins in the windows of Macy's, even though I felt more like a crash-test dummy. My head was still pounding despite the Advils, and I couldn't even look down at the soggy remnants on my plate. I needed some air. "If you'll excuse me," I said, "I'm going to use the ladies' room."

Both James and his father stood when I did. "It's right down the stairs where we came in," James said.

The second I was out of sight, I bolted back down the grand staircase and out the front door with as much decorum as I could muster. I took a few steps across the lawn and, steadying myself on an antique birdbath, breathed deeply, sucking in as much oxygen as possible.

"Nice day," someone commented.

I looked up and saw a grandfatherly man, smoking a cigarette. He had soothing blue eyes, the color of beach glass, and a benevolent expression. "Yes," I agreed.

"Too stuffy in there for you?" he asked, stressing the word "stuffy."

"Yeah," I smiled.

"Me too," he said. "Cigarette?"

"Uh, sure," I said, figuring that since my liver was already rotting, I might as well start damaging another set of vital organs. Smoking was another slippery slope. You started with one drag after a long night of work, then begin to associate smoking with winding down and de-stressing. The next thing you knew, you were smoking every time you were a little agitated or annoyed.

I put the cigarette in my mouth and he lit it with the signature Cartier lighter. "I'm Charles."

"I'm Cassie," I said, relieved that he hadn't offered his last name, so I didn't have to say mine and thereby disappoint everyone in the vicinity because my family lineage didn't trace back to Queen Victoria.

"Having some brunch?" he asked.

"Yeah, some friends of mine are members here," I said, taking a long, satisfying drag.

"What do you think of the Maidstone? It's lovely, isn't it? And all the members are theoretically lovely as well."

"Theoretically?"

"Yes, theoretically," he said, puffing on his cigarette. Then he leaned in with a devilish grin. "In reality they're all a bunch of assholes."

I laughed, nearly choking on the cigarette smoke. "Yeah, it's a pretty tough crowd in there."

"I used to be director of admissions of the club back in the sixties," he said. "But when I told them my plans for opening the Maidstone doors to minorities, well, that was the end of my term. They like to keep it pretty homogenous. Most of them boast that they can trace their heritage back to the *Mayflower*."

I looked around at the Aryan-looking members putting

at the eighteenth hole and thought about all the fair-haired people dining upstairs and the fair-haired children bathing in the swimming pool. I imagined Adolf Hitler himself was running the Maidstone and only granted access to members of the master race. "It's pretty WASPy, huh?" I asked.

"Well, that's not entirely true," he said. "We do have a token Jewish member and a token black member, and if you're lucky, you might be able to see a Catholic or two."

"I'll keep my eyes peeled," I said.

"Well, if you'll excuse me, I'm going down by the pool to buy myself an eight-dollar bottle of water."

"It was nice meeting you," I said.

"The pleasure was mine."

I put out my cigarette on the birdbath and collected myself. I would've liked nothing more than to follow Charles to the pool and smoke cigarettes with him all afternoon, but James and his intimidating father were waiting for me upstairs. If I was going to salvage any semblance of a future with James, I knew I had to march back upstairs with a confident smile and try my hardest to win his father over.

I walked into the foyer where two little strawberry blond girls, about eight years old, were racing up and down the grand staircase with abandon. My first thought was worry that they would fall and break their necks, and the second thought was that my mom would never in a million years have allowed me to carry on like that in a nice country club. No one seemed to care what these two were up to, though, and they acted as if they owned the place. I guessed their nannies had the day off.

As I popped into the ladies' room for a quick freshen-up, I suddenly desperately missed my mom. I felt entirely out of my element and was overcome with homesickness. I yearned for my comfortable, cozy kitchen at home and the plain old Bisquick pancakes with Log Cabin syrup and Oscar Mayer bacon that my mom made every Sunday morning. I looked around at the old-fashioned pink and turquoise "ladies lounge" with wooden lockers and plaques saying LADIES CLUB CHAMP, and wondered where James's mom was, and why he rarely mentioned her and clammed up whenever I tried to ask about her. Martin had piqued my interest when he mentioned the divorce. Even a much younger girlfriend for Mr. Edmonton—a Lily or a Pearls Girl, some sort of potential female ally—would have been better than nothing.

When I arrived back in the dining room, James and his father were sipping coffee, not saying a word to each other. Mr. Edmonton had reopened his newspaper, and James was looking out the window. I couldn't imagine sitting across a table from my father and not talking to him. Whenever my family got together we babbled on nonstop, practically fighting for airtime.

"Are you finished, miss?" the waiter asked when I returned to the table. Even though I hadn't touched my eggs, I nodded and he took my plate.

"So, Mr. Edmonton," I began, "how do you know Martin Pritchard?" I hoped that bringing up Martin, a mutual "friend," would be a good way for me to start over.

"He sold me my first Rothko," Mr. Edmonton replied, stone-faced.

"Oh, that's great. I love Mark Rothko. Martin and Lily stopped into Spark to say hello the other night when I was bartending."

"You're bartending out *here* too?" Mr. Edmonton asked.

Out of the corner of my eye I could see James cringe, and I immediately knew I'd said something wrong. But I didn't see how I could get away without answering his father's question, so I forged ahead.

"Yes, I'm working two nights a week at Spark—"

"Let's get the check," James interrupted, silencing me. I looked down, utterly humiliated.

As we stood up to leave, I noticed a girl about my age having brunch with her parents at a table to our left. Her flaxen hair was pulled back with a black headband, making her look like a grown-up Alice in Wonderland. As she delicately picked at her Waldorf salad, the telltale string of pearls around her neck caught my eye. I imagined that she'd been coming to the Maidstone since she was born and was probably a skilled golfer and played lawn tennis with talent and grace. Her peaches-and-cream skin was flawless, and I noted with envy that there wasn't even the slightest hint of darkness underneath her translucent aqua eyes. I thought about how earlier that morning I'd come home from work with my skirt saturated in grenadine and grime underneath my chipped fingernails. Standing there with James and his father, I would have sold my soul to trade my disgusting share house, money woes, and grueling lifestyle for the life that that girl lived: manicured nails, brunches at the Maidstone, and pearls.

James and I walked to the parking lot in silence a grand total of forty-three minutes after we'd walked in. Once we were both in the car, I felt so claustrophobic I thought I was going to explode. I couldn't take it any more.

"I can't do this," I erupted, my voice shaking.

"Can't do what?"

"*This*. I feel horrible about myself. Your father won't even talk to me. You got mad when I brought up bartending. What do you want me to say? I'm a bartender, James. I'm sorry if that embarrasses you." I was verging on tears, but my last ounce of pride wouldn't let the proverbial damn break just yet. I searched his profile for a reaction. Nothing. He made a left out of the Maidstone parking lot and started veering west on Further Lane. "Where are we going?"

He didn't answer me. He swerved in and out of back roads I'd never known existed until we arrived at Main Beach in East Hampton, where we'd had our first kiss.

"Cassie," he began. His face was red, and he looked incredibly frustrated. This is it, I thought. He's going to break up with me and marry Amanda Hearst or Alice in Wonderland from the Maidstone. I sat there with a racing heart. His reticence stoked all the fears burning inside me. He turned to look at me and said suddenly, "I love you."

"What?" I felt like I'd been shot in the gut.

"I love you. I'm sorry about my dad. He's an arrogant asshole. He doesn't even talk to *me*. Who cares about him? You're the only person I want to be with." I felt myself thawing, warming as his words sunk in. My anger melted away, and I couldn't even remember what I'd been saying. He was still gazing at me. I smiled at him and thought, I love you too.

Thirteen

BAY BREEZE

My brand-new, three-inch, baby pink, crocodile Sergio Rossi heels (which had cost more than I made in an entire weekend at Spark) sank into the gravel parking lot as I turned to admire the yachts docked at East Hampton Point. The forty-foot bows bobbed lazily in the tiny wakes of Three Mile Harbor, as crew members mopped their decks industriously. The sun was setting, and a delicate bay breeze swept the hair off my shoulders. James tossed his keys to the valet and grabbed my hand, lacing his fingers with mine.

We walked up the red-carpeted ramp of

the yacht club's restaurant to the outdoor bar where dozens of bronzed faces vigilantly watched everyone who entered or exited the scene. As I followed James past an open kitchen emitting all sorts of mouthwatering smells, I felt like a starlet about to work the press line of a major premiere. For a second it seemed like the room took a collective breath and paused to watch our arrival. But two steps later we'd blended in with the tanned, toned, and (mostly) blond crowd. Handsome, clean-cut bartenders wearing crisp white shirts and Maui Jim sunglasses were shaking bay breezes to the rhythm of the live reggae band that was stationed on the deck overlooking the bay, and the air vibrated with warmth and activity.

Cocktails and a light bite at East Hampton Point were a Sunday evening ritual for anyone who was anyone in the Hamptons. And now, it appeared, I was someone. I surveyed all the twittering socialites who were "dressed down" in Cynthia Rowley sundresses (the designer was an East Hampton local) and Michael Kors espadrilles, and even spied Betsey Johnson herself in a glorified sarong of her own design, swaying her dreadlocks to the island beats. I decided that if people were really confident in their wealth and status, they could afford to pull off the whole "beachy" look every once in a while.

I hung back slightly with Glen and Tom as James approached the five-foot-ten hostess, who looked like she'd feel more comfortable on the runway at the Ungaro spring fashion show than behind the oak podium at the front of the restaurant. She was wearing a minuscule white dress that hugged every inch of her perfectly toned body, and her long blond hair was pulled back into a purposefully tousled ponytail. "We'd like a table for eight, please. The name's Edmonton."

"I'm sorry, Mr. Edmonton," she replied, barely looking up. "The wait's at least an hour."

I couldn't believe it. If James and his crew had to wait over an hour for a table, I figured this place must really be exclusive.

"Let's get a drink at the bar," James suggested. "We still have to wait for the girls to get here anyway."

We walked over to the outdoor bar where I settled myself in a giant director-style chair and envied the bartenders who had been getting a great tan all summer while they concocted their island specialties (which to my trained eye were nothing more than Malibu coconut-flavored rum mixed with juice). At that moment, I would've given anything to trade the sweaty maelstrom of Spark for this perfect seaside bastion of summerness. I promised myself that if I was still bartending the following summer, I'd make sure to score a job at an outdoor location. In deciding what to order, I thought of Rosalind and the Pearls Girls who were en route to join us and how they were always demurely sipping champagne or white wine, and ordered a glass of Chardonnay.

James had picked me up at Animal House a little after six. Tom and Glen were in the backseat recapping the weekend's earlier highlights, and it became clear that they were both infatuated with Elsie. It seemed that her little show for P. Diddy a few weeks ago had sparked a fascination, and they begged me to divulge everything I knew about her.

"You guys, she's a cokehead," I said with a chuckle. "Don't get me wrong, she's a nice girl, but she looks a lot better at night, if you know what I mean. She doesn't look too hot when the sun comes up."

"Ouch!" Tom said.

"Come on, Cassie," Glen pressed as we made a right on

Three Mile Harbor Road. "She's hot as hell and her body's *smoking*."

Mine would be too if I spent all my tips on plastic surgery, I thought wryly, but decided to keep my mouth shut. I rolled down my window and peered out into the vast wooded plots of the area north of Montauk Highway known as the Springs, transfixed by the metamorphosis in the Hamptons scenery. As we drove along narrow, winding roads, traffic was practically nonexistent: not a Hummer in sight.

"Is that a trailer park?" I'd asked, pointing out the window to a clearing in the woods where I saw a cluster of dilapidated trailers. Clotheslines were strung in between them and small barefoot children darted in and out of the drying clothes.

"No way," Tom said. "The Springs are ghetto compared to the rest of East Hampton, but not *that* ghetto."

"It totally is," I said. "Look."

As the Range Rover wound its way down the road, we all caught a quick glimpse of a young Hispanic woman with a baby slung over her hip walking toward one of the trailers carrying a bag of groceries. I thought back to my first trip out to the Hamptons with Martin and Lily, and all the workers I'd seen who seemingly "disappeared" during the peak season.

"That's crazy," Glen said, genuinely surprised. "I never knew they were out here."

"Me neither," James said. "I can't believe I've never noticed them."

A couple of weeks earlier while riding an early-morning Jitney past the 7-Eleven in Southampton, I'd looked out the window and seen droves of Latino men milling around.

"Illegal workers," the woman in the seat next to me had whispered knowingly. She looked like a hippie, with her

Birkenstocks and long, flowing skirt, but then I'd spied her Hermès Birkin bag and realized she was really a "Trustafarian," the Hamptons breed of hippie—a bleeding-heart liberal living off daddy's trust fund. "They line up in East Hampton at the train station too," she said. "Some town residents are trying to crack down on the builders and contractors who hire them. My heart goes out to them."

Migrant workers apparently flocked to the Hamptons and were available for any kind of physical labor—farming, landscaping, construction—and were much cheaper to hire than legitimate labor because they would work for less than minimum wage. Also, with only one road leading out to the Hamptons and traffic forever at a standstill during the summer months, it was hard for established landscaping or construction companies to get their equipment and laborers back and forth. The migrant workers settled in the Hamptons and were thus easily accessible. But the residents were unhappy about it.

A week or so later I'd read a letter to the editor in the *East Hampton Star* from a resident complaining that dozens of migrant workers were cramming themselves into tiny share houses so they could live in the Hamptons affordably. She was concerned that the property value of her own home would nosedive due to her numerous new neighbors. We'd never received any complaints at Animal House, even though our landlord had long since figured out that we were way over legal capacity. I was sure no letters to the editor would be written about a bunch of white yuppies boozing it up all summer long.

I'd also read a similar letter in the East Hampton *Independent*—this one complained of "five or six cars in *one* driveway" of a share house inhabited by migrant workers. I found this interesting because in every driveway on Further

Lane there were at least five cars. After all, every Hamptons family needed an SUV, a sports car, a convertible, a minivan, a vintage pickup truck, and a hybrid (to assuage their SUV gas-guzzling guilt). It appeared that even though the workers dug their pools, built their houses, reaped their fields, and beautified their gardens, the residents of the Hamptons would prefer for them to magically disappear at the end of their seventeen-hour workday.

"The girls are here," James announced, interrupting my activist musings.

I turned around and saw Rosalind and the girls parade into the restaurant as if they were entering a cotillion, blowing air kisses and picking their way distastefully through the boardshort-wearing crowd with NutraSweet, beauty pageant smiles plastered on their faces. Like the rest of the patrons of the yacht club, they had "downgraded" to Sunday beach wear: different pale shades of C&C California tees, and buttery suede Manolo flip-flops. I was surprised to discover that I towered over them when they weren't wearing heels. While Charlotte and Abigail normally wore their hair blown out and expertly styled, today it was pinned back in "messy" buns to protect it from the bay breeze. Buffy had pulled her fair locks into an immaculate ponytail, and Rosalind's hair, immune to the humidity, was resting neatly on her shoulders. I guessed that the four pairs of Chanel sunglasses perched atop their perfect noses had probably cost a total of about $2,000.

"Can I get you ladies a drink?" Tom asked.

"I don't know what I want." Charlotte pouted. She turned to me. "What are you drinking?"

"The house Chardonnay," I answered. "It's good."

"Let's see the wine list," Rosalind said sourly. "I detest wine by the glass."

"Hey, isn't that Betsey Johnson?" Buffy asked. I looked over at the trendy designer who amid all the lily-white people dancing awkwardly with the band was the only one who really fit in. Her multitonal dreadlocks brushed against the African lead singer as she bumped her hips against his.

"Yes," said Charlotte. "We're doing the PR for her new collection. She's totally nuts. And apparently her daughter Lulu is quite a piece of work."

"I met her daughter!" I interjected excitedly. "She was in Spark the other night. She was totally *wasted*, and she'd gotten sick all over her dress. It was really gross . . ." I trailed off, feeling like an asshole. Why had I been talking about Lulu Johnson's puke? These girls always brought out the idiot in me.

"That's disgusting," Rosalind sniffed.

A half hour later we were seated at a large round table with a dazzling view of the sun as it made its descent over the glittering bay. I made sure to sit in friendly territory between James and Tom, as far away as possible from the Pearls Girls. A cute brunette waitress wearing sneakers, khaki shorts, and a sweat-moistened brow bustled up to the table, looking a little harried, but still with a broad smile on her face.

"Hi, guys, how are you this evening?" she asked.

"Great!" I said. "How's your shift going?" I saw Rosalind and Buffy exchange a look.

"Can't complain," she said. "It's a beautiful evening."

"A bottle of Pellegrino," Rosalind spoke up. "With a lemon *and* a lime."

"Coming right up," the waitress said, reaching for her pad. "Can I get you guys anything else to drink? I see you already have a bottle of wine." But everyone else had already turned back to their conversations.

"I think we're fine, thank you," I said finally.

The waitress smiled at me and tucked her pad into her apron. She was starting to walk away when Rosalind called out, "Actually, I'd like to take another look at the wine list. This Riesling is too sweet."

"We have a nice California Chardonnay," the waitress offered.

"Vintage?"

The waitress looked flustered as she wracked her brain to visualize the wine list. "It's from Sonoma . . ."

"I said *vintage*."

"I'm not sure. Let me check," the waitress said, but before she'd gotten very far, Rosalind started ordering.

"And the grilled shrimp salad with no dressing, no avocado, no onions, and no carrots," she said.

The startled waitress turned around, whipped out her pad, and frantically started writing down the order.

"I'll have the same," Abigail said.

"Me too," echoed Buffy.

"Same for me," said Charlotte. It was uncanny—whenever Rosalind placed an order, the others followed suit, like a chain of dominoes falling one by one.

"And you can forget the wine list," Rosalind added. "Just bring me a bottle of Château d'Yquem. I trust you have the '97."

Our waitress then turned to the boys, who ordered two filets, medium rare, and a surf 'n turf for James.

"And for you, miss?" the waitress asked. I looked into her tired eyes and wanted to give her a hug. It wasn't easy running around all day catering to the dining and drinking whims of the Hamptons elite. She was probably exhausted and miserable, just as I often was during a shift—only she didn't have the buffer that alcohol provided. When obnoxious customers got on my nerves, I could at least drink half a bottle of Patrón with Jake.

"I'll have the lobster roll, please," I said, adding, "Thank you so much."

"I hate lobster salad," Buffy announced after our waitress had finally escaped. "Too much mayonnaise."

"I loathe mayonnaise," Abigail agreed.

"But it comes with fries, and the fries here are off the hook," Tom countered. *Off the hook?* I thought, trying to mask my amusement. Whenever rich white guys used gangsta terms, I had to laugh.

"I haven't had a French fry since junior high," Charlotte boasted as if it were her greatest accomplishment.

Our waitress reappeared seconds later with the mandated sparkling water, and the second bottle of wine, which she presented to Rosalind, who nodded haughtily. The waitress quickly opened it with a loud *POP*. Rosalind frowned at the noise.

"Sorry," the waitress apologized.

She poured a small sip into the glass and Rosalind swished it around and smelled it deliberately before taking a sip. She pushed the glass away, grimacing.

"I don't like it. It's much too oaky. Take it back and bring me a different vintage. Do you have the '94?"

"I think so," the waitress said evenly.

"I'll try that."

I'd never in my life—even at Finton's—seen someone refuse a bottle of wine after tasting it. I looked at James for his reaction, but he was busy admiring a cigarette speedboat skimming the harbor.

After another ceremonious uncorking and tasting, Rosalind said reluctantly, "I don't love it, but I guess we'll keep it. Otherwise, we'll be here opening wine all night."

I stole a glance at the Pearls Girls, all of them sitting up straight, their knees touching, like Queen Elizabeth. Like so many times before, I found myself studying them. I couldn't imagine what their life was like. What did they do during the day? Go shopping? Visit the spa? Sit around eating lettuce? Their daily activities (especially of the mental variety) were a complete mystery to me.

Well, not a total mystery: I could make a few intelligent guesses. They probably all came from a long line of heiresses who didn't do all that much. However, in this day and age, it wasn't exactly fashionable for a young woman who went to a good school to loaf around and live off family money and not work. It was all about appearances. From what I could ascertain, they all worked either in PR or, in the case of Rosalind, as a muse, after striving for their "MRS" degree from whatever Ivy League or southern university they'd happened to attend (where they'd pledged the same sorority as their mother and grandmother). The big PR firms were chock-full of Pearls Girls just killing time until they got married and possibly had a kid or two. Once that happened, they could officially return to their lives of leisure and give up their "careers."

But what went on inside their blond heads? Did they agonize about their place in the world and what it all meant? Or did they just go from party to after-party, shop to showroom, and manicure to pedicure, never growing intellectually, emotionally, or spiritually, and just feeling entitled to everything that came across their path, not even considering how it got there?

"God, my nails are a mess. As soon as I get home, I'm getting a manicure, pedicure, and oxygen facial at Bliss," Rosalind said.

"Oh, me too," echoed the other three. And I guess I had my answer.

Our food arrived, and I dug into my lobster roll, handing Tom a bread plate full of his favorite fries. For a while, only the sound of contented chewing and forks clinking against china could be heard. Then, as our waitress was busy taking the orders of a family seated at the table next to us, Glen whistled to get her attention.

"Glen, what are you *doing*?" I asked, unable to contain myself.

"I need a beer," he responded obliviously.

"If someone whistled at me like that at Spark, I'd kill them," I muttered under my breath. I half hoped that James would hear me and agree, but he remained absorbed in his lobster tail.

As I sat there wondering what it was about these people— at least some of whom I generally liked under other circumstances—that made them utterly oblivious to their own indecency, I remembered James telling me that he'd grown up with a baby nurse, a full-time live-in nanny, a cook, a butler, and several maids.

"What's a baby nurse?" I'd asked him.

"Someone that's hired to take care of the baby from when they just come home from the hospital until they're four or five months old. They live in the nursery, change diapers, feed the baby, stuff like that."

"But isn't that the mother's job?"

"I guess, but a baby wakes up a lot of times during the night, and the mom's recovering, you know, from the labor and everything, so she needs to rest. It's just a lot easier on everyone to hire help."

I thought about my mom, who'd had three kids all two

years apart with no maids, butlers, cooks, or nannies, and certainly no baby nurses. When my brother was born, I'd been two and my sister was four, and my mom had managed just fine without any help other than my dad. In fact, she'd always told us that it was the happiest time of her life.

With visions of baby nurses from Trinidad and Tobago and tuxedo-clad butlers from England running wild in my head, I finally understood why Tom, Glen, and the Pearls Girls treated waitresses, maître d's, and valets like their own personal servants. They were used to having people wait on them hand and foot and had grown up with a very real sense of entitlement.

The interesting thing was that Tom and Glen had never treated me rudely when I waited on them at Spark. They clearly viewed me as being different from the average "server," but I couldn't pinpoint exactly why. Maybe it was because I was dating their best friend, or maybe it was because I'd gone to a good school and they knew I planned to do more with my life than sling drinks. It was hard to discern what made people "acceptable" in their eyes and worthy of their respect. Until tonight I'd always thought that Glen and Tom—unlike Rosalind and the girls—were really down to earth, unimpressed by their pedigrees and affluent upbringings. But now watching them bark at the waitress made me see them in a whole new light. You can always tell how decent a person really is by the way they treat the people who work for them. I looked over at James and saw that he had grown visibly uncomfortable. He'd read my mind, and knew I disapproved of his friends' treatment of the waitress. He squeezed my knee under the table, but I still felt disappointed and alone.

"I've got it," James said when the check arrived. He shot

me a smile to reassure me that he'd be leaving the waitress a huge tip to make up for the incessant demands of our table, and tucked his black AmEx into the black leather folder.

"Nope, it's my turn," Tom objected, grabbing the check, tossing James's card on the table and then replacing it with his own black AmEx. "You paid for the table at Tavern last night."

"We're staying for drinks at the bar, right?" Glen asked.

James looked at me and asked, "Do you want to stay for drinks, or do you want to head out?"

"I told Annie to meet us here when she's done with dinner," I said, "so we might as well have another drink."

The waitress came and collected the card. "I'm gonna run to the ladies' room," I said to James.

As I stood up to leave, he pulled me down toward him and planted a warm kiss on my sunburned lips. I loved when he kissed me in front of the Pearls Girls; it made me feel wildly victorious. He was by far the best catch of the clique, and he was all mine. And he appreciated my democratic manners, even if they didn't. On my way to the bathroom, I pulled our waitress aside and slipped her $40.

Well-heeled New Yorkers turned into Hamptons pumpkins after 8:00 P.M. on a Sunday, when they tore back to the city at breakneck speed, kids and nannies in tow. As a result, the restaurant crowd at East Hampton Point thinned considerably. The bar, however, was still hopping with a younger set of people in no hurry to leave the gorgeous summer evening behind.

As I crossed the deck, on the way back from the bathroom, I could see James's head, high above the rest of the flip-flopped crowd, and flashes of the blond head he was talking to. I hurried over and put my hand on the small of his back. He moved aside to reveal Annie.

"Cassie!" she exclaimed. We'd just seen each other only a couple of hours before, but every time Annie saw me, her face lit up, she threw her arms around my neck, and she acted like we hadn't seen each other for ages. She was the very best kind of friend to have.

"Hey! How was dinner?"

"*So* much fun. Bobby Van's is officially my favorite restaurant in the Hamptons. And André was amazing. He called ahead so there was a bottle of Dom waiting for us at our table, and he knew everyone there. Literally everyone."

"Wow," I marveled. Leave it to Annie to land a date with the famed hotelier who was also rumored to be dating Uma Thurman. Annie's inhibitions about double-dipping were inversely proportionate to her intended's level of star power. She'd met him the night before in VIP at Spark.

"I ordered you a blue margarita. They're amazing, and they'll knock you right on your ass." Annie beamed.

"Sounds good," I said, and even though no self-respecting bartender would be caught dead drinking a blue drink, we raised our neon turquoise glasses.

"Hey, girls!" a familiar voice called from behind us.

We turned around and saw a copper-toned Travis in a green T-shirt, worn-in khaki shorts, and his signature Reef flip-flops standing right behind us, Bud in hand. "Travis!" Annie squealed. "What are you doing here?"

"Yeah, I thought you spent your Sundays slamming PBR on the front lawn with the rest of the shirtless," I teased.

"I'm classing it up, ladies," he said, laughing. "Joining the civilized world."

"Really?" Annie asked.

"No, not really. I'm here with Camilla. She says it's the 'only' place to be on a Sunday."

I turned around and saw a decked-out Camilla gushing with the Pearls Girls. "Oh my God!" Air kiss. Air kiss. "You all look *fabulous* . . ."

"Baby, do you need a drink?" James asked, coming up behind me and wrapping his arms around my waist.

"James, this is Travis," I said. "Travis, James." My worlds were colliding. Even though Martin Pritchard had told me that the Hamptons were four times the size of Manhattan, they'd suddenly been reduced to the bar at East Hampton Point.

"It's nice to finally meet you," Travis said, shaking James's hand. "I've heard a lot about you."

"Nice to meet you as well," James said, giving him that thousand-watt smile that blinded me every time. If his banking career didn't work out and his trust fund ran out, I thought, he could always make a living doing toothpaste commercials. Travis turned to try to get the bartender's attention and, under Camilla's instruction, ordered the Pearls Girls a bottle of the most expensive Sancerre.

James pulled me aside and kissed me. "You look so beautiful in that little dress," he said huskily. I nuzzled into his neck.

"I love you," he whispered. I turned to face him. He was so handsome and he looked at me like he couldn't bear to lose me. He made me feel so taken care of that all my doubts from the dinner debacle receded.

I took a deep breath. "I love you too."

L ocated on the border of the residential West Village and the fashionable meatpacking district, James's luxury co-op building was equipped with a gym and an impressive roof deck, complete with a pool. The minimalist lobby had been designed by Philippe Starck. Martha Stewart, Calvin Klein, Nicole Kidman, Kelly Ripa and Mark Consuelos, and countless business billionaires lived in his building. There was no option to rent, and the apartments started at $2 million for a studio. James's father had given him a two-bedroom as a college graduation gift. Driving back to the city after dinner at East Hampton Point, James had handed me my very own set of keys.

"I know you don't have air-conditioning in your room, so now even if I'm out of town, you always have a place to crash where you can get a good night's sleep," he'd said, handing over the keys to his kingdom. To me, it was a very symbolic moment. I no longer had to sleep in a sixth-floor walk-up—I slept in the ritziest building in town. And I no longer had to take the Jitney or train—I had my own personal chauffered Range Rover. I'd moved up in the world. James had gone from my Hamptons fling to my full-time boyfriend.

That night, using my keys for the first time, I let myself in and dropped my bags on the cool marble tiles in the foyer while James took the car to the garage.

After a feast of cookie dough ice cream, we fell asleep on his couch watching *Serendipity*. James would never admit it, but he was a huge fan of the romantic comedy. His alarm bleated at promptly seven the next morning, and I awoke to a brand-new week.

Through half-closed eyes, I watched him shower, shave, and get dressed. I felt like a stay-at-home wife, a lady of leisure, and a small part of me didn't mind at all. He leaned in to kiss me good-bye and smelled so fresh and delicious that I had to struggle not to throw my arms around his waist and pull him back to bed.

"What're you going to do today?" he asked, bending down so he was at my eye level.

"I was going to write a little," I said.

"Why don't you stay here? You can use my computer and printer or whatever else you need. I'll try to get out early tonight and I'll take you to Da Silvano for dinner."

"Okay, maybe I will." I buried my head in the pillow and issued a muffled "I love you" to his back.

"I love you too," he called before the door clicked softly shut.

I stayed in James's Helmut Lang boxers and Calvin Klein undershirt all day, lounging in his luxurious air-conditioned apartment, ordering Movies On Demand and catching up on all the *Sex and the City* episodes I'd ever missed. Looking out the window at the sweaty bodies battling the humidity on the blistering pavement, I thanked my lucky stars that I didn't have a day job and didn't need to put on a restricting suit and brave the city heat.

At around four, I decided it might be a good idea to at least try to get some work done. His Apple G5 and attached printer seemed to pulsate in the corner, inviting me into the warmth of their silver glow. The bev nap notes stuffed in my bag were crying out to be transcribed into my notebook. So I settled into his deluxe office chair and admired the opulent rosewood desk that looked like it had once belonged to Alexander Hamilton.

I couldn't resist the urge to take a little "look" through the top desk drawer. Nothing but stamps, faded business cards, a stapler, and some old cell phone bills. I slammed the drawer shut, determined not to be one of those creepy girlfriends who snooped and spied on their trusting boyfriends. But I just couldn't help myself and slowly creaked the next drawer open, and started sifting through all the papers inside.

Soon a frenzy came over me. I couldn't find anything interesting in that drawer either (I didn't know exactly what I was looking for, but I knew I needed to unearth at least some small secret), so I systematically studied every single item in the next drawer. But the pictures, bank statements, and correspondence revealed nothing more than what I already knew: he was a multimillionaire, he went to Yale, and he was close friends with Tom, Glen, and the Pearls Girls. I slammed the drawer shut with frustration and maniacally wished I could crack the code to his e-mail account.

At the bottom of the final drawer, I came across a battered copy of *The Great Gatsby* and fell in love with James all over again. The pages were tattered and the binding was held together by masking tape—by the looks of the book, he'd read it at least a hundred times. I was just about to snuggle back into his thousand-thread-count sheets with the novel when another book caught my eye.

I lifted it out of the drawer. *The Hamptons Blue Book* was written in bold silver script across the cerulean blue hardcover. It was roughly the size and thickness of a novel. It appeared to be a kind of phone book for the Hamptons, and I started leafing through it. Each entry had a last name with an address and phone number, followed by a list of all the first names of the family members along with the college they attended and the year they graduated. I paged through the E's until I found Edmonton: 17 Lily Pond Lane, (631) 555-6564. James Richard II; Yale 1970. James Richard III; Yale 1998. Martin Pritchard was also in the little blue book. I learned he had two daughters, Rebecca and Erica, both of whom had graduated from Cornell and then attended Johns

Hopkins Medical School. As my search continued, I found Rosalind's family entry, and discovered that every member was a graduate of Harvard. All of the other Pearls Girls were in the book, along with Tom and Glen. I remembered that Jake had lived in the Hamptons his entire life. I wanted to look him up, but I didn't know his last name.

I heard the locks to the door being turned and immediately threw both books in the drawer, slammed it shut, and scurried out into the hall just as James walked in. He loosened his Paul Smith tie and tossed his briefcase on the floor. "I'm so glad you stayed!"

"What are you doing home so early?"

"I pulled some strings," he said with a wink as he collapsed on the brown leather couch and pulled me onto his lap. "Because I needed to see you. What have you been up to all day?"

"What's *The Hamptons Blue Book*?" I asked suddenly, surprising myself with my lack of control.

"Why do you ask?"

"I don't know . . . I was just wondering."

He looked at me accusingly, and I immediately tried to cover my tracks. "I was looking for a pen to write down some ideas and . . ."

James pulled my face close to his and kissed me. It appeared he wasn't mad. He actually looked kind of amused.

"So what is it?" I asked.

"I don't know," he said. "It's stupid."

"Is it like a phone book?"

"Not exactly."

"Then what?"

He let out an exaggerated sigh and, with a mock British accent, said, "It's the *Social Register* of the Hamptons." He rolled his eyes and continued, "Cassie, it's stupid. Some obnoxious anonymous committee gets together every year and comes up with a list of the so-called important families in the Hamptons. It's ridiculous. Whatever."

I could feel my stomach turn. "So it's a book of all the rich people in the Hamptons so they know who's acceptable for them to associate with? So they don't *accidentally* mingle outside of their caste?"

"Cassie, I told you it's stupid. I'm embarrassed that I'm even in that book. I hate it."

"You're not the only one that's in it. Tom and Glen are in it too, and Rosalind, Charlotte, Buffy, and Abigail. You're all in it."

"Who cares? It doesn't mean anything." I studied his green and gold eyes. "It doesn't matter, Cassie," he assured me again. "Now get dressed, and let's go to dinner."

I got up and went to the bathroom, turned on the water in his executive shower (with six water spouts, heated towels, heated tiles, a water temperature dial, and every Frederic Fekkai you could imagine), stripped down, and got in. I couldn't stop thinking about *The Hamptons Blue Book*. All this time I'd been trying to convince myself that the Manhattan/Hamptons caste system was all in my head, and now I was faced with concrete evidence that it actually did exist.

What really bothered me was that even if I made $100 billion, became a famous writer, philanthropist, or whatever, I'd *still* never be able to get into that book. *The Hamptons Blue Book* was reserved exclusively for people who came from a certain level of breeding. Somehow my gene pool was contaminated. The whole thing seemed so anti-American. What about the Horatio Alger stories? Rags to riches? Wasn't that the American dream? I'd read in middle school that Andrew Carnegie had been an immigrant laborer making two cents a week before he became the biggest steel tycoon and robber baron America had ever seen. I wondered if he'd be allowed in the *Blue Book*. With his working-class roots, he'd probably be chased off the course at the Maidstone.

So, we're not opening the doors to the general public until at least 1:00 A.M.," Shalina instructed the following weekend. "The guests from the White party will be the only people served until we decide that the *masses* can come in. Open bar—everything—including Johnnie Blue, the cognacs, all of it. Make sure your bar backs stock extra Hypnotiq and Cristal."

Every summer in the middle of August, P. Diddy hosted his famous "White Party" on the grounds of his Hamptons estate, which interestingly enough was located in the Springs. Even more ironic was the fact that it was the most coveted invitation in town—even the old-money residents who turned their noses up at "his kind" still wanted the opportunity to see and be seen at his event—P. Diddy was a bonafide Jay Gatsby. This summer, the after-party to the White Party was being held at Spark.

"Hand me two Heinekens," Jake barked an hour later when the party was in full swing. I grabbed two green bottles from the depths of the imports cooler, popped off the tops, and handed them to Jake, who was busy shaking a red devil. "This party fucking sucks," he grumbled.

I had to disagree. The place was more star-studded than the Planetarium at the Museum of Natural History. I'd never seen more celebrities in my life, and although I was trying to play it cool, I was a little starstruck, especially when I caught a glimpse of the Yankees' Alex Rodriguez and the Nets' Jason Kidd toasting up in VIP with Bruce Willis, Jared Leto, and Rosario Dawson.

"I fucking hate open bar. We're not getting tipped, and you know that bitch Shalina is going to pay us nothing for this," he went on, slamming an enormous shot of Patrón. "We only have three Saturdays left in the summer. This is fucking bullshit."

"At least it's cash bar from one on," I gingerly reminded him, as much for my own reassurance as his. "We'll make some money then."

"Cassie, you don't get it. We normally make money from ten to four. Now we're only making money from one to four. That means we'll make half of what we normally do," he said through gritted teeth as if he were explaining simple addition to a mentally retarded child. "Before you know it the summer will be over. This is our last chance to make some cash."

His words echoed in my brain and triggered a panic attack. How did the summer fly by so quickly? The cash we'd been making at Spark had been both a blessing and a curse. I'd been shopping with increasing frequency at Ralph Lauren and Scoop Beach and treating myself to $60 brunches at Babette's. Every time I went out drinking, I'd tip the bartenders and waitresses like I was Midas himself. Meanwhile I was up to my diamond-studded ears in credit card debt. I hadn't saved any money, and even though I'd made several small payments, I still owed Alexis's dad roughly $500. I hadn't counted on the money flow ending so abruptly, but Jake was right. The summer was quickly drawing to an end, and I knew I wouldn't be making this much dough at Finton's.

There was a momentary lull in drink orders, and Jake leaned in with a menacing look in his eyes as if he were about to hatch his plan to take over the world. "You better pull your weight if you want to finish out the summer here."

"What are you talking about?" I asked.

"You know what I'm fucking talking about. Don't pull that Virgin Mary shit with me," he growled. "Now listen, when you get exact change for an order, ring in only one drink and hit cash so the register opens, then put all the money in. The only thing the spotters ever look for is if the register opens and you put money inside. Then write down all the extra money you put in on a sheet of paper, and at the end of the night, when you're closing out, slip the money somewhere—in your shoe, your bag, whatever. We'll divide it up later."

I looked at him and didn't say a word.

"If you can't do it, I'll have you moved to the back bar where you'll be lucky if you can scrape together a hundred bucks," he whispered deliberately, spit flying out of his mouth and landing on my forehead.

His threats still ringing in my ears, I walked away from him to serve an older woman wearing a white pantsuit and draped in diamonds the size of golf balls. She looked like a clone of Elizabeth Taylor.

"What can I get for you?" I asked.

"Could I please have a glass of Cabernet?" she answered, blinding me with her ten-carat diamond ring.

I grabbed the wine bottle, but it slipped right out of my clammy hands and shattered, sending hundreds of maroon-tinted glass shards right in the ice bin. I called the bar back over to bring me a fresh batch of ice and leaned up against the bar to catch my breath. I didn't know what to do. If I didn't go along with Jake's plan, I'd lose my position at the front bar. I cursed Spark for being so damn dysfunctional. Jake was the so-called head bartender, and his modus operandi was to help himself to fistfuls of the owner's money. It was probably he who had gotten me demoted to the back bar earlier in the summer, I thought bitterly. As much as I couldn't imagine doing what he'd asked, I was terrified of finishing up the summer in even deeper financial hot water. It seemed I was screwed either way.

For the remainder of the private party, Jake happily made drinks for the guests without a care in the world. Before I knew it, it was one o'clock, but the party still wasn't over, and our chances for making legitimate money diminished with every passing minute. It wasn't until after two that the club opened to the public. Hundreds of screaming customers who'd been kept at bay by the ominous velvet ropes came rushing over to the bar to order cocktails. I took a deep breath and dug in for my newest misadventure as Bonnie to Jake's Clyde.

"Three Ketel tonics, two cosmos, and three Coronas," someone demanded.

"Ninety-four dollars please," I said.

He handed me $120. "Keep the change."

I saw Jake whip around at the sound of those three magic words and watch me closely. I walked over to the register and as nonchalantly as possible rang in two Coronas for $20 and the two Ketel tonics for $24, hit cash, and put the $120 inside. On a little pad next to my register I wrote down in tiny numbers, 76. I quickly turned around and nervously eyed the cameras, wondering if anyone had witnessed my crime. Everything seemed normal, so I continued making drinks.

"Two Mount Gay and tonics, and three Pinots," a woman ordered. I hated when people asked for Pinot. Pinot meant "grape." What she should have said was Pinot *Grigio* or Pinot *Noir*. Thankfully, we didn't carry Pinot Noir so the mystery was easy to solve.

"That'll be sixty dollars," I said.

She handed me $70. "Keep the change."

Nervously, I entered in only two of the Pinot Grigios, hit cash, and put the $70 in the register, changing my 76 to 122. Again I scanned the crowd anxiously, convinced I could see a suspicious man in a dark suit taking notes on my reprehensible behavior. But I decided it was all in my imagination, so I continued to take orders, make drinks, and ring them in, taking the occasional twenty or so for Jake and me. It was easier than I'd thought. Before I knew it the figure on my little cheat sheet read 200. I figured that was enough and spent the rest of the night ringing everything else in.

Shalina materialized around 4:00 A.M. and gave Jake and me $25 each for working the open bar for four hours. That equaled $6.25 an hour. She cheats us out of money, so it's only fair that we do the same, I rationalized. I promised myself I would never take money from Finton's—even though Laurel and Dan drove me crazy sometimes, they always took care of their employees and tipped us out more than fairly. Dan even tipped us when he sat at the bar and had a couple of cups of coffee (or too many glasses of red wine).

"I can't believe the night's already over," I said to Jake.

"How'd you do?" he asked, looking at me meaningfully.

"Fine," I said, sipping my fifth glass of Veuve. "Can you give me a ride home? James went to Tavern for Richie Akiva's birthday party."

"Yeah," Jake said. "Annie too?"

"No, she left an hour ago with this new guy she's dating."

The night might have been over, but I still had the little problem of how to remove the $200 from my register and slip it furtively into my makeup bag without any of my scandalous activity being caught on camera or by a spotter. My heart pounding, I collected all the money out of the register, stuffed it into the blue leather bank envelope, grabbed my makeup purse, and then bent down out of the cameras' sight line pretending I had to grab something from the lower cabinets. Squatting over the grimy bar mats, I pulled two $100s out of the envelope, crumpled them up in my left fist, and pushed them to the bottom of my makeup bag. I then sealed the envelope, stood up, and walked over to one of the tables where everyone was counting their money. My heart was still pulsating madly in my stomach, and I had so much adrenaline in my system that I felt like I'd just sprinted past the twenty-six-mile mark in the New York City Marathon.

We cleaned up and counted the money in record time, probably since we'd only been using our registers for under two hours. I grabbed the bottle of Veuve on our way out the door.

"So, what's the grand total?" Jake asked when we were safely sequestered in his car, driving home at the end of the night.

"I have an extra two hundred dollars," I said.

"Not bad for your first night, but you can do better," Jake said as he pulled into the Hess gas station down the street from Spark and parked the car. He pulled a wad of twenties out of his sock and tossed them on my lap. "Count that."

Sitting in the dark car in a deserted parking lot with hundreds of dollars everywhere and an empty bottle of champagne between my knees, I felt like we were either in the middle of a huge drug deal or in the executive offices of Enron. "Four hundred and thirty-five dollars," I said, amazed. Didn't anyone realize that there was that much money missing from Jake's ring? Together we'd stolen over $600.

"So that's an extra three-seventeen each," Jake said. "Not bad, so including our tips and the waitress tip-out, we made what—almost five hundred dollars?"

"Yup," I said. Five hundred dollars. If it wasn't for our little covert operation, we would have walked with less than half of that. It was oddly exhilarating. I was master of my own fate. I could cover next month's rent check and maybe even get a new dress for the upcoming charity clambake James had invited me to. But as we pulled out of the gas station and back out on the highway, the sun slowly rising over Montauk Point, what bothered me more than the iota of paranoia gnawing at my consciousness was the fact that I didn't feel guilty at all.

Fourteen

KAMIKAZE

"Eighty dollars," I said to the five-foot-ten, ninety-pound Giselle look-alike standing before me. I wondered if she'd ever eaten a carbohydrate. Maybe she was on the Hamptons cocaine-and-cigarette diet that did wonders for all the cocktail waitresses. She placed a $100 on the bar, and I could've sworn I caught Benjamin Franklin winking at me as he lay on the sticky surface, absorbing Johnnie Walker Black into his green skin.

"Keep the change," she said.

Her magic words sent a small shiver of excitement through me, even at the height of the crunch on my second-to-last Saturday night at Spark. I peeled the soiled bill off the bar, blotted it on a dirty bar rag, and after ringing $20 into the register, I put it in the drawer—no spotter would ever be able to say I failed to put money into the register. Then I wrote a little *80* on the scrap of paper next to my register, following the *40, 20,* and *20* I had already racked up. And it was only eleven o'clock.

For the first time all summer, I felt like I could really relate to Jake. Granted, I wasn't a raging cokehead, but the minuscule bits of money I was skimming off the astronomical Spark profits were addicting, and I could finally understand why he kept going to the bathroom to blow lines with increasing frequency and urgency as the night wore on. As *my* night wore on, I needed the fix of illicit cash more and more often. Adding dollar amounts to my list gave me a better buzz than shots. I envisioned myself a kind of Robin Hood—robbing from the rich to feed the poor. Only I wasn't helping deprived peasants suffering under the king's rule, I was helping myself.

I looked around compulsively. No spotters seemed to be in sight. Unless they were disguised as two gum-popping, big-haired Jersey girls who looked like they were headed for "the shore" (pronounced "shaw-ah") but had accidentally gotten on the wrong train. As they compared their prominently displayed belly-button rings, I decided there was no way they were working undercover. In my mind, all spotters were male, beefy, and dressed in cheap black suits. These girls definitely didn't fit the profile.

James appeared like a mirage behind the Jersey girls just as one was bending over to show the other the multichromatic butterfly tattoo located on her left butt cheek.

"Hey, baby," he said, leaning over the bar to kiss me.

"Be careful, it's a mess," I warned. "We're out of clean bar rags. I don't want your shirt to get dirty."

"I don't care about that," he said, leaning his body halfway over the lake of Johnnie Walker, taking my face in his hands and kissing me tenderly.

"I'm so happy you came in," I said, ignoring the people standing impatiently at the bar giving me pointed looks and waving their cash around. As the summer neared its end, I found I'd grown less and less tolerant of the pushy Spark customers. I felt I deserved a break from their incessant drink orders and demands for attention. I bent my body over the wide bar as far as it would reach to kiss James again, this time a little more heatedly. He tasted like an appetizing combination of spearmint gum, sexy saltiness, and a tinge of alcohol. I thought I glimpsed Rosalind in the crowd rolling her eyes at my display of affection, but as I'd already had roughly ten shots, I didn't care.

"Come on, James, our table's ready," Rosalind commanded from behind him. She was wearing a flirty pale pink dress and looked like a prima ballerina who'd pirouetted her way off the Lincoln Center Stage and all the way out to Wainscott. Her blond hair was pulled gracefully off her long neck, and she had a white leather Marc Jacobs purse dangling from her arm. Of all the girls, I had to admit that Rosalind's style impressed me the most. Pearls or no pearls, she always looked like she'd just pranced off the pages of *Vogue* and had a fashion sense that Jackie O would envy.

"Go on up. I'll be right there," he said, turning back to me. She pouted her cherry lips and stormed off across the bar and up the stairs to VIP. The bouncer saw her coming and quickly lifted the velvet ropes.

"God, she can be so aggravating," James said after

Rosalind was out of earshot. At first I wasn't sure I'd heard him correctly; I'd never heard him say anything negative about Rosalind or the other Pearls Girls. "She's so high-maintenance." I wanted to start listing my own set of complaints that I'd been harboring about Rosalind since Memorial Day weekend but was interrupted by Jake, who was sweating profusely as usual. His sweat reeked of Patrón, and his eyes were fairly popping out of his head.

"Do you have the bottle of triple sec?" he barked.

I pulled it out of my speed rack and handed it to him.

"Those bitches at the end of the bar keep ordering kamikazes," he grumbled, indicating the fake-and-bake Jersey girls. I turned back to James. "Did you guys get a table in VIP tonight?"

"Yes," he said, rolling his eyes. "But I think I'm going to stay down here with you. Can I get a Budweiser?"

"*Budweiser?*" I asked, aghast. "James, what if someone sees you?"

"Shut up!" he said, laughing. "I guess you're rubbing off on me."

I pulled the familiar molasses-colored bottle with the red label out of the cooler, twisted off the cap, and handed it to him. "You've gone from champagne in VIP to beer with the masses," I told him. "And I must admit, you look pretty hot with a Bud in your hand."

I reluctantly tore myself away from James and got back to furiously mixing drinks for the crowd, now three deep, which had continued to gather and yell impatiently during our interlude.

"Did you have fun at the barbeque today?" I asked James, midshake of a Moulin Rouge martini. He had invited me to come with him to a barbeque at one of the Pearls Girls' houses, but for once I just didn't feel like dealing with that crowd. After our dinner at East Hampton Point, my patience with them had worn extra thin. Even though I loved spending every waking second with James, I'd pretended that Annie was depressed about something (an occurrence as unlikely as snow flurries in July) and that I had to spend the day with her. Travis and the rest of the extended Animal House family had joined us (minus Camilla, who was also on the guest list for the barbeque), and we'd thrown the Frisbee around on the beach and splashed around in huge waves until we were all bright red and exhausted from the hot sun and exertion.

"Well, I wouldn't exactly call it *fun*," James admitted. "The caterers served frisee salad and watercress finger sandwiches, which of course none of the girls ate." I hid my amazement, but with every passing word out of James's mouth I couldn't help but feel that we'd turned a kind of corner. We were finally seeing eye to eye on that most important of topics: his friends.

"But you're coming next Monday, right?" James continued. "To the clambake?"

"Who's throwing it again?" I asked. If it was another Pearls Girls catered event, I'd at least remember to eat a burger or something beforehand.

"It's a benefit for the Children of America charity. Rosalind and I are on the committee."

"I'll try to make an appearance," I teased. He leaned in to nuzzle me, nose to nose, and I felt myself being transported away from the bar and onto the beach where we'd first kissed, the surf lapping at our feet . . .

"Hey! Gimme five shots of Cuervo chilled, two Goose martinis up with olives, and three Belvedere gimlets, rocks," a customer roared, pulling me back from my latest fantasy just as I was about to imagine James asking me to marry him.

At four on the dot the lights flooded on, illuminating the war zone behind the bar and encouraging the remaining stragglers to finish whatever they had in their eight-ounce plastic cups and head out the door. I reviewed my cheat sheet and deliciously totaled up the amount of the night's underhanded labor.

I gulped when I saw the total: $480. That was a *lot*. I guessed I had gotten a little overzealous, as I always did when given a challenge. Unfortunately, there was absolutely nothing I could do since it would look pretty suspicious if I started ringing drinks into my register at four-fifteen when there wasn't a customer in sight. I had no choice now but to keep the money. I hoped my ring was high enough, but then I thought about it realistically and figured I was safe—we had only one week to go and I would never have to see Shalina or Teddy or the ominous owners (not that I'd ever seen them in the first place) again. I felt curiously immune to getting into any real trouble.

I clenched the contraband in my sweaty fist and squatted down to quickly wedge it into my makeup purse, then grabbed my bag from where I had presciently stowed it on the bottom shelf and stood up, careful not to look anywhere near the cameras. I pulled the rest of my money out of the register, took the tip cup and all my credit card receipts, and entered the drunken, drugged fracas in the dining room, but not before grabbing two bottles of Bud for me and James. I pulled up a chair at the table where Jake had stationed himself.

"How'd we do?" he asked, buzzing through dollar bills faster than the mechanical counters at banks.

"*Really* good," I said, looking at him with a triumphant smile.

"Good," he said. He finished counting his register, put his money in an envelope, and went upstairs.

My dry eyes struggled to weed any fives, tens, or twenties out of the tip jar, so I could count and bundle the singles. But my brain was submerged in a deadly combination of Budweiser, Patrón, and champagne, and I was having trouble adding.

"Can I help?" James asked.

"Here," I said, handing him a fistful of bills. "Count these."

He wasn't nearly as drunk as I was, and he quickly rifled through the wad of cash and the rest of the tip bucket, neatly stacking the twenties, tens, and fives, and rubber-banding piles of a hundred singles. We counted in silence, punctuated by the cocktail waitresses' chatter.

"That fuckin' guy at 21 only left a fifty-dollar tip on a five-hundred-dollar tab. What a fuckin *asshole!* I wish I woulda looked at his receipt before he left, I would've kicked his ugly Eurotrash ass," Elsie slurred. She failed to mention that a 20 percent gratuity charge was automatically added to every single cocktail waitress tab, so in reality the guy had left her $50 on top of that. The waitresses were used to getting exorbitant tips in addition to the mandatory gratuity, because they neglected to inform customers that the tip was included. Elsie was smoking one cigarette after the other, lighting each new one with the butt of the previous one, and, as a result, was engulfed in a hazy cloud of smoke. In between puffs, she swilled out of a half-full bottle of Cristal that one of her "clients" had left on a table. Ariel, one of her cronies, was counting money while picking the almonds out of a salad she'd bought earlier at Citarella.

"I hate nuts on my salad," she lamented.

"Do you like them on your face?" Elsie smirked, and the bleached blond contingent guffawed in appreciation. I looked over at them, amused. Garth Brooks played in my mind: *I got friends in low places, where the whiskey drowns . . .*

A shadow suddenly fell across my work space, and I looked up to see Teddy towering over me. "Cassie, I need to talk to you," he said.

My heart dropped. I'm caught. He knows I'm stealing. He's going to fire me.

"Okay," I squeaked.

"Meet me in my office."

James looked up from his counting as I followed Teddy up the stairs and into the office. To my surprise, Jake was inside sitting on the couch, smoking a joint and drinking Patrón. I searched his strung-out expression for clues on what was about to go down. But his eyes were focused in all different directions, and he seemed to look right through me.

"Have a seat," Teddy ordered. I pushed aside a dated issue of *Hamptons* magazine with Kristin Davis on the cover and sat down. My stomach was churning in agony, and I felt like I couldn't breathe.

"Cassie," Teddy began, "I've been watching you really closely all summer and tracking your sales . . ."

I could actually feel the adrenaline flooding my bloodstream, cranking up the old fight-or-flight response. How could I be so stupid? I thought. Who did I think I was? I should've known that Teddy would be tracking my sales and would automatically detect a recent plunge in my rings. The moment was positively agonizing.

". . . and with the exception of Jake, you're the highest ringer in the club."

It was a moment before it registered that Teddy was paying me a compliment. I looked up at him, confused, and said nothing.

"A couple of colleagues of mine are getting ready to open up a club in the city. It's going to be twice the size of Spark—the VIP room alone will hold three hundred people. We're working with a team of promoters from Lotus, Jet, and Marquee, and I can guarantee you it will be the sickest spot Manhattan's ever seen."

I nodded. I had no idea where he was going with this.

"I'm trying to nail down the staff right now, and Jake suggested I offer you a position behind the bar."

"We'll be able to make twice what we make here if we really bang it out," Jake offered through his chemical haze.

"Are you interested?" Teddy asked.

"Um . . . yeah," I said, feeling not only enormously relieved but incredibly flattered. All the pent-up fear evaporated, and I felt as light as a feather. Only months ago I had flunked out of bartending school and had to take a job at a no-name bar where I was barely getting by—sometimes making less than $100 a night. Now, after working at the hottest spot in the Hamptons, one of New York's leading promoters was asking me to accompany him on his next venture. I'd graduated into the ranks of Jake, Elsie, and the girls who followed Teddy from hot spot to hot spot like disciples.

"Great," Teddy said. "Finish counting your money. I'll be in touch."

I left the office and walked through VIP toward the stairs. But halfway down I suddenly felt conflicted. I had expected to go back to Finton's after Labor Day, but that meant I'd be making about 75 percent less money than I'd made during my Spark shifts. I felt manacled by golden handcuffs to the enormous sums of money I could make at high-volume clubs. Furthermore, while the Spark staff and clientele nauseated me a lot of the time, it was still exhilarating to be a part of the scene. I liked being close to the glamour of it all, even if I was participating in it only from my vantage point behind the bar. And everybody there—Jake, Teddy, and even the cocktail waitresses—had grown on me. I guess because we were all in it together, trying to make enough money to avoid working a miserable day job in corporate America.

But I still wasn't sure I was ready to leave Finton's. True, it would mean a salary cut, but I never felt pressured and stressed out like I always did at Spark. No one ever pushed me to steal at Finton's, and I didn't live in constant fear of losing my job. And despite his questionable motives, Dan Finton had been good to me, giving me a job when I had no experience and changing my schedule so I could bartend in the Hamptons.

What really perplexed me was that Teddy thought so highly of my performance, while I was stealing hundreds of dollars from right under his nose. I'd been waiting for punishment for my debauched behavior, and instead I'd been rewarded. I went downstairs to finish counting and thought about the twisted world in which I was somehow entrenched. I now had a job at the latest in the string of New York VIP clubs because I'd been stealing with Jake, in part from his friend Teddy, who was actually the one hiring us in the first place.

But any remaining anxiety disappeared as I sat in the passenger seat of James's Range Rover on the way home with $890 in my pocket. I washed down the sesame bagel I'd bought at Twice Upon A Bagel with the Bud I'd swiped on the way out the door. I wasn't going to be losing any sleep that night.

H ey, kiddo," Billy called from behind the bar. Sean was counting out his register and getting ready to leave for the night, and Billy was meticulously scrubbing the bar, polishing the taps, washing glasses, and wiping down bottles. After all these months, I still admired the genuine pride Billy took in his work as a bartender. He kept his "office space" immaculate.

"Hey, guys!" I leaned over the bar and grabbed a cloth napkin to wipe the sweat off my brow and lower back. "It's ridiculous outside. You can hardly breathe it's so hot."

"How're the Hamptons?" Billy asked.

"They're great," I said, sliding behind the bar and checking out my face in the mirror. I had melted mascara oozing down my cheeks.

"It's gonna be tough for you to leave that gig," Billy said as I scrubbed the black smudges off my face and dabbed my cheeks with ice cubes.

"Yeah, but you know, working until seven in the morning can really take its toll on you."

"Definitely. But if you're walking home with five or six hundred dollars, it softens the blow."

"Try seven or eight at least."

"Seven or eight hundred dollars in one night?" Sean asked, stunned.

"Sometimes even more," I answered proudly. I loved watching people's reaction to the magnitude of cash you could bank (either legitimately or otherwise) as a bartender in the Hamptons. The funny thing was, every time I told someone about it, I found myself exaggerating more and more. I was like a seafarer telling tall tales. Pretty soon I'd be telling people we *never* walked with less than a grand.

"I've never made that in a *week*," Sean said. "Hello there, love," he added, pulling me in and kissing my cheek. "You look ravishing, as usual."

"Thank you, sugar," I said. I'd picked up cocktail waitress lingo. They always called their customers and fellow workers "sugar," "baby," or "honey." I always overheard them saying "Can I get you any cranberry juice, sugar?" Or "Would you like Red Bull with that, baby?" And sometimes: "Honey, how about another magnum of Cristal?"

"So Spark's kicking your ass?" Billy asked. He was organizing the beer in the coolers into neat stacked towers.

"Everyone's just a little crazy there, you know? I mean, we drink like a million shots every night, and half the staff take coke breaks every other minute, and this one guy I work with, who's sort of like in charge of the bartenders, he takes money from the register and keeps it for tips." I threw that last bit out there deliberately to gauge Billy's reaction. Of course I had no intention of telling him that I too was guilty of taking a little extra cash.

He didn't even blink. After twelve years of bartending in New York City and the Hamptons, Billy had pretty much seen and heard it all. "It's a rock star world, kiddo," he said. "After a while it hardly fazes you. You just have to keep your head on straight and not get swept up in all of it, 'cause it can be pretty fucked up."

And it certainly was. I mulled over the chain of deception in my head. Bartenders stole from the promoters, who stole from the owners, who stole from the well-to-do clientele, some of whom ironically had their own problems with thievery. The week before I'd read an article in the *Observer* about certain scions of the upper crust who had shoplifting and embezzlement problems. And look at Winona Ryder—what did she need to steal for? All those people were staging one big ploy for attention. Except for me, of course. I just needed the extra cash at the moment and then I promised myself I'd never do it again.

"We had this one guy working here a couple of years ago, stealing tons of money," Billy went on. "Dan caught on pretty quickly and canned him. It's just so stupid to do that. An owner *always knows* when an employee is stealing."

"Really?"

"Yeah, Dan said he stole a couple grand in less than a month. I heard through the grapevine that the guy couldn't get another bartending gig in the city again. That's the thing—if somebody fires you for stealing, whether it's true or not, word gets around to all the other bar owners and you're *fucked.*"

I gulped, but I calmed myself down by thinking that I would certainly never come close to stealing thousands in under a month, even though there was so much money floating around at Spark that they probably wouldn't even notice.

"There she is!" a voice suddenly boomed from the entrance. I turned and saw Baby Carmine strutting into the bar, accompanied by a short, plump woman with long black hair. Even though it was a virtual inferno outside, the woman was draped in a full-length chinchilla coat and adorned with more gold and baubles than King Tut's tomb. Baby Carmine was in a white linen suit, with a shiny, black silk shirt underneath. Of course the top three buttons had been left open so his diamond-encrusted crucifix was visible, gleaming underneath a web of wiry chest hair. His sapphire pinky ring twinkled in the light that reflected off his giant gold Rolex. I noticed that the woman was wearing a matching Rolex, although hers was partially veiled by a tangled lattice of diamond tennis bracelets. "Cassie, this is my wife, Olympia."

"It's nice to meet you," I said. She reached over the bar, clamped my face in between two bejeweled hands, and kissed me on each cheek.

"Honey, I've heard so much about you!" she enthused, in a nasally Fran Drescher–New York accent.

"How are you, doll face?" Baby Carmine said, grabbing my jewel-less hand and kissing it.

"Long time, no see," I said.

"Yeah, well, I was kind of on vacation . . . on a very exotic island," he said with a wily grin, flashing his gold-capped teeth.

"Yeah," I said, "You look very relaxed."

He laughed ironically. "I think we're gonna grab some dinner, gorgeous," he said, escorting his fur-clad wife toward the dining room.

"Come see me for a drink when you're finished," I requested, smiling at Mrs. Baby Carmine.

I watched them promenade through the restaurant, a blur of sparkling jewelry and plush glossy fur, thinking that Baby Carmine and Olympia were eerily reminiscent of P. Diddy's entourage with their bling-and-logo mania. I could have cut them out of the Finton's background and dropped them into Spark right next to the rappers and they would have fit in perfectly—minus the fact that they were white, Italian, and a good twenty years older. In their wake, I felt the curse of the nouveau riche in America. In the words of Bruce Springsteen, *You end up like a dog that's been beat too much till you spend half your life just covering up.*

Not that I blamed them. I could relate. There was nothing I liked more than flashing my new (real) Gucci sunglasses or having the tag on my Juicy sweats peek out at just the right moment—especially when I was feeling insecure around the Pearls Girls. I'd read somewhere that Americans defined wealth by the class above them. Therefore, nothing was ever enough. It was a material addiction—the more you had, the more you wanted. But it was also a major source of conflict for me, because growing up I'd been taught to appreciate everything I was lucky enough to have and value things like family and friends above all material possessions. In the microcosm of the Hamptons, I'd been infected with acquisitive fever, and I didn't know what the antidote was.

"Cassie!" Laurel barked over the intercom. I ran over to the phone and picked it up. "Can you work this weekend?" she snapped.

"Uh, no, this weekend's Labor Day, and it's my last weekend in the Hamptons."

"Well, when can I put you back on the schedule?" she demanded.

"I guess the weekend after Labor Day," I said, feeling my anxiety level surge. I still hadn't made up my mind about whether I should follow Teddy and Jake to the "sickest spot Manhattan's ever seen" or stay loyal to Finton's. At the moment, I was committed to both jobs.

"Fine," Laurel said, and hung up. I mentally added her name to the "con" list for staying at Finton's and turned back to the bar.

"Why don't you bring this over to Baby Carmine's table?" Billy said, handing me a cold bottle of Dom Perignon and two chilled champagne flutes.

"Doesn't he have a waitress?"

"Yeah, but this is on the house as a present from Dan and us. It's a big night for him. He just got out of jail again."

"*What?* I thought he said he was on vacation on some exotic island."

"I don't know if you could call Riker's Island exotic." Billy laughed.

"Oh my God!" I gasped, peering out into the dining room to catch a glimpse of my mobster friend who ran Mulberry Street. He had his hand on his wife's thigh and was looking at her lovingly. "What was he in for?" I asked.

"I don't know, the usual: racketeering, drugs . . . You should do the honors. He fucking loves you."

I grabbed the bottle, the flutes, and a champagne bucket filled with ice and presented the gifts to the recently released prisoner and his consort. "This is from Dan and Billy and me," I said, using a napkin to muffle the sound of the cork popping. "Welcome home."

"Thanks, beautiful," Baby Carmine said. His wife beamed at his side as I poured two glasses. "Thank you, Dan," Baby Carmine called across the restaurant, lifting his glass.

I followed his gaze and was surprised to see Dan Finton sitting in a booth with Martin Pritchard. Dan signaled me over as I submerged the bottle of champagne in its icy bath. I plastered what I hoped was a relaxed, friendly smile on my face and walked over to them.

"Cassie, why don't you join us for a second and taste this Pinot Noir that Martin brought back from his friend's vineyard in Oregon? It's magnificent," Dan said.

I didn't get it. Why was Dan suddenly being warm to me again? The last time we'd spoken, he'd accused me of having questionable priorities, and now he wanted to ply me with wine?

Feeling like I had no choice, I slid in next to Dan in the dimly lit booth. Martin handed me a sparkling Riedel Bordeaux glass and poured a small amount of wine into it. When Finton's had first opened, one reviewer commented that the wineglasses were so big, "you could drown a kitten in them." I took a sip of the velvety Pinot Noir and let the warm liquid linger on my tongue. "Delicious," I said, mentally adding the fact that I could sit around drinking expensive wine with the owner midshift to the "pro" list for staying at Finton's.

"Martin just invited me to come play golf with him this weekend at Shinnecock, so if I have time, maybe I'll swing by Spark afterward and see what you've been up to all summer," Dan said. He was so mercurial. Maybe he figured that the summer was almost over, and I'd be coming back to Finton's full time, so why not take me back into his good graces.

"I didn't know you belonged to Shinnecock," I said to Martin. "I thought you belonged to the Southampton Country Club."

"Yes, well, they don't have golf there, my dear. Truth be told, I'm not much of a golfer anymore since I injured my back," Martin said, chuckling under his breath and shooting Dan a devious look. I cringed, thinking he no doubt meant that he'd thrown out his back swinging with Lily, Denise, and Bill rather than a five-iron. "But the course is beautiful, and all my friends out there are members."

"It's the number-one course in the country," Dan said.

"I've never been there," I said. "But I had brunch at the Maidstone a couple of weeks ago with James and his father. The course is right on the ocean and—"

"Who's James?" Dan interrupted.

I looked at him, momentarily confused. Dan had met James at least five times. "James Edmonton, my boyfriend, whose dad is friends with Martin. You guys have met a few times when he's stopped by the bar." I thought I saw Dan's face darken, and I quickly turned away and fumbled with my napkin. "Anyway, it was really nice."

"Ah, the Maidstone," Martin mused. "Lovely place. It's one of the few institutions in the Hamptons that's still almost exactly as it was when it first opened, over a hundred years ago. The rest have *bent with the times*, so to speak."

"Oh, really?" I asked. I harkened back to the genial conversation I'd had with Charles, the feisty ex-director of admissions at the Maidstone, who'd tried to diversify the club at the expense of his position.

"Of course. The Maidstone is incredibly traditional," Martin went on. "Their committee is dedicated to discerning who should and should not be admitted. The newer clubs in the Hamptons aren't nearly as selective," he scoffed. "For example, National, in Southampton. Some younger men with no family connections in the Hamptons who did well in the Internet boom of the late '90s decided simply to start their own club because they couldn't get into any of the established ones."

"That was smart of them," I said evenly, trying to nip in the bud what threatened to be another one of Martin's diatribes about new money encroaching on the sanctity of the Hamptons WASP aristocracy.

"National's actually really beautiful," Dan said. "A friend of mine belongs there. The staff waits on you hand and foot. They literally wipe the sweat off your forehead and spritz you with Evian. It's hysterical."

"It's tacky," Martin groused. "That's what those people don't understand. When you go into a club like the Maidstone, it's casual because it's a country club, for

Christ's sake! The members don't want the staff fawning all over them. They want to be left alone."

"Exactly," Dan agreed, suddenly switching his position. "The members of National need to have waiters and caddies falling all over them because it makes them feel important."

"Tasteless," Martin sneered.

And yet, here were these two men who, combined, were presumably guilty of adultery, sexual harassment, elitism, and other deviant behavior. Both of their lives were all about self-affirmation and self-aggrandizement. As far as I could see, they were prey to the same (if not worse) pretenses as the members of National.

"Do you like the wine, Cassie?" Dan asked.

"Yeah, it's great." He poured me another glass.

"When Lily and I were in for dinner the other night, she had a glass of red and she loved it," Martin said thoughtfully. "What are you pouring?"

"It must have been the El Coto Rioja that Cassie liked when I had the employees do a tasting a couple of weeks ago. It's our new wine by the glass," Dan said, smiling over at me and putting his hand over mine just a touch too long. "What can I say? She has exquisite taste."

I smiled back, pulling my hand out from under his. I had to admit, inappropriate touching aside, that I liked the fact that he saw me as something more than a bartender, as someone with tastes and opinions to be respected. At Spark I was a commodity, a bartending machine, handpicked strictly for my ability to turn out drinks as fast as possible. If I did have a moment to mention to a customer that I'd gone to an Ivy League school and was an aspiring writer, they didn't really seem to care. The allure of intelligence just didn't register on their radar screen the way the possibility of a fuck or even the promise of a drink did. But in the city, in my little Finton's microcosm, it was different. Dan genuinely valued my knack for intelligent conversation, for astutely managing his customers, and for giving suggestions that enhanced the bar's appeal.

"Don't you think you ought to get behind the bar, Cassie?" Laurel had appeared over my shoulder wearing a tight, fake little grimace that I guessed she was trying to pass off as a smile.

"Laurel, the bar's dead. She can sit for a few more minutes if she wants," Dan replied.

"That's okay, I'm going right now," I said.

"And I posted next week's schedule in the kitchen," Laurel snapped as I followed her back to the bar. "You're on Wednesday, Thursday, Friday, and Saturday."

Suddenly my dilemma had snowballed. I cursed myself for not being more disciplined over the summer and paying off my debts like I should have. I weighed my options and decided to try a different tack, figuring compromise was always the best way to go.

"Laurel?" I asked timidly on my way toward the bar.

"What?" she spat.

"Um, the promoters at Spark actually asked me to pick up a couple of shifts at a new place they're opening this fall. I didn't tell them yes, because I obviously wanted to talk to you first," I lied. "We could figure out how I could do both. I could do a couple of shifts there that wouldn't interfere with my schedule here . . ."

"Absolutely not." Her voice lashed like a whip. "It's a strict Finton's policy that no bartender here work anywhere else in the city."

"But a lot of bartenders work at different—"

"That's the policy, Cassie."

I didn't remember reading that in the Finton's manual. I settled back behind the bar, sullenly wondering what to do next. I kept forgetting that being honest in the bar world got you nowhere and, in fact, telling the truth usually involved serious repercussions.

"Cass," Billy called, "a friend of yours is here."

I looked up and saw Jake studying a menu, sitting on the bar stool directly underneath the television. He was dressed in an oversized hooded FUBU sweatshirt over a T-shirt that read MEN ARE FROM MARS, WOMEN SUCK PENIS. His sleeves were rolled up, revealing thick Pony sweatbands on his wrists. A matching mustard yellow Von Dutch trucker hat was tilted sideways over his disheveled hair à la Ashton Kutcher 2002 (when young Ashton convinced the white male population that a slight tilt of the hat could make even the richest suburbanite look tough).

"What up, Momma?" he called.

"Hey! You're about the last person I ever expected to see here."

"Well, I was in the neighborhood."

"You want a drink?"

"Yeah, what do you have on tap?"

"Guinness, Bass, Harp, Stella, Yuengling, Carlsberg, Sierra Nevada, Newcastle . . ."

"I'll have a Bass," he said. I grabbed a pint glass and started filling it, amazed that Jake was being so tame and only ordering a beer.

"Here you go," I said, placing the beer on a crisp bev nap.

"And a Patrón neat."

Knowing that Jake would obviously want a double, I grabbed a highball glass and the squat bottle of tequila. I put both his drinks on my comp check (another "pro" on the Finton's list—I could always buy drinks for my friends as long as I accounted for them on a separate check).

"Do you wanna order food?" I asked him.

"Yeah, I'm starving. I haven't eaten since yesterday, and I haven't slept in like three fuckin' days either." Typical Jake, I thought, wearing his wanton disregard for sobriety like the Red Badge of Courage. "How's the burger?" he asked.

"Amazing."

"Done. Medium rare. Cheddar."

"You got it." I punched in the order.

"So Teddy and I just got back from a meeting with the guys that own Rain in Miami, and they're gonna invest in his new spot. They think they can open it as early as next month, and they want to call it *Thunder*. Sick, right?"

"That's great," I said, biting my lower lip.

"They already have all these parties lined up, and they hired like *a thousand* promoters. The place is gonna be packed every night. It's gonna be sick. We're gonna be able to make like two grand a week working only two or three nights."

I looked around to make sure Billy wasn't picking up on his use of the word "we." The loyalty to Finton's I'd been feeling only moments earlier was quickly dissolving in Jake's enticing promises about making crazy cash. Maybe I could finally pay back Alexis's dad, get rid of the rest of my credit card debt, settle my student loans, and start a savings account. Or more realistically, I could buy that dress I'd been eyeing in the window of C. Ronson for when James and I hit the Manhattan social scene this fall and finance a much-needed vacation to Cabo.

"Man, this place is fucking dead," Jake said, looking around. "You'll be lucky if you can scrape together fifty bucks tonight. This sucks."

"It's not that bad," I said. "It's really relaxed, and we get to do pretty much whatever we want."

"Yeah, but who cares if you're not making any money? I mean, you're not here to make friends."

"Yeah, but we do okay."

"Cassie, this place is in the middle of fuckin' nowhere. Who puts an Irish pub in Little Italy?"

"I know. It *is* in a weird location. I think a lot of people have trouble finding it."

"Don't sweat it. You got one more month in this place, and then Thunder will open and you'll start making money again. And the best part is, you get to work with me, and we'll *kill it*. We're the fuckin' franchise, baby."

Despite Jake's relentless attempts to look and sound hard core, his messy hair and swollen eyes, coupled with the wide-eyed enthusiasm that took over when he talked about our new gig, made him look like a baby recently woken up from an afternoon nap. He really wasn't a bad guy.

"Hey, Billy, come down here and meet Jake," I called. "He's my partner at Spark."

"Good to meet you, bro'," Jake said.

"You too, man," Billy said.

In his pressed white shirt, ironed slacks, red tie, and apron, Billy was a perfect foil to Jake's Bacchus. It occurred to me that I was witnessing the life cycle of the career bartender evolving right before my very eyes. Billy was an older, more seasoned manifestation of Jake. They were both behind the bar for the long haul, with no discernable aspirations other than wiping down bottles and serving cocktails. But Billy had obviously grown out of the stage where he stayed up every night, drinking his face off and drugging even harder. I looked at them both, and the characteristics they had in common came into focus. Both of them were mired by separate addictions: Billy smoked a pack of cigarettes a day and could down a liter of Jameson without blinking his sexy blue eyes, and Jake was a cokehead with a Patrón problem. But in their own way, they were both charming and sexy, and women loved them. There was something undeniably chemical about them, and they were redolent with the allure of the nocturnal underworld. Then again, maybe I found them both oddly fascinating because I was afraid of sliding down the same slippery slope they pioneered.

Fifteen

SLOE
COMFORTABLE
SCREW

Like hardened icing on a cupcake, the parched sand crunched under my bare feet, its brittle shell giving way to softer, smoother sand as I followed the sound of steel drums along the shore. A hundred yards from the parking lot at Atlantic Beach in Amagansett, three white tents framed by tiki torches protected an army of porcelain-skinned Pearls Girls from premature aging due to the harmful UV rays of the late August sun. I'd never seen so many Pearls Girls in my life—all of them dressed in a rainbow of brightly colored Tracey Feith dresses. Their laughter tinkled like bells in time with the glasses being passed, and they struggled to balance their Sauvignon Blancs as their four-inch stilettos sank into the sand. To avoid sinking myself, I'd decided to remove my new Prada heels in the parking lot and carry them dangling from my hand, praying every single Pearls Girls would notice the letters inscribed on the insole declaring PRADA in bold black letters.

I'd already been introduced to the Hamptons caste system at the Southampton Country Club, the Bridgehampton polo match, and the Maidstone. But none of those experiences quite measured up to the perfection on display before me. The tiki torch flames danced along to the licks of the ocean breeze, and the soft thrumming of the steel drum band seemed to move in time. And if all this wasn't enough to clue me in that this little event was a sizable step up from your average rustic New England clambake, my hunch was confirmed by the elaborate lobster buffet set up underneath the central and biggest tent of all. Chefs in crisp white uniforms complete with tall white hats were presiding over each station armed with tongs and oversized spoons to dispense the fruits of the sea to the young preppy crowd. There would be no holes dug in the sand for a fire pit, no metal garbage cans filled with seaweed, and no eating with your hands at this clambake.

As I grabbed a white plate that looked like genuine bone china and got in line for an appetizer of mussels and French peasant bread, it suddenly hit me that it was Labor Day weekend, and the summer was almost over. I looked out at the water, realizing that in a few days I'd be back to living full time in the concrete jungle with no ocean escape to look forward to at the end of the week. It had been a whirlwind summer: I'd fallen in love, worked at one of the biggest clubs in the world, written a screenplay, and now I was waiting on line for bread at *the* upper-crust event for young up-and-comers in New York society.

The irony that a Pearls Girls charity event was being held on Labor Day, the signature holiday of the working class, was not lost on me. One look around this posh party assured me that the only working-class people I'd be seeing (aside from me) would be the ones serving food and drinks.

"Hi, Cassie," a soft soprano voice cooed behind me. I turned around and saw Abigail approaching me, sipping a glass of white wine.

"Hi," I said.

"I love your dress. It's beautiful," she said, fingering her pearls with her perfectly manicured fingers.

"Thanks," I replied, shocked. I couldn't remember another time when Abigail or the other girls had complimented me on anything, and finally, after all these weeks of trying to withstand their obvious disapproval, one of them had actually said something nice.

"Is it new?" she asked.

"Yup," I said, reveling in her admiration. I'd been eyeing the soft azure dress in the window of Saks on Main Street in Southampton for the last few weeks and had finally broken down and bought it for the clambake. I was $750 poorer, but I rationalized the purchase by promising myself I'd wear it a lot. The only problem was that it was pastel, and I'd figured that one of the Pearls Girls would probably have me arrested by the fashion police if I wore summer colors after Labor Day.

"I love it, it's so bright and feminine," she purred, taking another delicate sip of her wine.

"Thanks," I said, still not quite believing I was having this conversation at all. Normally, the girls only talked to me out of obligation when James was around. But James had left my side and was now talking to a young banker type I'd seen a couple of times at Spark, so I couldn't figure out why Abigail had approached me of her own volition. I wished Annie was there; she would've died to witness this conversation, but she'd had to fly home to Brazil for her cousin's wedding.

"So who's going to be there tonight?" I'd asked James earlier. He looked effortlessly handsome in his baby blue Lacoste sweater, white button-down with the sleeves open and rolled up over the sweater, and crisp beige pants. We were speeding down Ocean Avenue toward the clambake, running late because I'd been tearing apart my room for the last forty-five minutes looking for my notebook, which I couldn't find anywhere. I could tell James was annoyed at the delay, but I was sick to my stomach at the thought that I'd lost it or, worse, that somebody else would find it.

"Everybody," he'd said tersely.

"Will any of the kids that the charity benefits be there?"

"Nope."

"I was thinking it would be nice if Rosalind and the girls were forced to mingle with underprivileged children—give them a little dose of reality," I'd teased.

"Cassie, come on. They're not *that* bad," he said. I looked over at him, confused and a little hurt. Only a week earlier he'd been going off about how high-maintenance they were, and now he was sticking up for them. Then again, as everyone was fond of reminding me, they had been his friends since birth.

"James, I was just *kidding*," I'd reassured him.

"I can't believe we're so late," he'd groused, consulting his platinum Patek Philippe watch. In the end, I'd chalked his irritation up to stress—he was, after all, part of the clambake committee, and he wanted the event to be a big success for the charity. And being late because of my disorganization probably hadn't helped.

"Red or white, miss?" My thoughts were interrupted by the mussel chef who stood over two steaming metal pots of shellfish. One was full of mussels marinating in a tomato garlic chutney, the other mussels stewing in a white wine and saffron bath.

"White, please," I said, thinking that red sauce and a pale blue dress could be a lethal combination. He dutifully shoveled mussels onto my plate. "Thank you."

"I'm going to go place some bids at the silent auction," Abigail told me, of course declining to take any mussels of her own. "Charlotte and I are trying to win the month at a vineyard in the Chianti region. I'll see you later. It was lovely chatting with you." She waltzed away and vanished into a sea of blond hair, pink pashminas, and pearls.

I dipped my crusty bread into the mussel broth and relished the briny flavor. Since the curtain was drawing to a close on my Hamptons summer, I decided to leave the shelter of the tent and savor my last dose of sun. On my way out, I found James sitting at a table draped in Battenberg lace talking with two elfin blonds I didn't recognize.

"There you are," I said.

"Hey," he answered, rising from his seat. "Ladies, I'm going to get some dinner. It was great catching up with you."

"You too, James," the blonds purred in unison.

"Who were those girls?" I asked.

"Just some friends of the family."

"Why didn't you introduce me?"

James tugged at the collar of his sweater uncomfortably. "To tell you the truth, I don't remember either of their names," he confessed.

I looked at him deliberately, studying his eyes. They

looked like tiny pieces of a Fabergé egg. He seemed distant. "You're not mad at me, are you?" I couldn't help asking.

"No," he said, startled. "What are you talking about?"

"Nothing. I don't know, you just seem a little distracted. And you disappeared right when we got here . . ."

"I was gone for like five minutes," he protested.

He had a point. He wasn't gone that long. *Why was I acting like such an insecure freak?* "You're right. I'm sorry. I guess I just missed you."

"Let's get something to eat," he said, taking my arm.

"The mussels are delicious," I raved as we headed back toward the buffet line.

"Did you have any lobster?"

"No, not yet."

At the head of the lobster line, there was a station that supplied plates, metal crackers for the shells, tiny oyster forks, Wet Naps, and lobster bibs. "Oh, I love these," I said playfully, donning the plastic bib with a bright red cartoon lobster depicted on it.

"Don't do that." He grimaced, yanking the bib off my neck and looking around as though he were concerned that somebody might have seen.

"I was just playing around," I said flippantly. "What's the big deal?" But beneath my laid-back exterior, I felt like I'd swallowed a spiny lobster whole and it was stuck somewhere in my throat. "I'm going to go get a drink," I muttered, turning away quickly and leaving the tent.

I made my way across the sand, allowing the breeze from the ocean to clear my head. I walked up to the tan bartender standing behind the only bar set up in the sun. He was wearing Ray-Ban sunglasses and enjoying some downtime as most of the crowd had opted for the bars set up in the shade.

"Hey! How are ya?" he asked, tossing a shot glass up into

the air and letting it spiral a few times before he caught it behind his back.

I was impressed. "I'm doing okay, how are you?"

"Can't complain," he said, looking pleasantly surprised
at my friendliness. I doubted that too many people at the
benefit had taken the time between their white wine sipping
and networking to ask how he was doing. "It's a perfect day.
I'm on the beach, in the sun, looking out at the ocean."

"Yeah, it's definitely great weather for a clambake," I
agreed.

"What can I get for you?"

"Two Buds, please," I said, figuring I could offer James
his new favorite beer as a peace offering. The bartender was
right—the setting was perfect and there was nothing to carp
about. It was my all-time favorite part of the day at my all-
time favorite time of year: around six o'clock in the evening
at the tail-end of summer. The sunlight was radiant with just
the slightest bit of haze, which gave the whole scene a dreamy
effect. The air was perfectly warm and comfortable, and the
chatter of flocks of seagulls mingled with the sound of the
surf crashing on the beach. I desperately wanted to capture
the moment and was overcome by a bittersweet feeling—a
tinge of the end-of-summer blues. The last days of summer
were slipping away and fall was just around the corner. I
needed to relax and enjoy myself and stop overanalyzing
everything.

"We don't have Bud," the bartender said, shattering my
reverie.

"What?" I asked, disappointed. "Well, what do you
have?"

"Stella and Paulaner."

"I guess I'll take two Stellas."

"Coming right up."

"I bartend too," I told him. "Over at Spark." With other bartenders I enjoyed displaying my Spark credentials like a Purple Heart.

"Wow. That must be a great gig."

"Yeah, it's been pretty amazing. Do you just work private parties?"

"Well, this summer I worked for Claws on Wheels caterers doing all these charity events. It's not great, but at least it's steady. This year was some sort of record-breaker—there were like fifty benefits. Were you at this clambake last year?" He pulled two green Stella bottles out of a red ice-filled cooler.

"No, this is my first time."

"The weather's much better this year. I worked it last year and it was overcast all day. It never actually rained, but it looked like it was going to, and all these frantic girls were running around trying to get everything inside the tents. It was the funniest thing I'd ever seen."

I gleefully imagined Rosalind and the girls bemoaning the moisture's effect on their perfectly styled hair as they wobbled around, their $1,000 Christian Louboutin heels sinking into the sand, trying to get all the silent auction merchandise to shelter. I giggled. "I'm sorry I missed that."

"What's this charity for anyway?"

"It's called Children of America," I said. "They raise money for inner-city kids." I pulled out the little booklet I'd been handed when we'd arrived. Rosalind was on the cover along with several other Pearls Girls, posing like beauty contestants, flashing their pearly whites and holding up a banner that read "Help Save America's Urban Youth!"

The bartender paged though it, smiling sardonically. "A charity for inner-city kids, and the whole brochure looks like a freakin' Ralph Lauren catalog," he quipped.

"It's pretty bad," I agreed with a smile. It felt good to talk to someone who actually recognized the inherent hypocrisy in events like these. Leave it to a bartender to get right to the heart of things. I looked up at him conspiratorially. "Wanna do a shot?"

Without hesitation, he grabbed the bottle of Patrón and filled two squeaky clean shot glasses. Tequila was definitely the shot of choice of the Hamptons bartender. "I'm Ben," he said after we shot our tequila.

"Cassie," I said, leaving a $10 bill on the bar top. "Thanks for the beers."

As I made my way back to the tent to find James, two perfectly coiffed Pearls Girls fluttered by me. I caught a snippet of their conversation.

"I'm *exhausted*," the first one moaned. "This is the fourth benefit I've been to this weekend alone."

"Tell me about it," her friend agreed. "No one parties in the Hamptons for the sake of *partying* anymore, there's always something to *benefit*. It's getting to be a little much."

"Did you hear that Marnie Porter has to have the Blue Moon Ball at their estate *next* weekend, *after* Labor Day, since all the rest of the summer weekends were taken up?"

"No! Really?! That's *horrible*! How did Children of America get Labor Day weekend?"

"The Guild Hall benefit got moved to last weekend because the Johnsons were leaving for St. Tropez this weekend, and Rosalind can make anything happen."

I shook my head, barely disguising my disgust, and taking note of their benefit-chic outfits, which, combined with all the tasteful jewelry that dangled from their wrists and ears, had probably cost somewhere in the high six-figure range. These women would probably have been appalled to learn that ten or twenty years prior, benefits in the

Hamptons had started as a way for the nouveau riches to get out of their summer estates and meet one another. I'd read an article in the *Times* on the train last week about how all these poor rich people were locked up in their mansions with no way to show off their wealth until the summer benefit season began in earnest. Snide old-money people called them "pay parties," since the people (presumably of the less established, new-money variety) who weren't invited to any dinner parties or nonbenefit get-togethers could pay their way into the charity path and hence get some well-deserved recognition for themselves or their homes. The Children of America benefit was relatively cheap at $350 a ticket, but I'd heard about benefits that regularly cost up to $50,000 for a table of ten. Buying tables at benefits seemed to be what you did when you graduated from buying tables with bottle service at Spark.

I finally found James underneath the tent walking toward his table with a plate piled high with lobster, spinach salad, potato galette, and grilled asparagus. "Hey, baby," I said, offering him the beer. "They don't have Bud so I grabbed you a Stella."

"I already have a drink," he said, gesturing toward a brimming flute of champagne on the table.

"Oh. Okay," I said, clutching the rejected bottle of beer. "I guess I'll go get some lobster."

James took his seat without saying a word. What the hell was going on? I turned on my heels and walked away, half-expecting him to follow me. But when I looked back, I saw him sitting there, chatting away with some people I didn't know, as if he didn't have a care in the world. I marched up to the beginning of the central buffet line and grabbed a plate and some hardware. This time I shunned the bibs, berating myself for having been so childish before.

"Hey, you work at Spark, right?" someone asked.

I turned around and saw a handsome investment banker—looking kind of guy sipping on what I would have bet my life was a Jack and Coke. He was wearing taupe linen pants, a soft yellow short-sleeved Polo shirt, and a rodent-like smile.

"Uh, yeah," I said. Though I'd enjoyed my little bonding session with the bartender outside, at that exact moment, I didn't need someone announcing to the crowd that I slung drinks for a living, especially considering the inexplicable turbulence with James. Being "recognized" in the Hamptons was a double-edged sword. On one hand, it was nice to enjoy a little celebrity, and it often helped me get free drinks from fellow bartenders. Also, it was sometimes fun to be fawned over by the peons who couldn't gain admittance to Spark and hoped they could get on the coveted list by befriending me. On the other hand, when I was dressed up in an expensive frock, carrying expensive shoes at a social event populated by socialites and heiresses, I hated being reminded of the fact that I was inexorably working class and would have to leave the party hours before everyone else so I could rush to Spark and set up my station behind the bar.

"Cassie, right?" he asked.

"Uh-huh."

"Do you remember me?" I hated that question. Only rude people asked it, putting the other person right on the spot. And I wasn't in the mood to be polite.

"No."

"My name's Simon. I was at Spark a couple of weeks ago. I had a tab with you at the bar, and I asked for your phone number."

I looked at him, hoping that something in his face would jog my memory, but I had zero recollection of him. I'd probably served close to ten thousand people throughout the summer, and most of the younger male Spark crowd looked exactly the same to me. Plus, a lot of the guys who went out on a Saturday night in the Hamptons were on a raging mission to hook up. As the night wore on, their possibilities became bleaker and bleaker, and after 3:00 A.M., you'd see a lot of good-looking guys going home with some pretty banged-up-looking girls out of sheer desperation. "Last call" could sometimes be the biggest albatross of the female bartender, because stragglers were still lurking around, hoping to hook up. I, the lone female left, frequently became the last resort for the desperate and horny. It was at this point that the bouncers generally yelled, "If you're not sleeping with the help, get the hell out!" Ever devoted to their mission to get laid, the guys would then approach the bar and proposition yours truly in a final effort to get some summer lovin'. Needless to say, the offer was not that appealing. Inebriated guys were *always* slurring pickup lines to me at 4:00 A.M.—how was I supposed to remember this one?

"Anyway," he continued, "when I called the number you gave me, it was for Pepperoni's Pizza Parlor."

My face turned the color of the steamed lobsters. Now I remembered who he was. A couple of Saturdays before he'd been hanging around, wasted out of his skull, and Annie and I had thought it would be funny to give him a phony number. The Pepperoni's delivery menu was in plain view behind the bar. I never thought I'd see him again.

I laughed uneasily. "Whoops! Sorry, I must have accidentally given you the wrong number."

His smile had long vanished. "So what are *you* doing at the Children of America clambake?" he asked.

"What do you mean?"

"I'm just surprised to see you here. Although, come to think of it, what an excellent opportunity for someone like you to do a little gold-digging."

I felt like I'd been slapped. "Excuse me? I'm here because my *boyfriend* is on the board of Children of America and he organized the whole clambake."

"Who's your boyfriend?"

"James Edmonton," I proclaimed, savoring the weight of his family name.

"Edmonton's your boyfriend?" he asked doubtfully.

"Yes," I said, my voice rising an octave or two.

"I'm in his group at Goldman."

I nodded distractedly.

"And he's never mentioned you."

My head spun as I tried to process the implications of what he'd just said. I wracked my brain but couldn't think of a good defensive comeback. My arsenal was empty. I gave him my best death stare and retreated. I needed to find James.

Navigating my way through clusters of future Stepford wives and young brokers boasting about their latest conquests—deals, girls, houses, cars—I searched frantically for James, quaking with rage. I couldn't believe the audacity of that guy. I stopped short and drank down half of my beer in one gulp, then briefly thought about seeing if the bar had any Jameson, but decided to keep looking for James instead. I stalked determinedly around the perimeter of the party, following the soft glow of the tiki torches. I barely registered the crystal-clear sky, which was just starting to freckle with brilliant white stars. I finally found James standing beside the silent auction table, a glass of champagne bubbling in his left hand. He was surrounded by a group of younger guys in their early twenties. Each one of them was hanging on his every word, their little hearts leaping in admiration beneath their Valentino sports coats.

". . . I don't know about that, but he's certainly in better shape than he was last year in Aspen. We were staying at Little Nell, and Carson over here got so drunk at this party at Caribou that he went back to the wrong room . . ." James began, but before he could finish, his words were drowned out by the group's overzealous laughter.

Even in the middle of my exasperation, I couldn't help but think how great he looked. Just the muscular shape of his forearm sent a little tingle of attraction through me. We needed to make up immediately from our little tiff or whatever it was so we could have hot makeup sex down the beach, out of everyone's sight. I had plenty of time for a romp in the sand before I had to leave for work. But first I had to tell him how the little weasel he worked with had insulted me.

I walked purposefully up to him, determined to lure him away from the crowd. "Hey," I said, pushing through his groupies and arriving at his side.

He gave me a half-smile and said nothing.

"James," one of the guys called out, "tell us the one about when Carson crashed his Vespa into that old woman in St. Barths!"

I tugged on his sleeve, looking up at him imploringly.

"That's a good one," James said, laughing dryly and ignoring me. "You see, Carson is the little brother I never had . . ."

Why was he ignoring me in front of all these people? What the hell was going on?

Finally, sheer embarrassment snapped me out of my stupor, and I abandoned the group. I knew I needed to talk to

James, but I wasn't about to make a scene. I'd show up at his house after work if I had to. In the meantime, I needed another drink.

"Hey, Cassie," Ben said as I approached the bar, and suddenly I envied him. While I was struggling to survive a series of never-ending awkward social encounters, he was safe behind the bar—protected by a thick piece of wood from vicious socialites and neglectful boyfriends. "How's it going?"

"I need a drink."

"That bad, huh?

"Sort of. I hardly know anybody here, and my boyfriend's ignoring me . . ." I knew I was probably revealing too much information to a guy I barely knew, but the words just flowed—I needed to talk to someone and none of my usual allies were there. A bartender was understandably the best stand-in. I'd been on the other side myself countless times.

"Two Stellas?" he asked sympathetically.

"Just one, thanks."

"You'd better make it two," said a male voice behind me.

I turned around and almost fainted with relief. Travis, dressed in cargo shorts, a worn-in T-shirt that read ST. JAMES FIRE DEPT. ANNUAL 5 MILE RUN: 1985, and Reef flip-flops, had materialized out of nowhere. He stuck out like a sore thumb amid the overdressed bankers in pressed button-downs and sparkling Asprey cuff links.

"It's so good to see you!" I said, flinging my arms around his midsection like a little kid. I nearly knocked him over with my embrace.

"Hello, Cassie," a female voice from behind him greeted me. Travis stepped aside to reveal Camilla, who, with her immaculate updo and strapless white dress, looked like Audrey Hepburn on the way to the prom.

"Hi, Camilla," I said. "How are you?"

"Fabulous!" she announced. "If you'll excuse me, I have to find Rosalind and see if I can be of any help. The poor thing has been working so hard to make sure tonight's a success for the charity. She's such a saint."

"I'll meet you under the tent in a few minutes," Travis said.

Camilla turned to him with a flicker of disdain in her eyes and then hissed under her breath, "You could have at least worn a decent shirt." She wobbled off, and I was impressed by her ability to maintain her debutante posture while walking in the sand wearing five-inch heels.

"Is everything okay between you guys?" I asked.

"Whatever." He sighed, then changed the subject. "You don't have to work tonight?"

"I do. I just promised James I'd come by for a few hours. What time is it?"

Travis consulted his Nike running watch. "Quarter to eight."

"That's it?"

"Did you want it to be later?"

"I just feel like I've been here forever," I said with a sigh, gripping the sand with my clenched toes and digging a small hole with the ball of my foot. "I guess I should call a cab soon. I have to be at work at nine-thirty, and they always take like an hour to come."

"Why don't you just take my car?" Travis offered.

"Are you sure?"

"Of course," he said, rummaging through one of his many pockets and retrieving his keys. "It's parked over by the bathrooms. I'll just get a ride to the Talkhouse later with someone here."

"Don't be so sure. It's not exactly a Talkhouse crowd," I grumbled.

"Are you okay?" Travis asked. "You seem a little off."

"I'm fine." I sighed. "I think I'm just stressed because I have to be at work later. I hate always having to be worried about what time it is."

"You guys want a shot?" Ben interrupted.

"Sure," Travis said. "And I'm almost ready for another Stella."

"Sure thing. I got plenty of them. They ordered twenty cases, but you two are the only ones drinking beer. One more for you, Cassie?"

"Uh . . . no, thanks," I said, suddenly feeling self-conscious. "I think I'm gonna to switch to wine. A glass of white, please."

"Coming right up," Ben said, as he finished pouring the three shots of Patrón. The three of us raised our tequila.

"To helping inner-city children in Harlem, Detroit, and Compton," I said, the irony clearly registering in my voice.

"Cheers," Travis and Ben echoed, downing the fragrant liquor and slamming the glasses on the bar.

"I'm gonna go find Camilla and get something to eat. I'm starving," Travis said, grabbing his second Stella.

"Okay. I'll see you back at the house later. Thanks for letting me borrow your car."

I didn't know if it had something to do with the aged tannins or what, but this summer I'd learned beyond a shadow of a doubt that the more expensive wine was, the drunker it got you. It was a mathematical certainty. I glanced down at the bottle on the bar. The fact that Ben was pouring Chalk Hill 1997 Vineyard Selection Botrytis Semillon ($225 a bottle) like it was Beringer White Zinfandel was irrefutable evidence that I was at a Pearls Girls–sponsored event. My head buzzing with the wine, Patrón, and Stella, I once again determined that I needed to find James and smooth everything over before I left for work so I wouldn't suffer an anxiety meltdown behind the bar.

The central tent was now a Pearls Girls beehive—swarming with thin blonds alive with the buzz of self-congratulation over what a "fabulous" job the committe had done on organizing the event and how generous they all were to help the less fortunate. James was nowhere to be seen. I was about to check the dessert tent where François Payard himself was whipping up Grand Marnier soufflés and caramelized Alsatian apple tart tatins when I noticed Abigail at the silent auction table inscribing her name and bid on a trio of Me&Ro bangles.

"Abigail!" I called out to her.

She looked surprised to see me. Nervously she dropped her pen and straightened her dress. "Cassie! I thought you'd left."

"Have you seen James?"

"What?"

"James. Have you seen him?"

"Uh . . . I don't know, I . . . uh . . ." It was the first time I'd ever heard a Pearls Girl stutter. They were usually perfectly poised and articulate. "I . . . uh . . . I think he might have left. I saw him walking toward the parking lot a couple of minutes ago."

"Thanks," I said, darting out of the tent and sprinting down the beach. My mind was racing faster than my feet. Why would James have left without saying good-bye? What was happening? What had I done? I arrived at the parking lot panting, relieved to find that his Range Rover was still there. The passenger door was open and I could see him standing behind it. "James!" I called breathlessly, avoiding broken glass as I walked across the pavement in my bare feet.

He looked up, alarmed. His face was white and a map of guilt spread slowly across his features.

"Oh . . . Cass," he stammered.

"Are you leaving?" I asked desperately. "I've been looking everywhere for you. I have to go to work soon, but I couldn't leave without—" My sentence came to an abrupt halt as shock strangled the words in my throat. There was someone sitting in the passenger seat. I'd recognize those platinum locks anywhere.

"Hi, Cassie," Rosalind purred. Her slim legs were dangling out of the car, her short skirt barely covering them. She made no move to get up when she saw me, and a smile played at the edges of her perfect, heart-shaped mouth, as she wrapped her arms intimately around James's neck.

I was the first one to look away, but not until a sickening, feverish feeling almost knocked me off my feet. What the hell had I just stumbled on?

James cleared his throat. "Uh, Rosalind? Could you give us a minute here?"

"Sure." She slid out of the car and leisurely strolled away, the click of each Jimmy Choo heel on the pavement driving a stake right through my heart. She stopped only a few feet away and leaned against a vintage Mercedes, examining her nails, watching us out of the corner of her eye. I looked back and forth between her and James in horror.

"What the fuck is going on, James?" I shouted. I was cursing *and* yelling, which meant I was drunker than I thought. I felt that damn spiny lobster crawl back up my throat to lacerate the back of my tongue.

"I don't know, Cassie. I'm just really confused right now . . ." His voice trailed off lamely.

"Confused about *what*? I don't understand. I thought everything was going great. What the hell happened?"

He looked down at his hands—the same hands that only days ago had been holding my face while he kissed me and told me he loved me—and said nothing.

"Answer me, James. What the fuck is going on?"

"I said I don't know. I have a lot on my plate and . . ."

"A lot on your plate? What the hell is that supposed to mean?"

"Maybe I just need a little time or . . ."

"Time for *what*?" I burst into tears of fury and confusion.

"Why don't I come over tomorrow and we can talk when you're not so drunk."

"I'm not fucking drunk!" I wailed.

He looked at me sadly and shook his head. I watched in shock and disbelief as he left me standing there and made his way back to the clambake with Rosalind.

"Wait! Where are you going?" I yowled.

He didn't turn around.

I stood there, dumbstruck, in the parking lot—the pain and humiliation was unbearable. I finally stumbled over to Travis's Galant, which was parked two rows from James's Range Rover. Still crying hysterically, I somehow managed to start the car and ram the gear into reverse, gunning out of the parking space.

I swerved the vehicle sharply to the left, skidding on sand and sideswiping a garbage can. My knuckles were colorless from clenching the steering wheel, and my heart was zipping around my rib cage as though I'd just finished competing in a triathlon. I made a left on Ocean Avenue and barreled down the narrow road toward Montauk Highway, the canopy of trees, the perfectly coiffed hedgerows, the masked mansions a colorful, indecipherable blur around me.

As I suspected, Montauk Highway was bumper-to-bumper. I hate the fucking Hamptons, I thought.

The scene at James's car haunted me. I didn't even know what it was that had just happened. Had we broken up? Maybe something else was bothering him, and Rosalind was just consoling her old friend. Or were they somehow involved with each other? I didn't know what to think. I was in shambles.

It took me nearly an hour to drive the roughly five miles to Spark, where the parking lot was already teaming with Jaguar XKs and Bentley GTs. By that time the tears had stopped and I was completely numb. Surprisingly, I was only twelve minutes late. I swerved the car into a parking spot in the back by the Dumpsters. I held my breath against the stench of the trash and sprinted inside.

"You're late," Jake said reprovingly.

"Shut up!" I snapped, tearing right past him and the tempest of activity already swarming around the bar. I took the stairs two at a time to the employee bathroom. Once inside, I collapsed on the toilet. I wanted to cry or scream, but nothing came out, so I sat there, shell-shocked, staring mutely at the tiled wall, only dimly aware of the minutes ticking by. Finally I put on my stupid uniform for the last time and checked myself out in the mirror. I looked like a wild woman. My hair had frizzed in the ocean breeze and my bloodshot eyes looked like they were straining against their sockets. I splashed cold water on my face, dabbed concealer on my dark circles, and smoothed on some lip gloss. I sprinted down the stairs, nearly tripping over the bouncer who was guarding the velvet ropes of VIP like Cerberus guarded the gates to the underworld.

"This must be the lovely Cassie," a man said just after I'd snuck behind the bar. He and the man sitting next to him were both drinking frothy pink martinis with cherries in them. When they raised their pink glasses to their puckered lips, they extended their pinkies like Miss Manners herself. Impeccably groomed, legs crossed, wrists bent, and heads permanently cocked to the side, the duo was so flaming I was afraid the bar might actually catch on fire.

"Yup, my partner in crime," Jake said.

"Love your lip gloss, cutie pie," one of them said. "It's Nars Baby Doll, isn't it?"

"Um, yeah. Actually, it is."

"I knew it!" he squealed, clapping his hands excitedly.

"And your bronzer!" the other man exclaimed, bubbling with excitement. "Don't tell me—Laura Mercier! I love her products. You know what they say, bronzer's all fun and games until you look like you've been hit in the head with a pumpkin! Oh, but not Laura's bronzer. It's so natural. It looks great on you!"

"Thanks," I mumbled, grabbing a Budweiser out of the cooler, twisting the top off, and taking a long satisfying gulp. Normally, in the beginning of the night when the lights were still turned up and Shalina was stalking behind every corner, I would never drink so openly, but I was already too drunk, tired, and devastated to care. Besides, it was my last night. What was she going to do, fire me?

"Cassie," Jake said, noting my brazen Bud-drinking before the clock had even struck ten. "This is David Goldstein and Todd Silverman, the owners."

"What?!" I gasped, almost dropping my beer into the ice

bin. These were the ominous owners, who watched us all with their evil eyes in order to protect their profits and interests? They looked so harmless. I felt like Dorothy must have when she peered behind the curtain to discover that the almighty Wizard of Oz was nothing more than a feeble old man.

I tried hard to match their enthusiasm. "It's nice to finally meet you."

"Likewise!" they warbled in unison.

"It really is *so* great to meet you, Cassie," David went on. "We've been watching you all summer on the cameras, and you always look so adorable in your little uniform. Great legs. Are you a dancer? Your calves are divine."

"Uh . . . thanks." All summer long I'd pictured the owners as big, scary Mafioso-type men from Long Island, watching my every move on camera, ready to drop the hatchet at any point if I failed to go back to the register and account for every single drink I made. Instead, they'd been watching me more like the Fab 5 did at the end of every episode of *Queer Eye for the Straight Guy*.

Shalina stalked up to the bar and snapped her fingers, calling "Jake, Cassie, over here!"

Reluctantly we both trudged over. "I'll make this brief," she started. "I know you probably both think tonight's 'anything goes' since it's the last night of the season. I just wanted to let you know that we've hired a bigger team of spotters and beefed up the camera and security systems. We'll be watching everything in real time, and if anything underhanded or illegal is going on or so much as a dollar is missing, the perpetrator will be escorted directly to the police station and will never work in the Hamptons again."

I just stared at her dully. This was typical Shalina fare— never once thanking any of us for working our asses off all summer to line her pockets with cash, but instead threatening us. Hamptons rumor had it that employees in the clubs would drink or steal or do drugs right behind the bar on the last shift of the summer season, since they could no longer be fired. Little did she know that all those things had been going on right under her nose (or up other people's noses) all summer long.

I hung my head and took my place behind the bar. At the rate my night was going, I would be on Prozac by morning.

The crowds continued to file in. Even as I started making drinks, I kept both eyes pinned to the door, praying fervently that James would show up at any second to apologize, tell me he loved me, and save me from my misery. I felt dazed and torn apart—the events of the clambake played a slow torturous loop over and over in my mind.

"Hey, sweetheart!" Burberry Plaid Man's annoying voice interrupted. "Let me get two Gooses with cranberry, three Ketel Red Bulls, a Sapphire and soda, and a Tanqueray tonic."

I grabbed seven cups, but by the time I filled them with ice, I'd already forgotten the order. "Two Gooses with Red Bull and a Ketel tonic and what else?"

"No," he said impatiently. "You got it all screwed up. It's two Gooses with *cranberry* . . ."

"Let's do a shot," I yelled to Jake, ignoring Burberry Plaid Man altogether.

Jake looked mildly amused. He grabbed the bottle of Patrón and poured us each a hearty dose of tequila.

"Let's do another one," I said after I'd sucked the first one down.

"Relax, tiger. I don't think you need another shot," Jake said. "You're already drunk."

"Talk about the pot calling the kettle black," I slurred. "Fine. Who needs you? I'll do one by myself." I filled a plastic cup with about four ounces of tequila and slammed it. I savored the burn of it going down—for the briefest moment, it took my mind off my misery. The numbing effect of my shock was starting to wear off, and at the moment, I didn't want to feel anything. For the first time, I could understand the incessant drinking of Finton's regulars who came in night after night and drank by themselves.

The music seemed to get really quiet, and the lights started to smear across my vision. Burberry Plaid Man and the other patrons reaching over the bar and waving cash looked like they were moving in slow motion. Their faces seemed distorted—their lips looked like melted wax sliding off their faces as they shouted drink orders. My night had only just begun, and it was already a throbbing blur, even worse than my surreal car ride over. There were so many digits already marked on my "cheat sheet," I might as well have been taking the money directly from the customers and putting it right into my wallet. But truthfully, I didn't know where any of the money was. I'd been tossing some of it right into the tip jar and ringing some stuff in. I was in no shape to keep accurate records, and I knew my register would be dramatically over or under at the end of the night. Plus, I kept getting in Jake's way.

"Move, Cass! What the fuck is wrong with you?"

"Jake?" I whined.

"What?"

"I don't feel good. I need to go to the bathroom."

"Hurry up."

Holding on to the railing for support, I slowly pulled myself up the steps to the bathroom one by one.

"I'm sorry, VIP only," the bouncer said, barely looking down at me.

"I work here!" I shouted through clenched teeth, pushing past him.

VIP was already jumping, and even though I knew James was still at the clambake, habit forced me to scan the tables of the privileged for his strapping form. I hurtled myself through the door that led to the employee bathroom and the office.

"Cassie!" Teddy called from behind his desk.

"What?"

"I need to talk to you for a minute."

"I can't. Jake needs me downstairs and I have to go to the bathroom." I was hyperconscious of my speech, worried that Teddy would detect my obvious drunken slur.

"Just get in here. It'll only take a second."

I stumbled in and found Teddy leaning back in his chair with his feet up on the desk. The latest issue of *Variety* magazine was spread open in front of him.

"I just wanted to congratulate you," he said, gesturing toward the opened magazine. "I read that you guys are selling your screenplay to Rising Star Entertainment. That's amazing!"

I looked up, my eyes question marks.

"Check it out," he said, handing me the magazine. There in bold black print under the *Film* heading in "The Week" section of *Variety* read:

> *"Rising Star Entertainment is in the process of negotiating a deal with novice producer James Edmonton of Catch 22 productions to produce "Glass Slipper," a Cinderella story about a dejected prostitute in New York City. Jennifer Love Hewitt and Freddy Prinze Jr. attached to star.*

A wave of shock crested over me. *Jennifer Love Fucking Hewitt? Freddy Fucking Prinze Jr.? And there was no mention of my name?*

All of a sudden the air felt thin, as though I'd arrived at the top of Mount Everest and I couldn't suck in enough oxygen. My lungs ached for air, my vision clouded. I stood staring at the two sentences in front of me, any happiness or sense of accomplishment that the summer had sown melting out of me and collecting in a puddle at my feet. My mind wouldn't accept what I was reading, but the inevitable conclusion couldn't be denied. The proof was right there on the page. On top of inexplicably ripping my heart out, James had stolen my screenplay and was selling it to Rising Star Entertainment.

I dropped the magazine and walked zombielike into the bathroom. I locked the door and finally exploded into tears. I picked up the air freshener can and hurled it at the mirror, hoping a real crash would somehow take the sting out of my world crashing down around me. But the glass didn't even shatter, and the clatter of the can as it fell to the floor was drowned out by the *thud-thud-thud* of the DJ's bass.

I stumbled out of the bathroom and down the stairs past a girl offering to give the bouncer a blow job if he would let her and her two friends into VIP. I didn't know why I was headed back behind the bar in my emotionally decimated state. Maybe because that was the only place I felt safe.

"Where the fuck have you been?" Jake roared when I walked back behind the bar. He didn't break his rhythm, holding six plastic cups in his right hand, smoothly pouring five Ketel on the rocks with his left. There were customers lined up ten deep, and even Jake, the head bartender himself, couldn't handle the volume.

"Three cosmos, two Jack and Cokes, and a glass of champagne!"

"Two Amstels!"

"Six shots of Cuervo chilled and two So Co limes!"

"Ketel tonic, Captain Diet, Stoli Ras and seven, a Bud, and a sloe comfortable screw!"

Their cries blended together in a devastating roar of drink orders that further clouded my mind. How was I supposed to serve this angry mob when I could hardly stand up? The congested air, the loud music, and the drinking made everything seem so surreal. For a moment I couldn't discern if this was really happening. I didn't know if I was asleep or awake.

"What are you doing? Get to work!" Jake ordered. I grabbed two beers out of the cooler for a young guy in a gray Izod pullover vest.

"Twenty dollars," I burbled. My words were colliding like bumper cars.

The guy handed me a bill and I walked over to the register and rang it in.

Then I started assisting another customer.

"Hey!" the man in the pullover shouted. "I gave you a fifty. You owe me another thirty bucks!"

At a snail's pace, I shuffled over to the register and took out $30 for the guy. My brain and heart were throbbing to the rhythm of the bass in the pulsing hip-hop. It felt like I'd swallowed one of Spark's speakers.

When I looked up again, the customers seemed to have multiplied, as though they were undergoing mitosis right before my very eyes.

"What do you want?" I slurred to a double-processed blond who had used way too much Clarins self-tanner.

"Two Sour Apple martinis and a Jack and Diet," she commanded.

I was too uncoordinated to locate a shaker, strainer, and

the Sour Apple Schnapps. I could hardly see, and the neurons in my brain weren't firing anymore. They had short-circuited in a sea of alcohol and emotion. I decided to ignore her and help another customer instead.

"What do you want?" I asked a guy who was waiting near the register.

"It's about time," he grumbled. "Gimme two red devils, three Long Islands, and one Long Beach." He pulled out a thick wad of money, unclipped it, and started to count out bills.

I stopped short and glared at him. "Listen to me," I hissed sloppily, pulling him by the neck of his shirt in toward me. "I am not some punching bag or servant for you to walk all over. The least you could do is say 'please' and 'thank you' when you fucking order a drink from me, asshole." I shoved him roughly away.

"What the fuck is wrong with you, you crazy bitch?"

"What did you say to me?" I asked menacingly.

"Everything okay?" one of the bouncers called from the doorway.

"No. This guy was rude to me," I said. I honestly couldn't even remember our exchange from a minute before, but I knew I felt slighted by him. And for the first time all summer, I was determined to do something about these obnoxious, entitled Hamptonites.

The bouncer dragged the customer out by his collar without another word. The guy's face had turned purple and the veins in his face and neck bulged under the bouncer's tight grip.

"You'll fucking regret this! I'll slap a lawsuit on your asses so fast your heads'll spin!" I could hear him continue to scream the whole way out.

Waving a white bev nap over my head in surrender, I collapsed on the cooler, letting my heavy head droop onto my neck as if I'd just been hanged on the gallows.

"What are you *doing*?" Jake demanded, poking me violently in the thigh. "GET UP!"

I couldn't muster the strength to speak or move. In quick succession Rosalind's face, James's face, the beach where we first kissed, the hours spent working at my computer, the angry Spark crowd, and James's "I love yous" penetrated what was left of my conscious brain.

At that moment, Elsie came up to the bar. "Hey, Jake! I need ten Red Bulls for one of my tables," she called. And then, noticing me in a heap on top of the cooler, she said, "Oh my God! What happened to her?"

"She's fucking wasted." Jake sneered. "I don't fucking believe this."

Although it was strictly against the rules for a nonbartender or bar back to enter the sacred space behind the bar, Elsie climbed over and grabbed my face in her magenta-taloned hands. "Come on, baby, what's the matter?"

"Everyone's being mean to me. I'm having the worst night of my life," I sobbed into her ample bosom. Her silicone implants felt hard, like those inflatable stability balls at the gym. "I need to go home."

"Shhhhhhh," Elsie soothed. She looked at me with such sympathy it made me cry even harder. "Everything's going to be okay. Let's go outside. You need some air." She put her arm around my waist and helped me off the cooler. "We'll be right back," she called to Jake.

If I wasn't so drunk with tequila and heartache, I probably would've been shocked to find that crass Elsie had a nurturing side. "James wants to dump me and marry a fucking Pearls Girl, and he stole my screenplay," I blurted as she dragged me through the thick crowd of hipsters. I struggled to make sense of the blurry forms, still maniacally keeping my eyes open for any member of James's crew.

We left the cool, climate-controlled environment of the club and headed to the netherworld of the employee parking lot reigned by two enormous Dumpsters. There really was nothing like the smell of restaurant waste in intense humidity. When the aroma of overripe fruits, discarded vegetables, moldy cheeses, and raw meats intermingle, the result is repulsive. Add the stench of rotting beer, stale rum and tequila, with a generous sprinkling of squirming maggots and flies the size of hummingbirds, and you had the sickening stench of the Spark employee parking lot. I immediately thought I was going to be sick, but it helped to be removed from the insanity inside. Elsie guided me through the garbage littering the ground to the far side of the Dumpster, shielding us from the view of any errant drunks, or the kitchen guys or bar backs, who were forever bringing out new bags of squashed plastic cups and empty beer and champagne bottles.

The closeness of muggy summer air matched the thickness that had taken up residence inside of me. My blood seemed to coagulate in my veins, and my thoughts moved at a glacial pace.

"How do you feel?" Elsie asked.

"I feel like shit. I can't go back in there. I'm exhausted."

"I know what you're going through. Trust me, I'm thirty-four years old. I've been through this a million times. Men are scum. You'll get over it."

Before I could object that I'd never get over James Edmonton, her words registered. She's thirty-four fucking years old and still cocktail-waitressing? At the rate I'm going, I'll be bartending at my own fiftieth birthday party.

"Cigarette?" she offered. I took one and lit it with shaking hands.

Then, out of her pocket, Elsie pulled a tiny ziplock bag, the kind that were ubiquitous at Spark. She produced a key and dipped it into the bag, covering the gleaming metal edge with a lump of white powder. Then, she cupped her free hand under the key, raised it to her right nostril, and sniffed deeply, closing her eyes briefly. She patted the bottom of her nostril with her finger to make sure she got every last bit. She repeated the steps for the other nostril. Carefully Elsie dipped the key into the bag a third time and handed it to me.

Sixteen

HANGOVER

I opened my eyes slowly and pain-fully. My head felt like it'd been flattened by a steamroller. Sharp shooting pains originating somewhere be-hind my eye sockets echoed in my head, sending tremors of nausea down my spine. Inside my stomach a tempest of acid, alco-hol, and emotion raged. At some point earlier that morning, I'd gotten out of bed and made a dash for the toilet, but only got as far as the garbage can on the far side of the room before throwing up. I'd then staggered down the hall to the bathroom, where, after retching again, I lay with my cheek pressed to the cool tiles of the floor for about twenty minutes. Eventually I made it back to my bed and slept fitfully. I tried to keep very still as even the smallest shift in position caused shock waves of nausea to ricochet through me.

Outside my window, another storm was gathering. It was as if Mother Nature herself were mourning the end of summer, causing the leaves to quiver on their branches and making the tall beach grass dance manically in the fields behind Animal House. Inside everything was ghostly quiet. A wraithlike calm had settled over the old farmhouse. Gingerly I heaved my body into a sitting position. My bones ached when I moved, and immediately my arms and legs were covered in a rash of goose bumps. I had the chills, the kind you get when you're coming down with a bad case of the flu or after you experience intense déjà vu. All summer long I'd been abusing my body, and it was finally letting me know it had had enough.

I imagined the fruits of the depravity from last night had collected in a pool at the base of the parietal lobe of my brain, where a lot of scientists believe the soul resides. I was pretty sure I was damaged permanently, and at the very least, my soul was scarred. When I tried to make it out of bed, I felt like I was inching through quicksand.

I looked down at my dirty feet as I planted them on the musty wooden planks. I finally knew why they wouldn't let us bartend in open-toed shoes. Last night in my rebellious stupor, I'd dared to wear flip-flops behind the bar. Each toe was now encrusted with sludge after marinating all night in the alcoholic sewer that existed behind the bar at Spark. My feet stuck to the dusty oak floor as I limped through the upstairs hallway.

"Hello?" I called, my hoarse voice echoing through the empty rooms, until the sound was consumed by vapid silence. I hobbled down the carpeted staircase. "Is anybody home?"

The house was completely vacant. There wasn't a pizza box or PBR can in sight. Dust particles had already settled on the broken table in the dining room, and the rusty wind chimes sang eerily on the porch. The decrepit wall clock in the kitchen read 3:37. While I was passed out, everyone had packed up their summer gear and left for the city. For the first time since Memorial Day, the house was deathly quiet. Over the summer I'd gotten used to the grunts and roars of my Animal House–mates, and there had been something distinctly comforting about knowing they were always out in the backyard drinking beer and playing football. Just when I actually wanted to hear them egg each other on to do a keg stand, I was alone with my thoughts.

After three months of happy oblivion, I'd finally had my first *real* insight into the Hamptons. I could finally sympathize with the Jakes and Elsies of the world. I'd been wrong to dismiss them as losers. I now knew exactly how they felt, drowning or blowing their problems away—even if the problems were as simple as not having any direction in life—in the oblivion of coke and booze. They woke up the next day at three in the afternoon, out of their skull with depression and coming down hard. The only light at the end of the black tunnel was going back to work and starting the eradication of their problems or unhappiness all over again. The cycle was born.

I threw on a hooded sweatshirt, slipped on some flip-flops, donned my $12 huge, dark black sunglasses from TJ Maxx that hadn't seen the light of day since my Gucci splurge a month and half ago, and walked outside, slamming the rickety screen door shut. All of the chairs on the porch had been folded up and piled neatly on the side of the house.

The hundreds of empty beer bottles littering every available surface were gone, and someone had even swept up the cigarette butts and food wrappers. The tidiness of it all scared me—it was like a family had died and their long-lost relatives had come to pack up their belongings.

Hoping food would calm the storm in my intestines, I started walking east on Main Street through Amagansett toward the Farmer's Market. The entire town was jarringly vaporous—the gathering storm had brought the fog in off the water and the air around me felt damp and cold. I passed the Amagansett Ice Cream Club where I'd enjoyed many a cone and found that it was already closed for the season. A sign on the door read THANKS FOR A GREAT SUMMER. SEE YOU NEXT YEAR!

It took me a minute to adjust to what I was hearing: nothing. With the startling volume of the silence, I became conscious of just how quickly the Hamptons had emptied out. In the fifteen hours since the clock struck midnight on the last official day of the summer season, Amagansett had settled back into its position as a quaint, quiet seaside town. There was no traffic on Montauk Highway—all the Hummers, Porsches, and Jags had mysteriously vanished overnight. I half-expected tumbleweed to come rolling down the median. I passed the Talkhouse, which was always bursting at the seams with noise and activity, but the only signs of life were two stray cats feasting on bar trash piled in the alley beside the Amagansett hardware store.

Even the Farmer's Market had already downsized. They'd dismantled the mouthwatering outdoor display of locally grown produce and closed down the deli counter, cheese shop, and bakery. In the green courtyard, where tanned New Yorkers usually drank coffee and munched on chocolate croissants, there were now piles of stocked boxes and crates ready for winter storage. Eager for human contact, I smiled at the Bahamian cashier while she rang up my Poland Spring water, Canada Dry Ginger Ale, and saltine crackers.

"It's really quiet today."

"Yeah, it really clears out after the holiday," she replied in her melodic island lilt.

Clutching my remedies, I left the market and headed back through town. So many beautiful homes, and all of them were already closed up for the winter. I couldn't believe people lived in them only three months out of the year.

Witnessing the aftermath of the mass exodus out of the Hamptons, and being the only one left behind, I felt stranded and suddenly wanted to get off Long Island as fast as possible. It was September and I needed to get back to New York City where I belonged.

I was nibbling on the saltines and sipping ginger ale as I walked, and placebo or not, they really helped my hangover. My mom had always given us crackers and ginger ale when we had upset stomachs, and as I munched on the salty wafers, I felt another sharp pang of homesickness. I wanted my mom. I wanted my family. I hadn't gone home to Albany once all summer. I'd been too caught up in my glamorous Hamptons existence to be bothered to take the Greyhound up north.

The rain started to drizzle the second I passed Gansett Green Manor, but I didn't quicken my pace. The cool drops actually felt cleansing and soothed my headache as they moistened my hair and dripped down my face. With the charcoal sky as a backdrop, Animal House looked lonely and desolate when it came into view.

I started to traipse across the soggy front lawn but stopped dead in my tracks. Parked in the driveway was

James's Range Rover. As the threat of an imminent confrontation entered my consciousness, my mind started reeling with questions. What was he doing here? What did he want? What am I going to say to him?

Cautiously I approached the house. He was sitting on the porch looking the most disheveled I'd ever seen him. His hair was unkempt and, judging by the dark circles shadowing his eyes, I suspected he'd also had a rough night. The very sight of him made me feel like I'd been punched in the stomach by someone the size of a Spark bouncer.

"Hey," he said quietly as our eyes locked in an inexorable stare. I felt a phantom pain in my heart in the now-empty spot he had filled only yesterday.

"What are you doing here?" I wanted to get in his Range Rover and run him over and drag his body down Montauk Highway, but at the same time I prayed that his presence on my porch was a sign that he really did love me and regretted everything that had happened the night before. There had to be a perfectly logical explanation for his behavior.

"I need to talk to you," he said.

"About what?" My voice was shaky.

"Cassie, you need to let me explain . . ." he began.

I stood there speechless on the lawn, the raindrops dampening my crackers and loosening the dirt on my filthy feet.

"Come on, get out of the rain," he urged. "I just want to talk."

"Then talk." I climbed the stairs to the porch and leaned against the wobbly railing at a safe distance from him. I wasn't about to let him touch me (even though more than anything I wanted to crumble in his lap and let his strong chest muffle the sound of my sobs while he stroked my hair). I became excruciatingly self-conscious in the truest sense of the word—I was painfully aware of every move I made, of each raindrop that slid down my face, of the rate at which I was breathing. So aware, in fact, that I swore I could actually feel my hair growing out of my scalp.

It was a moment before he began. "Last night, before I picked you up for the clambake, I got into a fight with my dad. He told me I wasn't allowed to see you anymore."

The force of his words rained down on me like nails. While this news shouldn't have come as a shock, hearing it uttered by James out loud felt like being drawn and quartered on a scaffold by a skilled executioner. The kind of executioner who could pull your still-beating heart out of your chest cavity with his bare hands and show the pulsing muscle to a bloodthirsty crowd, all while you were wholly conscious of the electric pain and mortification that was consuming your body.

"He threatened me with my trust fund. He actually told me he'd cut me off completely if I continued to date you. You have to understand—"

"I'm sorry, James," I interrupted, rage creeping into my voice, "but I *don't* understand. I've never had a trust fund."

"That's not the point, Cassie."

"Then what *is* the point?"

"The point is . . . He's my *father*, and . . . You don't understand where he's coming from. You don't know what he's been through."

"No, I don't. I don't know anything about your father because he won't even talk to me, even when I'm sitting across a table from him."

James took a deep breath. His eyes looked watery. "He doesn't mean to be like that. He just—"

"What?" I wailed.

"My mother," he said, barely audibly.

"What about your mother?"

An agonizing pause followed. I could hear every single suicidal raindrop meet its demise as it splashed onto the waterlogged lawn. Finally James spoke.

"She was a counter girl at the Clam Shack when my father met her."

Confusion precipitated all around me. I tried to imagine an Edmonton, especially James's mother, whom I'd always pictured as Princess Diana of Wales, serving fried clam strips and beer-battered shrimp at the dilapidated Clam Shack on Montauk Highway.

"Are you being serious?"

"They met when they were like eighteen. My father used to see her all the time when he summered out here. They fell in love and got married, even though my dad's family was obviously against it. Anyway, she left right after I was born. And she took almost everything because my dad was too in love with her to ask her to sign a prenup. She even tried to take me, but my dad's lawyers wouldn't let that happen."

I felt like I was experiencing some sort of internal earthquake. The tectonic plates of my bones were shifting and colliding. James's father had fallen for a counter girl at the Clam Shack who left him and took his money?

I finally knew why no one else ever mentioned her. I tried to adjust to the image of Mr. Edmonton as a lovelorn victim. In my wildest dreams, I'd never imagined feeling sorry for the man, but suddenly I knew *exactly* how he felt.

"How come you never told me about this before?"

"I don't like to talk about it."

I should have realized sooner that our relationship had a fatal flaw. We'd never talked about his obviously dysfunctional family history, and likewise he'd never asked me anything about my family beyond the few details and stories I'd volunteered.

Still, I had to get to the bottom of an even more pressing issue. "That doesn't explain why you stole my screenplay."

"What are you talking about?"

"I read in *Variety* last night that James Edmonton was in the process of selling a screenplay about a downtrodden prostitute to Rising Star Entertainment. There was no mention of my name."

My accusation didn't seem to faze him at all. His face was the picture of serenity. "Cass, I did *not* steal your screenplay. Like I told you, I've been shopping it around to some people, but nothing's come through yet. I had a couple of meetings with Rising Star, but that's it. Obviously I'd never do anything without your input. We're in this together."

"If that's the truth, then why haven't you told me about any of these meetings? Am I supposed to find out by reading the trades?"

"No. Listen, you're absolutely right. I should've told you, but I've just had a lot on my mind, and there's a lot of bullshit in Hollywood, you know, and most times nothing ever even comes out of it. I didn't want to get your hopes up. I'm really sorry."

I didn't know what to believe. Maybe he was telling the truth.

"Cassie, come on. You know I'd never do anything to hurt you," he continued. "I love you."

Suddenly I was furious. "If you love me, then what the hell were you doing with Rosalind in the parking lot?"

My question startled him. "*Nothing.* We were just talking, I swear to God."

"Give me a fucking break. Her legs were practically wrapped around you."

"Cassie, I promise, nothing happened. We were just

talking. I've known Rosalind my entire life. She's one of the few people who really understands my family, and I needed to talk to her about everything that was going on with my dad."

"Fine. But you didn't need to maul each other while you talked, did you?" He said nothing, and his silence only fueled my fire. "And I know about how you two have been practically betrothed since birth. Camilla told me all about it. I didn't think arranged marriages still existed, but maybe it'll help both of your fathers' fortunes if you two join kingdoms."

He walked over to where I was standing and took my hands. "Cassie, what are you talking about? You're completely freaking out for no reason. Nothing is going on between me and Rosalind." He laced his fingers in mine, squeezing my hands tightly. "Yes, our fathers have been trying to get us together since we were kids, but so what? I want to be with *you*. I love *you*. You know that, don't you?"

I dropped my head and studied the gray chipped paint on the old wrap-around porch. I couldn't meet his gaze, and I couldn't answer his question. I was so confused. I didn't know what to believe.

"Listen." He sighed, pressing his forehead against mine. "I'm having dinner with my dad tonight, and if the timing's right, I'm going to try to talk to him about us. I just don't want to upset him, you know?"

And then something clicked inside me. All the insecurity, embarrassment, awkwardness, desperation, and anxiety that had been bubbling beneath my surface all summer long erupted. I couldn't hold it in anymore. I looked up at him, tasting the bitter disappointment of seeing for the first time who he truly was. And, by extension, who I had become.

"You don't want to *upset* him? Why would you upset him, James? Because you're still dating a trashy barmaid? And what about upsetting *me*? I've been trying so hard. I spent all the money I busted my ass for all summer buying dresses, and shoes, and bags for your polo matches and your charity events and your lunches at your dad's country club. And you know what? I don't want to do it anymore. I'm tired of being embarrassed by the fact that my dad's a fireman or that I'm from Albany and went to a public school, God forbid. My parents love me more than anything in the world, and I have a great family. I should be proud of that. Not ashamed because their names aren't listed in the fucking *Hamptons Blue Book*, or because my mom drinks White Zinfandel, or because Marshall's is my sister's favorite store. I'm tired of being uncomfortable around your friends and your dad because I'm a bartender. I work hard, and I support myself. So what if my parents couldn't afford to buy me an apartment as my graduation present and I can't live off a trust fund?

"Do you even know how fucked up this world you inhabit is, James? The Hamptons are nothing but a bunch of selfish, shallow, boring people spending money trying to impress each other and cover up the fact that their lives are hollow and meaningless. How are these people really your friends? Doesn't it bother you the way they treat other people? All that's important to them is their own superiority—their rank in this fucked-up world.

"So go ahead and marry Rosalind. You can have your wedding at the fucking Maidstone and go off and breed members of the superior race. And you won't have to trouble your father's lawyers with any pesky prenuptial agreements."

I took a deep breath. I felt like I'd been exorcised. All the toxic thoughts and insecurities I'd been harboring all summer had been purged from my system, and I felt an overpowering sense of relief, as though I'd finally stepped back into my own skin. James stood there processing my testimonial. It was a long time before he spoke.

"So this is it?"

A large part of me still ached at the thought of letting him go, but I knew I had no other choice. "Yes."

"What about your screenplay?" He looked fairly miserable.

"You can have it. It's total garbage about a poor girl who needs to be rescued. I can't believe I even wrote it, and frankly, after this summer, I really don't want my name attached to it."

He nodded slowly and then wordlessly turned and walked away. Any doubts I had dissolved as he descended the porch steps. He didn't even have the guts to fight for me. I watched him cross the lawn and climb into his Range Rover. I listened to the engine spring to life and the unmistakable sound of his tires crunching on gravel. I watched as he backed out of the driveway and then sped down the wet road until the vehicle was little more than a glossy black spot in the distance. I did all this with just the slightest hint of longing. And not longing for him. Longing for an ideal that I thought I'd captured.

The same eerie calm that had seized the house now took over my body. It wasn't numbness. It was something else. I went inside and quickly packed up all my things. There was a 5:14 Manhattan-bound train leaving Amagansett, and I was determined to be on it.

As the lush East End scenery whizzed by the window on

my last commute back to the city, I remembered I still had one last item of unfinished business to take care of before I left the Hamptons for good. I pulled out my cell phone and dialed Teddy's number. Of course he didn't answer. Promoters were never awake at the ungodly hour of 5:30 P.M.

"Teddy, this is Cassie. I'm calling to tell you I'm not going to be able to take the job at Thunder. I appreciate the offer, but I think it's better for me not to work there, because I've got a lot of other things I want to focus on this fall. But good luck with it. Bye."

I snapped my phone shut and peered out the window. As we coasted by a farm somewhere between East Hampton and Bridgehampton, I glimpsed two men working in the fields, harvesting the last of the summer strawberries.

Cassie! Get over here!" Billy called from his end of the bar where he was pouring baby shots of Jameson. He handed one of them to me.

"No, thanks."

"You're *still* in detox?"

"Yup."

"I'm proud of you, kid," he said. "Cheers."

"Cheers." I lifted up my glass of club soda to meet the chorus of raised Jameson shots.

"Ugh! That is the nastiest thing I've ever tasted. Why do we always have to do Jameson?" Alexis grimaced, slamming her lipstick-stained glass on the mahogany bar. She'd had a long week at Morgan Stanley and was using yet another one of my Thursday shifts to "unwind."

"It'll put some hair on your chest," Billy smirked.

"Give her some more wine as a chaser," Annie suggested. "And I'll take another Amstel Light. Travis, you want another one?"

"Sure. Budweiser, please." Travis smiled at me.

"Can I bum a smoke?" Alexis asked me.

I smiled ruefully. "Lex, you know I quit."

"Hello, darling!" Martin bellowed at that exact moment, making his grand entrance. He came up to the bar and, taking my hand in his, tried to pull me in for his usual wet kiss on the cheek, just a little too close to my mouth. I politely extracted my hand before he could pull me any further and smiled at him from the other side of the mahogany bar top.

"Hi, Martin. Ketel and tonic?"

"No, no, dear! Summer's long gone. I'm back to Johnnie Black and soda."

"You got it."

I fixed his drink and handed it to him, just as Laurel came clicking by.

"Laurel, I'm taking Friday and Saturday off next weekend," I told her. "I already asked Sean and he said he'd cover the shift for me—I'm heading home to Albany to see my family for a few days."

I waited for the inevitable frown and sigh, but it didn't come. Surprised, I went back to my station at the service end, where I watched with amusement as Dan Finton affectionately introduced Martin to the newest waitress, Sarah. With her wide blue eyes and long brown hair, she had an uncanny resemblance to . . . me. Apparently she had just graduated from college and moved to New York—Dan had met her at the gym. She was looking for a job, and Dan was *always* on the prowl for new talent.

"Sarah!" Laurel barked, holding up a steak knife and

staring into it. "I thought I told you to always make sure you can see your reflection in the silverware before you place it on the table. I can hardly see myself at all. If you keep this up, I'll have no choice but to let you go. . . ."

C ass, I already cleaned up my end, do you mind if I head out? I gotta get up early tomorrow morning to work the day shift," Billy asked as he untied his apron and slipped it off his waist.

"No, that's fine. I'll lock up. I still have to count out my drawer. Want to give me your tip money and I'll divide it up?"

"Yeah. Here you go."

A minute later I handed him a stack of bills. "Two hundred and five dollars each. Not bad." Especially since I had already covered my rent. Two days before I'd filled two huge shopping bags with all my frivolous summer purchases. Just when I'd thought I was starting to get over the pain of everything that had happened, opening my closet forced me to relive the events of the entire summer—from the pink Calypso dress I'd worn to the Bridgehampton polo match, to the blue dress from Saks I'd worn to the clambake—all over again. I'd taken them to Tokio 7 consignment shop on Seventh Street, where I'd gotten just under $1,000 for all of the items. A fraction of what I'd actually paid for them, but I thanked God anyway for small favors.

Billy threw his messenger bag over his shoulder and exited out the side door.

"I've got an early-morning meeting tomorrow," Travis said regretfully. "So I guess I'd better be going too. Are we still on for tomorrow night?" He leaned in over the bar and took my hand.

"Definitely." I smiled at him.

"You sure you're okay to close up alone?" he asked.

"I'll be fine."

When they'd all gone, I looked around the empty bar, remembering how afraid I'd been to be left there alone when I first started working afternoons. Now it felt like all the ghosts were at peace and wouldn't be bothering me anymore.

I hit "No Sale" on the new Oasis computer and my drawer opened. I counted out the money, adjusted my credit card tips, and filled out a report. We'd run out of envelopes to drop our cash in, but Laurel had told me on her way out that there was a secret stash in one of the storage cabinets that lined the bar. I squatted down, careful not to let my bare knees touch the grimy bar mat, and tried to slide the cabinet open. Lime juice and liqueur had hardened the inside of the cabinets, making it difficult to open them. I pulled as hard as I could without derailing the door, and at last it slid to one side. As I pawed through dusty bottles of Amaretto and triple sec, I finally located the envelope reserves. I was just about to close the cabinet when a black-and-white marbled notebook caught my eye. I felt my heart flutter with hope.

I knelt down on the mat. The wet rubber felt slimy on my knees as I reached back into the depths of the cupboard and pulled the book out.

It was my long-lost notebook. *Cassie Ellis* was carefully inscribed on its tattered cover. I walked out from behind the bar, my register and tips completely forgotten, and took a seat on one of the bar stools. Paging through my records and observations of the summer, I realized what it was that I had in that notebook—a tangible documentation of my struggle to fit into the East End world of wealth, status, and power.

That night in Finton's, I finally saw the truth. The real me had always been there, even when I was afraid I'd lost her forever. I turned to a fresh page, but before my pen hit the paper, I glanced up at the ceiling and caught sight of the four carved mahogany devils. Images that had once seemed so sinister couldn't hurt me anymore. I started writing fervently.

ACT I

SCENE I

INT. FINTON'S BAR AND

RESTAURANT—EARLY EVENING

A brunette walks into a bar . . .

ACKNOWLEDGMENTS

To all of the VIPs in our lives . . .

To our families—Lynn Erickson, Molly Shear, Jack and Dorothy Toomey, Kerry Toomey, Jack Toomey, and all the rest of our extended clans—you are our rock. Without your unconditional love and encouragement, we would never be who we are or where we are today. We love you with all our hearts. And even though bartending wasn't exactly the profession you had in mind when you told us we could "be anything we wanted," we thank you for never losing faith in us.

To our friends—thank you for your unfailing love, advice, and support. We guess it's payback for all the free drinks we've given you over the years!

To our Matts—what are the chances that both of us would meet the loves of our lives behind the bar? Thank you for putting up with our mood swings and moments of self-doubt, and for being "the men behind the women."

To Elisabeth Weed, our agent extraordinaire—thank you for taking a huge chance on us and believing from the start that two bartenders had a story worth telling.

To Ann Campbell, our unbelievably talented, industrious editor—thank you for being the essential ingredient in our Perfect Manhattan.

To the rest of the Random House team—Ursula Cary, David Drake, Laura Pillar, and Julia Coblentz—thank you for sharing our philosophy that all business meetings should be conducted over drinks.

To David Halpern—thank you for discovering us!

To Chris Onieal and all the Onieals staff and regulars—thank you for all the good times, schedule flexibility, and endless inspiration.

To the Hamptons—thank you for providing a backdrop that is both beautiful and bizarre. Honestly, you can't make this stuff up!